Gina was smiling at me expectantly. She came into my arms, naked and smooth and warm. There was a small, springy click as, embracing me, holding me, she fired the automatic hypo-gun we carry, that she'd got out of my coat, through my pants and the big muscle of my rump.

I just hoped that, working hastily in bad light, she'd managed to charge the ingenious little weapon with the right capsule, the green one. The red and orange ones kill.

MAKING LOVE.
MAKING WAR.

MATT HELM
THE DETONATORS

Fawcett Gold Medal Books
By Donald Hamilton:

The Mona Intercept

MATT HELM SERIES

The Ambushers

The Annihilators

The Betrayers

Death of a Citizen

The Infiltrators

The Interlopers

The Intimidators

The Intriguers

Murderers' Row

The Poisoners

The Removers

The Retaliators

The Revengers

The Shadowers

The Terrorizers

THE DETONATORS

Donald Hamilton

FAWCETT GOLD MEDAL • NEW YORK

A Fawcett Gold Medal Book
Published by Ballantine Books

Library of Congress Catalog Card Number: 85-90629

ISBN 0-449-12755-9

Manufactured in the United States of America

First Edition: July 1985

‖‖‖‖‖‖ CHAPTER 1 ‖‖‖‖‖‖‖‖‖‖‖‖‖‖‖‖‖‖‖‖‖‖‖‖‖‖‖‖‖‖‖‖

THE GIRL Mac had sent to me, presumably because he didn't know what else to do with her, was a very proper young woman in a severely tailored gray flannel business suit and a severe white silk blouse with a neat little ascot thing at the throat. Nicely constructed, of slightly less than medium height, she had a grave oval face dominated by very serious gray-blue eyes. The mouth, although adequate in size, didn't look as if she'd ever taken advantage of its potential for laughter. A shy, pinched, reluctant little smile was the best she'd managed for me so far. Well, it wasn't exactly a laughing situation.

She had a lot of fine light-brown hair pinned up about her head in a ladylike Victorian manner, displaying a graceful neck. The hair was light enough that she could have become a striking little blonde without a great deal of effort—a simple rinse would have done the job. The fact that she hadn't made the effort said a lot about her. She wore very little makeup, just a touch of lipstick; and her face was pale, but that could have been the result of the awkward and distressing circumstances that had brought her to me. I noticed that her hands were quite attractive.

1

Locked in her lap as she sat facing me stiffly, on a small straight chair she'd chosen in preference to the mate of the comfortable number in which I was sprawled, they were slender, shapely hands, but not too small to be useful. The nails were well cared for but trimmed fairly short, with clear, colorless polish, very discreet. No blood-red talons here.

However, she'd yielded to conventional femininity in a couple of respects. Her neat black pumps, which matched the purse in her lap, had fairly high slim heels that did nice things for her pretty ankles; and her smoky stockings were very sheer, emphasizing the pleasant shape of her legs. But unlike most modern young ladies, who're happy to display their erogenous zones to anyone who cares to look, Miss Amy Barnett still hadn't let me determine whether she was wearing panty hose or sustained the smoothness of her nylons with more elaborate feminine engineering. So far she'd managed her narrow skirt with faultless modesty. But I would have bet a considerable amount of money on the tights. She didn't look like a girl who'd go in for frivolous lacy garter belts and cute little bikini panties; and she certainly didn't need the support of a girdle.

"Well, after all, he *is* in jail and he *is* my father," she said a bit defiantly. "Even if I haven't seen him since I was a child."

It was a mass-produced hotel room in a mass-produced hotel near the Miami waterfront. The Marina Towers, if it matters. Never mind what I was doing there. Actually, it was done, and I'd been making arrangements to return to Washington when the phone had rung and Mac had instructed me to sit tight and expect a visitor. He'd also given me the background of the situation and apologized for dumping the job on me because I was handy, since there were personal reasons why I might find it distasteful—but personal doesn't count for much with us. If it did, there were also personal reasons, which Mac seemed to have forgotten, why I didn't mind as much as I might have.

"But I gather you don't approve of him," I said to the girl facing me. "Even though he is your pop."

"How can I? The work he does . . . used to do! If you can call it work! I was terribly shocked when Mother explained it to me all those years ago—I was seven at the time—explained why I no longer had a daddy, why she'd had to leave him. But I understood perfectly. I mean, what else could she do when she finally learned what he'd been hiding all those years, what kind of a man he really was." Amy Barnett hesitated. "But now that Mother's dead he's my only living relative, Mr. Helm, and I felt obliged to come when I learned he was in trouble." She shook her head quickly. "No, that's not quite accurate. I was already trying to locate him when I heard about that."

"You've had no contact with him since your mother walked out on him and took you with her?"

She didn't like the way I'd expressed that, but she decided not to make an issue of it. "Well . . . well, afterward he tried to write me from time to time, like on my birthdays, but Mother made me send his letters back unopened, so after a while he gave up. Except for the last letter that came quite recently, right after her death, that let me know how to get in touch with the government agency he worked for, if I ever needed any kind of help. Your agency. He wrote that now that he was retired he'd be traveling outside the country for a while, where he'd be hard to reach. He wanted to be sure I was taken care of, now that Mother was gone." She gave me that pinched little smile again. "Of course, I have a very good job managing an office for a group of doctors; I also have

3

some nurse's training and plan to get my cap eventually. In other words, Mr. Helm, I've been taking care of myself perfectly well for several years; but he seemed really concerned about me. I was feeling very much alone in the world, so I called the number he'd written right away. I did feel that I was betraying Mother in a small way; but it really wouldn't hurt just to see him and talk to him a little, get to know him a little, if I could catch him before he left the country. Would it?" She shook her head abruptly. "Only, when I called I learned what . . . what he'd done now, where he is now."

"But you still flew down here to see him," I said. "All the way from Cincinnati, Ohio."

She shrugged resignedly. "I'm just stubborn, I guess. I started this and I had to finish it, even though I don't know how I'll pay for the ticket I charged to Visa yesterday, not to mention the hotel bill here. But I guess I've had a few doubts—I mean, Mother was a *little* unreasonable at times. However, it seems that in this case she was perfectly right." Miss Barnett's lips tightened primly. "Apparently, my father, a retired professional man of violence, now smuggles drugs and resists savagely when arrested, putting several police officers into the hospital! Not exactly a parent to be proud of, would you say? But I do feel I should face him once, myself, so I'll know . . . *know* Mother made the right decision all those years ago."

"Sure. Anybody else you want to lock up or execute without a trial while we're at it?"

There was a brief silence, while the big gray-blue eyes—mostly gray at the moment, I noticed—studied me carefully. Amy Barnett nodded slowly.

"I see. You feel I'm condemning him without a hearing?" When I didn't speak, she went on quickly:

4

"But that's exactly what I'm here for, to hear what he has to say!"

"But you've already made up your mind about him, haven't you? Or let your mom make it up for you?"

She frowned. "You don't like me very much, do you, Mr. Helm?"

I said, "You seem to have made a fine recovery, Miss Barnett."

"What do you mean?"

I said, deadpan, "Oh, the way he used to kick you around the room after beating up on your poor mother. Battered child, battered wife. But it's all healed now, I see. But the memories remain even after all these years, of course. The way he strangled the cat with his bare hands and chopped up the dog with a carving knife, blood and guts all over the place, horrible. Naturally your mother had to snatch you away before the disgusting, degenerate brute crippled you for life, or even murdered both of you in your beds. Right?"

She looked bewildered. "I don't know what you're talking about! Actually, Daddy was very fond of old Buttons, our springer spaniel. And he certainly never laid a hand on . . . Oh, you're being sarcastic!" She licked her lips. "I'm sorry. I'm a little slow today, Mr. Helm."

I said, "Yes, ma'am. Sarcastic." I got up and walked across the room to the dresser. "Would you care for a drink?"

"Thank you, I don't drink."

Picking up the bottle, I glanced at her over my shoulder. "And I don't suppose you smoke, either."

She shook her head minutely. "Anybody'd be a fool to do that to themselves in view of the scientific evidence." ·

I said, "And I've noticed that you don't swear. No vices at all, Miss Barnett? Do you fuck?"

She wasn't going to let me shock her into silence.

Her voice was very stiff when it came, but it came: "I'm not a virgin, if that's what you mean. But I . . . I wasn't impressed with it as a form of casual entertainment the . . . the few times . . ."

Se stopped. When I turned and walked over there and looked down at her, I saw that her ears were quite pink. I took a deep swallow of the drink I'd made myself.

"Miss Barnett."

She looked up warily. "Yes?"

"Will you accept my humble apology?"

Her eyes widened. "I don't understand."

"I'm sorry for giving you a hard time," I said. "But then you've been giving me a pretty hard time, too. There's no way you could know it, but a considerable number of years ago my wife left me, taking our three children with her, just the way your mother left your dad; and for exactly the same reason. So when I hear of a man who's done his best, within his limitations, to be a good husband and father, being deserted by his family for beautiful moral reasons relating to the type of work he's chosen for himself, I find it hard to be sympathetic with the family that left him; I'm on the other side. But at least my wife—ex-wife—didn't brainwash my kids into thinking that their daddy was a monster or prevent me from communicating with them occasionally, although in our business it's usually best to stay pretty much away from people you love so nobody gets the bright idea of using them against you. So I have." I raised my glass to her. "Anyway, I apologize for getting personal. Your vices, or lack of them, are really no concern of mine, right? But you did go pretty heavy on that professional-man-of-violence stuff. We're very sensitive fellows, we professional men of violence."

"I'm sorry. It was pretty tactless of me, wasn't it?" But her heart wasn't in the apology; she had more

6

important things to worry about than my sensitive feelings. She drew a long breath and glanced at her watch. "Well, judging by what I saw from the taxi that brought me from the airport, Miami traffic is pretty awful. If we're going to get there during visiting hours, we'd better start driving, hadn't we?" Her voice turned disapproving. "As soon as you've finished your drink, of course."

I said, "Don't worry, ma'am. I hold my liquor pretty good. But if I do feel a drunken stupor coming on, I promise to turn the wheel over to you."

DRIVING THE rental car across town with the girl beside me, I reviewed what I'd been told about the situation. I'd already known, of course, that Doug had long been a victim of the Slocum syndrome. Old Joshua Slocum was the first man to sail alone around the world. Men, and a few women, have been dreaming of following in the wake of his clumsy *Spray* for almost a century now, and even doing it. Well, there's nothing like a good dream to sustain you during the long dull day stakeouts and night vigils involved in our profession. Some men make the time pass by dreaming of climbing high mountains, or catching big fish, or shooting deer or elk that have enormous antlers. Some dream of food or liquor or women, or various combinations of the above. I don't suppose there's anything wrong in dreaming about boats.

Retired for medical reasons—he was getting on toward that age anyway—Doug set about turning his dream into reality. He bought a husky thirty-two-foot fiberglass sailboat hull, double-ended. The ones that are sharp at both ends are supposed to be more seaworthy, according to some authorities. According to others, not. But Doug had been sold on the virtues of that pointy stern that would part the raging seas gently as he ran before the howling gales in the great Southern Ocean.

I knew, because I'd done a job with him during which we'd had time for some idle talk before things got very busy and he'd had to save my life a bit, that he'd originally planned to do the whole construction job himself. However, now that retirement was a reality, he had a number of old aches and twinges, and some new ones, to remind him that nobody lives forever. He decided that if he wanted to carry out his sailing plans, he didn't have time to waste on building from scratch. So he acquired a ready-made hull—apparently they were available in all stages of completion—and finished and rigged it to his own specifications in a little less than two years.

He was a midwestern boy who'd never seen an ocean until World War II sent him overseas; but since the dream hit him he'd spent his free time—the little we get—in learning seamanship and navigation. Now he took a few more months to get acquainted with his new ship, with progressively longer cruises from his home in St. Petersburg, on the west coast of Florida. Feeling himself ready at last, with some knowledge of compass and sextant, and a little practical experience in handling his boat under a variety of conditions, he embarked upon his epic voyage, first heading south to Key West, at the tip of the Florida Keys.

From there he planned to head up the east coast of Florida to Miami, where he'd take care of any deficiencies in boat or supplies that had come to his attention. Later, as the seasons permitted, he'd proceed to Bermuda, the Azores, and the Mediterranean and make his way through the Suez Canal and the Red Sea and across the Indian Ocean to Australia.

After that, the palmy islands of the South Seas beckoned.

Well, that was the master plan. Remember, this was no crazy kid with wild hair and a yen for publicity, but a sober and very tough and competent gent of mature years, who'd spent a lot of his life working out, in his spare time, the details of his voyage and accumulating the charts and other publications required. With no family responsibilities except for the daughter he'd never been allowed to know since her childhood, whose welfare he'd nevertheless provided for—there was money waiting in Washington if she should need it—he felt free to indulge his romantic vision. If other people thought him nuts, too bad about them. Let them buy retirement homes in Florida or Arizona if they chose. His choice was the boat.

However, when he reached Key West he wasn't feeling very well. Ironically, considering his medical history, he wasn't hit by a flare-up of one of his old injuries, but by a simple touch of stomach flu. He saw a doctor and got himself fixed up with antibiotics, but he was too impatient to get on with his voyage to rest a few days, as recommended. Instead he took along a young man he met on the dock to help him sail the boat as far as Miami, about a hundred and fifty miles. He figured that by the time they got there he'd be well enough to manage alone once more. But as they rode the Gulf Stream north along the Florida Straits, the kid slipped down into the cabin to smoke a cigarette that wasn't tobacco.

There was an instant showdown when Doug, in the cockpit, got a whiff of the smoke drifting out the main hatch. He wasn't about to jeopardize his boat and his dream by having on board any illicit substances, as they're known in the jargon. There may even have been a bit of a struggle, which was a laugh. Although no longer young and not altogether well, a trained man like Doug would have had no trouble tying an untrained, spaced-out kid into fairly painful knots. He searched the shabby pack and threw overboard the illegal stuff he found there. After docking in the big marina in Miami, he tossed the punk ashore with his belongings and told him to get lost, fast.

The following day, as Doug was preparing to tackle the next leg of his long-planned voyage, feeling pretty good again, the Coast Guard descended on him, guided by an anonymous telephone tip. They found a small cache of marijuana hidden on the boat where they'd been told to look—apparently the punk hadn't kept all his smoking materials in his pack. Although Doug identified himself politely and asked them to call Washington, they'd heard that I'm-an-important-guy-and-anyway-I-wuz-framed routine before. They impounded the boat and called the police to take Doug away and charge him, or whatever the legal procedure is in such cases. Mac wasn't specific about the details.

Anyway, the cops got into the act somehow. When Doug protested, they apparently got a little rude and physical. Public servants ourselves in a sense, we don't react at all well to being manhandled by our fellow workers in the governmental vineyard, city, state, or federal. We've had to take too much shit from the real enemy, whoever he may be at any given time. One thing led to another and somebody made the mistake of bouncing a nightstick off Doug's head. . . .

Well, that was the Doug Barnett story as I'd pieced it together from what I already knew and what I'd been told over the phone. Fortunately, one of the Coastguardsmen who remained intact had a sharp pocketknife and knew how to perform an emergency tracheotomy on a crushed larynx, so the baton-happy cop survived. The three fracture cases were hauled

11

off to the nearest hospital for splints and casts. The walking wounded were patched up so they wouldn't bleed all over everything while they waited for proper dressings to be applied in the emergency room.

Douglas Barnett, subdued at last, was dragged off to jail. Eventually he got to make the phone call to which he was legally entitled; and Mac passed the word to me, as well as, I had no doubt, to various influential personages at various levels of government. We take care of our own. Maybe Doug shouldn't have blown his stack like that; but Mac knows perfectly well that the work he wants done would never get done by a bunch of docile characters who, falsely accused, would hold out their wrists for the handcuffs without argument. He also knows it's money in the bank. I mean, the word gets around. Next time one of our people asks politely to be put through to Washington to clear up a misunderstanding, maybe he, or she, will be shown a phone instead of a bunch of overbearing cops.

"It's all so stupid!" said the girl riding beside me in the rental car. "I mean, even if he was innocent, why did he have to fight them like that?"

I said, "When a man has spent his life fighting, he finds it pretty hard to stop, Miss Barnett. And you don't really believe he was innocent, do you?"

"Well . . . well, they did find that horrible stuff on his boat, didn't they? Drugs, ugh! How *could* he? And people always do say they were framed, don't they?"

I said, "Maybe it's just as well I've had very little contact with my own kids. This way I can keep my illusions. If they have so little faith in the veracity of the man from whom they've inherited half the genes they carry, I don't want to know it."

She glanced at me quickly and started to speak, then checked herself. When we reached it, we found

12

the jail to be located in a massive building that looked reasonably modern and handsome on the outside. Inside, although the interior decoration was pretty sharp, if a little worn, it was basically just another king-sized cop-house. There's something about a bunch of big men swaggering around in uniform with guns and clubs that arouses in me an atavistic hostility. I guess I just want to tell them I'm pretty tough myself, so don't give me that hard cop look unless you're ready to back it up, Buster. Childish.

We went through the usual visitors' red tape and were put into a waiting room. I gestured toward a chair. "Rest your feet," I said to the girl. "You said you wanted to see him alone and it's all arranged; but I'll see him first, if you don't mind. Business. After that he's all yours, lucky man."

When an escort arrived for me, I left her sitting there primly, knees together, skirt modestly in place, underwear still a mystery even though I'd watched her entering and leaving a car, an operation that usually reveals everything revealable. But it was a mystery that no longer interested me greatly. I mean, the very proper and modest ones are usually a challenge—you like to see if you can't at least win a relaxed and friendly smile from the inhibited lady— but the masculine curiosity Miss Barnett had aroused in me originally, because she was really a rather pretty girl, was fading fast. Her mother had done too good a job on her.

I was shown into a small visiting room and heard the door shut solidly behind me. It wasn't too bad a room. It was clean and had a table and some reasonably comfortable-looking chairs. It also had illumination enough to shoot a movie by, even with fairly slow film; and they should have no trouble with the sound, I figured, since the place was undoubtedly already miked and wired. There were no windows.

Doug Barnett was sitting in one of the chairs when I came in. He nodded at me but he didn't get to his feet and hurry forward to shake my hand; we don't go in much for effusive greetings. Or partings, for that matter. And maybe rising wasn't all that easy for him at the moment. I started to sit down in the nearest chair, on his left.

"The other one, if you don't mind, Matt," he said, gesturing to the identical chair on the other side of him.

"Sure," I said. When I was seated, I said, "I'm supposed to ask if you want us to cart this joint away brick by brick and sow the foundations with salt like the Romans did with Carthage so nothing would grow there again, ever. Or is it all right if we just blow it up and leave the debris where it falls?"

He didn't answer that. He knew it was just a fancy way of telling him the old team was behind him. We're not a buddy-buddy outfit, but there is a certain *esprit de corps* that surfaces at times like that. We spent a moment taking stock, since we hadn't seen each other for a while. Although I was senior in the organization, having been in it practically from the start, Doug was considerably older. He'd come to us from some other nasty outfit, like maybe the old OSS after they'd sanded it smooth and painted it pretty and called it CIA and he couldn't stand it any longer. He was a husky man with shoulders broad enough to make him look shorter than he really was. Actually he stood, when standing, only an inch or so under six feet. He looked better than I'd expected. I guess they'd cleaned him up fast when the pressure came on from Washington. He was neatly shaved and wearing a clean white shirt and clean dark trousers that looked a little too dressy for his well-worn brown moccasin-type boat shoes, the kind with the patent no-slip white soles.

He was watching me steadily with his head cocked a little to the side. His tanned, smooth face, which didn't betray his age, was unmarked. He still had most of his hair. Where it wasn't gray, it was considerably darker than his daughter's; apparently her fairness had come from her mother's side of the family. A spot had been shaved on Doug's head to make room for a lump of white tape, presumably where the police club had split the scalp. That was the only visible injury; but they're very good at demonstrating their disapproval of obstreperous prisoners without leaving marks that'll show in court. I'm not criticizing, really. They have their methods, and we have ours.

"Tell Mac thanks," Doug said. "I had no right to drag him into it."

"To hell with that," I replied. "Nobody really retires from this crazy outfit. You know that. It works both ways. If you're ever needed again, really needed, you'll be called."

"Well, I thought a long time before I dialed that emergency number; but it looked as if they were going to bury me so deep nobody'd ever find me. And I . . ." He stopped and drew a long breath. "I'd heard the girl was looking for me. I wanted to see her again, Matt. My little girl. Just once before . . . Is she here?"

Well, people do get mushy about their kids, even fairly tough people. "She's outside," I said.

"So she came!"

I said quickly, "Don't get your hopes up, *amigo*. She's been brainwashed most of her life. You're an evil, violent man. Brutally beating up half a dozen helpless little cops and coastguardsmen and smuggling nasty marijuana are exactly what she expects of you. She's just surprised it wasn't coke or heroin."

He grinned at me crookedly. "You don't pull any punches, do you?"

I shrugged. "You'll see her in a minute. What would be the point in letting you entertain any fond expectations, even briefly? To be blunt, your daughter is a fairly impossible, stuffy, little female prick. But she did come."

"Yes," he said. "And if anything happens to me, you'll look after that impossible, stuffy, little female prick for me, won't you? Because you owe me one and I'm asking."

I nodded. That was the second personal matter involved here, the fact that he'd once saved my life.

"You didn't have to say it."

"Sorry. I had to know. She's got nobody else, now that that self-righteous bitch I married is dead."

"Consider it signed and sealed. But Mac has pulled the right strings, and you'll be out of here in a few hours. Maybe you can make your peace with her and do your own looking-after."

He shook his head. "It's a nice thought, but I doubt that what's between us can be changed in an afternoon, after all the years her witch-mother had to work on her. And I may not have too much time, if you know what I mean; so let me give you a quick rundown on the arrangements I've made for her, just in case." After he'd finished, he said, "Well, that takes care of that. Now, what about the boat?"

I said, "That's the tough part. The Coast Guard is apparently being sticky. Pressure is being brought to bear, and we're looking for that creep you were dumb enough to invite on board, to get a confession out of him. But it'll be another few days, at least."

He grimaced. "Bunch of uniformed pirates! What do they do with all the vessels they steal? Oh, excuse *me*! Impound. Confiscate. For a bit of grass worth a few hundred on the street—even assuming it was my grass, which it wasn't—they grab themselves a boat worth fifty grand easy. What the hell kind of justice would that be, even if I were guilty? Legal larceny!"

I said, "Take it easy. Don't flip all over again. And incidentally, you didn't do so well the first time, did you?" I stared at him hard. "Granted, that seems to've been a good enough blow to the throat, judging by all reports, and you couldn't know that Coast Guard guy would be so handy at doing emergency surgery with his little knife. But as for the rest, just a bunch of piddling little fractures and lacerations. Very bad for the team's reputation. We're supposed to be the guys who leave them dead, Mr. Barnett."

He stared right back at me with his head held at that odd angle. "You know the answer, Matt. That billy club didn't do me a damn bit of good in the vision department. I haven't recovered from it yet and probably won't. Cop bastard."

I nodded. "I just wanted to be sure. Anything I can do?"

"There's nothing anybody can do. That was checked out by the medical experts a long time ago. They told me at the time not to let people bounce things off my skull, ha ha; that's why I was retired, although we didn't publicize it. But thanks anyway. Now let me talk with my daughter, please."

"One self-righteous young lady coming up."

"Matt . . ."

"Yes?"

"Don't tell her about my eyes, damn you. Not before I've seen her, at least."

"Is that fair to the girl?" When he didn't speak, I said, "If that's the way you want it. Be good."

"I tried that, and they took my boat away and locked me up in here."

"Well, be careful," I said.

AMY BARNETT was gone less than half an hour. When she returned I saw from her pale, resentful face that the family reunion hadn't turned out well. She said a polite good-bye to her police escort, and we made our way out the door, down the elevator, and out into the Florida spring sunshine. She didn't say anything until we were driving away. Then she opened the neatly buttoned jacket of her flannel suit and turned one of the car's air-conditioning vents her way.

"If I were staying in Florida I'd have to get some lighter clothes, I guess."

"But you aren't staying?"

"No. When I get back to the hotel, I'll see about getting a flight back to Cincinnati tomorrow. It's too late today." She glanced at me a little defiantly. "There's nothing to stay for. I found that out in there."

"He was just as you expected?" I said. "No surprises? Exactly the same wicked man your mother always told you, right?"

"I don't want to talk about it."

I spoke deliberately: "Pretty well preserved for his advanced years, though, wouldn't you say? Nice and tanned and healthy after all that sailing. Or were you so busy reciting all your mother's old grievances that you didn't really look at him at all?"

She studied me for a moment. "What are you trying to tell me, Mr. Helm?"

I said, "Hell, you spent twenty minutes in there. Why should I have to tell you anything? You're a smart girl; you can see things for yourself. If you bother to look." When she didn't speak, I asked, "Where did you sit?"

She frowned. "Well, I started to sit down in the nearest chair, of course, but he said he'd rather have me on the other side of him." She looked at me, puzzled. "Does that have some kind of mystic significance?"

I said, "No peculiar mannerisms that caught your attention?"

"Well, he did hold his head to the side and kind of peer at me, but I thought that was just a nervous habit he'd acquired since I last saw him all those years ago . . . Mr. Helm, will you stop this, please! Tell me what you're driving at!"

"There's something else," I said. "You're shocked at the amount of damage he did in the fight. We're shocked at the amount of damage he didn't do. I mean, we never fight for fun, just for keeps. That's the way he was trained; yet there wasn't a single lousy dead man on that dock when he got through. A very poor performance, even for an agent who's been retired for a while and hammering on a boat instead of practicing his lethal skills."

She shivered. "What a horrible attitude, to criticize a man for *not* killing!"

I said, "Jesus, that knee-jerk humanitarianism! From a dame who doesn't even bother to find out why her own father had to be retired. Why don't you practice a little of that bleeding-heart stuff at home, Miss Barnett?" Driving one-handed, I worked a paper out of my inside jacket pocket and passed it to her. "One of our people, the one who's negotiating for Doug's release, stopped by and gave me this while I was waiting for you. Read it."

There was a little silence. At last she turned to me, aghast. "But this medical report says . . ."

I said, "Apparently there was a light plane that crashed; I gather Doug made it crash. It was the only way he could accomplish his mission, his last mission. I don't know what it was; as a matter of fact, I didn't know any of the details before, only that he'd been retired with a disability a year or two back. But it seems he was knocked unconscious by the crash. He was in a coma for a while; later they had to go in and relieve the pressure or something. Dig out bone splinters. Whatever. As a would-be nurse, you can probably decipher the jargon of that report better than I can. They put the lid back on and sent him to a place we have out west to recuperate. They were just about to turn him loose, put him back on active duty, when the trouble started."

Amy started to speak but checked herself. She stared at the official-looking paper in her hand.

I went on as I drove: "It's all in there. Blurred vision in the left eye. Violent headaches. Brief dizzy spells that were almost momentary blackouts. They ran their fancy tests and scans on him. The consensus was that something was going bad in there and would get worse. While they could go in again and try to fix it, the operation might leave him a vegetable; and what was in there probably wasn't fixable, anyway. Recommendation: immediate retirement. Advice: take it easy, live right, and avoid any more blows on the head. Prognosis: maybe two years, maybe five, you want fortune-tellers, yet?"

Amy Barnett whispered. "Oh, my God!" So she wasn't totally incapable of blasphemy.

I said, "Apparently he decided to carry out the plans he'd been developing for years, get the boat, fix it up, and sail it as far as he could. Why sit around waiting for the dark?" I shook my head irritably. "And I'm guessing that the reason he didn't kill anybody in that marina hassle was that he just wasn't seeing very well after being cracked by that police club. I think he felt something go very wrong inside his head when he was hit and knew he didn't have left even the few years of vision he'd been promised. Half-dazed, he instinctively used his best shot on the guy who'd hit him, who was right there within easy range. After that, I guess, he was hurting pretty badly and just fighting shadows as they came at him."

"But he didn't act as if . . . I mean, I'm sure he could see me, just now."

I nodded. "After a fashion, sure, but he obviously has to work at it. My guess is that both eyes are affected now, but the left is worse than the right, which is why he doesn't like to have people sitting on that side of him." There was a little silence. Amy Barnett glanced back over her shoulder and started to speak impulsively; but I cut her off: "No, I won't take you back there. What do you want to do now, offer to hang around and tie his shoelaces and hand him his white cane because you're so sorry for him?"

"Why didn't you tell me?" she whispered.

"He asked me not to. He was running a little test, I guess, to determine just what kind of a brat he'd begotten—was she going to accept her remaining parent at last even though he was behind bars, or was she just going to tell him how much she disapproved of him? He didn't want the exam complicated by a lot of cheap sympathy. And you flunked, so you can get your damn airplane ticket and go home to Cincinnati.

21

As you said yourself, there's nothing to keep you here."

There was a little silence. At last Amy Barnett drew a long, ragged breath. "You really hate me, don't you!" she whispered.

I was shocked. "Don't be ridiculous! I've only known you a couple of hours; why in the world would I—"

"You do!" she breathed. "And isn't it wonderful for you, to have somebody to hate at last! After all these years of forcing yourself to be generous and understanding about the way your own family left you. So kindly, so tolerant, gritting your teeth all the time to keep from letting anybody know the way you *really* felt. But now you can take it out on me, all the hurt and anger you've been keeping bottled up inside yourself all these years. Telling yourself all the time that you're just doing it because of your sympathy for my poor daddy, who was betrayed by my mother and me in exactly the same way!"

Mechanically guiding the car through the dense Miami traffic, I told myself that she was executing a typically feminine maneuver, defending herself by attacking me—quite unreasonably, of course. The only trouble was, I realized, that she wasn't being all that unreasonable. In fact she was perfectly right: I was using her to unload some old private anger and frustration. Which, I suppose, said something unpleasant about me, but that was no great surprise. However, the fact that she was capable of reading me so accurately indicated that there was more girl there than I'd seen. Or wanted to see?

I said rather stiffly, "Very shrewd analysis, Dr. Barnett."

She licked her lips. "I'm sorry. I shouldn't have said that. But you hurt me. Not that I didn't deserve it."

I said, "All right. I surrender. Don't hit me again;

I'll be good, ma'am." I glanced at my watch. "But I can't take you back there now; according to the man who gave me that medical report, they should be getting ready to release him, and we don't want to confuse things by trying to get to see him. You know the red-tape circuit. But if you want to put off your flight home and talk with him in the morning, I'll let you know where he's staying. Well, I was told it'll be the Coral Shores hotel, but I'll get the room number for you. Of course, he won't make it easy for you. He's a proud man, and he'll know you've changed your mind about him simply because you've learned of his condition."

"Everybody's been too proud, including me." She swallowed hard. "I wanted to tell him how lonely it was nowadays and how much I needed somebody, him, and the words wouldn't come. And then, somehow, we started talking about Mother, and he was so sneering and contemptuous that I got mad and . . ." She shook her head quickly. "I shouldn't have reacted so defensively. I should have remembered all the years he's had to brood about it. I really meant to be very reasonable and understanding. I'd like to try again."

"I'll see what I can do," I said. "In the meantime, may I make amends for my prejudiced behavior by buying you dinner?"

She shook her head and gave me that meager little smile of hers. I thought I'd like to be around some time when she cut loose with a real grin.

But her words were reasonably friendly: "Reparations aren't necessary, Mr. Helm. But I'm pretty tired. It's been a long day. When we get back to the hotel, I think I'll just retire to the room you were kind enough to arrange for me, have room service send up a hamburger, and go to bed early."

Around nine o'clock that evening I got a call from

the local man who'd slipped me the copy of Doug's medical report, earlier. We don't have agents all over the world like some outfits, but we do have part-time people in various strategic places including Miami. They aren't used for heavy work; they just serve as eyes and legs. This one's code name was Jerome. He reported that Doug, upon his release, had allowed himself to be escorted to the hotel room arranged for him; then he'd disappeared. Jerome was annoyed. He hadn't been warned that the man whose welfare he was supposed to be looking after might try to give him the slip. But the room had been empty when he'd stopped by to see if there was anything further he could do, and there was no note to indicate where Doug might have gone.

"Did you check the marina?" I asked. "His boat's still there, isn't it?"

"Yes, they've confiscated so many vessels hauling drugs they don't know where to put them all; their official dock, wherever it is, is full up," said the voice on the phone. "No, I haven't had a chance to get over there; I just called immediately to let you know he was gone. I'll head right down there."

"Hold everything." I thought for a moment, then said, "To hell with it. The way he's feeling, if he's going for the boat, you'll have to shoot him to stop him. Let him run. Let the Hooligan Navy worry about the damn boat; they're the ones who grabbed it. We'll stay clear."

"Okay, but I still think somebody could have told me he might sneak off. . . ."

I made a note to warn Mac, in Washington, that our current man in Miami would bear watching. We'd had a very good part-timer there named Brent, but he'd quit and married the boss's daughter; and Mac was now a grandpa. A six-pound girl, if it matters. But Jerome was obviously not of Brent's caliber; and any agent in an escort situation who thinks more about his own feelings than about the person he's been assigned to help and protect has to be used with caution. It occurred to me it was something I could well bear in mind myself.

I went to bed. It seemed that the phone rang again almost immediately; but my watch said it was four-thirty in the morning.

"Mr. Helm?" It was Amy Barnett's voice. "Mr. Helm, I just got a telephone call from the coast guard. My father's gone absolutely crazy; he's stolen back his boat and put to sea!"

"Isn't that a contradiction in terms, Miss Barnett? If it's his boat, how can he steal it?"

"Oh, stop it! You know what I mean. They're going out after him, and they want me to come along; I can't imagine why."

"I can," I said. "They want you to witness the fact that this time they picked him up very gently and legally."

"They want you, too. Representing your agency, I suppose."

"I'll be with you in a minute. Bring a heavy sweater, if you've got one. The Gulf Stream is supposed to be a warm current; but I understand it can still get pretty chilly out there in the Florida Straits."

The moment I put the phone down it rang again. That was the U.S.C.G. with my official invitation to the hanging.

|||||||| CHAPTER 4 ||||||||||||||||||||||||||||||||||||||||||

THE COAST Guard vessel was a sizable boat as boats go, but it was not one of the long, lean, junior-grade destroyers you sometimes see wearing that slanting orange stripe up forward on their wicked-looking white hulls. Our transportation, although it carried the same stripe, was less naval in appearance: a husky, beamy, planing-type vessel in the forty-foot bracket. It bristled with antennas and searchlights, and the deckhouse was crammed full of interesting electronics gear. At least I suppose it was interesting to somebody.

I recognized a radar set; also a Loran, since I'd once had to master one in order to find my way home on a boat with a very dead crew I'd helped make that way—well, most of the way home; we ran into a little more trouble eventually. Fortunately, there had been an instruction book handy, and I hadn't found the apparatus all that difficult to figure out. However, there were other black boxes here that I couldn't identify, also with touch-type keyboards and luminous windows displaying magic numbers that undoubtedly meant something to somebody. There were also radios of various persuasions: SSB, VHF, and even a little CB stuck into a corner like an afterthought.

There really wasn't much room left for people, but I helped Amy brace herself in a neutral corner.

She'd lost some of her prim and proper look; it's hard for a girl to look prim in jeans. The round collar of a neat white cotton blouse showed above a light-blue sweater that emphasized the blue of her eyes and played down the gray. Her soft light-brown hair was still, or again, neatly pinned up about her head. I reminded myself that I must not be prejudiced against her because of an ancient hurt of my own, for which she had not been responsible. It shouldn't be hard to treat her fairly, I told myself; she wasn't bad-looking, even in pants. Then the cabin lights went out. On deck they went through the routine of casting off the lines, and finally we were off.

"I don't think it would be advisable to sit down, even if there were someplace to sit," I said above the muted rumble of the engines. "I don't know how fast this thing travels, but some of them can break your back when they really start to go, if you aren't prepared to absorb the jolting with your knees."

They'd given us a mystery man for company, wearing khaki uniform pants like the rest; but his navy-blue watch cap and turtleneck sweater carried no insignia of rank. He was a compact man of medium height with regular WASP features and a dark Mediterranean skin—it had to be more than just a deep tan—but his eyes were gray and the shape of his face was strictly Anglo-Saxon. Well, we're all kind of scrambled genetically these days, but I had a hunch the Swedes and Scots in my own ancestry got along a little better than the widely diverse racial types, whatever they were, that had produced him. Thick black hair and strong white teeth. Age fifty, give or take five. Now he showed the fine teeth in a tolerant smile at my assumption of nautical knowledge.

"It shouldn't be that uncomfortable, Miss Barnett,"

he said. "There's not much sea running out in the Straits this morning, and we won't be making that much speed. We won't need to. He can't have got very far. We should have his location by radio by the time we get out the channel."

Gray daylight was sneaking up on us now; and the lights of Miami—or was it Miami Beach here?—were going out along the heavily built-up shoreline as we threaded our way between the buoys of a pass leading seaward that was unfamiliar to me. But then, while I've had to learn how to handle boats after a fashion in the line of duty, it's not my sport. I'll take a horse or a four-wheel-drive vehicle and some nice desert or mountain scenery any time I'm offered a choice; to hell with a lot of salty water that leaves you sticky when you swim in it and can't even be used to mix a drink with.

I said, "His location is no problem. Why should it be? Didn't anybody bother to look at his maps? Excuse me, charts, sir."

He didn't look like the kind of man who'd be impressed by a lot of greasy sirs; but when you're dealing with the uniformed services it's always best to play safe. There was no telling what rank he held, but there was no mistaking the fact that he had some. Respect is cheap and doesn't hurt a bit. At least I've never found it very painful, although I've worked with some younger agents who'd much rather be tortured than polite.

"Belay the sirs," he said. "The name is Sanderson. What do you mean, Helm?"

I said, "If I know Doug Barnett, he'll have it all worked out on paper, where he's going from here. He's a very systematic guy with a very systematic master plan. He told me about it once. As I recall, after Miami his next stop was to be Bermuda, about a thousand miles away, out in the open Atlantic."

Sanderson was watching me closely by the dim glow of the instruments around us. "We figured he'd head straight across to the Bahamas," he said. "Less than fifty miles. We do have certain arrangements with the authorities over there, but we've got to be diplomatic about taking advantage of them. Once he's in Bahamian waters, it'll take a certain amount of red tape to get him back."

"Bullshit," I said. "You talk as if you're dealing with some kind of criminal in flight. As far as Doug Barnett's concerned, he's an innocent man who was attacked by pirates masquerading as law-enforcement officers. They stole his boat and beat him up and kidnapped him . . . Don't argue with me, sir. I'm not the guy you're chasing. I'm just telling you the way his mind is working. Remember he's carried a badge of his own for a good many years; your pretty uniforms and fancy collar decorations don't mean a damn thing to him. I don't mean he's nuts or anything. He simply refuses to accept your authority anymore; and he's just taking back his boat going right on with the cruise you interrupted so rudely. If you leave him alone, everything will be fine. If you don't, well, he's ready for that, too."

"He broke the law—"

"What law says you can beat a sick man over the head for unknowingly having a couple of ounces of pot on his boat?"

"The captain or owner of a vessel is responsible for whatever is found on board."

I stared at him unbelievingly. "You must be kidding? You mean that if I invite three friendly couples for a sail on the big yacht I don't have, the pretty wife I don't have will have to take the women into one cabin while I take the men into another. And then we'll strip our guests and examine all their bodily orifices for contraband—my nonexistent wife will have the harder job there, since she'll have an extra orifice to deal with in each case. And then I'll slice open the shoulder pads of the men's jackets while she breaks off the heels of the women's shoes and does some jacket work herself, not to mention some dress work, to make sure nothing's hidden there. We'll rip open any suspicious seams of all their garments. She'll hack apart the women's purses and I'll chop apart the luggage. You never can tell what's hidden inside a purse or suitcase lining, can you? And then at last I'll tell our happy, naked guests to haul their ruined belongings to their cabins. Sorry about that, folks; the law says we're responsible, so we had to make sure. Now, if you can find yourself some clothes that aren't in rags, you can get dressed and we'll have a nice drink to the lovely cruise we're going to have." I grimaced. "Jesus, Sanderson! I thought drugs were *your* job. Are you going to issue a badge to every boat owner so he can enforce your laws for you while you play golf or go fishing? Talk about passing the buck!"

Sanderson's dark face was impassive. "If you're quite finished with your lecture, Mr. Helm, perhaps you'll condescend to tell me where you think your colleague really is."

I glanced at my watch. "It's five-thirty in the morning. Doug apparently disappeared around nine last night. Say it took him an hour to reach the boat and get it under way, and another hour to get clear of the harbor, that's eleven o'clock, right? So we can figure he's been on course for six and a half hours. What speed does his boat make? There's not a hell of a lot of wind and he doesn't have much power, does he? Most sailboats don't, as I recall."

"A two-cylinder Volvo-Penta diesel. A little over twenty horsepower."

"Well, you know more about this stuff than I do,

but even if he's really pushing, six knots is about as much as he's going to get out of that heavy boat even using both power and sail, isn't it? Six knots times six and a half hours comes out to thirty-nine nautical miles. Oh, I forgot, there's the Gulf Stream. Two knots of favorable current? Three? Say two and a half, average; I heard somebody use that figure once. Times six and a half, is what?"

There was a little pause; then Amy Barnett said softly, "Sixteen and a quarter miles. But—"

I said to Sanderson, "Okay, tell them to look about fifty-five miles up the line."

"What line, Mr. Helm?"

I shook my head irritably. "What's the big problem? Hell, he made no secret of his plans; he's been telling everybody about them for years. I told you, he's heading for Bermuda, only he can't sail a direct course there because the Bahama Islands are in the way, right? He's got to get out of the Florida Straits and into the Atlantic before he can settle on his final course. So he'll figure to pass the northern end of the Bahamas reef by a safe margin before he swings northeast toward Bermuda."

"You make it sound very simple, Mr. Helm. However, the fact is that Barnett is a fugitive from justice; he'd hardly adopt such an obvious—"

I sighed. "Goddamn it, why won't you *listen*? He doesn't give a good goddamn about your justice, Mister. This is a government agent just like you, except for being slightly retired, who asked for a little consideration from his fellow government agents and didn't get it. Now he's making his own rules and to hell with yours. To put it another way, he's giving you one more chance to be reasonable; and speaking for myself, why can't you do it? We have a fairly efficient and useful organization, Captain Sanderson or whatever your rank is. One day you may need a little help from us. So leave it now; let him go. Forget those two ounces of pot or however much it was, or go find the man to whom it really belonged; and we'll forget the way you pushed our man around and beat him up when all he did was ask for a little break as a colleague recently retired from government service. Just one little phone call, but he wasn't allowed to make it!"

After a moment, Sanderson spoke without expression: "So you think Barnett is heading for Matanilla Shoal, at the upper end of the Bahamas. But that's well over a hundred miles, closer to a hundred and twenty, if I remember the chart correctly."

I looked at him bleakly and shrugged. "Very well, sir. If that's the way you want it. You'll find your quarry somewhere on a line between here and Matanilla Shoal, wherever the hell that is. Probably about halfway there."

"Why are you telling me this?"

I said, "Hell, finding him is no problem. You'd eventually have spread your search wide enough to manage it without my help. But just what do you plan to do when you find him?"

His gray eyes studied me thoughtfully. "An unarmed man in a slow boat shouldn't present a tremendous problem, Mr. Helm."

I laughed in his face. "You're dreaming, Sanderson. What makes you think he's unarmed?"

"We confiscated a rather fancy stainless-steel pump shotgun hidden behind the backrest of the main cabin settee."

"So now you're guilty of robbing him of his boat, his liberty, his eyesight, his future, *and* his gun. Haven't you done enough to him?" The brown-faced man watched me without speaking. I said, "Don't count on dealing with an unarmed man, *amigo*. That shiny, obvious pumpgun was just something to keep

you happy if you looked. Or any other official interested in firearms. There'll be other weapons on board—
you can bet on it—hidden away well enough that
even your hotshot searchers couldn't find them. We
make enemies in our line of work. Doug would be
prepared to deal with a vengeful character settling an
old grudge. And I understand there are real pirates
around these days in certain waters, not just the ones
in fancy sea-cop uniforms hijacking people's boats
under a pretense of legality. No, don't think for a
moment he'll be an easy, unarmed mark a second
time. One way or another he'll be ready for you. So I
ask you again, how do you plan to deal with him?"

"Just a minute."

Sanderson moved forward to where the young officer in command of the boat stood beside the helmsman.
There was a brief conference, which was moved to
the chart table. Presently one of the radios was
activated. The sound of the motors made it impossible for me to eavesdrop. It was full daylight now, and
we were out in open water with the wedding-cake
skyline of Miami Beach receding astern. I saw that
Amy Barnett was regarding me with hostility.

"What's the matter with you?" I asked.

"You don't have to *help* them track him down, do
you?"

I sighed. "For God's sake! What do you think this
is, a Boy Scout jamboree? First of all, as I just said,
they'll find him easily enough without my help now
that it's daylight; why be obstructive for nothing?
Second, Doug knows perfectly well that we—I—have
to cooperate with the local authorities even though
we don't like it. He wouldn't want it otherwise. He's
spent most of his working life with us; he wouldn't
want us to jeopardize the whole agency just for him.
As a matter of fact, that's the one bright spot in this
hassle. We're the ones who got him turned loose; if

he does a lot of damage now, we'll be held responsible. Of course, if he's hurting badly enough and they make him mad enough, he could forget it. Keep your fingers crossed. Here we go."

The conference was over. The young skipper spoke to the man at the wheel, and the boat swung to the left—excuse me, to port. The lazy sound of the big motors under our feet increased in volume. I steadied the girl as the boat surged ahead. Sanderson returned to us.

"I'm afraid it may be a little rougher than I promised you, Miss Barnett," he said. "We may have farther to go than I thought; we'll have to use a little more speed." He glanced at me. "There's a hundred-and-ten footer on patrol up ahead. The *Cape March*. She's moving in to intercept."

"Tell her to stay clear when she gets there," I said.

He studied me for a moment. " 'Yacht *Seawind* to be located and taken under observation; no other action without further instructions.' Satisfactory?"

"As far as it goes," I said. "But let me explain something about our organization, Sanderson. We're a bunch of screwballs, as you may have noticed. Certain things were left out of us, or trained out of us, or beaten out of us. Like a normal reverence for human life, and that includes our own human lives. In other words, we were taught that if we gotta go, well, we gotta go; let's just see how much company we can take to hell with us. Are you following me?"

"More or less." His voice was dry. "You sound rather like a bunch of rabid wolves, Mr. Helm."

"Hey, you're getting the idea," I said. "And when you see a rabid wolf trotting dumbly up the street with slaver dripping from its jaws, you know the disease has got it and it's making its death run and you'd damn well better not get in its way. Well, Doug Barnett is out there making his death run, Mister.

He can only see out of one eye, to amount to anything, and that one's on its way out, thanks to you and your club-happy cop friends. His head is aching enough to drive him crazy. He knows he's through, things are going irreversibly wrong inside his brain, and there's nothing left for him but a lousy ending in the blind, black darkness. Remember, this is a man who's spent his life dealing in violence, and your uniforms don't mean a thing to him any longer. The old training rule is maybe you sometimes have to stand still for one blow or bullet, but nobody—*nobody*—ever gets two free shots. You've had your freebie, as far as Doug Barnett is concerned."

Amy Barnett started to speak in protest, but Sanderson's calm voice interrupted her: "What do you expect him to do, Mr. Helm?"

I said, "I can't speak for him, only for myself. But I can assure you, if I were Doug on that sailboat up ahead of us somewhere, I'd be waiting hopefully for a bunch of you self-righteous, legalistic, uniformed bastards to come sailing within range all fat and sassy and self-confident. And I'd laugh and laugh as I emptied clip after clip into you, and to hell with the fact that we're supposed to be working for the same government. It didn't bother you when you had me arrested and clubbed with a nightstick and thrown in jail, so why should I give it a second thought? I'd make damn sure I got enough of you to force you to shoot back and kill me. I'd figure that after what you'd done to me, the least you owed me was a nice quick death. Doug may have other ideas, but I wouldn't count on it."

"I see."

Sanderson frowned at me for a moment; then he turned abruptly away and moved forward once more to speak to the skipper, who picked up a microphone. Again I couldn't hear what was said but I didn't have to: the word was being passed that the subject might be armed and mentally unbalanced and highly dangerous. Sanderson stood there awhile talking to the skipper. The boat roared on northward. The jolting wasn't too bad, but it's surprising how incompressible water can be at that speed; every now and then we'd slam into something that felt like concrete. I tried to steady the girl beside me, but she shrugged my hand away.

At last she burst out with the thing she'd been brooding about: "How could you talk about my father that way? You made him sound like a madman!"

I said, "Well, *there's* a sudden access of filial devotion! A bit slow, aren't you? If you'd given him something to hang around for yesterday, like a reconciliation, he might not be out here today looking for death in the large economy package." Her face lost color, and she looked away. I was sorry I'd said it. I went on quickly: "Anyway, I thought it was myself I was representing as the madman. And if you'd think about it a little instead of going off half-cocked in your usual immature fashion, maybe you'd see that the more dangerous and crazy I make your daddy sound, the less likely they are to go charging up to him at full throttle with a lot of arrogant demands and ultimatums designed to make even the mildest character flip his lid."

She drew a long breath and looked up at me. "I see. I'm sorry. I didn't realize you were deliberately exaggerating. . . ." Her voice trailed off. She looked away again. "And I wasn't aware of displaying any conspicuous immaturity, Mr. Helm."

I grinned at that, and she gave me a resentful glance and didn't speak again for a long time. In bright sunshine, under a clear blue sky, the boat charged on up the Florida Straits. It's a fifty-mile slot, as Sanderson had indicated, between the solid, densely populated mainland of Florida, and the widespread reefs and often uninhabited islands and islets of the Bahamas. We'd long since lost all land from sight.

I spoke to the girl: "Doug put you in my charge. Did he tell you that? If anything should happen to him, I'm your substitute papa."

She started to speak quickly, perhaps in protest, then she smiled instead, rather maliciously. "Then you'd better stop ogling my nylons hoping for a better view, hadn't you, Mr. Helm? I mean, when I'm wearing nylons. Under the circumstances that's practically incest, isn't it?" Her smile faded and she shook her head quickly. "I've been getting along without a father most of my life. And if I did have to pick a new one, it certainly wouldn't be you."

"Nobody asked you," I said. "Who the hell gets to pick their parents? No, shut up and listen while we've got a little time to ourselves. I'm to tell you that there are twenty-five thousand dollars available to you at any time just by calling the Washington number you called before. You can use it to buy diamonds or ice cream cones or a fancy sports car. If you want. But he put it there originally for emergencies, like if you lost your job or got sick or something while he was off sailing where he couldn't be reached. And when he dies you've got two hundred grand coming, more or less, depending on how the lawyers make out with the IRS. It's Babcock and Phillips, St. Petersburg, Florida. Can you remember that? Well, if you forget, they'll get in touch with you."

She licked her lips and said stiffly, "Of course I can't accept it."

I said, "You really are a bitch, aren't you? You won't even give him the satisfaction of leaving his daughter in pretty good shape financially! This is danger pay he's saved up over the years because he had nobody to spend it on, just the boat. Where do you think he'd rather have it go, to his own flesh and blood or some lousy charity? Or the IRS? Think about him for a change instead of your lousy little pride and your lousy little self."

She drew a long breath. "You don't exactly practice the bedside manner, do you? Did he tell you all this just before he saw me?" When I nodded, she breathed, "If he was thinking of my . . . my welfare then, why did he have to be so *impossible* when he talked to me only a few minutes later?"

"Well, it can't have been an easy scene for either of you, after all the years."

"All right, I'll talk to the lawyers, when . . . if there isn't anybody else who's better entitled to his money."

"He said not."

"So you've done your duty and given me the information. Now you can take off your daddy hat and be your simple, lecherous self again."

I grinned. "What's the matter, are you ashamed of your pretty legs, Barnett? But you're wrong. I haven't done quite all of my duty. There's one more thing."

"What thing?"

I spoke carefully: "I told you once; I've stayed away from my own kids because I didn't want anybody ever getting the idea of using them against me or punishing them for something I'd done. It's an occupational hazard we all face. And you're Doug Barnett's daughter and somebody out of his past with a grievance might just possibly decide to take it out on you if he's unavailable. So if you ever run into a situation that looks even slightly menacing, that you don't quite understand, call us right away. Same number, collect. If I'm available, I'll come running; if I'm not, somebody else will. And that goes for what might be called non-service-connected problems as well."

She frowned. "What does that mean?"

"I'm sure you can manage your life without our assistance under normal circumstances," I said, "but you haven't had much experience with violence. If anybody threatens you in a physical way, a rejected boyfriend who won't stay rejected, for instance, or some syndicate jerk who doesn't like the way you're testifying in a court case, or even just the gang of dead-end kids you have to pass on your way to the bus or subway or whatever they have in Cincinnati, just pick up the phone. Or, hell, if you just get into a bad bind of any kind and need help. Somebody'll come solve the problem for you, diplomatically, financially, or otherwise. Me, if I'm around." I regarded her for a moment. "What I'm trying to say is that we take care of our own, Miss Barnett. You're not alone. Regardless of what happens here, you've got a family of sorts, maybe one you disapprove of, but that's often the way with families. Keep it in mind."

She hesitated. I sensed that her impulse was to reject us and everything we stood for as her mother had done; but she checked whatever she'd been about to say and nodded.

"Thank you," she said gravely. "I can't imagine that I'll ever have occasion to take advantage of the offer, but . . . well, thank you."

Up forward in the deckhouse they'd been on the radio again. Sanderson made his way back to us, steadying himself by the overhead handrails.

"We've got Barnett located," he said to me. "He hadn't come nearly as far as you estimated. The *Cape March* just picked him up less than ten miles ahead. She's closing in on him, but cautiously, as you advised."

I nodded. "Okay, I misjudged him. I knew he wasn't fleeing, but I thought he might goose it just a little, to get as far as possible before he was spotted. However, he wouldn't normally have used the motor here even though the wind is pretty light, would he? With the favorable Gulf Stream current to help him, he'd have been doing it strictly under sail and saving his fuel to get him through real calms on the long passage ahead. So I guess he told himself he damn well wasn't going to let you panic him into going even a fraction of a knot faster than he ordinarily would. . . . Christ, what was *that*, a sonic boom?"

Even in the deckhouse, which vibrated with the noise of the powerful engines below, we'd all heard it, or felt it: a short, hard clap of sound. As we started unanimously for the doors leading out on deck, the boat's skipper turned quickly with the microphone in his hand.

"Admiral, it's the *March!*" he called.

Sanderson hurried forward. I guided Amy Barnett outside and steadied her on the narrow side deck. We couldn't see it at first; then I spotted and pointed out to her the little round smoke cloud just separating itself from the horizon ahead and rising deliberately like a released balloon, gradually losing its tight, hard shape as the breezes worked on it. Sanderson appeared in the deckhouse doorway, or whatever you call it on a boat. His face was grim.

"Was Barnett carrying explosives?"

I looked at him for a long moment; then I shrugged. "We had a case a while back, somebody who used sailing yachts as floating bombs. As a matter of fact it was my case, but Doug could easily have heard about it; and while he bought his hull ready-made he finished it himself. He could have built anything into it he wanted to, including a self-destruct apparatus for when things got really tough."

Amy said desperately, "Stop it! Stop talking as if this is a polite tea party. . . . What *happened*?"

I said, "Obviously he blew himself up when he saw he was caught. The only question is did he take their goddamn cutter with him, I hope?"

She looked pleadingly at Sanderson. "Tell me!"

"Helm is right, Miss Barnett. I'm sorry." He stared coldly at me. "But I have to disappoint you, Helm. Barnett made no attempt to damage the *Cape March*. When he saw the ship taking up station astern, he raised them on the VHF and said he'd been expecting them, but it had been a hell of a fine good-bye sail. He suggested that it might be well if they fell back a bit now and stuck their fingers in their ears. They could see him sitting in the main cabin hatchway; he had one of those wind-vane gears that let boats steer themselves. He grinned at them over his shoulder and threw them a mock salute; then he reached down into the cabin and . . . well, the whole boat simply disintegrated and disappeared in the violent explosion that followed. He must have had something fairly potent packed away in that bilge."

After a little, I spoke deliberately: "God, what an opportunity missed! I'd have coaxed your damn toy warship alongside before I pushed the bang-button. Well, Doug always was a softhearted slob."

We stared at each other for a moment longer. Amy Barnett was making tearfully indignant noises, but she didn't understand. Maybe in the next century the women's libbers will have us all weeping and wailing pitifully in time of grief; it's supposed to be very therapeutic. Meanwhile, girls still do it one way and boys another, and Sanderson and I were both boys together in that moment.

He knew what I was telling him. He knew how I felt about Doug Barnett. He also knew how I felt about him.

THE FREAK'S name was Ernest. Ernest Love, he said. Well, I suppose it could have been. He was almost too good to be true, or too bad to be true. He had a scraggly reddish beard, maybe to make up for the fact that his scraggly reddish hair started fairly well back from his forehead, leaving quite a bit of bald pinkish scalp exposed, although he wasn't very far along into his twenties. It gave him a prematurely aged and rather degenerate look.

He had small greenish eyes and a long thin nose and big bad teeth with wide spaces between them. He wore ragged jeans, a dirty green jersey with dirty white letters across the front—NIX THE NUKES— and worn-out jogging shoes. I wondered whatever happened to Keds, but it's all Adidas these days, or reasonable facsimiles thereof. Ernest Love needed a bath very badly; but what he really wanted, he said, was information.

"Who the fuck do you think you are?" he demanded. "What the fuck do you think you're doing?"

They always ask who the fuck you think you are and what the fuck you think you're doing. Our man in Miami, Jerome, who'd tracked him down with help and brought him to my hotel room, held him by the arm. Beside Ernest Love's scrawny, ragged, antisocial figure, Jerome looked solid and conventional, although he, too, was in jeans and jogging shoes—a husky beachboy type, very tanned, with golden locks almost as long as his captive's straggling red hair. The two of them made me feel quite ancient, brought up as I was in a bygone age of sneakers and haircuts.

But that was irrelevant, of course. I thought of a small round cloud of smoke on the horizon; and I looked at Ernest Love and thought he was a hell of a thing to bring about the death of a good agent who'd survived the best homicidal efforts of truly dangerous enemies. We don't go in for friendship much in the business, and Doug had been an abrasive guy to work with anyway; but that made no difference now. I looked at Ernest Love and felt a strong desire to pistol-whip him a little, and then maybe kick him in the balls a little, and then maybe boot the shit out of him a little, just a little, when he fell down screaming and hugging himself. I told myself I was a reasonably civilized person and didn't do such brutal and barbaric things. Well, at least not unnecessarily.

I said, "I'm a friend of Douglas Barnett's, Mr. Love. Somebody framed him on a drug charge, and one thing led to another, and he wound up committing suicide. Would you know anything about that, Mr. Love?"

"Barnett? I never heard of any Barnett!" There was innocent, self-righteous indignation in the redhead's voice. Then his assurance wavered as the rest of what I'd said penetrated. "What . . . what do you mean, framed?"

"An anonymous phone call to the Coast Guard telling them to check out a thirty-two-foot sailing yacht called *Seawind*. And exactly where on board to look."

He licked his lips. "Oh, Christ! *That* boat?"

43

"That boat."

"Who remembers what they call themselves? Was that his name, Barnett? Jesus, man, I didn't mean nothing. I mean, shit, the guy hassled me so I hassled him back, that's all. Getting all holier-than-thou just because he owned the fucking boat! Roughing me up and throwing overboard most of my . . . Christ, do you know what that shit *costs* these days? So after I got ashore I made a phone call. Why the fuck should I let him get away with shit like that? Okay, I made a phone call. What are you going to do about it?"

I said, "Me? Shit, man, I'm not going to do fuck about it. I'm just going to turn you over to another friend of mine. Did you ever hear of Giuseppe Velo?"

"Velo?" He frowned. "Wasn't he a Mafia bigshot? I thought he was dead."

I shook my head. "No, but you'll wish he were about an hour from now. And for two or three hours more, depending on how long you last. No, old Seppi isn't dead, not quite, and he kind of owes me a favor. Anyway, he says that now that he's retired his boys need exercise. They're getting fat and lazy with nothing to do except guard the body." I turned to Jerome, who was watching with a certain amount of disapproval. To hell with him. I said, "Call the lobby and have Velo's wrecking crew come up here and haul this away, will you? And then turn up the air-conditioning a couple of notches and see if we can't get the stink out of here."

Ernest Love licked his lips. "But . . . but what are they going to do to me?"

"Do?" I said. "I don't know what they're going to do and I don't want to know, Mr. Love. I'm a respectable employee of Uncle Sam; how would I know anything about things like that? Strictly against regulations. Hell, a man could get into trouble doing *that* to people, even to a cheap creep who drove his best friend to kill himself." I thought Doug Barnett would be surprised to learn about our fine relationship, wherever he was. To be sure, he'd saved my life once, and I'd promised to look after his daughter in return; but it had been all in the day's work. However, it sounded impressive. I said, "Later, they'll bring me your confession so I can clear Doug's name. What they do with you when they're through with you, what's left of you, is no concern of mine. Who'll miss you? They have their own ways of putting out the garbage. I don't pry into things that are none of my business."

There was a knock on the door. Jerome went to open it. Old Seppi, from the Miami Beach penthouse where I'd called him, had done very well by us. The first one in was menacing enough, an obvious ex-pug not quite big enough for a heavyweight, and perhaps not very good in the ring considering the way he'd got his nose and ears and eyebrows battered, but still nobody you'd want to tackle without a shotgun. But the second one was truly spectacular, over six feet tall and very black, with his head shaved in a peculiar manner. What a gent of African ancestry was trying to prove by wearing an Iroquois Indian scalplock, I couldn't say—if there was a message there, it wasn't being delivered at my address—but even though it was a recognized TV getup it made him look as mean as a king-sized rattlesnake, and I think it was what did the job.

At least Ernest Love was clutching at my arm in a panicky way. "Oh, Jesus, man, can't we make a deal? Hey, you want a confession, I'll give you a confession. . . ."

The rest of it kind of went by me; I wasn't listening any longer. Because there was real terror in his eyes now, and I realized that everything that had gone

45

before had been just an act: fake arrogance, phony defiance, pretend fear.

Waking up at last, I looked at the bald spot and saw the very faint reddish stubble where the hair had been shaved away for effect. I looked at the carefully soiled jersey with its protest legend. I looked at the artistically frayed and dirtied jeans and the skillfully broken-down shoes. I remembered that we've got a costumer in Washington who's a real artist at turning out convincing clothes for any role, flashy or shabby. And the skin of neck and knuckles grimy enough to pass at a glance but lacking the ingrained dirt of weeks. All good enough to fool an unsuspicious audience—a sucker named Helm, for instance; and the young man was a fair country actor, too. But he hadn't expected to be thrown to a couple of syndicate man-breakers.

He'd obviosuly thought—and the people who'd sent him had thought—that I'd keep it in the family and, if persuasion was needed, apply it myself. It had been expected that if things started getting too rough—if I started getting too rough—Mr. Ernest Love, whatever his real name might be, would be able to stop it with a few words; that he could save himself by identifying himself and telling me what a ridiculous patsy I'd been, to be taken in by this elaborate performance in which he'd played only a minor role. He was panicking now because he knew that somebody'd misjudged the situation badly. He knew that unlike me, Seppi Velo's goons wouldn't be stopped by anything he had to say. But he was just a bit player in this farce. The comic relief, of course, was being supplied by one M. Helm, while Amy Barnett added feminine interest to the cast; but the leading man was obviously Doug Barnett himself.

I couldn't flatter myself that I'd suspected the hoax

consciously; but I must have sensed something wrong when I broke the rules and asked old Seppi to send me some truly impressive muscle to blast things apart. Now I started remembering the little things: Doug Barnett in jail with a neat patch of tape on his skull, looking just a bit too tidy and unbruised for a man who'd recently taken on two law-enforcement agencies bare-handed. I remembered the subtle way he'd called my attention to his failing vision. I remembered the uncharacteristically sentimental way he'd referred to his daughter, overacting a little there; and how, according to her report, he'd pulled exactly the same weak-sighted routines on her before picking a fight with her about her mother that had probably been deliberate.

It would take time to make sense of it all; but how could I forget the dramatic boat ride up the Florida Straits with the camouflaged Coast Guard admiral passing on to me a lot of dramatic radio dialogue that I never actually heard—hell, anybody can talk into a mike and pretend to listen—all leading up to selling me, and Amy Barnett, a clap of sound and a ball of smoke?

Most clearly of all I remembered the fact that the coast guard's 110-footer, the *Cape March*, supposedly in the danger zone, had escaped unscathed. But I'd worked with Doug Barnett in the past and, regardless of what I'd said to Sanderson, I knew he was really no more Mister Nice Guy than I was. If he'd *really* been driven to despair and suicide, and some of the people responsible were within reach, as they had been, he'd have made damned sure he wouldn't have to take the long, dark journey alone. . . .

IT'S ROUGHLY seventy miles from Miami up to West Palm Beach. I took the turnpike, joining the spring flight of Cadillacs leaving their Florida wintering grounds for their nesting grounds up north.

The motorized Chevrolet roller skate I'd rented for the previous job, because it was small and inconspicuous, had legroom only for a dwarf—I hadn't noticed it so much in city driving, but a seventy-mile run brought it clearly to my attention. Oddly enough, the rather diminutive Japanese have caught on to the fact that their American customers often have long legs; but the big men in Detroit still figure that only small people buy small cars, reminding me of the days when firearms manufacturers used to think that only peewee-handed people used peewee-caliber guns. If you had a big mitt like mine you were practically doomed to shoot a roaring, thundering .44 or .45 because you couldn't get a good grip on anything smaller.

The cramped driving conditions didn't improve my disposition. I was followed, discreetly, at a distance, by a small white Volkswagen Rabbit. I took the first West Palm exit as directed and slowed as I came off the ramp, letting my escort slip by. The driver, a middle-aged woman, gave me the all-clear signal as she passed. To hell with her. I spent most of an hour making sure she was right and nobody hostile was tailing me. I mean, I might eventually kick somebody's rump for the trick that had been played on me; but I'm a pro and I don't blow an elaborate operation, such as this seemed to be, just because I'm mad. After confirming that I was clean, I proceeded to the indicated rendezvous, a small, pink motel that was shaded, if you don't mind a slight exaggeration, by a few ratty palm trees. I parked between a large sedan and a small station wagon. When I knocked on the door with the right number, in the indicated way, Mac opened.

It was something of a shock, since I'd thought he was speaking from Washington when I'd called there angrily a couple of hours earlier and had gotten no sympathy, just instructions to proceed to this place with utmost care. But they can make telephone circuits do funny things these days. I looked at the familiar, lean, gray-haired gent with the black eyebrows who, while I've sometimes seen him look a bit tired, never really seems to get any older. Maybe he sold his soul to the devil years ago in return for eternal life, except there's no evidence he ever had one to sell.

His neat gray business suit reminded me of Amy Barnett, whose neat gray business suit had also been a bit too substantial for Florida in the spring. For some reason I found myself wondering what the girl was doing now. But of course I knew what she was doing, since I'd put her into a taxi early that morning, before I got involved with the Ernest Love problem, and aimed her at the Miami airport. By this time, barring unscheduled delays, she was riding a plane home to Cincinnati, if she wasn't there already.

"Come in, Eric," Mac said. He always uses the code names for official conversations.

I walked past him into the shabby motel unit. There were the usual stylized works of motel art on the wall: a cute little Indian boy facing a cute little Indian girl. The big double beds had either not been slept in last night or they'd already been made up, not likely, since a breakfast tray—apparently sent over from the all-night restaurant next door—had not yet been removed. The breakfast had been for two people, one of whom had had the works: steak and eggs, hashed browns, toast, and coffee. A pretty good trencherman. The other had settled for a continental breakfast of rolls and coffee and left one of the rolls in the basket. A frugal eater. Mac. I took Ernest Love's confession from my inside jacket pocket and tossed it onto the cluttered table beside him.

"Too sad about Doug Barnett," I said. "But here's the proof of his innocence. At least his memory will be forever bright. And ours."

Mac picked up the paper and gave it a brief glance before dropping it into the nearby wastebasket, which was the fate it deserved. There wasn't a word of truth in it, of course. There had been no hassle on board the *Seawind* on the way up from Key West and no drugs thrown overboard, there had been no hidden marijuana left on the boat, and there had been no anonymous phone call to the authorities; but I'd made Love confess to his supposed guilt in detail, in writing, because I was feeling mean. Or maybe I just wanted somebody else to look bad for a change.

"You were not authorized to investigate further," Mac said. "And you were certainly not authorized to employ outside help."

"It did the job, didn't it?" I said. "It broke your phony hippie into little squirming pieces. After a look at those two goons, he couldn't stop talking. And he was so eager to write whatever I told him, true or false, that he'd have confessed to sinking the *Lusitania* if he could have figured out how he got that iceberg to the right spot. What the hell is wrong with Pac-Man, sir?"

"Pac-Man?"

"I mean, if you simply have to play games." I faced him for a moment; when he didn't speak, I glanced toward the bathroom door and said, "Well, let's have the great resurrection scene. I suppose, since he's officially defunct, our shy friend in there wanted to make absolutely sure it was the right man knocking on the front door before he showed himself; but he must be getting tired of sitting on the potty by this time."

But apparently Doug Barnett had been standing by the door, listening to our conversation. Now he emerged from the bathroom and walked straight over to the dresser that held some glasses, an ice bucket, and a bottle.

I said sourly, "He moves pretty good for a dead man, doesn't he, sir? And sees pretty good for a blind man."

Doug Barnett, bottle in hand, glanced at Mac, who shook his head. Doug poured two stiff shots, dropped ice cubes into them, and came over and handed me one.

"If you want a splash of water—I seem to remember that you like your Scotch partially drowned—the faucet's over there. Hi, Matt."

"You bastard," I said. "I suppose it was your idea to let me make a jackass of myself."

"That's right," he said. "I recalled, from our long-ago foray together, that you're an okay operative and a damn good shot, but a lousy actor. I figured you'd be more convincing if you didn't know it was an act. Admiral Sanderson says you put on a hell of a show for him."

"For him?"

"Well, for the girl."

"For Amy? You went to all that trouble—we all did—just to make your daughter think you're dead? Why?"

Mac stirred, glancing at his watch. "I have a plane to catch . . . Eric."

"Yes, sir."

"This is Abraham's operation." That was Doug's code name, don't ask me why. We've never figured out how he picks them. Mac went on: "He's been on it for over two years; but it seems to be gaining momentum now and developing ramifications we never anticipated. You were brought into it, reluctantly, because you were on the spot and available and because you were eminently suitable in more ways than one. Abraham will explain. I flew down to make certain there would be no misunderstandings. The mission is his and you will take your instructions from him. Any questions?"

"No, sir."

That wasn't true, of course. I had plenty of questions. I'd been on quite a few cooperative ventures where I'd had to defer to high-ranking stuffed shirts from other agencies, but this was the first time in a good many years that I'd been ordered to work under one of our own people; and as I've said, regardless of age, Doug Barnett was technically junior to me in our table of organization. Not that we pay much attention to technicalities. I realized that Mac was watching me closely. Perversely, I found myself a little annoyed that he'd felt the need to fly clear down here to give me the word, as if he didn't trust me to take his orders unless they were delivered personally. However, it was also, I decided, his way of apologizing for putting me into an unfamiliar and uncomfortable situation, and maybe for the hoax that had been pulled on me. And maybe there were other reasons. I could think of one: When you have a kennel of good fighting dogs you're careful to keep them from tearing each other apart.

I said, "Correction. I would like to ask one question, sir. The audio-visual effects out there in the Florida Straits. How were they rigged?"

Mac said, "Is that relevant? . . . Very well." He looked at Doug. "Tell him."

Doug made his report without expression: "After I'd picked up the Coast Guard one-hundred-ten-footer, or it had picked me up, and it was cruising along nicely in *Seawind*'s wake, I bore off a bit so the mainsail was between us and they couldn't really see what I was up to in the cockpit. I pulled on mask and tank and flippers and dropped overboard, after starting the bang clock. I went deep; that ship came right over me. Even though I'd used a five-minute delay, which should have let the boat get well clear at the speed it was moving, I got quite a jolt when the charge fired. I surfaced cautiously and saw that *Seawind* . . ." Doug cleared his throat. "That *Seawind* was gone and the *Cape March* had stopped to search through the floating debris over there about half a mile away. Pretty soon they gave it up and got under way again and disappeared over the horizon. So I just inflated my vest and drifted with the nice warm Gulf Stream for a couple of hours until I heard the helicopter; then I used a dye marker to cue it in. The helo crew was in on it, of course, and the top brass and radioman on the *Cape March*, and Admiral Sanderson and the skipper of your boat; but we tried to keep the information circle as small as possible. Satisfactory?"

Mac glanced at his watch again. "Is that what you wanted, Eric?"

"Yes, sir." I went on to explain: "I wanted to know that this mysterious operation, whatever the hell it may be, is important enough that Doug really sacrificed his precious boat to it instead of faking the explosion in some way. Well, if it's that important, I guess I can sacrifice my precious pride or whatever it is I'm sacrificing. But I certainly wasted a lot of fancy speeches out there on the water. I even had the seagulls and pelicans weeping pitifully for my poor, brave buddy Barnett."

Mac smiled thinly. "Well, I'll leave you two to work it out. Good luck." He turned at the door. "Incidentally, Eric, the *Lusitania* was torpedoed. It was the *Titanic* that hit the iceberg."

The door closed behind him. We heard the smooth, nostalgic sound of the big V8 sedan starting up outside and moving away; a sound almost as obsolete, these economical four-cylinder days, as the clip-clop of a horse-drawn carriage.

"Well, now you know," Doug said.

He whistled a few bars of the old *Titanic* song: "It was sad, it was sad, it was sad when that great ship went down." Then his face changed and I knew he was remembering a not-so-great vessel that had just gone down, taking a lifelong dream with it. It seemed a large personal sacrifice for him to have made on the altar of his official duty. I couldn't help thinking that he could have achieved the same result in a less costly way; but then Doug Barnett had always gone in for elaborate and meticulous operations with props and costumes and characters all as authentic as he could make them. Here he'd used a real boat, his boat, and he'd also employed an almost-genuine pot-smoking villain; he could have dispensed with both with a little finagling. I remembered that it had driven him crazy to work with me, since my style is just the opposite: I like to barge in heedlessly and just shake the tree hard to scare the monkeys out.

But still, he'd made a bigger and more expensive—to himself—deal of it than seemed absolutely necessary; and I reminded myself not to overlook the possibility that Doug Barnett had something driving him here in addition to duty that helped him resign himself to the loss of his boat. Furthermore, I warned myself, it seemed a hell of a fancy charade to put on for just one young girl. . . .

I said, "A personal question, *amigo*. Since we're going to be working together, I think I'm entitled to know what shape you're really in. Should I carry along a few nice books in Braille to keep you entertained if things go bad?"

"We'll be working on the same project, but if things develop as I expect we won't be working together, thank God," Doug said stiffly. Then he grinned. 'It's a legitimate question, I guess. Fifty percent loss of vision left eye, right normal. Occasional headaches that are real bastards. But no progressive deterioration has been noted as yet; if anything, my condition has improved over the past year. Okay?"

"So your airplane accident, if you want to call it an accident, wasn't faked?"

"No, that was for real, dammit, but I was originally scheduled to go back on limited duty after I got on my feet again; only something came up that made it advisable for me to announce my retirement."

"And when that didn't convince somebody that you were harmless, it was decided to have you commit suicide."

"Something like that. Now it's my turn. How did you know it was a setup?"

"Know?" I said. "Who the hell *knows* anything in this racket?"

"You had a couple of syndicate thugs standing by."

"There were a some loose ends, false notes, whatever you want to call them. Things didn't quite jell. I figured if I squeezed that lemon hard enough—Ernest Love, for God's sake!—I might get some useful juice out of him; and if I didn't, then I could relax and figure it was just my suspicious nature acting up."

Doug laughed. "You know why our mutual friend, just departed, *really* made that plane trip clear from Washington, don't you? He had to bring us together for the job, and he knew that you'd be sore when you learned how you'd been used. He also knew that we aren't true bosom buddies in spite of what you said out there when you thought I was dead, for which I thank you. He came because he wanted to be present when we met, so he could prevent a killing."

It was the same thought I'd had earlier. I studied him for a moment. "Whose killing? Which way was he betting?"

Doug grinned. "It would be interesting to find out, wouldn't it? Who's the toughest boy on the block around here? Who's the fastest gun in town? Kid stuff. And it wouldn't get the job done."

"Anyway, I don't pick on senile, half-blind old men," I said without expression. "And you were perfectly right. I did put on a better act because I didn't know I was acting. So tell me about the job. And the girl. She seemed like a nice enough kid to me. Why is it important to have her think she's fatherless as well as motherless?"

"They all seem like nice kids to you. That's why you're so eminently suitable for part of this mission, the part that concerns my daughter." He frowned at me. "Did she make any arrangements for getting in touch with you again?"

I shook my head. "But I nobly offered her my strong right arm and my shining sword in case of need. Call any time. Sir Matthew is willing."

"Ah, I knew I could count on you! Well, I think you'll find the need will arise fairly soon, if we have Miss Amy sized up correctly. In fact, while I'd like to buy you lunch, I don't recommend the room service here; and I think you'd better get back to Miami as soon as possible and wait for her call. Now that I'm dead, it's fairly certain she'll try to attach herself to you. We're counting on it, in fact."

I said, frowning, "This is still your daughter we're talking about?"

"Don't give me that blood-is-thicker line!" There was sudden anger in Doug's voice. "Why do you think I picked you, anyway? I could have turned her over to one of those cold young Casanovas who hang around the office in Washington. But you've got a warm, sentimental streak where women are concerned. It'll get you dead one day, but right now I'm making use of it. I'm not asking you not to sleep with her if the mission requires it. I'm not even asking you not to kill her if you have to. There's a job to be done and we're going to do it. All I'm saying is—" He stopped and cleared his throat. "All I'm saying is, don't hurt her any more than you have to."

After a little, I said, "I still don't know what this is all about, but she didn't look like much of a menace to me. Are you quite sure we're thinking of the same girl?" He didn't answer that, and I said, "Okay. The man says you're the boss, so we'll play it your way. But why send me back to Miami? Unless the airlines screwed up again, the kid's in Cincinnati by this time."

Doug shook his head. "No, she isn't. She missed her flight, deliberately. At the very last minute, while everybody was milling around waiting to be sent aboard the plane in relays, filling it from back to front the way they do nowadays, she slipped out of the waiting room and disappeared, letting her checked suitcase travel to Ohio without her."

"You had somebody covering her?"

He nodded. "Yes, but in the boarding confusion they lost track of her and didn't realize she'd vanished until her section was called and she didn't appear to present her boarding pass at the gate."

I frowned. "So now she's wandering around Miami with nothing but the clothes she's wearing and the money in her purse, which can't be much. At least she talked very poor when she described how she'd come to make the trip."

"I wouldn't be too concerned about my daughter's destitute condition," Doug said dryly. "If she really needs help, she has plenty available, I assure you. But we're hoping that you're the one she'll turn to in her hour of need. It will be interesting to hear what her story will be. A sudden emotional crisis, probably." He stared at me grimly. "I know what you're thinking. I'm not sounding very fatherly, am I? But I've had a good many years to get over my original attack of paternalism, years during which my letters were returned and my bitch-wife told my little girl all about her evil daddy. And give me credit, Matt. I have made provision for her long-run security if she survives her present foolishness. It stands, even if she hates me so much she's willing to be used against me. Also, I did pick you to deal with her, not because I like you but because you're a softy in certain respects."

"Yes, you said that," I said. "Okay, I'll beat her gently, if I have to beat her. Tell me why I may have to."

Doug Barnett regarded me bleakly. "The fact is that whatever you think, my daughter is not a nice kid. Blame it on the divorce, blame it on her mother, blame it on me; it doesn't matter. I know she looks pretty good, maybe a little too goody-good, that prim-and-proper act she puts on, but among other things she's been arrested and she's spent time in jail. Granted that the causes were all very noble, and that she doesn't go in for shoplifting or fraud or arson; these kids never seem to know how to draw a line between legitimate protest and criminal activity. She's been in on several pretty rough demonstrations that could have had her up on serious charges. To put it bluntly, she's an erratic little screwball with idealistic pretensions and I'm afraid it's got her into real trouble at last."

It seemed to be my week for being wrong about people. He was talking about a girl I'd never met. I couldn't visualize the tidy and controlled young woman I'd met screaming wild obscenities in a protest march and being knocked down by the fire hoses and hauled off to a cell all bruised and bedraggled.

"What kind of trouble?" I asked.

"We learned quite recently, when the man was spotted in Cincinnati, that my daughter's recently been shacked up with somebody whose record we both know, somebody I've actually been tracking for the last couple of years while I pretended to take up boatbuilding in my retirement. I don't for a moment think they got together by accident. He knows I'm after him, and I think he sought her out specifically because she was my daughter; more specifically because she was my daughter who'd been taught to detest and despise me. And I don't think she just happened to start looking for her dear old daddy by accident either, even though I did write her a note after her mother's death. I think she was following the very careful instructions of her lover, Mr. Alfred Minister, and the organization by which he's been hired."

I whistled softly. "Minister? Our inhibited young lady sure picks her company!" Then I asked, "Hired to do what?"

"That's what we have to find out," Doug said.

|||||||||| CHAPTER 7 |||||||||||||||||||||||||||||||||||||||||||||

OFFICIALLY, OUR specialty may be called counter-assassination, as opposed, say, to counterespionage, or counterintelligence. We're the good guys with the guns who go after the bad guys with the guns when they're too mean for anybody else to handle—although I've heard doubts expressed in some quarters as to just how good we are. Some folks just don't like guns no matter who uses them. I don't suppose they liked the club, the spear, or the bow and arrow, either.

Anyway, in the line of duty, we have to keep track of a lot of people, mostly dangerous people. Among them, Alfred Minister was easy to remember, because he had a quaint conceit: his aliases were always ecclesiastical. We had records of him operating under several different names reflecting the same theme, like Aloysius Pastor or Alan Priest. It was a proud signature of sorts, like an artist placing an identifying scrawl in the corner of his canvas.

Minister was very good at his art. He could blow up practically anything with practically anything. Give him a little acid and something for it to chew on and he'd cook you up a nice batch of nitro in the kitchen sink and show you how to set it off very simply; but for his own use he preferred more exotic explosives detonated in more complicated ways.

Driving back to Miami, I didn't pay much attention to what was behind me after an initial check to make sure nobody'd managed to pick me up at the motel: Doug's continued existence was still a secret. Beyond that, there was nothing to be gained by being fancy, since I was returning to the Marina Towers, where anybody could find me who wanted me. As I drove, I reviewed what I'd just been told; also what I hadn't been told, like the real reason Doug Barnett had been officially retired to devote his time, almost two whole years, to the Minister case and nothing else. We don't usually pay so much attention to a lousy dynamiter, even one who's a virtuoso.

Doug had handed me a condensed dossier to look through as we talked: *Minister, Alfred M. Forty-four, five six, one eighty-five. Light Brown. Blue. Distinguishing marks: none known. Psychological characteristics: professionally obsessive, personally sadistic. No weapons training or experience. Expert explosives.* There was a long list of the man's professional achievements ending with: *Buenos Aires 1981; Tel Aviv 1983.* The last, I remembered, was an El Al airliner that had been blown up right after takeoff by an ingenious pressure-sensitive device, killing all on board. The PLO had paid for the job and claimed credit for it, but the subsequent investigation turned up the fact that the actual work had been done by a certain Mr. Archibald Deacon.

I frowned at the rear of the inoffensive car ahead. It wasn't easy to accept the fact that this was the man with whom pretty little nonsmoking, nondrinking, nonswearing Amy Barnett was deeply involved: a middle-aged, balding butterball who liked to demolish people publicly and torment them privately.

"And this outfit he's working for now?" I'd asked Doug Barnett.

"You won't believe it," he said. "After doing his last job for a bunch of wild Arabs, our explosive friend has now gotten himself hired by a supposedly respectable pacifist outfit called the People for Nuclear Peace."

"Weird," I agreed. I hesitated. "Is Amy a member?"

"Naturally," he said. His voice was bitter. "If there's any screwball save-the-world group around, my little girl will be on the list. Not that I'm opposed to saving the world in principle—we're all working on that—it's the half-baked way they go about it in practice." He made a wry face. "The PNP is the brainchild of a wealthy Cincinnati dame named Georgina Williston who may or may not have all her marbles. We know she's spent some time in an institution, but we don't know what for. She's got enough money to pull down the medical curtain and keep it pulled. We haven't found a hole or a crack in it; and we can't force it open officially, because we can't afford to reveal our interest yet. The woman recruited Amy personally. Actually, the kid probably couldn't have qualified otherwise in spite of her brilliant protest record. It's a fairly restricted group of very wealthy citizens like the Williston dame. I guess they're interested in preserving what they've got, since they've got such a lot of it. Well, you can hardly fault them for that. But when they hire a guy like Minister, you start to wonder."

I asked, "Is your theory that this rich dame deliberately got Amy into her PNP outfit for Minister's benefit?"

"It seems likely, doesn't it? I mean, if they're going to use the Preacher for something—God knows what—they've got to pick the ticks off him first, don't they? Ticks like me. And now that I'm officially dead, ticks like you. After that brothers-in-arms act you put on, you're the obvious candidate to replace me on the Minister job, aren't you? And here's the girl telling them you offered her your services in case of need; would they waste it? A spy in the enemy camp is always useful. If somebody else inherits the Minister assignment, tough. She thanks you for your help and goes home. But if you get it, there she is all tender and trembling, begging you not to leave her all alone in this big cruel world; you promised her poor dead daddy you'd look after her, didn't you? And from then on she'll stick to you so closely she'll be able to report every move you make; and though she's hardly qualified to take you out when it's time for that, she'll be in a good, trusted position to set you up for it. Shit!" He cleared his throat angrily. "I keep remembering her sitting on my lap when she was four years old. Cute as a button. And what's that got to do with anything now?"

I said, "You're making quite a dragon lady out of this daughter you hadn't seen for some seventeen years until yesterday."

He stared at me bleakly. "I've got to, don't I? I'm running this thing. I've got to treat her like any other member of the opposition. I've got to figure out the very worst she can do, the very worst she can be, and plan accordingly. Hell. I can't do her any favors at all, because I'm too damned involved; I won't know if I'm doing them because they make sense or because I'm her papa. So any breaks she gets, any consideration she gets, will have to come from you. And then only because you think it's safe, not because she's my kid, damn you!"

"Sure," I said. After a moment, I asked, "What's the target?"

"Minister's target? That's what we have to find out, like I said."

"No hints, no clues?"

"We only got onto this PNP outfit recently, remember, when the Preacher was spotted in Cincinnati." Doug grimaced. "I said he and Amy were shacked up, but that's a slight exaggeration due to paternal dissillusionment. They weren't actually living together, and they were very discreet about their meetings. Not to say secretive. They had a hidden little basement apartment where they'd get together. Considering Minister's known habits, I don't want to think about what went on there. They'd come and go separately. Our local man, keeping an eye on Minister after he'd been spotted while waiting for somebody with experience to take over—unfortunately I was in the hospital for my semi-annual checkup—only saw her coming there once; but he was smart enough to follow her and identify her. Smart, but maybe not the best shadow in the world. At least Minister seems to've realized, a few days later, that he was under surveillance; by the time I got there he was gone, and we haven't managed to pick up his trail since."

"But you figure Amy doesn't know we're aware of her Minister connection."

"More important, we're gambling that Minister doesn't know we're aware of his Amy connection. But he'd hardly have sent her here to pull the long-lost daughter act on me if he were." Doug drew a long breath, dismissing the subject. "Back to the PNP. We ran the membership list through the computer and found that the Bahama Islands seem to be a very popular vacation spot these days for people from Cincinnati with antinuclear leanings."

It seemed to be that, disturbed by his daughter's behavior, he was being a little too hard on all protest movements.

"Practically everybody's got antinuclear learnings these days except the Pentagon and the Soviet High

Command," I said. "I wouldn't mind a bit seeing the bomb stuffed back into its box myself; the world was a simpler place without it. But then, gunpowder complicated hell out of things, too, when it came along a few centuries earlier. But we learned to live with that." I frowned. "A lot of wealthy people visit the Bahamas."

"The computer says the statistics are out of line," Doug said. "We haven't had time to work it out in detail, and we don't even have all the data yet, but indications are that Mrs. Williston's well-to-do friends in the PNP don't seem to go anywhere else, recently. No vacations to Paris or London or the lovely fiords of Norway. No tours of the mysterious Orient. No 'round-the-world cruises. Just the damn Bahamas. So if my daughter does make a play in your direction, as I firmly believe she will, that's where I'm sending the two of you. Of course, you'll swear her to secrecy, and you'll have a fancy cover—we're arranging it for you—and you'll go through all the proper secret agent motions, very hush-hush; knowing all the time that she's reporting your every word and move to her PNP friends."

"The old decoy act, in fact," I said. "And what will you be doing while I'm holding their attention by playing wooden duck out there?"

"You won't be entirely a decoy," he said. "At least there's an odd situation out in the more distant islands of the Bahamas that seems worth investigating. The Coast Guard lost a boat that was snooping around down there a few weeks back. They were trying to get a line of the operations of a big drug dealer named Constantine Grieg. The funny thing is that the PNP also seems to be interested in Mr. Grieg, born Griego. Greek mother, Latin father. Headquarters, Nassau. Our antinuclear friends have been spotted in that vicinity."

"Jesus," I said. "What the hell kind of peace group is this, anyway, involved with a mastermind of drugs and a high-powered bang-bang expert?"

"When you find out, let me know," Doug said. "Anyway, I'll be playing dead and keeping you covered, and following any leads that turn up, in my ghostly way."

I said sourly, "I suppose I'll be sailing some kind of a boat; there's no other way of poking around those islands except by plane, and I fly even worse than I sail. And keeping a small boat covered inconspicuously out in open water isn't easy, *amigo*."

"I know," he said. "We'll do what we can; the rest if up to you." He hesitated. "What I'm going to say will sound crazy, Matt, but there's a coincidence that keeps nagging at me."

I nodded. "It popped into my mind, too, while you were talking. You're thinking of the Nuclear Disarmament Conference that opens in Nassau in a very few weeks? But I can't think of a single reason why these people would hire an explosives expert to sabotage an antinuclear conference. It makes no sense at all. After all, they're sincerely dedicated to banning the bombs and nixing the nukes themselves, aren't they? Or do you suspect the PNP of being a cover for something else?"

He shrugged. "I don't know what I suspect them of, yet, but our investigation has turned up no indication that they aren't a perfectly genuine bunch of wealthy idealists." Doug made a face. "But on the other hand I wouldn't bet too high on the dedicated sincerity of most of the conference delegates, or of the nations they represent, particularly the big nations that already have expensive stockpiles of nuclear weapons. Public opinion forced them to hold this disarmament meeting at last, but I doubt any of them have major concessions in mind." He shook his head.

"But as I said, as far as the PNP is concerned, the conference may be coincidental. At least we certainly can't commit ourselves to a theory that doesn't begin to make sense."

"So?"

"So we ignore the conference, at least for the time being, and just ask ourselves the general question: Why would a bunch of rich and respectable save-the-world idealists hire a man like Minister to blow up anything, and what would they pick for him to blast? And what the hell kind of interest could they have in a bigshot drug dealer? Not that none of them ever touch the stuff; but with that much money they're bound to have their own sources." He paused, then went on without expression: "It seems probable that my daughter knows the answers, or knows the people who know the answers."

I said, "While I'm waiting for the Preacher to come out of hiding and take a shot at me so you can clobber him, I'll see what I can do about finding out what she knows. Always assuming that she does make contact with me."

"She will," Doug said. "I wish I didn't think so. I wish . . ." He paused again, and drew a long breath. "But she will."

But after the big rush to get me back to Miami that day without lunch, it wasn't until late the next day that she did.

IIIIIIIII CHAPTER 8 IIIIIIIIIIIIIIIIIIIIIIIIIIIIIIIIIIIIIIIIIIII

WHEN THE telephone rang at last I was watching a television show that was attempting to make me laugh and not doing a very good job. That evening after dinner I hadn't been able to find a single program that wasn't supposed to be funny except the news, depressing as always—well, I should have been cheered by a segment proclaiming that the forthcoming Nassau Nuclear Disarmament Conference was going to save the world, but somehow I found myself unconvinced—and some rock-and-roll, which I'm too old-fashioned to understand even nowadays when they give you weirdo pictures to go with the text.

I'd run out of reading matter and all I had to entertain me was the damn little screen with its funny men and women. They were funny standing up and they were funny sitting down. Lying in bed they were hilarious. Even the weathermen cracked jokes, and the local Spanish channel had them rolling in the aisles, judging by the facial expressions and the cackles on the sound track. It scared me a little, the thought of a whole continent shaking with the uproarious laughter emanating from a hundred million living rooms. I'm not one of the highbrows who want TV to be forever uplifting and educational, and God forbid that naive, impressionable, young fellows like me should be exposed to sex and violence; but while comedy is all right in its place, whatever happened to tragedy, or romance, or just plain action and adventure?

It had been a long, boring wait, over twenty-four hours of waiting; and I had to check the impulse to make a wild lunge across the room and spear the jangling instrument on the first ring. Instead, I turned off the TV, walked over there deliberately, and sat down on one of the big beds. Even then I let the phone ring two more times before I picked it up.

"Ye-es?"

"Mr. Helm?"

I drew a long breath of relief, but I was aware of a little disappointment, too; a kind of final disillusionment. I guess part of my mind had been clinging stubbornly to my first impressions of a stuffy young lady who'd had a certain prickly, innocent charm in spite of being totally impossible. But this was the right female voice making guilty contact as predicted. At least it was almost the right female voice. The enunciation wasn't quite as careful and ladylike as I'd remembered it. Stress, perhaps, or a deliberate imitation thereof.

"This is Helm," I said.

"Oh, thank heaven! I was afraid you might already have left town."

I said obtusely, "I'm sorry, I don't recognize—"

"It's Amy, Mr. Helm. Amy Barnett. I'm in terrible trouble and . . . Oh, dear, I've made such a fool of myself I'm ashamed to . . . But they snatched my purse and I haven't got a cent and if the nice Spanish lady in this place hadn't let me . . . You said if I . . . You said I could call you. . . ."

"Are you all right, Miss Barnett? Your voice sounds a little strange. That's why I didn't recognize—"

She giggled, an odd sound from a girl who'd seemed opposed to laughter on principle.

"My voice probably sounds a little strange because I am a little . . . strange. Well, that's one word for it. Very s-strange, for me. . . . Oh, dear, I've been such a terribly tragic figure and I've made such an awful spectacle of myself and would you come and get me, please, I haven't any place to stay and they snatched my purse so I can't even take a taxi. . . . It's the Cantina Colibri on Abeyta Street, two-oh-seven Abeyta Street. El Colibri, that means "the hummingbird" in Spanish. Did you know that?" She gave that unfamiliar little nervous titter again. "Why would anybody name a bar after a hummingbird? Silly!"

I passed up the opportunity for an ornithological discussion and said, "Sit tight. Two-oh-seven Abeyta. Colibri. I'll get there as fast as I can."

Hanging up, I got the little five-shot revolver I'd laid aside for comfort and clipped the trick holster into place under my waistband and made sure my loose-hanging sport shirt covered the butt with plenty to spare. Doug's theory was, of course, that the Preacher would let me run for a while before he tried to take me out, since he had me covered, or would have if the girl did her job right. Better a known pursuer than an unknown one. But I hadn't survived in the business as long as I had by trusting anybody's theories completely, not even my own. It could be a simple trap with Amy Barnett as bait. For the same reason, and because I was being led into a part of town with which I was not familiar, I took a taxi instead of getting the mini-Chevy out of the garage as I'd be expected to.

"Abeyta Street?" said the cabbie, a dark-faced man with a bushy black mustache. He gave a little shrug

71

indicating that it was my money, and if I wanted to waste it going to Abeyta Street, it was my business. "*Sí, señor*. Two-oh-seven Abeyta."

"Is something wrong with Abeyta Street?" I asked as he drove us away.

"*Calle* Abeyta not very good street," he said. "Cantina Colibri not very good place, *señor*."

I wondered what the hell the girl had gotten herself into, or wanted me to think she'd gotten herself into. As we proceeded farther from the hotel, I was glad I hadn't tried to make the drive myself. Suddenly, it had become a foreign country—well, a foreign city masquerading under the name of Miami—and I found myself resenting it slightly. After all, my own parents had been grateful enough to the new land that had welcomed them to learn its language and customs and bring up their son, when he appeared a few years later, as an American, instead of ganging up with a bunch of fellow square-heads and trying to build a Little Scandinavia here for themselves.

"There is El Colibri," the driver said at last.

"Park as close as you can and wait for me, please," I said. "I should be right out. Here."

I gave him a five on account and got out of the cab. It was one of those lousy situations where you have no guidelines. I mean, in my native New Mexico I'd have known what I was doing and what to expect, even in the Spanish-speaking section of town, any town. I can usually even get around in Mexico proper without starting a riot; but for all I knew these expatriate Cubans, or whatever the hell they were, reacted quite differently in spite of speaking the same language. Well, more or less the same language. I'd heard my New Mexican *amigos* poke fun at the clumsy Cuban manner of mangling the tongue of the Conquistadores.

It was a narrow, dark little street; and the place

was shabby, with faded lettering on the front. If the awkward-looking hummingbird painted on the sign had ever gotten off the ground, it would have been an aeronautical miracle. A couple of loungers out front eyed me silently as I approached. Inside the bar a moment of silence greeted my appearance. As I said, no guidelines. It was not that I was afraid of them, particularly; I was just afraid of making a mistake, call it a cultural mistake, that would trigger an altogether unnecessary confrontation. I hadn't come here to fight anybody.

The gloomy, narrow bar was off to the left of the door. There seemed to be some kind of a small eating place beyond, boasting slightly better illumination, like weak daylight at the end of a dark cave. Closer, there was a counter with a cash register and a case of cigarettes and candy. Behind it, a dark, hatchet-faced woman with severely pulled-back black hair streaked with gray sat on a stool making entries in an account book. She looked up inquiringly as I approached, a good sign. I had a hunch the bartender would have kept on polishing his damn glasses until I shot him through the left eye to get his attention, damn *gringo* that I was.

I drew a long breath and, by way of interracial diplomacy, summoned up some of my atrocious Spanish.

"*Señora, por favor,*" I said. "*Donde esta la Señorita Barnett?*"

The woman smiled. "Ah, you have come! The *pobrecita*, she has much grief. Also she is *muy borracho*. But do not scold her, *señor*. It is not necessary. She has sufficient shame already. You will find her in the café, that way."

I started in the direction she'd pointed, then stopped and looked back. "If there's a bill . . ." I said in a tentative way. "*La cuenta?*"

The sharp-faced woman gave me a look of contempt.

73

"Do I appear as one who cannot afford to provide a telephone call and a cup of coffee for a troubled *niña?*" she demanded. "Go, take her home! But gently."

So much for the bloody battle of the dangerous Cantina Colibri. I made my way through the cramped bar and entered the tiny café beyond. I was ready to be impressed by the show that had been prepared for me, if Doug had read his daughter correctly; but I didn't spot her at once. Only one of the tables out in the room was occupied at this late hour, by a rather young boy and girl, slim and handsome in the Latin way, both dressed in sloppy jerseys and grubby jeans. I remembered when we used to dress up a bit for dates with the opposite sex. It still seemed like kind of a nice idea.

Then something stirred in the booth at my right elbow and I turned quickly with my hand instinctively moving toward the gun in my waistband. There she was, hidden away in the corner, slumped on the bench seat with her elbows on the table, holding a mug of coffee with both hands and staring into it dully. She was still, I saw, dressed a little too warmly for Florida, in the same suit and blouse she'd worn when I put her into a taxi airport-bound; but after two days and a night they were, of course, no longer the same suit and blouse, nor was she the same girl. In spite of everything I found myself unprepared for the way she looked now. She became aware that I was staring at her, shocked at what she'd done to herself; and she raised her head defiantly.

"So you came," she breathed; and then she giggled. "I told you I was strange, didn't I? Spelled d-r-u-n-k. Oh, I'm so very, very drunk, Mr. Helm!"

"It's a good thing you told me," I said. "Otherwise I'd never have guessed."

"There you go, being sarcastic again!" She giggled once more. "Help me out of here, Mister Sarcastic

Helm. You do want to see the whole dishaster . . . disaster area, don't you?"

She gulped the remains of her coffee and, with another look of defiance, wiped her mouth crudely with her sleeve to shock me more and struggled out of the booth with a little assistance from me. Swaying there, she squared her shoulders with an effort, presenting herself for inspection with a certain inebriated pride that rather surprised me. It was as if she were admitting that it was all an act and asking me to admire the great drunk performance she was putting on for me and the great drunk costume she'd designed for it. I'd have expected phony shame—after all, she'd led the woman at the cash register to believe she was very much ashamed of herself. I'd have expected her to be, or at least pretend to be, painfully embarrassed by her disgraceful condition and distressing appearance; but maybe this was the clever way of doing it.

In any case, she'd really done a job on the neat and attractive young woman I remembered. Most of her fair hair was still pinned up after a fashion; but lank strands of it straggled down her neck and into her face, which had a soiled and red-eyed look. Her silk blouse sagged open untidily, limp and half-unbuttoned. It showed stains of old liquor and new coffee; and the built-in ascot tie hung untied, crumpled and grubby. She'd got ketchup, presumably from a forgotten hamburger, on the lapel of her now shapeless flannel jacket and a big spot of grease on the front of her now creased and baggy flannel skirt. Two days of abuse had pretty well demolished her fragile stockings. Her nice black pumps had become very dusty and badly scuffed.

Well, I'd seen bedraggled ladies before, they aren't uncommon in the business—I'd seen plenty of bedraggled gentlemen, too, of course—but the fact that she

75

would deliberately make such a clown of herself for my benefit changed my opinion of her in a fundamental way. I mean, I'd tried to kid myself that if she was collaborating at all with Minister and those who'd hired him, she was doing it reluctantly under duress, but to achieve this outrageous lady-lush effect she must have cooperated enthusiastically at the very least, if she hadn't done it all to herself.

I had a disturbing picture of her, in the privacy of a hotel room, say, sending out for food and drink and then using it to paint ugly stains on her nice suit and blouse. After that, a nail file, perhaps, to start runs in her pretty nylons and scratch and scuff her handsome shoes. And then maybe even going to bed fully dressed to give her sabotaged costume an authentically creased and wrinkled look to fit the demeaning act she was now performing for me. . . .

"Stand still," I said. "You can't go out of here looking like that."

I found that I was embarrassed for her and trying to keep myself between her and the rest of the room to shield her, which was ridiculous since she'd got herself into this state deliberately. Besides, everybody here had undoubtedly gotten an eyeful when she'd come stumbling in. But after all, it went with my part in this scenario: the rescuing hero. I buttoned up the gaping blouse and arranged the soiled ascot as neatly as its condition allowed, tucked her in a bit, and buttoned her jacket tidily. I dipped a paper napkin into a glass of water and used it to clean off her lapel; the stained skirt was obviously beyond such simple remedies, and there were other smears and smudges she'd have to live with a little longer. She'd have looked better without her hopelessly laddered stockings, but I couldn't see peeling them off her here.

She gave that giggle again. I remembered that I'd

once wanted to see her laugh, hear her laugh; but that had been another girl in another lifetime. Now the intoxicated titter was getting on my nerves.

"Those kids are whispering about me," she said happily. " 'See the drunk female *gringo*.' I really look a fright, don't I?"

I said, "If it's female, it's a *gringa*. Do you need to go to the john?"

"I've been to the john, I've been sick as a dog in the john. Bitch?" She tried for the giggle once more and choked on it. Her eyes were suddenly wide with the shame and embarrassment I'd looked for earlier. "Oh, I feel so awful and I look so dreadful! Please get me out of here, Mr. Helm."

It was a genuine plea, a moment of honesty, I thought, as she realized fully, belatedly, the shocking condition into which she'd gotten herself. Perhaps she hadn't intended to carry her performance quite so far. Perhaps she hadn't lied when she'd told me she wasn't accustomed to drinking. Perhaps, inexperienced, she'd had a few too many, trying to make her act look very convincing; and now she could feel herself losing control of the situation and becoming the sodden creature she'd only wanted to imitate for my benefit. . . . I steadied her as she swayed, and guided her out of the place and across the street into the waiting taxi, where she promptly fell asleep against me. I had to shake her awake and tidy her up again after paying off the driver. Then I helped her out of the cab and supported her as she stumbled across the sidewalk and through the hotel lobby.

"No raincoat," she said reproachfully. "I'm hurt. You didn't bring me a raincoat. No conshideration . . . consideration!"

She was over her moment of shame, I saw, and it was all just a great big happy joke once more.

"It isn't raining," I said.

"In the movies, the hero always wraps the poor beat-up heroine modestly in a big raincoat, or coat, or blanket, or something."

"You're not beat-up, you're just soused," I said.

She gave me the giggle again. "You can say that twice, Mister!" Oooh, am I shoused . . . soused! And I ushed to be shush a pure, shober little shing . . . thing. Oops!" Entering the elevator, she caught a high heel and almost fell, but I caught her in time and leaned her against the wall. She said, "It's all your fault, you know."

"It always is," I said.

"No, I mean it! You're the one who told me I'd killed him."

"Killed whom?"

"My father, of course."

I should have expected this, but it hit me hard anyway; and gave me a painful sense of guilt, reminding me of what I knew about Doug Barnett that she didn't. She might be playing ugly games, but I had a pretty mean line of deception going, too.

I said rather stiffly, "I don't recall saying anything like that."

"But you did!" she protested. "Don't you remember, you said that if I'd acted right and made friends with him, made a real effort to know him instead of quarreling with him, he wouldn't have been out there making his . . . what was that horrible thing you called it? Death run. Like an elephant going to the elephants' graveyard or something."

It was no time to argue about exactly what I had or hadn't said. To ease her away from the subject, I asked, "Is that why you decided to slip away from the airport and tie one on?"

She nodded several times with drunken emphasis. "Well, at first I just had to get away from all those people. Someplace where I could break down and cry for him, the daddy I'd deserted all those years ago; and now I'd murdered him. . . . Is this where we get out?"

"I hope so," I said. "If it isn't, we'll have to come back and try again, won't we?"

She thought that was very funny and giggled some more, forgetting that she was a murderess. Then we were in my room with the door closed. She wanted to admire her beautifully bedraggled self in the dresser mirror, but I set her back against a wall, hoping it would enable her to remain upright without my assistance. While she leaned there, I unbuttoned her jacket and the cuffs of her blouse, untied the ascot, and unfastened the blouse down the front and pulled it out at the waist all around, while she watched me gravely.

"Are you going to rape me?" she asked. "Is that why you're undressing me?"

"Do you want me to rape you?"

"Of course," she said with utmost seriousness. "And do all kinds of nasty and degrading things to me."

The trouble was, she wasn't kidding. I remembered the peculiar bedroom habits attributed to Alfred Minister. It was disturbing to think that this small, intoxicated girl, who still managed to cling to a look of disheveled innocence, probably knew considerably more about certain kinds of oddball sex than I did. Or maybe I was just envious.

I said, "Stand up straight so I can slip this blouse and jacket off you."

"Why don't you just rip them off? Be macho."

"It's tempting, but you've got to have something to wear; and I'm not much good at shopping for ladies' clothes. I'll see about having your suit cleaned in the morning." I worked the stuff off her, sorted it out, and draped it over a nearby chair. "Why do you want to be ripped and raped, Miss Barnett?"

She licked her lips and answered very carefully: "Because that's the way I am. I like to be hurt. I want to be hurt. When I'm hurt it's as if I've paid a little for all the horrible things I've done."

"What horrible things?"

"Leaving my father like that. And hating my mother all those years for making me leave him, and wishing she were dead so I could go back to him and tell him how much I really loved him; and now she *is* dead and I did it, didn't I? And now I've even k-killed him, too! Don't you understand atonement, Mr. Helm?"

It was do-it-yourself psychology/psychiatry in the handy zip-lock plastic bag: the poor, distressed, guilt-ridden girl who'd turned her tidy and pretty self into an instant bag lady because she was really trying to destroy herself. Who could suspect this poor, disturbed, semisuicidal young woman of any ulterior motives? Well, Doug had predicted that his daughter would produce an emotional crisis to make her actions seem plausible to me. For a long-distance daddy, he was calling the shots very well.

I asked, "Is that why you got so drunk, for atonement?"

She nodded again. "*Somebody* had to punish me for being such an awful person, even if I had to do it myself! Anyway, after watching him kill himself like that . . . It's supposed to make you forget, isn't it? Isn't that what liquor is for?"

"Well, that's one of its functions," I said. "But didn't it make you feel a little good at first?"

"Oh, I did feel quite . . . quite cheerful for a while, that was in the cheap room I'd rented, and I'd bought a bottle, one of those flat ones, not the round ones. One of the bigger flat ones . . ."

"A pint."

"Yes. Whiskey. Some kind of whiskey. It made me feel quite sinful, buying it. I'd never bought any liquor before. Daddy used to have a drink in the evening when he was home between assignments; it was one of the things Mother associated with him, so afterward she wouldn't have it in the house. I forced myself to drink the whole bottle, quite slowly, sitting there in my room watching TV. Well, trying to watch TV, trying not to think about *anything*, just feeling it working in me so warm and nice. I felt so lovely and wicked, and everything got so funny and I kept on giggling even when I couldn't get across the room anymore without knocking things down. And in the morning I found myself sprawled on the bed still fully dressed even to my shoes. Well, one of my shoes. I had to hunt and hunt before I found the other under the bed. I didn't have enough money to stay another day, so I got out of there feeling sick and headachy, and very self-conscious about my slept-in clothes. But I found a bar that was open and after a couple of drinks I felt almost human again and it all got very funny again, and I stopped caring about being a little wrinkled and grubby. I left that place and wandered around in a happy daze and had something to eat and another drink, and another. . . . I don't have any idea what happened to the rest of the day; maybe I finally passed out again somewhere. Then it was dark again and I found myself stumbling down that grimy little street with my stockings all torn and my suit all dirty and my purse missing. I remember vaguely somebody grabbing it and knocking me down when I wouldn't let go. . . ."

She stopped to listen to a man and woman moving down the hall outside, arguing bitterly in loud voices. She giggled.

"They're drunk, too," she said happily. Then she sighed and went on with her story: "Suddenly it wasn't a bit funny anymore. It was a crazy, hazy nightmare, feeling so awful and being such an awful, embarrassing mess in my good clothes with my hair all straggly right there on the public street. You know, like when you dream of being stark naked at a glamorous formal ball. And not being able to walk very well and terrified that I'd fall down and have to crawl and ruin my nylons on the concrete sidewalk, except they were already ruined, weren't they? And people staring and laughing at the staggering slob girl. . . . And not even knowing where I was. Finally I fumbled my way into that place and was very sick in the john, and the woman let me make that phone call—thank heaven I remembered the name of this hotel—and she gave me coffee to sober me up even though I told her I'd lost my purse and couldn't pay."

It was quite a gripping story. "The Amateur Lush's Progress, Or the Alcoholic Adventures of Amy Barnett." I tried to look properly impressed and sympathetic as I figured out the combination lock of her skirt and zipped the garment open along the side. I worked it down her hips, let it fall to the floor, and made her step out of it so I could drape it over the chair, although the way it already was, a few more creases hardly mattered. She watched me, standing there in her white slip, hugging herself in the classic "September Morn" pose of any lady caught without her shirt, although the room was not cold.

I asked, "Do you want to sleep like that or can you manage a shower first? You might feel better after a shower."

She looked down at herself and giggled. "Heavens, even my underwear is dirty! I'm really quite revolting, aren't I?"

"That should cheer you up," I said. "Revolting is what you want, isn't it. . . . My God, what did you do to your arms?"

I hadn't really looked at her directly since I'd started peeling her, not wanting to remind her that she was alone in a hotel room with a strange man who was taking her clothes off. Now I saw that her bared upper arms were faintly striped, mostly behind, with fine pink lines that had obviously once been considerably redder and angrier; in another few days they'd be healed to the point of invisibility.

Amy Barnett regarded me for a long moment; an unreadable look. She bent down and caught the hem of her slip and pulled the garment off over her head and let it fall. She wasn't wearing a brassiere. She hooked her thumbs into the waistband of her panty hose—it occurred to me that I'd finally got the answer to that question, at least. She looked down proudly.

"Wow, I really fixed my hose, didn't I?" She laughed at the startling appearance of her legs. "You can see I'm not a movie heroine. Their stockings never even get little runs, and here I'm positively in rags. . . . Ooops."

I had to steady her as she swayed and support her as she worked the nylon wreckage downward and stepped clear. She freed herself from my grasp and, straightening up quite nude, looked at me soberly for a moment. Then she turned away without speaking to display her back and buttocks and thighs, all crisscrossed with the same fine, fading lines. I found myself remembering being very sarcastic about her healthy and unblemished appearance, earlier—and all the time she'd been carrying these marks under her clothes.

I cleared my throat. "You seem to know some nice people, Barnett. Unfortunately, I can't do a thing for you. I forgot my little whip, and S-M isn't exactly in my line, anyway."

"S-M? Oh, sado-masochism. But sarcasm is still very much in your line, isn't it, Mr. Helm?" Amy licked her pale lips. "Do you think I'm crazy, to let somebody do that to me?"

I was aware of a disturbing change in her. Naked, she was no longer the almost sexless object of pity—or contempt, if you felt that way about drunks—that she'd been in her soiled and crumpled suit and disintegrating stockings. I couldn't help noticing that she had very lovely breasts. Not that I'm a bosom freak. Slim ankles and pretty faces do a lot more for me. Anyway, I told myself disparagingly, she'd never make it in the big-boob sweepstakes. However, I came to the reluctant conclusion that I'd put my money on her in the tender-tits division anytime—and I knew that I was being crude about it in my mind simply to keep from admitting to myself that I was affected. Well, all right, attracted.

I cleared my throat again. "What's crazy?" I asked. "Let's discuss your psyche tomorrow, Barnett. We can take up the subject of sex and rape at the same time. Right now it's time for a little pure shut-eye, unless you want to take that shower first."

She'd picked up the fallen slip and the blouse I'd laid aside. "I'm too filthy to get into a clean bed," she said quite steadily. "I seem to be sobering up a little. Maybe it's the coffee. I really would like to shower and wash out some things, if you don't mind. I think I can manage without falling on my face." A little malice came into her voice: "Do you think I'm pretty like this, Helm?"

"Go take your damn shower," I said.

She laughed softly. "I guess that's an answer. Do you have something clean I can use to sleep in, please?"

"I'm all out of satin nighties, but one of my T-shirts might serve."

It did.

IT WAS close to noon when I got back to the hotel room next morning. She'd been sleeping heavily when I left, but she was up now, sitting in one of the big chairs in front of the television set, which wasn't on. She was just sitting there. Well, she probably had a lot to think about, including a massive hangover, which, I reflected, served her right for putting on such a convincing intoxication act.

"I had to chase all over town to find a quickie cleaner," I said as I hung her suit on the rod in the little dressing alcove off the bathroom. Emerging, I said, "I hope you didn't feel deserted when you woke up. I thought you needed your sleep. Here." I tossed a small paper bag into her lap. "They didn't have anything very close to what you were wearing; apparently black isn't in, here in Miami. There was nude, beige, suntan, and brown; and petite, medium, and tall. I got you nude medium. Hope I didn't misjudge your taste or size too badly. How do you feel?"

She was curled up in the chair, wearing only her white slip, quite clean now—I'd seen it hanging over the shower rod when I shaved, earlier, along with her freshly washed blouse. The slip wasn't as fancy as some lingerie, but it did have a little lacy stuff top and bottom, rather pretty in a discreet way. Her bare shoulders were very nice, but they still showed the fading marks of the whip. I found that the sight made me feel surprisingly sick and angry. I'd seen people who'd been interrogated for real—I'd even participated in a few fairly brutal sessions myself, on both the delivering and receiving ends—so why should I care what this erratic, screwball girl did to herself for fun or let somebody do to her? Hell, she probably had an orgasm with every lash and loved it.

Her hair was pinned up very tidily this morning. She'd obviously shampooed it meticulously with the stuff provided by the hotel management and brushed it carefully. It was soft and shining again; and I'd probably be finding long, light-brown hairs in my comb and brush for weeks to come. Souvenirs. It occurred to me, belatedly, that she hadn't spoken a word since I came in. I'd done all the talking.

"Are you all right?" I asked, concerned.

She licked her lips. "I washed out your T-shirt," she said. "I hung it in the bathroom to dry. Thanks for the loan." She drew a long, shaky breath. "I can't believe it was me!" she burst out with sudden desperation. "I've never done anything like that before, honest. I must have had . . . some kind of a breakdown or something, to deliberately go out and make such a dreadful little fool of myself. You must think I'm perfectly awful!"

Well, it was the logical next move. Having showed herself in a very bad light necessarily, to give her a convincing reason for calling on me for assistance, she now had to repair the damage and make me understand that she was really a very attractive person after all.

"Did you get anything to eat?" I asked.

She shook her head. "I couldn't face it yet. Besides,

86

I didn't want to call the desk until I'd checked with you." A little color came into her face. "I mean, I didn't know if I, well, was really supposed to be in this room with you, if you know what I mean."

I grinned. "You're perfectly legal, Miss Barnett, in an illicit sort of way. I changed the reservation to double occupancy this morning, with a significant wink. I hope you don't mind being a fallen woman."

But it was no joke to her. She said bitterly, "After the way I spent the last two days I don't have very far to fall, do I? Mama, why is that nice-looking lady lying in the gutter in her nice clothes? Did . . . did I really beg you to, well, rape me? Did I really perform a drunken striptease for you and ask you to admire my nude body?"

I shrugged. "Don't sweat it, Barnett. I've seen naked ladies before. In fact, I once even saw another girl who wasn't quite sober."

"Having to drag me out of that place looking like *that*, and carry me up here practically paralyzed, and undress me like a baby . . . How can you ever have any respect for me again?"

It was really getting pretty soap-operatic. I was a little disappointed in her. She'd done better last night with that cocky, gee-don't-I-look-awful-ha-ha routine.

I said carefully, "Does it matter? Your suit's back in reasonable shape, your blouse and slip are clean and dry, and you've got replacements right there for the tights that kind of fell by the wayside. I bought some black polish so we can make your shoes look more or less respectable, good enough to get you where you're going, although I'm afraid they'll never be quite the same again. There's an afternoon flight to Cincinnati. Tonight you'll be home. Incidentally, I checked and they're holding your suitcase at the Cincinnati airport—it's actually across the river in Covington, Kentucky, but you know that—and you can pick it up when you get there. A week from now you won't even remember the Hummingbird Bar or the guy who spent an interesting evening buttoning and unbuttoning you. So what do you care about my respect?"

She licked her lips. "I see. You're sending me away."

I frowned in a surprised way. "Isn't that what you want? Excuse me if I've made a mistake, but you were on your way three mornings ago, when you were sidetracked by a bottle. I figured that was where you still wanted to go and made the arrangements accordingly. The flight leaves at three-twenty. You should pick up your ticket at the Delta desk half an hour early. If you want somebody to hold your hand, I'll run you out there; but you're a big girl now and I think you're capable of catching a plane all by yourself—now that you've got whatever it was out of your system, I hope. Oh, before I forget . . ." I took three bills out of my wallet and dropped them on top of the package in her lap. "Sixty bucks ought to do it. For taxis at both ends and maybe something to eat and drink along the way. If you don't like taking cash money from strange men, you can send it back to me sometime. The rest is on the house and please don't argue about it. I'm your surrogate daddy, remember? Okay?"

The big gray-blue eyes were watching me steadily out of the attractive face that showed few signs of recent dissipation.

"You'll be happy to get rid of me, won't you?"

I said, "Your pop asked me to look after you. I'm looking after you."

"But you don't really like me very much."

I said irritably, "Like! Respect! You sound as if we were planning a long and intimate relationship. If you really want my opinion, I think you're a nice but nutty kid who'd better see a shrink before she gets herself into more trouble than she can handle. Or than I can help her handle, although I'm perfectly willing to keep trying for the sake of a guy who once saved my life." This was strictly speaking quite true, I certainly owed Doug Barnett an important debt, but I didn't like the guilty way it made me feel, using the fact against his daughter under these circumstances. I went on quickly, "As I said before, call anytime. I probably won't be here much longer, but you know the Washington number, and they'll get word to . . . What's the matter?"

"I completely forgot! There was a phone call for you, oh, an hour ago. That's what woke me up. You were supposed to call Washington the minute you got back. I'm terribly sorry!"

I shook my head. "Don't be. All they want is to tell me about a lousy assignment I don't particularly want to hear about." I sighed. "Oh, well, duty calls. . . ."

Mac's timing was good. I'd called from a pay phone while I was out, and we'd made the arrangements— Doug was out of this little charade, of course, because we couldn't risk having the girl hear his voice. Now, even as I turned that way, the phone started ringing. I gave a rueful shrug for Amy's benefit, walked over, and picked it up.

"Yes, sir," I said. "Yes, she told me, I was just about to call. . . . What's that? How did the fool woman manage that? Well, get me another dame who knows how to sail, for God's sake. Or just some female who doesn't get too seasick, who'll make my cover look good and can help me pull the strings after I show her how. . . . No, I won't do it in a powerboat, dammit; I don't care how many freebies the Coast Guard offers us. If the people we're after are that nervous, they'll blast any fast powerboat that comes snooping around, as they did just a few weeks back, if you'll recall. The only way we've got a chance to survive, and locate the place the C.G. is after, is to look dumb and innocent, a nice stupid married couple in a slow, slow sailboat dragging a big deep keel, obviously the last thing anybody'd use for spying in those shallow waters. . . ."

I heard a rustle of movement and saw that Amy had walked over to seat herself on the side of her rumpled bed. She was starting to try on the panty hose I'd bought her, a fairly interesting operation. I forced myself to concentrate on the telephone in my hand.

"Hasn't the Coast Guard got a dame they can lend us?" I asked, and listened, and said, "Oh, Christ, bureaucratic morality, yet! Do they really think I'd ravish their tender lady seaman, seawoman, seaperson, or whatever the hell they call her? Well, haven't we got some competent old bag hanging around? She doesn't have to be young and beautiful. Christ, I'm not very young and beautiful myself; a stodgy middle-aged boating couple might be just the right cover. . . . Yes, sir. I'll await your call with eager anticipation, sir. No, sir, I don't mean to be disrespectful, sir. Good-bye, sir."

Well, it was a pretty obvious teaser, almost as obvious as the drunk-and-disorderly act Miss Amy Barnett had put on for me the night before. I sat for a moment after hanging up, staring grimly and picturesquely at the dead phone; then I shook my head as if to dismiss some unpleasant thoughts and looked across the room.

"Well, how did I do, nylon-wise?" I asked. I grinned as she pulled down her slip hastily. "They seem to fit all right. How about the color?"

"It's fine. A little on the light side, but . . . No, they're fine." She gave me an odd, shy glance. "It's the first time I ever let a man buy stockings for me, Mr. Helm."

I said, "I once visited Sweden, where my folks came from. They're pretty formal over there, or were back when I was there, and they had a little ceremony when two people got to know each other pretty well. In the case of two men, the senior took the initiative. In the case of a man and a woman, it was the lady's prerogative to suggest that it was perhaps not necessary for the gentleman to call her *Fru* or *Fröken*—Missus or Miss—any longer; first names had become acceptable. We've been kind of stuffy for various reasons, Miss Barnett. Would you care to make a move toward informality before we part company?"

After a moment, she laughed softly. It was, I realized, the laugh I'd been waiting for, the warm and pleasant laugh her mouth was made for.

"We *have* been kind of stiff and silly, haven't we, Matt? Yes, you have my permission to call me Amy."

"Well, Amy, you shouldn't make that flight on a totally empty stomach. If you'll get dressed, I'll feed you lunch in the restaurant downstairs. If you feel you're up to taking a little nourishment."

She nodded. "I think so. But Matt . . ."

"Yes, Amy."

"Can you use a child bride?"

There was a lengthy silence. After staring at her hard, I turned away and walked to the window, which looked out over a big street and a sunny park. Beyond that, I knew, was the city marina, called Miamarina, and I thought I could make out a mast or two, but the trees made it hard to tell. I heard again Doug Barnett's voice saying: *Now that I'm dead, it's fairly certain that she'll try to attach herself to you.* I found myself wishing he hadn't been quite so right about the daughter he hardly knew.

Her voice spoke behind me: "I couldn't help overhearing. You need somebody to play a female part on

91

a boat, and she doesn't really have to be a very good sailor, isn't that right?"

I said without looking around, "The dumb nautical broad who was scheduled to go with me had to play rescuing angel when somebody's brat fell overboard instead of just letting the little monster drown. She saved the kid all right but got an ankle smashed between the boat and the dock. The mission is not one that can be accomplished by a dame in a cast." After a moment, I went on, "Or by a nonviolent wench who thinks some weapons are worse than others, but all are pretty horrible." I turned quickly. "Here! Catch!"

Instinctively, she caught the gleaming object I tossed at her. Then, realizing what she was holding, she gave a little squeal of fright and dropped it on the hotel carpet and backed away from it as if it had been a live and rattling diamondback. I laughed shortly, walked over and scooped up the fallen revolver, swung out the cylinder, and reloaded with the cartridges I'd palmed while my back was to her.

I said, "Go home to Cincinnati, little girl. I appreciate the generous spirit behind the offer, but you really shouldn't try to play ball in the same league with us grown-ups."

"That wasn't fair," she said softly.

"A lousy little unloaded thirty-eight," I said scornfully, "and you panicked as if somebody'd tossed you a grenade with the pin out! Go back to your pacifist friends, Amy Barnett. What I need is a tough, trained, ruthless broad who can save me from a knife or bullet, not a dainty lady protest marcher who's going to save me from The Bomb."

"I can't go back," she said.

"What?"

"I'm afraid to go back," she said. "That's the other

reason I ran away from the airport and got so drunk. I'm terrified of going back to . . . to him!" She touched a whip-marked shoulder. "The man who did this to me! I couldn't bear to go back to *that* again!"

THE HOTEL dining room was one of the elaborate, dark, plushy ones—no cafés, cafeterias, or tea shoppes need apply. It wasn't doing much lunch business yet, and we were led directly to a table for two against the far wall. Amy walked ahead of me, following the head waiter. Her suit had cleaned up surprisingly well, considering the indignities to which it had been subjected. She looked trim and businesslike once more; apparently the same neatly dressed and very serious young lady who'd come to this hotel to see me a few days back. But I remembered that I had then taken her, along with some other people and situations, at face value, gullible me.

From my viewpoint behind her, the neck exposed by the smoothly pinned-up hair looked particularly slender and graceful. I wished I wouldn't keep finding, or refinding, nice things to like about this girl. Seated, I ordered a drink for myself—vodka martini, if you must know—after Amy had shuddered at the question and shaken her head emphatically.

"Okay, now let's hear about this terrible Cincinnati boogeyman," I said when we were alone.

"No, ladies first," she said. "Just how do you happen to know so much about my gaudy past, Mr. Helm? I never told you anything about my political activities that I can remember."

I said, "I told you once, you're one of the family; you're Doug Barnett's kid. And after offering so nobly to come to your rescue if you should ever need it, I thought it advisable to get a little background information on you." Well, that wasn't too far from the truth, although Doug had briefed me on his offspring's history without being asked. I went on: "I wanted to see just what I might be letting myself in for. It was quite a surprise. You don't look like a wild-eyed activist."

"Amy the Mouse," she said dryly. "I do keep trying very hard to be a proper little lady, but it keeps getting away from me. I keep getting away from me. In not very pleasant directions. Didn't you ever find yourself compelled to do things you didn't really approve of, even repulsive and shameful things? Not that I'm ashamed of fighting for peace; but things like drinking myself silly and . . ." She ran her hand over her shoulder as if feeling for the fading scars under her tailored jacket. Then she said stiffly, "So in addition to being featured in a number of police records, I'm also in the files of your agency?"

"Of course," I said. "So are my kids, if that makes you feel any better. Now, what about the villain with the whip?"

I'd been startled at having her throw the man we wanted right at my head, so to speak; I'd expected that she'd have been instructed to keep the association a secret. Yet perhaps this was the smart way of doing it. Maybe she'd even been given the cruel marks on her back deliberately, to let her use this approach when I saw them and, shocked, asked about them. The best cover is always the one that makes most use of the truth. This way, no matter how much we checked up on her, we couldn't accuse her of hiding anything. Hell, we might even request her assistance in apprehending the wicked pervert who'd hurt her. And of course she'd cooperate willingly, saying that she'd known he was a creep, look what he'd done to her; but she'd never dreamed he was a dangerous criminal, and if there was any way she could help us bring him to justice . . .

Amy hesitated at my question and drew a long breath. "Matt, will you let me do this my way, please? I'll tell you all about it in a little while, or as much as I can bear to, but it isn't really *significant*, is it? It has nothing to do with whether or not I can do the work you need done. You don't have to like or respect the person next to you on the assembly line, do you? As long as they use the right wrench to stick the right nuts onto the right bolts."

I said, "I tossed you the right wrench for the job and you dropped it as if it were red hot." I shook my head. "You're wasting your time, Amy. The idea is crazy. Even if I were crazy enough to take you along, gambling that your inexperience wouldn't kill us both, you haven't the slightest idea what you might be letting yourself in for."

She licked her lips. "Isn't that my worry? Don't you have any imagination at all? Hasn't it occurred to you yet, even after seeing my back, that I might be running away from something much worse than anything that can possibly happen to me on your silly little drug investigation? It is drugs, isn't it?"

I said, "Nobody said anything about drugs, sweetheart."

She said impatiently, "If you don't want people to hear, don't talk on the phone in front of them! I know that you're going to take a sailboat and go spying for the Coast Guard among some islands, presumably somewhere over in the Bahama Islands. Do I have to pretend to be stupid? What else could it be besides drugs?"

"What are you running from, Amy? Whom are you running from?"

She shook her head impatiently. "I'm running from me. I'm running from a me I don't want to be, that somebody's trying to make me into—"

"What somebody?"

"Oh, please!" she protested. "Please let me do it my way. I'll be glad to answer your questions, but just *listen* to me first! I don't know much about boats, and I'm afraid of guns and violence, but I can learn the one, and I . . . I think I can get over the other if you're patient with me. Anyway, isn't that exactly what you need to make a convincing 'cover'? That's what you called it, isn't it?"

"Cover is right, but—"

"You need me, Matt!" she said breathlessly. "I meant it when I said child bride. I'm twenty-five years old, but why do I think I go to the trouble of forever keeping my hair pinned up? Because, while it isn't terribly becoming like this, I look so awfully, pitifully immature with it down that nobody takes me seriously as a grown woman!"

There was a pause while the waiter put my martini glass in front of me and took our orders. When he was gone, I said, "Actually, I think you look very nice with your hair up."

She shook her head again, dismissing the flattery. "The point is, Matt, that I can make a very good stab at looking nineteen or twenty, in cute little white shorts and a very skimpy halter, and my nose and shoulders peeling because of course I don't have sense enough to protect myself from the hot sun. Squealing like a rabbit every time the boat tips, getting deathly seasick whenever the wind blows, and falling overboard with a big splash when I try to help by lowering the anchor or whatever you do with an anchor. And you doting on this pretty, clumsy, sexy child you've managed to catch and marry—"

"Sexy?" I said.

There was color in her face. "Well, we'll have to make the cushions squeak and the boat rock a little at fairly frequent intervals, but that shouldn't be hard to fake, should it? Or if you really want to . . ." Her blush deepened, and she drew a ragged breath. "I'm not a virgin, Matt. You've probably guessed by this time that I'm even somewhat further from being a virgin than I let you think when we first met. If . . . if you want to try to make love to me after I tell you all about me, that's all right; but we can work it out later, can't we? Right now, what you need is a convincing cover story, if that's the right phrase; and what could be more harmless-looking than a cute, helpless little blond bride on her honeymoon cruise— I'll use a pale rinse on my hair; I'll be the silliest, dumbest blonde you ever saw—and the somewhat older bridegroom who's obviously gaga about her?"

"Thanks for the 'somewhat,'" I said dryly. "The big catch, Amy, is that these people kill. It used to be that drug smugglers were mostly amateurs who weren't going to turn a simple drug bust into a case of murder; but it's all getting organized now by some very tough professional characters. And this isn't the Florida Keys—Condominium Alley—we're talking about. There's a lot of empty, watery space over there in the Bahamas, dotted with coral reefs and mangrove islands that haven't seen a policeman since Columbus hit San Salvador and thought he was closing in on the wealth of the Indies. Just for an example of what it's like: Recently with Bahamian permission the coast guard tried sending three agents into the area in which we're interested. They were disguised as enthusiastic Yankee anglers looking for new fishy worlds to conquer, in a fast, twin-screw sport-fisherman. Part of one of the men was found a couple of weeks later, the part that had washed ashore before the sharks could finish it. The other two pseudo-anglers, and the other half of the first man, haven't turned up yet and probably won't. . . . And if you can't even stand to have me talk about the gory details, how are you going to feel when those same gory details are staring you in the face? That little incident is the reason we got roped into this. The trouble is that the Coast Guard's people, like the three who disappeared, are pretty well-known to the drug Mafia. Well, we happen to owe the C.G. a favor at the moment, and our agency generally deals with totally different problems; so while my picture might be recognized in Moscow, it probably isn't known on Grand Bahama Island, or New Providence, or Andros. Or down in the Exumas and points beyond. So I'm elected, dammit."

She said stubbornly, "My face isn't known there, either, Matt."

I ignored this and went on: "They presumably disposed of the whole crew, fed it to the sharks, and ran the boat out into deep water—there are tongues of deep stuff sticking into most of those big shallow areas—and opened the seacocks, good-bye. Very unpleasant people. Come to think of it, as your mother undoubtedly told you over and over again, we're kind of unpleasant, too. But how am I going to do my unpleasant stuff, or even defend myself—us—if my pretty pacifist partner goes all hysterical every time I pull out my nasty, wicked, violent gun? So let's forget it and talk about the man who's terrified you so badly you can't even bring yourself to get on a plane homeward. If he's got you so badly intimidated, how did you get away from him?"

She started to speak quickly, obviously to continue

the argument; then she shrugged resignedly and said, "He was out of town for a while, long enough for me to work up enough courage to pack my bag and dash to the airport and buy a ticket here; fortunately they had a last-minute seat available. I'd got that letter from my father, remember? It occurred to me in my desperation that if I could see him and talk to him, Daddy might . . . might be able to help me."

"Help you do what?"

"Break away for good," she said. "I tried it once before, alone, but *he* just came after me and brought me back like a . . . like a runaway child, ugh. I had to have help from somebody strong enough to stand up to him. I . . . Where he is concerned, I have no willpower left at all. There are men like that, you know, who can turn women, at least nutty, susceptible women like me, into obedient zombies."

"So you didn't really come down here just to be nice to your poor old rejected daddy after all these years."

She winced. "I don't think I ever said I did. I just said I was . . . lonely and wanted to see him, didn't I? That wasn't bending the truth very much. Don't make me sound worse than I really am."

"Has this guy got a name?"

"Pope. Albert Pope."

From minister to pope. Our friend was working his way up in the world.

I said scornfully, "And Mr. Pope has the Power or something? Something so terrible that rather than face the prospect of going back to spit in his eye you deliberately set out to drink yourself blotto after twenty-five years of sobriety? This guy must really have transfixed you with his evil eye!" She didn't speak, she just sat there watching me gravely across the table; and I was ashamed of myself for bullying her. "Sorry. I just find it hard to believe, Amy.

You're an intelligent person, and I don't think you're a coward."

She licked her lips. "You don't understand. You're strong, you're normal, you don't have any ugly compulsive needs that a clever person can use to . . . If somebody tried to dominate you, persuade you to submit to crazy, sexy rituals of pain and humiliation, you'd just pull out your big gun and shoot them dead, wouldn't you?"

I laughed shortly. "Okay, you've got me all figured out, although you may have overestimated my normality slightly. But I'm still trying to figure you out and it's tough going. Tell me about this man. I suppose he's tall and handsome and dark and devilish-looking, a real midwestern Heathcliff."

"Well, he's not midwestern, I don't know where he comes from, really." She smiled faintly. "Actually, Albert is a slightly overweight businessman type with thinning blond hair, the last man in the world you'd expect . . . I suppose that's why it happened. I needed somebody kind and trustworthy who wasn't forever after me to smoke his stupid pot or accommodate his stupid sex. Albert looked so gentle and harmless after all the intense bearded creeps. . . . Gentle!"

"What happened?" I asked, after she'd been silent for a little, remembering.

She moved her shoulders in an awkward shrug, as if her clothes were still not quite comfortable against her recently lacerated skin. "My job at the clinic keeps me busy days, of course, at least during the week; but in the evenings and on weekends . . . I'd joined this antinuclear group, and part of their program involved lectures and seminars and other group activities, kind of missionary work. All those everlasting meetings and discussions! I guess I was, well, getting pretty fed up with all the protest jargon mixed up with marijuana and harder stuff, and the notion that I was letting down the team because I wouldn't make myself—my body—available to any whiskery fanatic who talked a good antinuclear fight. What in the world has sex got to do with . . . That wasn't what I'd joined them for!"

She paused while the waiter brought me a second martini. I noticed that after last night she no longer felt herself entitled to disapprove of my drinking habits.

She went on: "Of course I was proud that they'd asked me to join, although in my modest moments I wondered why they'd picked me for their elite save-the-world society. The People for Nuclear Peace sounds very democratic, but they're really a pretty snobbish group. I mean the inner circle around Mrs. Williston, not the ones who come for the free food and liquor and lectures. You know who she is? Mrs. Georgina Williston?"

"Yes, I know," I said. "Why did you join them, if you think they're snooty and don't enjoy their programs?"

"Well, it was flattering to be asked, and Mrs. Williston is a very persuasive lady." Amy hesitated. "Actually, I joined them because I'm crazy," she said softly.

"As good a reason as any," I said.

"I'm not joking!" She didn't like my attitude. "I went to a psychiatrist. He told me why I did all those things, joined all those movements, participated in all those demonstrations. Didn't I tell you last night? Not because I'm such a great idealist, but because . . . well, call it guilt. Expiation. I can't remember exactly what I did tell you last night. But the fact is that I want to be hurt, humbled, shamed, punished for being the wicked girl I am—I did tell you—and that even as a kid I gloried in the times when the police mauled me and threw me into their stinking jails all bloody and bruised and messy, even while part of me, the sensible part, cringed at the dreadful disgrace of it. Self-destructive, that's Barnett. Joan of Arc looking for a bonfire. The martyr syndrome. Of course those shrinks are great for telling you why you do things, but they're not much help in telling you how to stop doing them."

"And then Mr. Pope came along," I said.

She nodded. "Albert saw it at once, when he became a member of the Cincinnati chapter of the PNP. I don't think he gave a hoot about nuclear proliferation. I think he just knew it was a good place to hunt for . . . for the right kind of masochistic material. . . ." She was silent while the waiter put our lunches on the table. "Material like me," she whispered when he was gone.

There was silence while we attacked the contents of our plates. I noted that her hangover didn't seem to be affecting her appetite any longer.

"Matt," she said at last.

"Yes."

"I don't really want to tell you about . . . well, the nasty clinical details. It was just like last night experiencing the sickening humiliation of finding myself staggering down that sidewalk so helplessly intoxicated, looking so incredibly awful; I couldn't believe that dreadful, dirty, stumbling creature was me. But still . . . still, I was gloating just a little because this degradation was no more than I deserved. Justice was being done. Can you understand that?"

I said, "I'm not a psychiatrist, Amy. Don't ask me for understanding. I just shoot off those big guns."

She laughed shortly. "Watch out or I'll fall in love with you, the only man in the world who doesn't claim to understand me better than I understand myself." Her brief amusement faded. She drew a long breath. "Albert knew. He became the stern father figure forever punishing me for deserting my own father. The first time, I couldn't believe it was happening. I couldn't believe I'd let him persuade me . . . I couldn't believe *that* was me, modest and dignified me, all naked like *that*, letting myself be bound like *that*, and allowing *that* to be done to me. But I did allow it, Matt; I can't blame him, really; he didn't force me. Something made me obey him, even when he asked things of me that were utterly revolting. I can't even tell you about them. I couldn't ever tell anybody about them."

I said, "You might be better off if you did. But not over lunch, please."

She smiled faintly. "Aren't you afraid you'll spoil me with all this mushy sympathy?" The smiled died. "At first, of course, even though I couldn't seem to help myself, I hated the ghastly hurting indignities of it, the shameful abuses of my . . . my rather nice body. But it satisfied something black and ugly inside me; and then I found myself not hating it so much anymore. I found myself even beginning to . . . to respond to it sexually, no longer just enduring it as a kind of atonement. That was when I knew I was in *real* danger. That was when I knew I had to escape before he completely destroyed me, my will, my pride and self-respect, what little was left of them. Don't send me back to him, Matt. Help me. You promised my daddy you'd help me. Take me with you and help me find myself again. Please!"

THE BOAT was up on shore when we first saw her, stored in a boatyard near the Dinner Key Marina in Coral Gables, just south of Miami. Twenty-eight feet long on deck, with a bowsprit adding another couple of feet, she was sandwiched in between two larger and racier yachts that made her look quite small, but sturdy and seaworthy, by comparison. The mast seemed very tall, however. The propeller was solid and had three businesslike blades, a reassuring sight. Skinny, two-bladed folding props that reduce water resistance under sail are fairly common on auxiliary sailboats these days, but I'd heard horror stories of such props folding at the wrong moment or not unfolding at the right one. Considering my limited sailing experience, I figured I needed a totally reliable power system to get me out of the awkward spots I was bound to get myself into.

Two days later, with a fresh coat of very expensive antifouling paint on the bottom to discourage the weeds and barnacles—you'd think they mix those paints with gold and platinum instead of tin and copper, the prices they charge—our ship was launched. The name on the transom was *Spindrift*. Salty, perhaps, but not exactly original.

"Oh, Johnny, darling, look how nicely it floats, I think it's just *beautiful!*" My little blonde bride hugged my arm ecstatically as she watched a couple of workmen towing our boat to a nearby dock where more work would be done. "Can we . . . can we sleep aboard it tonight?"

Her expression said that sleeping was the last thing she had in mind. She was throwing herself into her sexy-child-wife act with as much enthusiasm as she'd employed for her bedraggled-lady-drunk routine. Sometimes I think acting comes more naturally to women. A man almost always feels self-conscious about pretending to be somebody else, while a woman apparently gets tired of forever being the same dull person and gets a big kick out of changing characters occasionally, even if the new character is slightly ridiculous or even somewhat disreputable. I once met a very nice, and very respectable, lady professor who was forced by circumstances to pretend to be a fairly wanton woman. She admitted afterward that she'd enjoyed every minute of it—far from home and with a good enough excuse to satisfy her stern professorial conscience, of course.

Amy Barnett—alias Penelope Matthews, Mrs. John Matthews—was wearing part of the yachting trousseau we'd bought her: blue boat shoes with tricky rubber soles, rather thin and very tight white pants, and a snug light-blue jersey with long sleeves. We'd decided to give her a few more days to heal before displaying her in public in a bikini, or shorts and halter, since it wouldn't do for people to think I tortured my young bride in private.

Her hair fell smooth and straight and pale to her shoulders. The do-it-yourself rinse hadn't done the job to her satisfaction so she'd had a beauty shop take it all the way to silver-blond. Like that, wearing the shining hair in that simple schoolgirl fashion, she looked much smaller; also, as she'd promised, much younger. Her fine little breasts peeked shyly through the soft blue jersey. The younger members of the boatyard crew thought I was a lousy old lecher, robbing the cradle like this; and if I found I wasn't up to the bridegroom job at my advanced age, would I ask for volunteers, please?

"Can we, darling?" Amy pleaded.

I said, "They've still got to install the Loran and self-steering, and do some work on the engine. We'd better not get the cabin all cluttered up with our stuff before they're through."

She pouted. "I'm tired of that old hotel. I want to move aboard that cute little boat right *now!*"

I glanced around. For the moment, there was nobody within earshot. I said softly, "Don't overplay it, sweetheart."

She whispered right back, "You run your act, mister, and let me run mine!" She pinched my arm painfully. "And who was it who said we had to *live* our parts every minute of every day? Matt, I mean, Johnny."

"Yes?"

"Thank you. Thank you very much for taking a chance on me."

"My pleasure," I said. "But maybe you ought to wait until the job is done and we're back here alive, if we make it back, before you thank me."

"It doesn't matter, really. Already I'm a different person, a rather silly little person, but one I like a lot better than that morbid, masochistic wench. . . . Well, all right!" she said petulantly, seeing a man approaching. "All right, if we have to wait, all *right*, but I'm just melting standing here in the hot sun, darling. I'll see you back at the hotel."

"Penny . . ."

But she'd flounced away. We watched her go, since the action of the neat little buttocks in the thin white sailor pants was not to be missed; then the man who'd come up said he was the yard's electrical specialist and I'd better come aboard and show him where I wanted the Loran installed. I'd told Washington that since I was going to try to make it without a human navigator to help me, I'd better at least have an electronic one, even though dockside rumor had it that Loran doesn't always function well in the remoter regions of the Bahamas. Propagation anomalies, somebody'd told me. Whatever that means.

There's a big mystique associated with seamanship. If you weren't born in a forecastle in the middle of a hurricane and didn't cut your teeth on a marlinespike, you'll never qualify. Well, hell, they told me just about the same thing about horses when I was a kid. The fact is, there are people with vested interests in just about every sport who get a big kick out of making their particular athletic activity seem too difficult for ordinary mortals to comprehend, let alone master. I've been known to tell beginners how hard it is to shoot straight, myself. Actually, making a boat or horse go where you want it to, or making a gun go bang in approximately the right direction, isn't all that tough once you've decided not to let the experts intimidate you; and I wasn't really worrying about the technical aspects of getting myself and my boat over into the Islands with a landlubber crew. The human aspects were something else again.

Before heading back to the hotel, I stopped at a pay phone near the yard gate. Doug Barnett, having set things up to his own satisfaction, had dropped out of sight completely, as befitted a dead man, and Mac was coordinating things from Washington. It didn't take long to get him on the line. He may be a bastard at times, or even all the time, but he's an available bastard.

"Yes, Eric?"

"Has she made any false moves yet? Or any moves?"

"There's been only one telephone call from your hotel room since the last one you were told about, to the clinic in Cincinnati where she's employed, asking for more time off. We recorded another call yesterday to the same number. Apparently an afterthought. She wanted a friend, female, to take a couple of plants from her apartment and look after them. Some kind of an ornamental cactus, I believe, and a philodendron. She'd had a neighbor coming in to water them, when she'd thought she'd only be gone a few days, but she doesn't want to impose on her any longer."

I said dryly, "It could be some kind of fancy code. Cactus. Philodendron. And watch out when she says chrysanthemum. That's when the shit really hits the fan."

Mac said, "A nurse who works in the same clinic was later seen carrying two potted plants from Miss Barnett's apartment building."

I said, after a moment, "Cincinnati's a long way to send a man to check on a telephone conversation, sir."

"He was already in the city, waiting for Minister to return."

"But Minister hasn't?"

"Correct. I'm afraid we must assume that the Preacher is now operating from a different base and that of the people we know, only Miss Barnett is aware of his present location."

"Mrs. Matthews, please," I said. "Mr. John Matthews here, at your service. Address, The Palms, Coral Gables."

"Yes," Mac said. "Which reminds me, somebody

has been making inquiries at the Marina Towers in Miami about that immoral Mr. Matthew Helm who lures intoxicated young ladies to his hotel room. Although that wasn't exactly the description used. We haven't been able to locate the man who was asking the questions."

I frowned. "That doesn't make sense, sir. Hell, they don't have to track me down; they have a tracking device planted right on me to let them know my movements. A cute little blonde tracking device. All they have to do is wait for her to call in."

"It would seem that there are two possibilities," Mac said. "Either Miss Barnett—Mrs. Matthews— has been silent so long that her associates in the PNP are getting worried and making cautious efforts to locate her, or . . ." He paused to let me complete the sentence for him.

"Or there's somebody else on the trail," I said. "An element we've overlooked. Nice thought. Well, all I can do is be ready to duck. That won't be easy on a twenty-eight-foot cockleshell bobbing around in the middle of the Gulf Stream, where we hope to be pretty soon."

"In the meantime, have you made any progress toward finding out what the young lady knows?"

"I haven't really tried, sir," I said. "I don't want to louse up everything by crowding her."

"That's the safe approach, certainly, but I'm under a certain amount of pressure, Eric. The international conference in Nassau is getting close. I've had it impressed on me that it may be our last chance, the world's last chance, and nothing must be allowed to jeopardize it. Even if we don't have quite so much faith in this gathering, we're obliged to give it an opportunity to succeed."

I said, "Yes, but we still don't know for sure that it's the target Minister and his backers have in mind.

In fact, there are no indicators whatever pointing that way except sheer geographical coincidence. And simple common sense says it just can't be."

"I have long since given up expecting simple common sense from fanatics of any persuasion," Mac said dryly. "All over the world fanatic patriots are destroying their own countries in the name of patriotism. Can we expect more rational behavior from an organization of fanatic pacifists or supposed pacifists—there's some question about how idealistic this wealthy PNP group really is—led by a rich, spoiled woman who's spent time in a mental institution?" Mac was silent for a moment; then he went on: "Actually, it doesn't matter, Eric. We want Minister anyway; and under the circumstances we must deal with him before the conference gets under way, to be on the safe side."

"Yes, that's what Doug told me."

"And in order to deal with Minister we have to find him. At the moment, the girl is our only lead."

"I hate to force it, sir," I said. "I'd prefer to let her set the pace; sooner or later she'll want to talk about herself some more, and about her demon lover. It's safer if I wait. Right now I'm in good shape. I didn't jump to accept her offer to come along; in fact I sneered at it and told her how impossible it was for me to even consider taking her. I made her practically get on her knees and plead with me to give her sanctuary of sorts. I think she's pretty well convinced that she talked me into it; but if I start asking leading questions about the whereabouts of her sadistic gentleman friend she could start to wonder if this conjugal voyage was really her idea after all."

"Well, do what you can. We don't have much time, and it will be quicker if you can persuade her to talk than if you have to wait for her, or her friends, to lead you to Minister somehow. Or him to you. Quicker, and much safer."

"Thank you for your concern, sir."

"In the meantime, of course, all you can do is go through the motions of carrying out your part of the Griego operation for the U.S.C.G. Abraham is investigating the connection between Constantine Griego and the PNP in a quiet way, both in Nassau and down in the lower Bahamas where it's believed the man has an important transshipment point where the drugs are unloaded from the ships coming up from the Caribbean and put into fast motorboats for delivery to this country. That's what the Coast Guard's ill-fated expedition was searching for. You will do likewise, up to a point. . . ."

"The point where I get eaten by a shark," I said dryly. "Yes, sir. I'll try to avoid repeating the Coast Guard experience past that point. But with my pretty little wife broadcasting my operations to the enemy whenever she gets the chance, it won't be easy."

"But it will take the pressure off Abraham," Mac said calmly.

"Yes, sir," I said. "Watching me make a jackass of myself again, this time under a false name with a phony marital cover trying to make a five-ton sailboat with a forty-foot mast look invisible, they'll be laughing so hard they'll never notice a dead man sneaking up on them from behind." I grimaced at the phone. "Aren't you going to tell me to be careful, sir?"

Mac said, "If I need to tell you to be careful, you're the wrong man for the job. Good luck, Eric."

He always wishes us good luck. It's really very nice of him. As I left the booth, I wondered why I'd felt compelled to refer to the girl in a more derogatory fashion than was absolutely necessary, as if I had no liking for her at all. You'd have thought I was afraid of admitting, to myself as well as to Mac, that I actually found her rather pleasant company in spite of what I knew about her.

To GET to the Bahamas, I first had to start the little
two-cylinder diesel and back the boat out of its narrow slip in the boatyard's cramped basin and get out
of the basin without hitting anything. Then I had to
find the Dinner Key Channel between the sheltering
islands and follow the channel markers out into Biscayne Bay without running onto the pale shoals on
either hand. Then we had to motor several miles
across Biscayne Bay and pick up the narrow channel
that ran close to the southern end of Key Biscayne,
again running the markers cautiously to avoid the
threatening shallows. Finally, passing the picturesque
old Cape Florida lighthouse on the tip of Key Biscayne,
I had to locate the offshore marker that would guide
us off the shallow coastal shelf—I believe it's actually
a coral reef—and out into the deep water of the
Straits of Florida.

That was all supposed to be easy sailing for any
competent yachtsman or yachtswoman. Next came
the hard part: finding the Bahamas.

"Do you want me to start fixing something for
lunch?" Amy asked as the U.S.A. fell astern at last.

I said, "Sure. A good stiff Scotch on the rocks with a dash of water. Have one yourself."

She shook her head. "My first bout with alcohol was hardly a glorious victory. I'm not in a hurry to try a rematch, thanks. But you'll have to translate. Teach me how to bartend. Just exactly what's a stiff drink and what isn't?"

I said, "The chances of your being a promising AA candidate are very small, but suit yourself. A normal shot is an ounce and a half. For me, let's try two ounces as a therapeutic dose. The jigger's hanging on the galley bulkhead next to the ice pick."

"Matt—I mean, Johnny . . ." She hesitated.

"What is it, Penny?"

She was studying me quizzically. "Do you know what you're doing . . . Johnny? You looked awfully tense back there."

I said indignantly, "What do you mean, woman? We haven't hit anything yet, have we? We didn't run aground, did we? Questioning the competence of the skipper comes under the heading of mutiny, a walk-the-plank offense. If we had a plank." I grinned. "No, Mrs. Matthews, I don't know what the hell I'm doing. My salty female partner was supposed to handle the boat; my job was the muscle and the guns. I've been on a lot of boats run by other people delivering me hither and yon across the water in the line of business, government business, but I haven't handled very many myself, and very few sailboats, and none on a hardship cruise like this with a heartless dame who deliberately lets the captain die of thirst at his post of duty."

Amy laughed softly. "I guess I'd better start reading that seamanship book on the cabin shelf, huh?"

"After I've finished it," I said. "I'm just working my way through A for Anchor at the moment. Does it worry you?"

"Being stuck out in the middle of the ocean with somebody who doesn't know how to sail?" She gave me an odd, crooked little smile. "No, not really. Strangely, it doesn't. It's the ugly things inside my head that worry me, the things that make me do ugly things to myself and let people do ugly things to me. Drowning isn't one of my big fears. Anyway, I don't think you're nearly as helpless as you pretend, nautically speaking. One drink coming up."

"Switch on the Loran while you're down there; it takes a little while to warm up. I'd better start making like a navigator as soon as we've finished lunch."

I watched her make her way through the hatch and down the ladder, a slim figure in jeans and a horizontally striped blue-and-white knitted shirt with an open sailor collar and short sleeves. The saggy pantaloons and baggy bloomers some females have taken to wearing these days have performed a miracle I'd have called impossible a few years back: they've succeeded in making girls in ordinary, well-fitting jeans look attractive. There was a time when I'd have said they shouldn't be let out of the barn until they'd got the manure all shoveled and were ready to bathe and don presentable clothing; but my current shipmate didn't look too bad to me at all, even with her bottom swathed in crude blue denim.

Although I kept telling myself that it was all an act and she'd naturally do her best to tug at my susceptible heartstrings, I found myself with a strong urge to cherish and protect the poor disturbed little thing. There was, of course, another factor involved besides sympathy. There always is. The lady was beginning to look good enough to me in other ways to create something of a problem, call it a propinquity problem. Well, I told myself firmly, there was obviously nothing to be done about it at the moment, confronted as I was by a lot of tricky navigation, with an unfamiliar boat to manage, and the land getting lower and lower on the western horizon.

After finishing my drink and devouring one of the Swiss-on-rye sandwiches Amy had constructed for us, I got to work and figured out where we were, electronically. I can't tell you how Loran works, except that there are numbered lines on most nautical charts these days representing the transmissions from certain land stations. Punch the right buttons on your magic box and similar numbers will come up in the two windows. Find the lines on the chart corresponding to those numbers, and where they cross is where you are. That's the basic theory; in practice you can make those silicon chips do almost anything on board short of cooking and hoisting the sails—the next step in our nautical progress, as I told Amy.

"That's the big jib up forward, rolled up like a window blind," I said, "but we won't unroll it yet. Next comes the little forestaysail. In a moment you can go up there and get the lashings off it; I think they're actually called stops. I thought the hinged spar at the bottom of that sail was a jibboom, but I was advised that jibbooms went out with clipper ships; it's called a club. Be sure you call it by the right name. You've got to call everything by the right name afloat, or the damn boat will sink like a rock. At least that's the impression I got from the dockside geniuses. Next comes the mainsail on the main boom. We'll start with that. I'm told the proper response is "Aye, aye, sir."

"Aye, aye, sir."

"Incidentally, falling overboard is frowned upon," I said. "One hand for the ship and one for yourself, as the old saying goes. Okay, give me a minute to figure out this crazy autopilot so I can let go of this stick, known as a tiller, and we'll get to work."

Setting sail is, I believe, supposed to be a five-minute job on a boat the size of *Spindrift*. It took us well over an hour. All the lines seemed to go to the wrong places, and if they were correctly led, we found them tangled in the rigging overhead when we tried to haul on them. The mast was equipped with little patent steps like certain telephone and power poles, so you could climb up to fix things at the top, but they seemed to have a devilish affinity for any rope that flopped within range. The sails themselves had been improperly installed. By me, of course. Nothing worked right the first time, or even the second, but at last we had the little sail hoisted forward of the mast and the big one hoisted aft of it, reasonably taut and pretty.

I turned off the motor and had Amy help me adjust things until the nautical speedometer said we were making maximum speed through the water, actually a gentle two knots with an occasional surge to three. Hardly America's cup performance, but good enough for a couple of landlubbers feeling their cautious way toward seamanship. By dinnertime there was no land on the horizon, although a yellowish dome of pollution haze astern let us know that Miami was still back where we'd left it. We ate in the cockpit, little pan-fried steaks and fresh vegetables she'd insisted on buying. I'm strictly a can opener–type chef myself.

"I'll do the dishes," I said. "No reason for you to have all the galley duty."

She said, "I'll do them. I don't mind. Then, if you don't need me, I think I'll lie down for a while. Those seasick pills are making me very sleepy. Matt?"

"Yes?"

"It's . . . it's very nice out here. Thank you again for bringing me."

"Wait till we've made it across," I said. "We've been lucky with the weather so far, but that's not to say we won't have a hurricane by morning, although the weatherman tells it otherwise. And there's one thing we'd better do while we have the ocean to ourselves. A little artillery practice. Can you bring yourself to get out the revolver I put away under the mattress of the starboard bunk, and the shotgun from its clips at the back of the galley locker? And the ammunition, for both, bottom galley drawer. You should get used to grabbing for them and handling them. You may have to do it for real sometime."

I was demonstrating how seriously I took this mission of searching out the secret island den of that wicked purveyor of chemical evil, Mr. Constantine Grieg—I had, of course, given her all the details to show how much I trusted her. Well, almost all the details. And of course I'd spoiled it, the sense of peace she'd been feeling; but she obeyed in silence and I put her through the basic drill. Open and close. Load and unload. Hammer cocked and uncocked. Safety on, safety off. Then I had her snap the weapons empty, working the mechanisms repeatedly.

At last I had her shoot the .38. I didn't make her fire the shotgun, although I let off a few rounds myself to check it out. It was a police-type Winchester pump in stainless steel, presumably just about the same gun I'd been told Doug Barnett had carried on his boat, a handsome weapon in a brutal way; but a twelve-gauge is really too much gun for a beginner, particularly a relatively small beginner who's been brought up to be afraid of guns. With that short barrel, and the heavy loads that were all I'd brought along, the noise and recoil were ferocious. I'd learned what I wanted to know. There was no need to hurt her.

Taking the weapons back below, she paused in the hatchway to look back at me. "You didn't teach me to hold the handgun in both hands as they do on TV," she said.

"Without one hand to steady yourself, you could have been pitched into the drink if the boat lurched, right?" I said. "Sure, you can make better scores on a paper target, or some people can, using two hands; but that doesn't do you much good if you're swimming, does it? Think about it."

She frowned at the guns she was holding. "I suppose you did this to remind me that this isn't really a pleasure cruise," she said a little stiffly.

"Something like that," I said. "And to give me a chance to deliver my famous lecture on the proper employment of firearms. Remember this: A gun is serious business. Once you point a gun at somebody you're a murderer; whether or not you get around to pulling the trigger is irrelevant. So you'd damn well better decide if that's what you want before you start waving the piece around. It's only in the movies that a pistol, or whatever, is a magic wand that bends people peacefully to your will. The cops have to try it because they're supposed to bring 'em back alive if they can. We don't. I don't point guns at people I'm not prepared to kill; and if anybody points a gun at me, I figure he means it, and I think about nothing but killing him until I have him totally dead. Or he has me; but somehow that hasn't happened yet. Forget that idiot drop-your-gun-and-put-your-hands-up nonsense. Do you remember the old TV show called *The Twilight Zone?*" When she nodded, I said, "The moment you aim a gun at somebody, you've moved into the twilight zone, baby, the killing zone, and you'd better be ready to finish the job and do them in fast before they do you. End of sermon."

She licked her lips. "I understand," she said quietly. "And I hope you noticed that I don't shriek and swoon every time somebody hands me a firearm. You just caught me by surprise that once. But I'd better warn you that I don't really think I could pull the trigger if the target was a man and not a milk carton. Not that I could hit it anyway, or him, dainty pacifist me. As we just proved. Good night, Matt. Wake me if you need me."

Well, the experiment had been a success, I reflected grimly as I watched her disappear down the hatch. I'd determined that she was quite ignorant about guns. It's something that's impossible to fake. But I found myself wondering if she was thinking, as I was, that we now had a rather lovely sunset, and a beautiful gentle sea with a light favoring wind. If recent nights were any guide, there should even be quite a presentable moon on display fairly soon. Two people who didn't have to play lousy games with each other could have had a very pleasant and companionable sail across the Gulf Stream tonight. And speaking of the Gulf Stream, the numbers in the lighted Loran windows were telling me I should steer even more to the east to allow for the current sweeping us north. . . .

She insisted on taking over the watch at two in the morning to give me a little rest. At four she woke me to report a small, winking light far ahead. I went on deck and timed the winks with my fancy digital watch: fifteen seconds. Great Isaac Light at the northwest corner of the Great Bahama Bank. Bull's-eye. With Loran you, too, can be a great navigator.

I'd already explained to Amy that while the little town of Bimini on the island of the same name was the closest Bahamian port of entry to the U.S, I'd lost nothing there. According to the guidebook it had a tricky entrance channel that I didn't want to tackle and the kind of endless shallow banks behind it that I didn't want to cross until I became a hotshot sailor, say a week from now. So we were bypassing Bimini and heading for Freeport on the sizable island of Grand Bahama to the north, staying in the deep water of the Florida Straits and the Northwest

Providence Channel, and making an end run around those particular banks. Sooner or later I'd have to learn how to get around in that shallow stuff, but I wanted a little more boating practice first.

"You can turn in again. I'll take her now," I said.

Amy shook her head. "No. I've had enough sleep. I like it up here."

"Well, curl up on the cockpit seat if you get tired."

She said a bit sharply, "Don't treat me like a baby, Matt. I may have a few screws loose in my head, but there's nothing wrong with my body."

"Not a damn thing," I agreed. "I've been noticing that."

She gave me a sharp glance and started to make some kind of a protest, then checked herself. In the red light from the binnacle, I saw a little secret smile come to her lips; the smile of a woman who's discovered, somewhat to her surprise, that she doesn't really mind being told that a man finds her desirable.

With daylight, we summoned our collective courage and unrolled the big jib, almost doubling the sail area and raising the speed to just about four knots. The good weather held. The Loran led us by the hand across the Northwest Providence Channel. It was a considerable thrill, after all those hours with an empty horizon, to see the hotels and condominiums of Freeport-Lucaya rise out of the sea ahead. Columbus and Magellan move over, please; here comes Helm.

Sails down, I managed to negotiate the entrance of the Lucayan Harbour Marina under power and take us to the customs dock without casualties. An hour later, legally admitted to the Bahamas, we were tying up in the slip that had been assigned to us off one of the long concrete piers and, after making everything shipshape, we celebrated our successful ocean passage by having a drink under the cockpit awning. At least I was having a drink. She was having canned pineapple juice. Ugh.

We had dinner in the cockpit. I helped her with the dishes afterward and found that I could hardly stand it, working with her in that tiny galley, after the days we'd already spent in close, but not intimate, association pretending to be man and wife. I mean, I'd conquered the raging sea, hadn't I? The victorious hero-navigator is customarily entitled to certain privileges, right? We'd both had showers in the rather rundown marina facilities, and she'd changed to crisp white sailcloth shorts and a rudimentary blue halter; and I couldn't bear to look at her.

"It was a long night, last night," I said, hanging up the dishtowel. "I think I'll hit the sack early, if you don't mind."

"Matt . . ."

"Here it's Johnny," I said.

"I'm sorry." I'd thrown her off-balance for a moment, but she drew a long breath and spoke softly: "Johnny, it's all right. I told you when we started this that it would be all right. If you wanted to." When I didn't speak, she said a little bitterly, "Or is it that I'm well, such a crazy little broad that you don't care to get, well, involved in that way? Is that why you're fighting it so hard? Fighting me."

I licked my lips and said stiffly, "I thought I was just being gentlemanly, not taking advantage of the situation. You made the offer, sure, but there were certain pressures, and you didn't sound particularly enthusiastic."

She said calmly, "I just didn't want to . . . to over-sell the merchandise." Then she swallowed hard and whispered, "Heavens, this is kind of silly, isn't it? Just standing here *talking* about it?"

The tired old seduction scene, I thought sourly, as she came into my arms. Amateur night in the whore-

122

house. But her lips were sweet and willing and her body was warm and nicely shaped and her hands were quick and helpful as, after the first clinging kiss, they assisted me in removing her halter and my shirt and guided my fingers to the fastenings of her little white shorts. . . . Then we were naked on the starboard settee berth trying the kissing bit again in an experimental and exploratory way while our hands became acquainted with each other's bodies as we prepared to proceed beyond mere childish osculation to the adult concerns of the evening.

I raised my head to look at her, wanting to see what kind of a passionate expression she'd put on her face, the damn little phony-blond tramp who'd led me here, all the way from Miami and into her arms at the behest of her lover, doing it all so skillfully that it was hardly fair to class her with the amateurs any longer. . . .

It was a mistake. I shouldn't have looked. She was watching me steadily and her face showed no imitation desire, no pretend passion, quite the contrary. What I saw was apprehension and a kind of innocent trust. Kissing had been all right, even kind of fun, but her wary expression said she knew all about what came next, the brutal indignities and shameful hurts she'd already experienced at the hands of a couple of clumsy, overeager college students and a twisted character calling himself Albert Pope. I had to do it, of course, because I was a man and all men had to do it; but she was counting on me, a nice guy for a change, to keep the humiliation and pain as small as possible.

I released her and sat up abruptly. I told myself that she was faking, she had to be faking; but I knew she couldn't be that good, nobody could be. She couldn't possibly be faking this apprehensive trusting innocence, any more than she could have faked her ignorance of guns. And it meant that we were wrong, everything

123

was wrong, everybody was wrong, all the clever, clever people, including that undercover genius, superagent Helm. I got up and scooped my jeans off the cabin floor.

She started to speak behind me, and the wrong name almost came out, but she corrected it. Her voice sounded puzzled and a little hurt.

"Johnny?"

"Put something on and come on deck," I said harshly. Then I found myself adding: "Please."

"Yes, Johnny."

"Turn out the lights when you come up. Please."

Blindly, I hauled on my pants and found a couple of glasses and dosed them with ice and Scotch. I reached out the hatch to set them on the bridge deck, then climbed out after them. In a moment, the cabin lights went out and she joined me in the cockpit, in a short ruffled white silk nightshirt that made her look about ten years old with her straight blond hair shining in the soft light of the marina—what light found its way under the cockpit awning.

I said, "Listen to me carefully, please. I want you to drink this because you're going to need it. Call it medicine. And then I want you to listen very carefully and keep your pretty mouth very shut. Don't say *anything*, do you understand? Whatever pops into your pretty head is bound to be wrong, so let's not confuse the situation with a lot of impulsive recriminations and accusations. Do you think you can do that?"

After a moment, she nodded. "Yes, Johnny."

I took a moment to review my decision. I was breaking security, of course. I was jeopardizing the whole mission, of course. And partly I was doing it out of a sense of guilt for the way I'd misjudged and deceived the small girl beside me—for the way we all had. But that was irrelevant. What was important was finding out what she really was, now that I was certain she wasn't at all the kind of person we'd thought her. After all, I did have a directive of sorts: I'd been told it was important to get the information about Minister she carried in her head, as quickly as possible. Doug Barnett would scream his head off if he knew what I was doing, but instinct and experience warned me we'd had enough trickery and deceit and concealment here. It was time for a little trust for a change. It was time to see what a little honesty could accomplish.

I said, "If you pass on what I'm going to tell you to anybody, anybody at all, the security freaks in Washington will have my balls for breakfast. I hope you understand that."

"I understand." She swallowed hard. "Is it about my father? Tell me!"

Apparently I wasn't the only one with instincts on this boat. I nodded and told her.

SHE SAT very still as I talked, listening in silence as instructed. She used both hands to hold her glass of whiskey—well, a plastic tumbler. On a small boat you keep real, breakable glass at a minimum. She gripped it very tightly, as if it were a defensive weapon she'd need any minute, and perhaps it was. Now and then she'd take a cautious sip from it as she listened.

The marina was quiet, as marinas go. Some anglers drinking beer in the cockpit of a sportfisherman down the dock laughed a bit loudly from time to time; and across the water in the next row of slips we could see a man and woman talking in the cockpit of a sturdy cruising powerboat bearing some resemblance to a commercial trawler. Occasionally the murmur of their voices reached us.

But the place was not crowded. I'd been told that Bahamian marinas seldom are these days. Since the islands gained their virtual independence from Britain some years back, the hospitality for which they were once noted has deteriorated significantly. Service and maintenance have slipped in most tourist facilities—I could testify that the showers and toilets here were badly neglected—sending a lot of the pampered luxury trade, the gold-plated sportfishermen and the luxury cruising yachts, to look for more congenial accommodations elsewhere. Considering that tourists are just about the only cash crop of the Islands, it seems like a shortsighted policy; but if I were black and had a pretty new country to play with all my own, maybe I'd be shortsighted, too.

"Well, there you have the bare bones of it," I said at last. When she didn't speak immediately, I asked, "How about a refill?"

Her voice was almost inaudible when she spoke: "You're bound to make an alcoholic of me, aren't you?" But there was no smile on her face or in her voice. "All right. I might as well. You may have to clean up after me, but you're used to that."

When I returned to the cockpit she was still sitting there, in her pretty nightshirt, motionless, looking at nothing in particular. I put the drink into her hands.

"Now it's your turn to talk," I said.

She sipped her whiskey and licked her lips thoughtfully, and looked at me. "It tastes almost good. Smooth. Not like that awful raw stuff I bought."

"It's Dewar's White Label Scotch," I said. "Cutty Sark and J. and B. are pretty good, too; and of course if you want to be fancy there's Ballantine's Pinch, but it costs. You probably got yourself a pint of Old Dynamite or Sammy's Swamp Juice or something. But any girl who can get tight enough to pass out on a pint can afford to use the good stuff."

"Matt . . ."

"Yes, Amy."

She stared at me blindly, her eyes big and dark. "How could Daddy do it to me? How could he bear to trick me like that, even if he really thought I'd been sent to spy on him and betray him? And how could he think that? Couldn't he just look at me and see that I . . . that I . . ." Then she was crying softly.

"No, please don't touch me! I'll be all right. I don't need any comfort from you!"

"Sure."

"And you!" she gasped, sniffing and mopping her eyes with the ruffled hem of her shirt. "You! How could you possibly think I'd do *that* to myself deliberately, make such a ghastly spectacle of myself, just a fool you? And the way you went along with all that cruel trickery! Letting me believe I'd seen . . ." She stopped and studied my face for a moment, then asked, "Did you know?"

I said irritably, "I just told you! I talked with Doug Barnett the next day in West Palm Beach. Of course I knew he hadn't killed himself."

"I mean before that." She was watching me steadily. "That first day, in Miami. When you took me to see him in the jail. And later when we were out in that Coast Guard boat with that handsome brown-faced admiral, whatever his name was. . . ."

"Sanderson. Antonio Sanderson."

"Did you know *then* that it was all a . . . an elaborate hoax?"

I said, "What the hell difference does it make? Don't kid yourself. If I had known, I'd have acted exactly the same way. I follow orders."

"No," she said quietly. "No, I don't think you'd have acted *exactly* the same way. That's just the point. So you didn't know, back then, that they were misleading me so terribly with . . . with my father's help, making me think he was a violent drug-smuggling criminal, making me believe I'd seen him commit suicide?"

I shook my head. "No. If it matters, I didn't know, then. I wasn't let in on the gag that early. They didn't consider my thespian abilities adequate; they thought I'd put on a better show for you if I thought the situation was genuine. As I did." I made a rueful

128

face. "You're right, of course. I got kind of carried away, as I wouldn't have if I'd been putting on an act. Jesus, anybody'd have thought your pop was my sainted older brother, the way I laid it on!" I glanced at the shadowed small face framed by the fall of pale hair. "But I don't get it. Isn't all this kind of irrelevant?"

"No." She raised her head. "No, it's the most important thing as far as I'm concerned. You."

I said grimly, "Then you're in a very bad way. If I'm your most important thing. Because I'm a pro, Amy. I do what I'm told, with a few exceptions; and if it means deceiving gullible little girls, that's just too damn bad. Let me go on to say that if anybody ever tries to use you for a shield while shooting at me, I'll shoot right back and to hell with you. That's the way we're trained, that's why I'm still alive when a lot of good men—probably better men in many respects—aren't. And if you're kidnapped, and the kidnapper threatens to cut you into little bloody pieces if I don't do certain things, I'll send him a sharp knife with a note telling him he might as well start slicing because I won't play. We don't ever play those sentimental hostage games, no matter who gets hurt, no matter who dies."

Her smile was faint in the darkness, but it was a smile. "Tough guy," she whispered. "The ruthless mechanical man who obeys orders no matter what! Oh, you're so tough. But you couldn't even make love to me under false pretenses, tough guy!"

I started to speak and found I didn't have anything to say that made sense. I watched a small outboard boat cruise by in the channel outside the lighted marina. In a little while the ripples it had made stirred the boats along the docks and splashed gently against *Spindrift*'s hull.

"I should be very angry with you, shouldn't I?" her

voice said softly. "Well, I was, but I should stay that way, shouldn't I? Instead of . . . I should detest you, all the lies you've told me, all the tricks you've played on me! But you couldn't do *that* to me, even though I was lying there naked, all kissed and caressed and breathless, just waiting for you to . . . what's the word, consummate?" The voice was almost inaudible. "Why couldn't you consummate, Matt?"

I hesitated; then I drew a long breath and said, "Hell, I started out to screw a sinister conspiratorial-type lady, strictly in the line of duty, of course; and suddenly I found myself about to ravish an innocent young girl. And as you say, under false pretenses. I guess the shock was just too much for my virility." I watched her for a little; when she didn't speak, I asked, "So where do we go from here?"

"Isn't that up to you?" Her voice was even. "Nothing's really changed, has it? I mean, if you really had an investigation under way, well, we can keep on with it, can't we? I don't mind. I have no place else to go. Noplace else I want to go. Of course, if you were only playing secret agent for my benefit . . ."

I shook my head. "The mission is genuine enough. We just dressed it up a little fancier than we otherwise might have in order to impress Mrs. Penelope Matthews."

She frowned. "That's what I don't really understand, Matt, all this terrific interest in me. What makes me so important? Even if everybody thought I'd come to Miami to spy on Daddy for the PNP, why all these elaborate games to gain my confidence? What is it you want from me, all of you? Information about Mrs. Williston's group or some of the other organizations I've joined? I shouldn't think I'd have much to add to what's already known. It used to be a standing joke among us that half of us were probably working secretly for the FBI. They keep pretty good track of all the offbeat movements. So why in the world—" She broke off and stared at me in a startled way. "You can't possibly be concerned with Albert!"

And there we were, at the subject I'd been reluctant to bring up myself. I'd left Minister pretty well out of my recital, wanting his name to come from her in the natural course of events; she might have resisted the truth if it had come from me.

I said, "You've got it, baby. We've been looking a long time for the man you know as Albert Pope."

There was a long silence. At last she licked her lips and said, "Just because . . . because he likes to be mean to little girls? It's not very nice of him, but it doesn't seem like a major threat to the world order."

"What did he say he did for a living?"

She shrugged. "I think he said he was retired from some kind of manufacturing business. Small, but big enough to leave him reasonably well off when he sold out, so he could devote himself to important matters involving the survival of mankind." She shook her head quickly. "The standard involved-citizen-of-planet-Earth speech. We get lots of those. Some are sincere, some are looking for publicity as noble public benefactors, and some, like me, are looking for beautiful martyrdom. I don't mean to sound cynical, Matt, but I told you, after learning the truth about my own motives from that psychiatrist, I was getting pretty disillusioned with all these wonderful movements. It's undoubtedly my fault, not theirs."

"And Albert?"

She shook her head quickly. "I never did figure out what category Albert fell into, really. If any. After the first time—our first date, if you want to call *that* a date—his political opinions seemed quite irrelevant. It was not an intellectual relationship. After a while I found that I'd stopped thinking altogether. Thinking had become too much effort, too complicated. I lived in a simple, fuzzy, woozy world of . . . of exquisite pain and ecstatic pleasure. If you want to call *that* pleasure. That's why I had to break away, while there was still a little of the . . . the thinking me left." She looked at me across the cockpit. "Who is Albert Pope, Matt?"

"His real name is Alfred Minister," I said. "He's the man responsible for blowing up the U.S. embassy in Buenos Aires when they were protesting U.S. support of Britain right after the Falklands business. An Argentine patriot group paid for it, but Minister did the work. The El Al airliner that exploded right after takeoff from the Ben Gurion Airport at Tel Aviv last year was also one of his jobs. The PLO claimed the credit there, but Minister rigged the fancy detonator. We have a list of several other definites, and a large number of probables and possibles that we haven't been able to confirm."

"Oh, my God!" Having allowed herself one of her rare blasphemies, she was silent for a little; then she swallowed and asked, "Is he doing . . . is he working on something special right now, that you know about? Is that why you're so concerned about him?"

"We hoped you'd be able to tell us."

She said sharply, "You mean you hoped you'd be able to trick me into telling you!"

I risked a grin. "You got it, sweetheart."

Her anger faded. She smiled faintly in response. "Yes, of course. It makes sense. If you thought I was a . . . an accomplice, that would explain everything, all the elaborate tricks and lies. Using me to trap . . . Alfred Minister. Albert Pope to me. But . . . I'm sorry. He never said anything to let me think . . . I had no idea what he really was; what he really did. I'm afraid I can't help you."

I studied her for a moment. She was a little too earnest about her ignorance, and her eyes wouldn't quite meet mine. I didn't think she was actually lying. What she was saying was true up to a point; she really hadn't known what Minister was, and she had no information about what he was working on at present. But she was withholding something, waiting for me to ask the right question.

But this was not the time to lean on her too hard and risk losing her confidence. I merely said, "Keep thinking about it. Something may come to you."

She said softly, "I always seem to wind up with no self-respect left at all! The fine idealist discovering that she doesn't care so much about saving the world; what she really wants is the lovely humiliation of being beaten with a nightstick and thrown into a smelly cell with a lot of common criminals! The dignified young professional woman deliberately getting herself so plastered that a man has to peel off her filthy clothes and hose her off in a shower. And now the proud beauty who'd convinced herself that a certain male individual found her lovely body irresistible, even though he had a very funny way of showing it. . . ." She grimaced ruefully, overdoing it slightly. "But Albert picked me for his . . . his strange pleasures only because he could use me against Daddy, isn't that right?"

"I'm afraid so."

"But he never did. Why didn't he?"

"Would you have let him?" I asked. "Okay, so you let him hurt you because you like being hurt; but would you have let him use you to hurt your father?" When she shook her head quickly, I said, "And Minister is pretty smart about people; he has to be. He discovered that in spite of the way you'd been brought up to hate your daddy, you didn't. That made you useless to Minister—well, in a professional way, at least. He checked you out thoroughly, to be absolutely sure; and maybe he hung around a little longer than necessary for reasons of pleasure, if you'll excuse the suggestion. Or maybe he thought he could overcome your filial devotion by getting you thoroughly enslaved, if that's the right word; hooked on his weirdo rituals. But you kept resisting that final domination, you kept trying to escape; so in the end he gave up on you. That must be why he disappeared, as he seems to have done. You have no idea where he may be now?"

It was the big question, and I made it as casual as I could. Her response was almost right—almost, but not quite.

"No, Matt. If he isn't back in Cincinnati, I have no idea where he is."

It was the truth. But something in her attitude warned me that again I'd asked the wrong question.

"He never returned to Cincinnati as far as we know," I said. Considerable experience at interrogation told me it was no use asking her directly what she was concealing; I'd have to get at it some other way. I went on smoothly: "We believe he just came to that city in the first place because you were there, recruited for him by the local chapter of the PNP. Minister knows we're after him, of course. He knows your dad's been after him ever since that Argentina business. I suppose he, and the people who'd hired him, figured that if he got Doug Barnett's daughter secretly involved, on his side, he'd have a certain edge. But when it became obvious to him that you were useless to him—that you'd never allow yourself to be used against your pop under any circumstances—Minister apparently just cut his losses and went underground." It was time to leave the subject, before she sensed that I knew she was still holding out on me a little. I said in a different tone, "You're sure you want to stick, Amy? Remember, this isn't a very safe operation. The people who tried it before us

134

are missing, one known to be dead, two presumed to be. There are several flights a day from Freeport to Miami. You could be home tomorrow."

It was the offer that would have been made by an honest agent, guilty and embarrassed about the way he'd treated this innocent girl and unwilling to expose her to further risks. I had to make it; but I hoped she wouldn't take me up on it. I'd paid high for the information I'd already received from her; I'd given her knowledge that could wreck the mission and probably get Doug Barnett killed, if she passed it on. Since I'd paid the price, I wanted to get as much as I could for it; and there was still something to be gotten. I waited for her answer.

She smiled a little crookedly. She said softly, "You're always waving plane tickets in my face, Matt. A sensitive girl might begin to think she wasn't wanted."

I said, after a moment, "Even a sensitive girl couldn't be that dumb."

She drained her glass and set it aside carefully. "I guess I'm not really an alcoholic; I don't want any more. But that much was very nice. I think . . ." She'd risen to look down at me, very serious and unsmiling now. "I think we should go back downstairs now. There was some . . . some unfinished business."

Now I was standing, too. I realized that I was being offered, among other things, total forgiveness. It made my tricky little maneuvers and machinations seem very cheap.

I spoke carefully: "You don't say 'downstairs' on a boat. You say 'below.' "

She was smiling again, in the semidark under the cockpit awning. "We always seem to talk around and around it, don't we?" she murmured. "What makes us so slow?"

Then she was in my arms, her small body smooth and warm under the pretty nightshirt that didn't stay on her very long after we reached the cabin downstairs. I mean, below.

||||||||| Chapter 14 |||||||||||||||||||||||||||||||||||||||||||||||||||

THE PUBLIC transportation system of Freeport-Lucaya is simple but effective. It seems that anybody who wants to run a bus is allowed to do so, as long as he runs it more or less along the established route—there must be more to it than that, but that's the way it looks to a visitor. Accordingly, independent buses of all sizes, some just ordinary little vans, some half a block long, in various stages of disrepair, wander at will along the pleasant palmy roads, mostly divided, with grass and trees between the opposing lanes. Since there are a lot of such vehicles, you never have to wait very long for one, but you may find yourself making a slight detour for a pit stop before you reach town. Price, sixty-five cents. American money cheerfully accepted.

We got out at the International Bazaar in Freeport, which is of course a tourist trap; but as tourist traps go it's colorful and interesting, a gaudy rabbit warren of little ethnic shops. In some of the shops you can pick up fairly good stuff at fairly reasonable prices if you know what you're doing. I stopped outside a jewelry store, larger than most, with the Oriental name of the owner painted in gold on black over the door.

"This is the place, if I remember right from the last time I was here," I said. "I think you need a jade necklace the worst way, don't you, darling? Go in and browse while I make my phone calls."

"Oh, isn't this cute and exciting?" My silver-blonde child bride rose on tiptoe to kiss me on the cheek. "But don't get lost, Johnny. I'd never, ever find my way back to that marina all by myself."

"I'll be right back."

I watched her disappear into the shop, in her snug white sailor pants and the blue-and-white jersey with the big sailor collar; a real little Jack Tar, female gender. Our relations were slightly strained this morning, but we were both being nice about it. It's only in the movies that all problems are solved the instant the hero and heroine hit the mattress.

Tired after a long overnight sail and a considerable emotional upheaval, not to mention one false start at love, we hadn't really set that bunk on fire with our passionate coupling when we finally got around to completing the act. In fact, while the job had got done after a fashion, it had been a fairly clumsy and self-conscious performance on both sides; so now in the morning we were being very cheerful and polite with each other.

However, it had cleared the cobwebs of sexual frustration from my mind and, lying in the bunk beside her afterward, I'd run through what I'd learned from her and realized that I'd probably found the answer to one question: Why had somebody been asking about us at the Marina Towers Hotel in Miami after we'd slipped away? It was, I decided, a hopeful sign. Even though Doug had completely misjudged his daughter, and the situation, the mission he'd set up around her might still work out.

Although last night had convinced me that Amy was quite innocent of any hostile intentions, she was still a member of the People for Nuclear Peace. If the other members of that well-to-do outfit were even slightly on the ball, they would know by this time that she'd flown to Miami to see her dad, and they'd know about Doug's supposed suicide. They'd know that she'd got herself into alcoholic trouble and been rescued by me; they'd know that she'd spent a night in my hotel room and that in the morning I'd run some fairly intimate errands for her, like having her clothes cleaned and buying her filmy undergarments. A potentially very promising relationship, from their point of view.

It seemed likely that although they hadn't planted her on me in the first place, they were by now tracking her hopefully—we'd been careful not to make it hard for them. They'd want to make use of her in the strategic position she'd achieved, close to the man who, now that Doug Barnett was apparently dead, was the biggest threat to their demolition genius, Minister, and the project they'd hired him for, whatever it might be.

That was one answer that came to me as I lay in the rather cramped berth feeling the warmth of the girl beside me and listening to her soft breathing. It also occurred to me that while I'd made some progress in learning about one Barnett, the behavior of another deserved much more careful study than I'd given it. Just why had Doug Barnett, supposedly retired, spent a couple of years on the case of one lousy dynamiter . . . ?

As far as I'd been able to determine on previous visits, there was only one public phone in the whole sprawling bazaar area, in a little courtyard toward the rear. It was in use when I got there. The user was a rather handsome, moderately tall, tanned female in her thirties who sabotaged her lean body with tentlike khaki shorts in the name of current fashion. I spent my waiting time visualizing the lady in well-fitting Bermudas, a great improvement. Then it was my turn to do battle with the Bahamas telephone system, soon confirming what I'd already more or less known, that the only practical way to talk overseas from one of their pay phones is to call collect.

Unfortunately, there was no reason why the man I was calling should want to pay to talk to me. I gambled on the fact that he was a reporter who made his living by his curiosity; but first I had to get the number of the *Miami Tribune*, which took some doing. Getting through the paper's switchboard wasn't easy, either, but at last I had a harsh male voice on the line.

"Spud Meiklejohn here. Why should I be interested in what a guy named Helm has to say?"

"You remember me?"

"Well, we were never introduced. But you are . . . were a friend of Elly Brand's. We met, just to say hello, in the Miami Airport a couple of years ago. As a matter of fact I don't think we even said hello. My business was with Elly, right?"

"You've got it."

"And Elly's dead, so what have we got in common worth talking about?"

A certain constraint in his voice made me fairly certain that, although it wasn't common knowledge, he was aware that Eleanor Brand, a journalist lady I'd known quite well, had been knifed to death on a Chicago street because of her association with me. The fact that the murder had been paid for later didn't change the fact that a very nice girl was no longer alive.

I asked, "You know what my job is?"

"More or less," Meiklejohn said. "One of those screwball Washington agencies."

"I need information. Fast information. And I don't want to go through Washington to get it, for various reasons I don't care to specify."

I heard a short laugh at the other end of the line. "You're starting to interest me. And I guess Elly would have wanted me to help you, damn you. So ask your questions." When I'd asked them, he said, "It'll take me a few minutes. Do you want to hold on or call back?"

I shuddered. "It was hard enough getting through once; I wouldn't want to try it twice. I'll hang on right here."

It did take a while. A stout gent in a flowered shirt who'd come up behind me thought it took too long and, by looking at his watch pointedly and jingling his change nervously, made his impatient opinion quite clear. At last Meiklejohn's voice spoke in my ear.

"Got pencil and paper handy? The following were killed in the blast or died from their injuries: Harlow Francis Catlin, fifty-five; Mary Elizabeth Parks, thirty-two, and her husband Oliver William, thirty-three; Miguel Alemán Perea, thirty-four; and Jerome Robert Shattuck, forty-four. Do you want the wounded?"

"Perea?" I said. "Hired locally?"

"No, he was a U.S. citizen. American born. Interpreter-translator, among other things."

"And that Parks couple?" I asked. "Who were they?"

"A couple of unlucky tourists who just happened to be in the embassy because he'd lost his passport."

"Okay, give me the injured."

"It's a pretty long list. Ranging from bystanders who got nicked by flying glass and needed only the Band-Aid treatment, to one poor dame who wound up in a rest home—right near here in Coral Gables, as a matter of fact—badly burned and mangled in a pretty permanent way."

I drew a long breath. "The woman's name?"

"Marsha Bettina Osterman, forty-three. Actually, Mrs. Osterman. Maiden name, Frelinghausen. Took a secretarial job with the glamorous foreign service because she was tired of her dull life as a Florida widow living on her defunct husband's pension and insurance. Got herself sent to Argentina just in time to get blown to pieces. Too bad. According to her pictures, she was a good-looking woman before it happened."

"Any others with serious injuries?"

"None that shouldn't be healed by this time, barring a few scars."

"Do you happen to know the name of Mrs. Osterman's rest home?"

"Yes, it's right here. The Krueger-Fischer Sanatorium on Crescent Drive. No number given. Coral Gables, as I said. Aside from the satisfaction of playing Boy Scout and doing my good deed for the day, what do I get out of this, Helm?"

"A bottle of booze and as much of an explanation as I can give when I've got the final answers."

"Make it Jack Daniels," he said.

That was the call I wasn't supposed to make. Having made one, I made another; then I checked in with the local control that had been established for the mission to impress people with how seriously we took all this. I spoke a code phrase to let them know the patient was alive and doing well, and got a phrase back that let me know there were no messages or instructions for me. Very professional undercover stuff, like in the movies. I hoped the opposition had an ear on the line so they could appreciate it. And even if they weren't equipped to listen in, I hoped they were watching and I wasn't playing to an empty theater.

I turned the phone over to the fuming fat tourist, who was working himself up to a fine coronary, and returned to the Oriental jewelry emporium to find that Amy had all the necklaces and bracelets in the store spread out on a counter in front of her. At least it seemed that way.

"Oh, Johnny, aren't they *beautiful*?" she said breathlessly when I came up to stand beside her. "How can I ever decide? You'll just have to make up my silly mind for me."

We got out of there minus a few travelers checks and plus a jade necklace and a couple of matching bracelets. In the sunshine outside, I checked her when she started up the sidewalk.

"Can you bear to pass up the casino, at least for the time being?" I asked. "And can you stand missing lunch?"

She glanced at me, surprised. "Of course, but where are we going?"

"How about Miami?"

"Are you serious? Sail all the way back there—"

"Who said anything about sailing?"

A taxi took us to the local airport. The tickets I'd ordered by phone were awaiting us, and the international red tape was minimal—U.S. Customs and Immigration checks you out right there in Freeport so you don't have to stand in line on the other side. I made a phone call from the Miami Airport, and we paused to get something to eat there, then took a cab to Coral Gables. The sanatorium was as pleasant as a place full of the aged and ailing can be, with white buildings surrounded by wide green tree-shaded lawns. I stopped at the reception desk inside.

"I'm Matthew Helm," I said. "This is Miss Amy Barnett. I called just now and arranged for us to see Mrs. Marsha Osterman."

I was aware that Amy was regarding me curiously,

wondering why I'd dropped our Mister-and-Missus cover, of course; but wondering more who Mrs. Osterman might be and why we'd come all this way to visit her. The gray-haired woman behind the desk checked a schedule and nodded.

"Yes, she should be ready for you. Mr. Helm . . ."

"Yes?"

"You're aware that Mrs. Osterman doesn't . . . communicate?"

"No," I said. "I wasn't aware of that."

"But she does seem to like visitors just the same. However . . ."

"What is it?" I asked when she hesitated.

The woman at the desk looked up at me soberly. "Mrs. Osterman doesn't know that her friend Mr. Barnett is dead. My condolences, Miss Barnett, but could you please refrain from mentioning your tragic loss? We don't feel she's ready for the shock quite yet."

I suppose I should have felt triumphant at having confirmed my wild guess about Doug Barnett's personal involvement; but it was hardly a triumphant occasion.

"We won't say anything about it," I said quickly, to save Amy from having to make a properly grieved response.

"Very well. Miss Pritchard, here, will take you to her."

Miss Pritchard was a sturdy young woman with dark-brown hair cut in a businesslike bang across her forehead. She wore a black linen skirt and a white cotton blouse and seemed to be a little self-conscious about them.

"I'm new here," she confessed as we walked. "I'm still not quite used to dealing with patients and not wearing my uniform. I guess I miss the authority or something; but we try to make this as little like a hospital as possible. It's really a lovely place for them, the poor dears." She paused at a door. "Here we are. You will be careful? Remember that she does see and hear, although you should speak clearly because there's still some residual hearing loss from the explosion. And she does feel. I think she feels very much. You mustn't hurt her. Just a minute." Miss Pritchard went through the door, which closed behind her. In a couple of minutes she was back. "All right. She's ready for you now."

||||||| Chapter 15 |||||||||||||||||||||||||||||||||||||||||||||

We get them at the place out in Arizona that we call the Ranch, too; the ones who didn't make it back in one piece. There are two kinds. There are the ones who hide their disablement and disfigurement in dark rooms; and then there are the ones who face you in the light and take perverse pleasure in watching you wince and swallow hard at your first sight of them. Mrs. Marsha Osterman belonged in the second category.

It was a fairly large, sunny room with an old-fashioned high ceiling and curtains at the two big windows. An effort had been made to temper the institutional atmosphere as much as possible, although the electric bed bore no resemblance to an antique four-poster. But the mahogany dresser and its mirror looked solid and moderately old, like stuff that had been in somebody's family for a while; and so did the two comfortable chairs for visitors. There were a couple of realistic paintings on the wall, in heavy frames, that appeared to be family portraits; and a couple of nonrepresentational modern things as well. It looked as if Mrs. Osterman had been allowed to furnish her room with a few of her own belongings, or, if she hadn't been up to doing it herself or hadn't really cared, somebody had done it for her.

However, like the hospital bed, the wheelchair struck a discordant note in the pleasant surroundings, as did its occupant. I'd seen as bad or worse before, but Amy gasped and gripped my arm fiercely.

I said softly, "Why get all upset? It's just some of your nice friend Albert's work. I thought you'd like to see what he does in his spare time, when he isn't whipping people."

"Stop it! She can hear you!"

Good girl. If she was thinking more of the feelings of the woman before us than of her own horrified reactions, she was going to be all right. But it was really pretty grim. The figure in the wheelchair was wearing a handsome bed jacket, violet, with some white lace at the wrists and throat; and there was a blanket across the knees, except that there were no knees. Professionally, I found myself separating the blast damage from the burn damage. Apparently the woman had lain helpless with the shattered legs, later amputated, while the fire worked on her—I hoped she'd been unconscious at the time. The left hand was a burn-scarred claw, and most of the left side of the face including the eye had been seared away. The right side of the face and the right hand were still human. The hair, where it still grew, was thick and black and glossy, carefully arranged to minimize the effect. Well, a little. The remaining eye watched us steadily out of the ruined face.

I drew Amy forward. I remembered to speak slowly and clearly: "I'm Matthew Helm, Mrs. Osterman. A friend of Doug Barnett. He may have mentioned my name sometime." It seemed that I was forever being forced to claim a friendship that didn't really exist. There was a slight change in the seated figure to tell

147

me the woman was tuned in and receiving. "And this is his daughter, Amy," I said.

There was a long silence; then Mrs. Osterman's good hand lifted in a small, beckoning gesture. I was prepared to urge Amy forward, but the girl was always better than I gave her credit for being. She stepped forward quickly, took the older woman's hand, and, after a moment, pressed it to her cheek; then she was on her knees beside the wheelchair, crying, and Mrs. Osterman was stroking her hair gently.

"Oh, my dear, we could have been such good friends!"

It was a harsh whisper. The lips, badly distorted on the left side, hardly moved. Amy looked up, startled; then she took the older woman's hand again and kissed it, jumped to her feet, and ran past me and out of the room, still sobbing.

To break the silence that followed, I said, "If you're wondering about her hair, she became a blonde for a job she's doing for us." I stepped closer, so I wouldn't have to speak so loudly. "Is there anything I can do for you, Mrs. Osterman?"

The figure in the wheelchair didn't speak, but after a moment the shoulders moved slightly as if shaken by silent laughter at my dumb question.

"Oh, Of course." I studied her for a while. "You could have asked Doug. . . . No, I see. He loves you. You love him. You don't want him to have it on his conscience. What about my conscience, ma'am?" Again she didn't speak, but her answer was quite clear, and I grinned. "Okay, so you don't give a damn about my lousy conscience. Fair enough. But I'll have to ask you to hold off for a few days, preferably longer, so it won't be too obvious who gave it to you. Make it easy for them to call it heart failure or something."

She was trying to say something, but apparently

the words she'd brought out for Amy were the only ones available to her today. I studied her face carefully.

"I see. You have no plans for using it very soon; you just want to know it's there if things get unbearable." I saw her head move in a slight nod, and I went on: "In that case, I'd better warn you that you may get some bad news shortly, Mrs. Osterman. Don't let it rush you into anything you weren't planning on anyway. Wait to make absolutely sure. All kinds of rumors get around, and a lot of them aren't true, if you follow me. Now, where's a good hiding place?"

She was watching me carefully; obviously she would have liked to question me, but the words wouldn't come. At last her hand moved slightly toward the dresser. I went over, reflecting that a woman in her condition who'd have a big mirror in her room was obviously a woman who never kidded herself much about anything. I saw the jewel case lying there; when I touched it, she nodded. I brought it back and placed it in her lap, noting that she had some function left in the crippled hand; it could hold the case steady in a clumsy way while the fingers of the good hand worked the lock. I turned away to get at the little capsule I carry—the key to the big black door. It's not mandatory except on certain types of high-security, high-risk assignments, but I've been around too long and know too much about our operations to feel quite comfortable without it.

When I turned back, she'd selected a ring with a rather large opal; as I watched, she pressed a tiny concealed catch with her thumbnail and the jewel swung up like a miniature trapdoor, revealing a golden cavity. I placed the death pill inside. She snapped the ring closed.

"Real Borgia stuff," I said. "I'll put it back for now. When you start wearing it, they'll think it's a good symptom, a nice bit of vanity that shows you're beginning to take an interest in life at last. I suppose we could call it our little private joke. Bite hard and swallow fast when you want to go. Good-bye, Mrs. Osterman."

I took the jewel case back to where I'd gotten it and hesitated. It was really time to leave, but I found myself returning to the wheelchair instead for some reason. I guess I wanted to say some final, wise words that would help her; but there were no such words. She was a proud and brave and intelligent woman facing years of imprisonment in this dreadful remnant of a body. Well, I'd given her the means to escape. Whether or not she empoyed it was up to her.

Abruptly she held out her good hand, and I took it. I thought she was trying to speak again, but the words still wouldn't break through. Instead, watching me steadily for a sign of flinching, she took the other hand, the ugly one, and placed it on top of mine. I grinned down at her.

"Lady, you scare little girls, but you don't scare me. I wish . . . Ah, hell!"

She pressed my fingers lightly and released me. I turned and walked quickly out of there. Amy and the nurse were waiting in the corridor. Miss Pritchard glanced at me sharply and hurried in to see her patient. Amy had dried her wet face, but her eyes were still pink. She started to speak, but I shook my head.

"Let's get out of here."

Outside, it was sunny and pleasant, that is if you overlooked the canes and crutches and wheelchairs. I opened the door of the waiting taxi for Amy, slid in after her, and told the driver to take us back to the airport.

I spoke at last: "You're a good man, Barnett. You did fine in there."

Amy whispered, "You might have warned me!"

"Shock effect," I said. "Did it work?"

She didn't answer directly. "Who *was* that poor woman?"

I said, "I'm not in the mood for rhetorical questions. You're a bright girl. You know perfectly well who she was."

"Somebody Daddy was . . . is fond of?"

"I would say the lady had been elected to be your stepmother, wouldn't you? Judging by what she said in there."

"How did you find out about it? About her?"

"We don't normally spend too much time on explosives experts who aren't very good with weapons. I mean, anybody can handle them, the only hard part is catching them. Our specialty is the guys nobody else can handle, if you know what I mean. Yet suddenly this particular dynamiter wound up on our high-priority list. Whenever-wherever. I figured that the last job he pulled before his appearance in such select company must have touched a nerve somewhere. The Buenos Aires job. It couldn't be just that he hit an embassy; people are always blasting U.S. embassies these days and nobody seems to think much about it. Or do much about it. And there was an awful lot of Doug Barnett in the story. So I checked the list of casualties. Except for a young married woman accompanied by her husband, the dead were all men; and to the best of my knowledge your daddy is strictly heterosexual. He might have flipped on account of a brother or something; but I'd never heard he had a brother, and the name Barnett wasn't on the list. But among the injured, terribly and permanently injured, was a handsome widow. . . . Okay, it was thin. It was a gamble. However, as I said, I needed to shake you up a bit, show you what kind of a guy your boyfriend really is, what kind of suffering he's responsible for. If my vague hypothesis about Doug and this unknown lady was correct, so much the better. Two birds with one stone."

After I'd finished talking, the taxi ran on for a while along a hot sunny boulevard filled with stinking traffic. At last Amy glanced at me warily.

"Why . . . why would you want to shake me up, Matt?"

"You know why. You're holding out on me," I said. She started to voice an indignant denial but fell silent. A little color came into her face. I went on: "Feeding me all that crap about your self-respect taking such a beating because the man you'd allowed to do all those mean things to you didn't really love you; he'd just picked you because you were your daddy's girl. Well, that's why he picked you in the first place all right. But I watched you while you were saying it, and you were a kid with a warm little secret. I think you have some reason to believe that after a while your beautiful body, and your beautiful you, came to mean a little more to Alfred Minister—Albert Pope—than just a means to a business end."

She drew a shaky breath. "It isn't fair! I go sailing with a man, and he can't sail worth a hoot, but he turns out to be a sneaky clairvoyant!" After a little, she said defensively, "There isn't so much love in the world, Matt, that we can afford to betray any of it lightly."

I said, "I hear the words. What do they mean?"

She licked her lips. "You know so much about me, I'm sure you already know there were two boys in college; but all they really wanted was to get my skirt up and my panty hose down. But Albert—I can't think of him as Alfred—was different, or became different very quickly. All right, what we did together, what he liked to do, wasn't very conventional or very nice, but . . . Oh, dear, I don't know how to say it! Love is such a big word and maybe it doesn't apply to the violently possessive way he feels about me. Let's just say that even though I don't really *like* him—I'm afraid of him and I hate the power he has over me and what he wants to turn me into—I couldn't bring myself to betray something he'd told me in confidence under, well, rather intimate circumstances. There's got to be a little loyalty, doesn't there? Anyway, I'm afraid it won't help you much."

She was silent for a while, perhaps waiting for me to persuade her to continue; but I sensed that she'd already convinced herself and didn't speak. At last she went on without being urged.

"Once, after we'd made love, he told me not to worry if he disappeared someday without warning. He said if it happened he'd let me know very soon where to join him. He . . . he didn't seem to have any doubt that I'd come." After another little pause, she said rather bitterly, "You see, your shock treatment worked. After seeing Mrs. Osterman, I can't keep quiet any longer. If that's what he does to people, he's obviously got to be stopped. But it really isn't much of a clue, is it?"

"That depends on the message he sends and how soon it comes," I said. "Did he give you any idea how he planned to get in touch with you?"

She shrugged. "I assumed at the time he meant a simple letter or phone call."

I said, "You won't mind if we monitor your mail?"

She shrugged again. "You're probably doing it already."

We probably were. I said, "And if he should somehow manage to get in touch with you secretly . . ."

She looked at me directly. "I suppose you had to

say that. Yes, Matt. If there should be a . . . a contact,
I suppose you call it in your jargon, I'll let you know
immediately. Even though I'll feel like Salome holding the bloody head of John the Baptist or whomever
it was she gave the chop to. I . . . I haven't had so
many lovers that I can bring myself to consider one
expendable, even a pretty weird one. Matt?"

"Yes?"

"You were in that room for quite a while after I
ran out."

I said, "I just stayed to ask Mrs. Osterman if there
was something I could do for her."

Her eyes were steady on my face. "Was there?"

"I think you'd better reconsider that question, doll.
Don't ask unless you're sure you want to hear the
answer."

She shivered slightly. "I guess I already know the
answer. It's . . . not as nice a world as I thought
when I was a little girl. But then, I was a rather
stupid and sentimental little girl."

"I bet you were cute, though," I said.

She smiled a little at that, but not very cheerfully.
Well, it hadn't been a very cheerful day.

|||||||| CHAPTER 16 |||||||||||||||||||||||||||||||||||||||||||

AT THE Miami airport, we found that we had a couple of hours to wait for the next flight back to Freeport, Grand Bahama. I arranged to have a fifth of Jack Daniels black delivered to a certain gent at the *Tribune*. We bought some magazines at a newsstand, and Amy settled down to read in a waiting area while I used one of the nearby phones. After the endless Bahamas communications hassle it was a relief to be back, if only momentarily, in the U.S.A., where making a call from a pay phone wasn't quite as difficult as putting a man on the moon.

"Where are you, Eric?" Mac demanded after I'd identified myself.

"Miami, for the afternoon," I said. "Waiting to catch a plane back to Grand Bahama and our private yacht, junior grade."

"Your instructions—"

I interrupted rudely: "I don't mind playing second banana to Doug Barnett, sir. I just wish he'd get his goddamn act together. Our goddamn act. And if he doesn't tell me things I need to know, and you don't, then I damn well have to find them out for myself. Where the hell is he, anyway?"

"As a matter of fact, he's right here in Washington for the day. He'll be on the line shortly."

I said harshly, "Why wasn't I told that this was a personal vendetta on his part? I don't have the least objection to helping him settle a private score, but I don't see why I've got to do it blindfolded."

Mac said, "Perhaps Abraham has been overly security-conscious, knowing your casual attitude. But the target is a legitimate one."

I said, "Sure. You legitimized it for him, put it on the list so he could go after it officially. Fine. I'm the last man in the world to complain, sir. I can remember your doing as much for me quite recently. That Chicago business involving Elly Brand. And in both cases you could soothe your official conscience with the fact that the private interest, mine back then and Doug's now, coincided with the public interest. Well, I've just been visiting a victim of Minister and his explosives—"

"You've seen Mrs. Osterman?"

"That's what I flew back to Miami for," I said. "It wasn't a good thing to see, and I'll be very happy to help Doug eliminate the blast-happy sonofabitch responsible. All I ask is to be treated like a grown man with a gun, not a little boy with a cap pistol."

"What do you need to know, Eric?"

"How can I tell, working in the dark? Let me lay it out for you the way I've got it figured to date, and you tell me the parts I've missed and the parts I've got wrong."

"Go on."

I looked over my shoulder at the waiting-room bench where Amy was sitting, engrossed in a fashion magazine. It seemed an odd choice for her, since even for her present sexy-blond incarnation she'd selected a fairly conventional wardrobe, without much regard for the curious dictates of current fashion. But maybe she was interested in reading about how the other half, the superstylish half, lived. She rose and, with a wave of the hand to me, headed for the nearby restrooms.

I said into the phone, "Let's start with the Buenos Aires bombing in which five embassy employees and visitors were killed and Mrs. Marsha Osterman was so badly hurt, not to mention the lesser casualties. Afterward, presumably, there was official pressure on you to retaliate in the name of the U.S. against those Argentine terrorists and the specialist they'd hired for the job. There always is, after every such outrage. But we haven't got the manpower to go chasing after every murderous little political action group that thumbs its nose at Uncle Sam or every guy who knows how to set off a stick of dynamite. Right?"

Mac said, "I refused to consider a punitive expedition against an organization of rabid patriots on their own soil. That type of gunboat diplomacy is always counterproductive. If we support one country against another, we can expect the citizens of the other to dislike us. As for the explosives expert involved, however, it isn't altogether a bad idea to let independent specialists like Minister know they should be a little selective in accepting employment. I said I'd take the matter under advisement."

I nodded. "And while you had it under advisement, I figure, Doug came to you and asked permission to go after the guy directly responsible for his lady's brutal injuries. To hell with the fanatics who'd merely paid the bills, they'd at least had a political grievance; but Minister had done the job strictly for money, in cold blood. Or maybe Doug just handed in his resignation and told you he was off to track down Minister if it took the rest of his life."

"I refused to accept the resignation," Mac said.

"Sure," I said. "Instead you told him to relax, you could make Minister an official agency project, since you'd already been asked, and assign it to him. And in order to permit him to work on it without attracting attention, he was to exaggerate the injuries received in his recent plane crash and take disability retirement and make a big thing of building the boat he'd been talking about for years. You can cover a lot of territory, I believe, while picking up pieces of nautical equipment at bargain prices. So Doug worked hard at learning everything he could about Minister's background and habits so he'd be ready when the guy resurfaced, which he did for that Ben Gurion Airport job. I presume Doug got fairly close to him there, but not close enough. No score. Then Minister was reported living in Cincinnati on more or less intimate terms with a young lady named—surprise, surprise—Barnett. That must have been quite a shock to Doug Barnett, in a couple of different ways."

"I can assure you that it was, Eric; aggravated by the fact that before he could respond to the report, Minister had slipped away again."

I frowned at the wall, working it out. I said, "Doug's late ex-wife had made no bones about hating him and everything he stood for, meaning us. Now he jumped to the conclusion that, brainwashed for years by her mother, Amy was knowingly aiding and abetting his enemies—well, one of his enemies. But that was personal. On the professional front, it was obvious that the Preacher had learned who was tracking him. It could hardly be a coincidence, his making a play for the daughter of the man who'd been assigned to get him. So Doug figured out a dramatic, if slightly complicated, way of becoming officially dead, leaving him free to operate unsuspected while I dealt with the girl and took whatever heat was going around. Thanks loads, Douggie—boy!"

"You're welcome, Eric," said a new voice in the phone.

I said, "Oh, there you are! The mastermind himself."

"What have you got for us besides a lot of gripes, hotshot?" Doug Barnett asked

I said, "What I was told to get. Pretty complete information about your little girl's motives and intentions *vis-à-vis*—I've always wanted to use *vis-à-vis* in a real sentence—*vis-à-vis* a certain individual she knows as Albert Pope. But you won't like how I got it."

"Tell me."

I told him. There was silence after I'd finished. Then Mac started to speak on one line, and Doug started to speak on the other, and they both stopped.

I said, "Well, which one of you is going to stomp me? Make up your cotton-picking minds."

Doug said in a strangled voice, "You can't be serious! You're telling us that you blew the whole operation, deliberately, to a subject known to be collaborating with the opposition!"

I said, "Known? What's known to you, *amigo*, isn't necessarily known to me."

"But—"

"Let me point out that I've had a lot more opportunity to study this so-called subject, who happens to be your daughter, than you have. And let me also point out, while we're on the subject of this so-called subject, that all this crap about your bitch-wife keeping your little girl away from you all these years is just that. Crap. Under the circumstances, no court in the land would have denied you visiting privileges or prevented you from exercising them, if you'd really worked at it. But you discouraged pretty easily, didn't you?"

"You sonofabitch—"

I said, "Cut it out. You forget that I know what

I'm talking about; I've been there. We're not family men, either of us. Marriage seemed like kind of a nice thing, and we gave it our best shot, but our best shot wasn't very good, was it? And there's something kind of claustrophobic about domesticity, anyway, isn't there? So when the lady decided to bail out with the kid or kids, using whatever excuse came handy, we ranted and raved about our empty homes and broken hearts, but we were really kind of relieved, weren't we? And I kept in touch with my kids a little because my ex-wife made it easy, but you lost contact with your little girl because your ex-wife didn't. And although you do like to act the martyred papa—don't we all—you were just as happy not to push it, weren't you? So don't tell me what you *know* about a daughter you haven't even talked to, to amount to anything, since she was eight."

Doug said harshly, "You always were a sucker for attractive young girls; I should have known better than to trust your judgment with this one."

"You wrong me, *amigo*," I said. "I'm a sucker for attractive middle-aged girls, too, and even attractive old girls."

Mac's voice came over the line: "This is becoming quite irrelevant. We're wasting time. Eric has chosen to trust the young lady in question, whether rightly or wrongly remains to be seen. In return for his faith, misguided or otherwise, he has obtained certain information. It remains for us to decide how we should act on it. Eric?"

I said, "Amy believes that Minister will get in touch with her somehow, as he promised, because he can't live without her or at least doesn't want to—"

Doug's voice was scornful: "This is the Preacher you're talking about, not a lovesick college boy?"

I said, "That's a very nice girl you begat somehow. Screwy but nice. Pretty, too. We're all nuts about her, all us sinister characters on both sides of the fence. Got to make up to her somehow for that cold-hearted monster of a daddy who never made a real effort to see her all these years. Maybe it's true love with Minister, or maybe he simply can't bear to lose such a delectable morsel after working so hard to teach her his peculiar ways, but Samson had his Delilah, and Dillinger had his lady in red, if I remember correctly. It seems at least possible that Minister has his Amy, and we can't afford to disregard it. We don't have any other leads to him at the moment, or have we?" The brief silence that followed was answer enough.

Then Mac said, "Your suggestions?"

"She's got to be covered every minute of every day. As long as she's on the boat with me, okay; but I could be taken out, or just fall overboard. Or she could decide she's mad at me after all and run off. Or she could be snatched out from under our noses, willingly or unwillingly. While I trust her enough to take a chance on her as far as keeping Doug's suicidal secret is concerned—because I've asked, and because he's still her pop no matter what kind of a suspicious bastard he may be—I don't trust her not to leave me if Minister whistles. She says she's afraid of him, but there's some kind of a domination-submission complex working there that may be stronger than any affection or loyalty she may feel for me. But if she goes to him, somebody's got to be there to follow, whether it takes a boat, a helicopter, a submarine, a fast automobile, or just a pair of sturdy shoes Forget about me. I'll keep plugging along the lines we've already laid out, searching for that mystery island of Constantine Grieg's, and maybe I'll come up with something and maybe I won't; but the girl is a definite thread leading directly to Minister and it must not be broken. Concentrate your manpower on her and to hell with me, no matter what happens."

Mac's voice said, "Abraham?"

"I suppose it's all we can do, under the circumstances," Doug Barnett said grudgingly.

I said, "If she keeps her mouth shut, we're in good shape. They'll all be watching me and expecting no trouble from you, resting in your watery grave. On the other hand, if she does tell them about the little suicide that wasn't, they'll guess you're hanging around with nefarious intent; but what the hell, we've all dealt with situations where the enemy was alerted. You'll just have to tell the people watching her to be more careful, that's all. Just so they don't lose her. We can't afford that."

Mac's voice said, "Abraham?"

"Very well." Doug's voice was admirably businesslike, dismissing all personal conflicts. "Anything else?"

"Yes, information," I said. "If I'm going to close in on this hidden drug-smuggling harbor, assuming I can find it, I'd better know something about those two Coast Guard characters who didn't make meals for any sharks, at least we don't know that they did. In case they managed to survive after all, and I stumble on them hiding in the mangroves or somewhere."

Doug said, "I'll read you the vital statistics. . . . Just a minute. Here. The one who was lost was six one, two twenty, curly red hair, blue eyes. Anchor tattooed on left forearm. Name Michael Brennerman, chief boatswain. Number two: five nine, one fifty, black hair, brown eyes. No distinguishing marks known. Name Ricardo Sanderson, ensign. . . ."

"Sanderson?" I said. "Like in Admiral Sanderson?"

"Precisely. His son."

I said, "Hell, it's old home week. Everybody's got a personal interest in this case. Go on."

"Number three: five six, one thirty, blond, blue

eyes. No distinguishing marks known. Name, Molly Brennerman, yeoman. Wife of number one, if it matters."

"Yeoman or yeowoman? Yeoperson? Hell, I was told there were three *men* on that boat. Can't anybody give me the straight dope about anything?"

Mac's voice said, "I'm afraid the sexless official verbiage of the Coast Guard's preliminary report led me to make an unwarranted assumption about the gender of that boat's crew, Eric, which I passed on to you. My apologies." After a moment, he went on: "We have a little more information for you. The drugs are brought in by ship. Constantine Grieg concentrates on marijuana. Cocaine and heroin, being much more compact, are usually imported by other routes, often involving light planes. Grieg's marijuana-smuggling vessels are generally small ships, two thousand tons or less. A couple of hundred feet long, not more. Often less. They've got to be manageable in fairly confined waters at both ends of the voyage. Draft, fifteen feet or less. Normally, the cargoes would be transferred to smaller boats offshore, often to powerful speedboats of the ocean-racing type, as in the old rum-running days when the whiskey boats were just about the fastest craft afloat."

I said, "That's hardly new information, sir. They've been working that routine for years. And I thought we were looking for something besides, or in addition to, drugs."

"Yes. This PNP organization does seem to have become involved with Grieg somehow; but we haven't yet determined how. Or why. We may have to wait for you to find the answers there. As far as Grieg's drug operation goes, what I've described is the way it used to be done. There seem to have been a couple of interesting variations introduced recently. For instance, the problem with the offshore transship-

163

ment of the illicit cargoes has always been that, besides being obvious to passing traffic and to any airplane in the sky, even when the rendezvous is chosen for privacy, the operation is at the mercy of the weather. If it's blowing too hard, the small boats can't get to the ship offshore. We think they have therefore found, or constructed, a hidden harbor on this island of Mr. Grieg's where a small freighter can be concealed while unloading proceeds at leisure. It wouldn't have to be much of an installation. I'm told that islands with natural saltwater ponds are quite common in the Bahamas."

I said, "I can think of two offhand, sir. Up in the Abacos, there's Tilloo Pond on Tilloo Cay and the sheltered little harbor behind New Plymouth on Green Turtle Cay. I don't know what's down in the Exumas, never having been there."

"To be sure. The trouble is, the Bahamas charts are not very reliable, being based on fairly ancient surveys. There could easily be an uncharted, hidden pool of suitable dimensions on one of the many cays down in the remote area we're considering. If the entrance channel were dredged, and the basin deepened a little, perhaps, a ship the size we're considering could be brought in at night, tied up against the shore, and fully camouflaged by daylight. After all, the Germans once hid a large battleship in a certain Norwegian fiord."

I said, "Well, the *Tirpitz* wasn't exactly hidden, sir. Her location was soon known; she was just damn hard to get at. But the minisubs did the job in the end."

"Unfortunately, these waters are too shallow for submarines, even of the miniature variety. We'll have to trust to a certain sailboat, won't we?"

I said, "It looks as if I'll need a couple of torpedo tubes and a rocket launcher, with a few HMGs spotted around the deck for close-in defense. The trouble is, even just a light machine gun with mount and ammo would practically sink the poor little bucket, even if a spot could be found from which you could fire it among all that sailboat rigging. I suppose the theory is that our Coast Guard predecessors were wiped out because they got too close to this Hole in the Wall?"

"What did you call it?"

"A famous old outlaw hangout, sir," I said. "Out west. You could ride past those cliffs and never spot an opening, but there was a cleft in the rocks, if you looked hard, and a real little robbers roost inside. Like our mysterious hidden harbor."

"Yes. Very appropriate. We do assume that the Coast Guard's expedition managed to find your Hole in the Wall and was therefore eliminated."

Glancing around, I realized that Amy was still missing; but before I could panic I saw her returning to her waiting bench and opening her magazine once more.

I said into the phone, "And I think we must also assume that the body, the part of a body, that was apparently washed up by accident on a deserted beach may actually have been placed there deliberately to mislead us, a long way from the right area. You suggested that there might be another interesting variation from the normal drug-smuggling routine."

It was Doug who responded. "We have reason to believe that special arrangements are being made to receive a ship that, while she may be carrying the usual cargo, is abnormal in some way."

"What way?"

"We're waiting for you to tell us, pal."

"I'll see what I can do, but I feel the girl is still our best lead. Your best lead. But okay, as I said, I'll keep plugging. Before we sign off, let me give you a couple of descriptions and see if they match anything you've got in the working file. It may not mean anything, but they were hanging around the pay phone in the International Bazaar when I made some calls this morning—I announced my telephoning intentions fairly loudly to see who might be interested. First, a beefy male, say five ten or eleven, say two twenty. Say forty-five or fifty. Brown hair getting very thin on top. Red face. Bad temper."

After a moment, Doug said, "There are several overweight business types associated with the PNP, but it rings no bells very loudly."

"Okay, try this. Female, say five eight or nine, carrying no excess weight, nicely tanned. Dark-brown hair, expensive hairdo, short and trim, ears showing. Strong, straight nose, good mouth and chin, couldn't see the eyes for the sunglasses. Say midthirties. Legs very brown, handsome enough to overcome the handicap of low-heeled sandals."

Doug didn't hesitate. "Hell, that sounds like Mrs. Georgina Williston, the moneybags behind the PNP. We knew she'd left Cincinnati heading this way."

"You might have told me," I said. "I'm getting a little tired of being kept in the dark. And I somehow got the impression from you that Mrs. Williston was a dowager type with five chins and some missing brain cells. The lady I saw didn't seem to be missing anything important."

"Oh, my God," Doug said. "Isn't one dame at a time enough for you? Next job I manage, I'll recruit nothing but certified eunuchs."

OUR FLIGHT out of Miami was late. Even though the short jump across the water to the Bahamas—well, short by plane; it had taken us thirty hours under sail—barely let the big Lockheed jet get its nose into the sky before it was heading downward again, we didn't disembark at Freeport until dusk. The formalities were again pleasantly brief.

Afterward, with a handful of the other passengers from the U.S., we squeezed aboard a beat-up taxi, actually a vintage checker with jump seats, and were treated to a tour of the palmy, wedding-cake beach resorts before being deposited at our own hotel-marina complex. Since I was hoping to make an early start in the morning, we tracked down the off-duty dockmaster and paid the bill. When we reached her at last, *Spindrift* was still floating jauntily in her slip.

The tide was down, and it was quite a jump from the dock to the deck. I made it and caught Amy as she scrambled down after me. She was a pleasant, feminine armful, slightly damp and rumpled from all the hot-weather traveling. Vulnerable, like any lady at the end of a late party or a long day, when she can no longer use the defense that you really mustn't because you might wrinkle the clothes or muss the hair or smudge the makeup, since by this time they're a bit wrinkled and mussed and smudged already; and they've done their duty for the day, anyway.

She threw me a rather shy and uncertain glance as she freed herself, obviously knowing exactly what was in my mind, or on it. She spoke behind me as I turned to unlock the main hatch.

"If you're going to have your usual drink before dinner, make me one, too."

There was a note of defiance in her voice, but she wasn't defying me, just her own inhibitions.

"Goody, at last I've managed to corrupt her totally," I said. When I emerged from below, she'd kicked off her shoes and made herself comfortable along the cockpit seat to port, her feet up, a life preserver cushion behind her shoulders. I put one glass into her hands and seated myself to starboard nursing the other. I looked at her for a moment, wanting to ask if she'd known that Mrs. Williston was around, but I could think of any way of putting it that didn't sound like an accusation. "Tired?" I asked.

"It's been a long day. Matt . . ."

"Yes?"

"I don't want to seem . . . well, uncooperative, but I've had only one skinny airport hamburger all day and I'm very hungry."

"Sure. Down, Rover!"

"Nice Rover." She smiled faintly, in a preoccupied way. "Let's take our drinks downstairs . . . below. If you want another one, you can have it watching your pretty little bride cooking up a storm. Or is it considered bad luck to mention storms on shipboard?"

There were obviously things on her mind; but I sensed that she didn't want to tell me about them, and it was better not to pressure her. So we moved below, and I lounged in the compact main cabin watching her, in the tiny adjacent galley, as she found the last two steaks in the icebox, peeled some potatoes and cut them up so they'd cook faster, and broke out the last of the broccoli.

"Johnny . . ."

"Yes, Penny," I said.

Working at the stove, she didn't turn her head to look in my direction. She said, "You know practically everything about me, and I know hardly anything about you. Tell me something about yourself. The real you."

It wasn't very smart, and it didn't go with our Mr. and Mrs. Matthews cover at all. On the other hand, if anybody knew enough about us to listen in, he probably knew too much already. So as she made dinner I told her about a mission that had taken me to the wilds of Scotland—which are wilder than you'd think—and about the lady who'd accompanied me although she was officially on the opposing side, since it was supposed to be a joint operation for the good of humanity; and how she'd finally double-crossed me by slipping knockout drops into my coffee as we picnicked on the desolate moors.

"What happened then?" Amy asked when I stopped.

I shrugged. "The mandatory response. It's right there in the manual. If you're stupid enough to swallow a Mickey, and the situation is at all critical—and this one was—you have no choice. I shot her before I passed out, of course." I watched Amy look around quickly, shocked, and I said without expression, "You'd better flip those steaks before they burn."

"Yes." She licked her lips. "Yes, of course."

It was a pretty good meal, in the cozy little cabin, but a silent one. Several times she started to say something, but each time she changed her mind. Then we collaborated on the dishes in good matrimonial fashion, wifey washing, hubby drying. She put away the dishrag, and I handed her the damp towel, which she hung neatly over the rail above the stove that kept you from falling into the burners when things got rough. But we hadn't had it that rough yet. Nautically speaking.

She spoke at last without looking at me. "I'm all sticky after all that traveling and I smell of cooking; I'd like to take a shower." Then she turned to face me, startled by the laugh I couldn't help. "What's so funny?"

I said, "I was just betting myself that would probably come next. First the dinner and then the dishes and then the shower."

She licked her lips. "Yes, I know. I'm stalling. I . . . I wasn't much good to you last time and . . . and I don't really know if I want to try again."

I said, "You were sweet and honest; and now you're turning into a goddam phony. Where did you get the word, Amy?"

"Word?" She frowned. "I don't know what you mean."

"Was it in that Chinese jewelry store while I was making my telephone calls? Or later when you disappeared into the john so long in the Miami airport? Except for a few minutes in the sanatorium, which seems an unlikely place for a contact, those are the only times you've been out of my sight all day." After a long silence, I said, "No, I'm not clairvoyant, sweetheart. But I do this for a living, remember? What are your orders? What do they want you to do?"

"I thought . . ." She swallowed hard, then tried for a little indignation. "I thought we'd decided that I was really innocent!"

"You were, but you aren't anymore. Something happened today, didn't it? Somebody happened."

She stared at me bleakly for a long time. At last she asked, "Why did you tell me that horrible story?"

"You know why," I said. "We've had it very easy in a way. Lots of lies but no bullets. No violence at all. Only a distant noise and a puff of smoke on the horizon. Somehow, during all this peaceful time, you may have come to the ridiculous conclusion that I'm a nice guy. Just because after over a week in my company you still have all your teeth and can see out of both eyes and retain the use of both arms and don't limp on either leg. And maybe because, just like you, I was kind of awkward in bed the one time we tried it. Who ever heard of a dangerous secret agent who had a hard time getting it up, for Christ's sake? So I thought I'd better impress on you the fact that I'm really a very vicious fellow; and I hope you aren't letting anybody talk you into playing some stupid amateur tricks on this mean old pro."

She looked at me gravely and reached out to touch my face with her fingertips. When she spoke, there was sadness in her voice: "I wouldn't ever try to trick you, Matt." Then she turned away to take some stuff—a towel and a small beach bag—from the shelf over the port bunk that was her bunk when pulled out to its full width. At present, in its narrow configuration, it was serving as settee for the big dropleaf cabin table on which we'd eaten. She squeezed past me in the narrow space and turned to look back at me, her eyes oddly wide and shiny. She rose on tiptoe to kiss me lightly on the mouth. "I'll be back as soon as I can, darling. Be good."

I heard her make her way up to the dock and walk away. After a little, I moved out into the cockpit, wishing I still smoked a pipe—the antitobacco boys and girls may have done great things for our lungs, but they've deprived us of a lot of solace.

It was another pleasant Bahamas evening with the

water glassy calm between the docks. I could hear the heavy, sexy beat of rock-and-roll music from the vicinity of the hotel swimming pool. Well, the *thump*-bump-bump, *thump*-bump-bump of the waltz was considered very erotic and wicked in its time, I've been told, making susceptible young ladies quiver estatically inside their whalebone stays and lacy pantalettes and multitudinous petticoats.

I went below again, and, just to make sure, looked around her side of the boat and found that the purse we'd bought her to replace the one that had been snatched in Miami—with the passport, driver's license, and credit cards we'd got her to replace the ones she'd lost—were missing, of course. She'd said goodbye as clearly as she could without actually saying it. And I'd let her go because she'd served her purpose as far as I was concerned; she was Doug's problem now. We'd hoped she'd take off so he could follow, hadn't we? But it was still an empty boat without her.

Now I had to wait and see what the people who'd ordered her away had in mind for me. I didn't expect them to leave me lonely very long. However, I still had to go through the motions of being a moron, it's always expected of you; so I went searching for my lost love. I made a production of sneaking a peek into the LADIES, unoccupied at this hour, thank God. She wasn't there, and none of the three grubby shower stalls had been used very recently. She wasn't in the lighted pool area with its handful of guests and its little outdoor bar and its noisy loudspeakers; and she wasn't in the dark indoor bar with its dance floor and its powerful, blaring sound system that also fed the pool speakers; and she wasn't in the restaurant and she wasn't in the lobby.

I made the phone call that would be expected of me: *Subject contact lost, relocate ASAP*. Okay. I'd complied with the rules, the Hollywood rules that require everybody to be stupid and never figure things out for themselves. As if I wasn't bright enough to know, just from her behavior, that my child bride had slipped away from me deliberately after refraining from dirtying our relationship with some hasty and deceitful last-minute sex, although she'd probably been instructed to use it to keep me unsuspicious.

I walked back down to the docks. As I started out the long pier, I saw smoke rising from *Spindrift*'s main hatch. My first impulse was, of course, to break into a run; hell, my boat was on fire. Then I reminded myself firmly that it wasn't really my boat, and that a man in my line of work who rushes blindly toward a supposed disaster makes a fine target for somebody who doesn't like him. I checked myself and stepped quickly alongside one of the concrete lightposts at the edge of the pier—not a hell of a lot of protection, but it might deter somebody who wanted to be quite sure of his shot. Peering past the post, I realized that the smoke was too thin for a real fire. It didn't come from the hatch but from the cockpit area just aft.

When I approached warily, the woman lounging in the cockpit flipped the cigarette she'd been smoking over *Spindrift*'s stern. It made a little red arc in the night before it was extinguished by the water of the harbor. She'd changed from the fashionably wide shorts in which I'd last seen her, but her current costume was just as far-out: a voluminous white jumpsuit with billowy sleeves and baggy harem pants. It had narrow cuffs at the wrists and ankles and a wide gold belt at the waist. You'd have to search a week to find the woman inside all the droopy draperies. If you wanted her.

"Good evening, Mrs. Williston," I said, looking down at her from the dock.

"So you checked me out, after seeing me at the

telephone. I hoped you would; that's why I showed myself to you like that." She smiled up at me. "That's nice. I like intelligent men."

"But what do they think of you?"

She said, "I believe there's a vacancy in your crew, Captain. I thought I'd apply for the position. Two Bermuda races and one transatlantic cruise. I swing a mean sextant; and I can even cook a little if I have to. Since women's lib hasn't made much impression on the yachting scene yet, I usually have to."

I looked down at her bleakly. I was tempted to tell her to haul her fashionable ass the hell off my ship. I felt bereft and lonely and not up to coping with lean, tanned females in far-out costumes. But she'd apparently ordered Amy away for a purpose and come here for a purpose; and it was obviously part of my job— maybe even the most important part of my job—to find out what that purpose was. I shrugged in answer to her little speech and dropped to the deck below. It wasn't quite as far below as it had been. The tide was rising. I made my way aft.

"A drink, Mrs. Williston?"

She nodded. "Amy said you were a fast man with a bottle. I liked that."

"It's a wonder you've managed to live without me all your life, admiring me the way you do," I said dryly. "We've got Scotch."

"Scotch will do very well."

"Short or tall?"

"No water. Easy on the ice."

Drinks made and distributed, I shoved aside the gear she'd brought with her: a shoulder-strap purse and a canvas seabag, the modern kind that zips open lengthwise instead of making you dig down from one end when you want to find your clean socks. I sat down facing her.

"Where's Amy Barnett?"

"Alias Penelope Matthews?" The woman smiled thinly. "That really wasn't much of a cover, Mr. Helm, to use your correct name. It didn't take us very long to find you, after you tried to pull down the curtain, so to speak, in Miami. We traced you to the marina in Coral Gables, and it wasn't hard to learn, there, that you were heading for the Bahamas. We determined that you hadn't stopped in Bimini, or in West End at the tip of this island; but the third marina we checked here in Freeport . . ."

"Jackpot," I said. "And Amy?"

"She refused to have anything to do with the nasty plans we've worked out to deal with you. So we pulled her out of the action, shall we say, and here I am instead, you lucky man." After a moment, Mrs. Williston went on: "Your little girl is quite all right. She'll be taking the first plane home in the morning, that's all. Do I get her job?"

"Why would you want it?" I studied her handsome, tanned face for a moment before asking, "What nasty plans does your PNP have for me, Mrs. Williston?"

She gave me her thin smile again. "Hell, you're the macho establishment warrior who carries a gun and thrives on danger, aren't you? And knocks the ladies dead, one way or another. Why should you worry about the feeble plots concocted by a silly bunch of do-gooders represented by a helpless social butterfly like me? You can cope with them when the time comes, can't you? And in the meantime I *am* damned good with boats, and you apparently aren't. What's the bigger risk, my slitting your throat while you sleep, or your trying to get this tub to Nassau and beyond all by yourself? Hell, you'll either capsize her in a squall while you're still in deep water or run her onto a coral head the minute you try to negotiate those tricky banks."

It was an intriguing approach, the way she was

warning me in advance that I'd be taking an enemy aboard if I let her come. It was also a deliberate challenge: Was I scared of a pampered rich bitch in a fashionable umpteen-hundred-dollar monkey suit? That was supposed to get my machismo up in arms so I'd rush to embrace the danger and maybe even the dame herself; there was more than a hint in her attitude that while I might die if I made this passage with her, she'd see I died happy. All of which was totally irrelevant, of course. You don't survive in the business by accepting stupid challenges from arrogant females or anybody else.

While I didn't really look forward to handling the boat alone, I was gaining confidence with practice, and I didn't think it would be quite the suicide voyage she'd described; she was just another old salt trying to scare the pants off a gullible landlubber. And quite apart from any tricks she might pull, I wasn't anxious to share with this overpowering lady the cramped cabin of a twenty-eight-foot boat, particularly not this twenty-eight-foot boat, which carried strong memories of a girl I'd really liked.

But that was also irrelevant. This was what we'd been waiting for. I'd been sent here for bait, hadn't I? I'd been sent to draw Minister, or his employers, out of hiding; and here was the top lady of the PNP kindly offering herself as deckhand and dishwasher. I drew a long breath.

"If you're such a hotshot sailor, I suppose you can get us out of here in the dark," I said.

"Why ever not? The harbor is lighted like a football stadium. Once we're out of the land cut, all we do is head for the flashing buoy, leave it to starboard, and we're free and clear, next checkpoint Great Stirrup Light at the north end of the Berry Islands, sixty nautical miles away. That's assuming you do want to head for Nassau." When I nodded, Mrs. Williston said, "Just give me a minute to stow my gear and change my clothes. You can get the sail cover off the forestaysail while you're waiting. . . ."

|||||||| CHAPTER 18 ||||||||||||||||||||||||||||||||||||||||

IT WAS an overcast night, but the moon was lurking behind the thin clouds. We didn't make very good progress across the Northwest Providence Channel because the lady was a sailing nut and didn't believe the internal combustion engine was here to stay. Personally, in those light winds, I'd simply have fired up the diesel again—she'd turned it off after we'd cleared the buoy and set the sails—but she wasn't having any of that. Instead she wanted more canvas. Well, Dacron.

I hadn't paid much attention to just what sails had come with the boat, figuring I'd first master the basic threesome of mainsail, forestaysail, and jib; and probably, aided and abetted by the two-cylinder Yanmar, they'd do everything I needed done. Now we scrabbled around in the forepeak and found a couple of storm sails and a spinnaker—thank God the wind was in the wrong direction for that monstrous kite—and finally, hooray, a jib almost twice the size of the one already up. That one she called a jib topsail and didn't think much of. This beautiful new discovery was a Genoa jib, affectionately known as Jenny.

Next, working under the spreader lights with darkness all around us, steering by autopilot with *Spindrift* pitching gently in the slow swells of the channel, we had to haul the big sail onto the foredeck and crawl out onto the precarious bowsprit—my job—to slide the smaller jib, flapping wildly, out of the slot of the roller-furling apparatus and slide in its giant replacement instead. Also flapping wildly, despite the light airs. It took half an hour to get the big sail up and organized to Mrs. Williston's satisfaction; and she thought I was a pretty piss-poor sailor not to have worked out the proper locations for the strings and pulleys—excuse me, lines and blocks—ahead of time.

Finally we had to tidy up the foredeck and bring down the little forestaysail and furl it neatly again, because, she said after careful study, it was too small to pull worth a damn under these conditions and it disturbed the wind for Jenny. Then back to the cockpit, where she turned out the blinding decklights and disengaged the Tiller Master. Taking the helm herself, she had me crank in a bit on this winch and ease that sheet a touch—it took fifteen minutes more before she pronounced herself satisfied with all adjustments.

It's the great sailboat fallacy, as far as I'm concerned. It's a pleasant way of getting around on the water, it's nice and quiet, and the wind is free although the sails damn well aren't; but fast it isn't, so why not just relax and glide along at three knots instead of beating your brains out to make three and a quarter? Hell, if this dame really wanted an extra knot or two, all she had to do was turn the Yanmar key instead of working my tail off.

Then I decided that this was the wrong attitude. After all, it was a useful educational experience for me, watching a real sailing expert at work; and if she felt compelled to treat a casual passage to Nassau as if it were the critical competitive event of the Southern Ocean Racing Conference, who was I to spoil her fun?

Having been exposed to a couple of her high-fashion shore-going costumes, I'd expected her to produce something equally tricky to sail in, but she'd fooled me. A pair of dirty white boat shoes with the usual death-grip soles, a pair of well-washed white jeans with old paint stains on them, and an old gray sweat shirt, the kind with a hood, was the uniform of the day, or night. Satisfied with the sail trim at last, she spoke without looking away from the luff of the ghostly mainsail barely visible in the night.

"Three-hour watches, I think, don't you? I'll take her until oh one hundred. You'd better go below and get some rest."

"Yes, ma'am."

"Oh, Helm . . ."

"Yes?"

"How the hell did you and that child ever manage to get this boat all the way across the Gulf Stream? It's people like you who keep the Coast Guard busy, blundering out on the water without knowing a damn thing about what you're doing."

As I've said, you find them in every sport. The next time you reach the top of Everest, there'll be a mountaineering expert waiting to tell you sternly that you should be banned from the cliffs and slopes because you used the wrong color rope and didn't hammer in your pitons with the proper stylish stroke.

"Yes, ma'am," I said. "But we did get where we wanted to go, didn't we? And it's people like you who keep the undertakers busy, talking big about slitting people's throats—to a man in my line of work! I hope you realize that, having said it, you're dead if you come anywhere near my bunk after I turn in."

There was a little silence, broken by the rhythmic

surging sound of the bow wave as the big Genoa pulled us along as best it could with the wind we had.

"Oh, dear!" said Mrs. Williston at last, very softly. "Oh, dear, that *was* a stupid thing for me to say, wasn't it? I assure you, it was just a manner of speaking. I really have no designs on your life."

"You'll excuse me if I don't take your word for that," I said. "If you're not here to kill me, sooner or later, or at least put me out of commission somehow, what are you here for? The warning still goes. Don't make any moves that can be misinterpreted, Mrs. Williston, or feed me any funny-tasting foods, please. I can be a very sudden guy when I have to, or just think I have to."

She said, "Yes, you warned the little girl, too, didn't you? Or threatened her. Are you a very careful man who doesn't want any unfortunate misunderstandings? Or are you just a big blowhard who likes to intimidate helpless women, Mr. Helm?" Then she laughed softly. "All right. Get your rest. I won't come below at all. That's a promise."

I hesitated. "It might be kind of hard to keep, on a long watch."

She laughed again, more heartily. "My dear man, there's a bucket in the cockpit locker; and it won't be the first time I've squatted on deck. Go to sleep."

The cabin of a boat under way, even a sailing vessel under sail in light airs, is a noisy place full of creakings and gurglings and splashings. As I lay in my bunk drowsily, I heard the ratchety sound of a winch aft as Mrs. Williston cranked in the Genoa sheet slightly. A pan in the galley clanked metallically against something at the end of each roll. Somewhere above me on deck an unidentified piece of gear was going tick-tock against the mast . . . and I found myself thinking of a smallish girl with pale straight hair and blue-gray eyes and shy little breasts of surpassing loveliness, and I was teaching her, in my gentle and expert fashion, that she really wasn't significantly aberrant; in fact, with the right approach she could respond quite normally and adequately, even passionately, to the skillful ministrations of a wonderful, understanding, virile partner like me. . . .

A clattering crash inside the cabin shocked me awake. I sat up, grabbing the shotgun I'd removed from its locker to save Mrs. Williston from temptation. Something was rolling and rattling around on the cabin floor: a plastic bucket.

"Helm, wake up!" It was a sharp whisper from the cockpit. "Damn you, get up here, we've got company!"

I scrambled aft without bothering with my shoes, all I'd taken off to sleep. I climbed the companionway ladder cautiously, until I could see Mrs. Williston through the open hatch.

"God, I could have cut your throat a dozen times, the way you were sleeping! And I didn't want to leave the tiller and tip them off I'd spotted them. Or get shot trying to shake you awake."

"Where?"

"Port quarter. They're running dark, and they're hanging well back now; but they slipped and got too close a few minutes ago and the stern light caught them on the roll. One of the big fast macho jobs. Donzi, Cigarette, Magnum, you name it. I can't keep those damn thunderboats straight. Around thirty feet. Fifty to sixty knots, probably. Maybe more. We sure as hell can't outrun them with fifteen lousy horsepower, which is about what you've got down there, isn't it?"

"Right on," I said. "Any idea who's out there?"

She looked at me sharply in the glow of the instruments. "No friends of mine, if that's what you're thinking. If they were, I'd have let them take you asleep, wouldn't I? Instead of heaving a bucket at you." She threw a glance over her left shoulder.

"They can't just be tracking us to see where we go, that's no mystery. On this course it's got to be either the Berry Islands, or Nassau farther on. So they'll probably move in on us as soon as those ships get well over the horizon. Just in case we get on the horn or let off a distress flare or something."

She indicated two clusters of lights, like floating hotels, far off to port. Looking that way, I caught a glimpse of a shadowy boat shape, low and rakish, much closer and farther aft. Black or some very dark color, it was almost invisible in the night; I guess it was the gleam of the water curling off the predatory bow that had drawn my eyes to it.

"Maybe you'd better get on the radio," Mrs. Williston said. "It's hardly a job for Bahamas Air Search and Rescue, known as BASRA, I don't think they have any law-enforcement facilities, but maybe there's some kind of a government vessel cruising around here within VHF range, looking for pot smugglers or something."

I said, "Even if there is, it'll be too late getting here; those boys aren't going to hang around back there very long, knowing that sooner or later the moon will break through and spoil their surprise by showing them to us. Anyway, I don't think I want to bother the Bahamian authorities." I frowned. "Have you ever been shot at, Mrs. Williston?"

"No, and I don't want to be."

I said, "Who gets a choice? At least being shot at is better than being shot. How's your nerve?"

"Mister, I'm a big brown chicken. Guns scare me shitless."

"Sure. Well, we can wash out your pants afterward, if that's the only problem; and how is it we keep having these excremental discussions, anyway?"

She laughed shortly. "All right, tell me what to do."

183

I found myself liking the woman better. To be sure, she'd been infuriatingly dictatorial as long as we were dealing with her specialty, sailing; but apparently she was willing to take orders from me on the subject of my specialty, violence. Furthermore, only the good ones tell you what stinking yellow cowards they are. It's when they start telling you how brave they are that you've got to watch them.

I said, "Just steer the boat and behave naturally. Act shocked and scared and yell for me when they close in; scream at me to snap out of my drunken stupor and come save you from these terrible pirates. And drop into the bottom of the cockpit and stay there when the gunfire starts. That's important. Don't go rushing around. I've got to know where I have you so I know where I can shoot and where I can't."

She licked her lips. "Where will you be?"

"You'll see. Can you stay on course without the compass lights? Or any lights?"

"Hell, I'm steering by the wind, anyway. Yes, I can hold her steady. Helm . . ."

"Yes?"

"I hope you shoot as mean as you talk."

"Lady, that makes two of us."

I ducked back down into the cabin, fell over the bucket and set it aside, put on my shoes, and found a coil of rope up forward and hacked off several lengths with my pocketknife, probably ruining an essential piece of boat equipment, but to hell with it. Working in the darkness alleviated by the leakage of the instrument lights aft, and the glow of the masthead navigation light spilling through the Plexiglas hatch overhead, I used one piece to rig a sling for the shotgun and strung the others on my belt. I moved into the galley and filled my pants pockets with shells: buckshot to starboard, solid slug loads to port. Pistol ammunition aft, in the hip pocket; although it didn't look like a good spot for a .38 bellygun with a two-inch barrel. I checked the little gun in its waistband holster and slung the big gun across my back and moved aft.

"Ready?" I whispered.

Her voice came down the hatch. "They're still hanging back. Ready any time you are. As ready as I'll ever be."

"Here goes nothing."

I hit the boat's main switch, cutting all the electricity on board. That left us in darkness except for the vague luminosity of the moonlight filtering through the thin clouds. I hauled myself out the main hatch and ran forward and went up the mast like a scared monkey—more scared because I hate high places. I thanked God for the mast steps since I'm not much for shinnying up slick aluminum poles with seven pounds of shotgun on my back, not to mention the pistol and all the ammo.

Some fancy boats have two or more sets of spreaders to provide the proper angles for the shrouds supporting the mast, but *Spindrift*'s was a bread-and-butter rig with only one pair. I pulled myself up there and used one of the rope lengths from my belt to tie myself to the mast, forcing the rope through the slot between the taut mainsail and its track and running it over one of the mast steps as well, hoping it would hold if my whole weight should hit it.

That put me standing on the spreaders forward of the mast, facing aft some twenty-five feet in the air, with the whole dark watery world open to my left and the curving Dacron of the mainsail and Genoa blocking most of the view to my right. The boat was heeling only moderately, and the motion, although amplified at this height, wasn't too bad; but it was still a hell of a place to shoot a shotgun from. The mast and mainsail were in the way of a right-handed man expecting to do business to the left, since they would undoubtedly try to board from that side, the windward side, avoiding the sails and sheets and boom cluttering up the other side of the boat on this tack.

I was aware of a searchlight probing the sea aft of us now, as I freed the shotgun and unfastened the rope sling from the barrel. Leaving the rope still secured around the small of the stock, I tied it to the same mast step I'd used for my safety line. I worked the gun's action once to feed a shell from the magazine into the empty chamber—I'm not brave enough to go mast climbing with a fully loaded gun. I let the shotgun hang from its line, using my body to keep it from swinging while I dug into my pocket for my little knife and, finding it among the spare ammunition, pried the larger blade open.

Ready at last, I let myself become aware of the world below. *Spindrift* was still gliding along on the starboard tack without lights. Mrs. Williston had risen to stand at the tiller, a shadowy figure down there, her attitude suitably puzzled and worried as she looked aft at the beam of light that was searching the ocean astern, but searching in the wrong place. Apparently they'd been goofing off, overconfident, when our lights went out so suddenly. Temporarily disoriented, they'd lost us in the darkness and slid off course a bit; but even as I watched, the white finger swung our way. I leaned back behind the mainsail, but I needn't have worried about being seen; they weren't interested in masts and rigging and attached foreign objects. Having located us by our sails, the searchlight instantly swung down to pin *Spindrift*'s hull, and Mrs. Williston, in its beam. I heard big motors roar into life out there.

"Matt! Matt, come up here, somebody's coming at us very fast! What do I do?"

Still holding the tiller, she'd leaned forward to shout

down into the cabin. Good girl. Even if the words weren't heard at the distance, the action would speak for itself. Now the ghostly black hull with its gleaming white bow wave, hard to see through the glare of the searchlight, was approaching fast. Moments later, near enough, the oncoming boat squatted, the way they do, as the power went off and the noise of the engines subsided.

"Matt, for God's sake, forget that damn fuse box and get the hell up here! It's crazy, but I think we're being attacked by a bunch of Bahamian pirates!"

Mrs. Williston didn't lose her head in a crisis. She'd improved on my drunken-stupor story and loudly explained the failure of our lights, to keep the attackers unsuspicious. The overgrown speedboat was swinging alongside now, keeping its searchlight trained on *Spindrift*'s cockpit. I could make it out fairly well. No insignia on the hull. No red-flashing or blue-flashing lights. No loud hailer ordering us to heave to in official tones. No uniforms on the four men in the fancy, Naugahyde-padded cockpit. Okay. We hadn't gotten ourselves involved with a mysterious government patrol boat of some kind. Open season.

The wake they'd kicked up during their brief burst of speed rolled under us belatedly, causing the mast to swing like an upside-down pendulum. After the motion had subsided I stabbed with the little knife and opened a horizontal slash in the taut mainsail. I was braced for just about anything. Sails aren't my field of expertise, and I wouldn't have been a bit surprised if the whole big triangle of Dacron had exploded when punctured, like a kid's balloon. Maybe it would have, or at least split widely, in heavy weather; but in the light breeze we had, nothing happened beyond the simple slit in the sailcloth. I made a vertical cut downward from the inner end of the slit. Here I had to saw through a couple of tough seams before I'd opened an adequate triangular window in the sail, which would let me shoot from the right shoulder as I stood on the spreaders. I closed the knife and put it away. Below, a man was giving orders.

"You, lady! Keep both hands on the tiller in plain sight! Tell your boyfriend to get his ass topside, before I start shooting holes in his pretty helmsman."

"Matt! Matt, for God's sake don't try anything crazy or they'll kill me! Matt, come up here, please!"

Embracing the mast with my left arm, I grasped the dangling shotgun right-handed and shoved it through the hole in the sail. Safety off. It occurred to me that twenty-five feet would be a long way to fall, backward, to a very hard fiberglass deck, if the recoil kicked me off my precarious perch on the crosstrees in spite of my arm around the mast. Well, that was what the safety line was for, wasn't it? I had a picture of myself dangling helplessly in my rope sling while four men used me for target practice. . . .

"Matt, what are you *doing* down there in that lousy cabin, do you want them to shoot me? Oh, *please* come up here and do what they want! *Please!*"

Steadying the gun, I could see her leaning forward to make her desperate plea to the empty cabin. One man was at the near side of the powerboat's cockpit, aft, with a pistol aimed at her. Two others, just ahead of him, were getting ready to board us, one with a gun, the other with a rope; the speedboat's bowline. As I watched, the second man flung the rope across *Spindrift*'s cabin for later retrieval and pulled out a pistol of his own.

The fourth man was at the wheel on the far side of the attacking boat, holding the vessel steady alongside. It took a considerable amount of steering since those fast-powered craft don't handle well at low sailboat speeds. Once in a while he'd reach out to adjust the throttles a bit, or to adjust the searchlight, which he kept trained on our main hatch where I was supposed to appear. The glare was considerable; they probably couldn't have seen me even if they'd looked up to where I was perched above them in relative darkness, but none of them did look up.

I reminded myself that I'd equipped myself with a pump-action shotgun since it was less likely that an automatic would be disabled by the rugged conditions on a boat. However, while a pumpgun can be operated as fast as an autoloader by expert hands, it must be pumped; it won't cycle itself. I centered the barrel on the man covering Mrs. Williston and waited until a sharp roll of his boat caused him to steady himself by the cockpit coaming and let his weapon wander off target. I pulled the trigger.

A foot-long flame licked out from the short barrel of the Winchester. The noise was shattering in the night, and the recoil of the twelve-gauge, as always, was murderous. I was driven back against my safety line, but I kept my footing on the spreaders. *Pump, you stupid bastard!* I swung on the two would-be boarders who were looking up now, startled but still close together, fine; but I didn't know how much shot spread I'd get at that close range, so I concentrated on the near one and fired again, practically taking his head off. *Pump, you jerk!* Something slapped through the sail beside me, and I saw that the helmsman had released the steering wheel and pulled a gun. We shot simultaneously, and I saw the full charge of buckshot, twenty pellets to the load, hit him in the chest, tearing him open. I had no idea where his second bullet had gone, except that it hadn't hit me. *Pump, you slow-motion moron!*

Then I clung there, embracing the mast and breathing hard, because there was nothing left to shoot at. There were three bodies sprawled in the speedboat's plushy cockpit, now blood-splashed and ripped by flying lead. I had a vague mental image of something scuttling into the cabin in a crippled way while I was concentrating on the helmsman—presumably the second would-be boarder, fringed by my shot at his companion. I knew that Mrs. Williston had obeyed orders and found shelter in the bottom of *Spindrift*'s cockpit at my first shot, but she was up now, clinging to the rope that had been thrown aboard.

"Matt," she called. "Matt, do you want me to secure their bowline or cast them adrift?"

"Secure it."

I had a lot of adrenaline running around inside me with no place to go; and I had a hard time concentrating. Unload shotgun; pocket shells. Untie shotgun, fasten to belt, let hang there. Unfasten safety line and thread through belt; and why are you being so careful to preserve a lousy little piece of rope that's served its purpose? Come down mast very cautiously; you'd look pretty ridiculous falling and breaking your back now that it's all over. . . .

"Are you all right?" Mrs. Williston asked when I reached her. "That other man was shooting at you, wasn't he? Oh, God, my knees are still shaking!"

"I'm okay. How about you?" I asked.

"I'm okay. I didn't even wet my pants. God, there I go again, scatological Williston!" She looked up quickly as the sails started flapping and lunged for the tiller. "Christ, we're in irons. . . . No, she's paying off. What are you doing?"

I was hauling in the overgrown speedboat, which was now towing astern. I studied it as I did so. The forward part was decked over; but the resulting cabin was undoubtedly rather low and dark, although there were a couple of ports in the side, closed, and a hatch in the deck, open.

"There's a live one in there, somewhere," I said.

"At least he was live enough to crawl into his burrow. I'd better go dig him out. Keep your head down; there could be more shooting."

"Can't we just turn the boat loose and leave it?"

"And have a shot-torn vessel found drifting with a lot of dead bodies on board; and a lot of international questions asked about the bloody Battle of the Northwest Providence Channel? Anyway, if the guy in there pulls himself together, he's still got several hundred horsepower against our fifteen, and several guns; he could make more trouble for us. And I would like to know who the hell sent him and why, unless you've got some answers."

She shook her head. "No. No, I have no idea what it's all about."

I sighed wearily. It was anticlimax alley. The great sea engagement was over and victorious Captain Hornblower was entitled to relax a bit, wasn't he? I shook my head in a meaningless way, trying to shake off the reaction, I guess. I got the rope off the shotgun and shoved a round into the chamber and four into the magazine, using the slug loads this time. Mrs. Williston, *Spindrift's* tiller between her knees, was holding the powerboat's bowline snug for me.

"Be careful," she said.

"Sure."

It occurred to me that this was quite a woman. She hadn't panicked during the shooting, and she wasn't puking at the sight of blood in large quantities. Whatever she'd been in the booby hatch for, they seemed to have done a good job of curing her. But it was no time to be admiring handsome ladies. I hauled myself onto the foredeck of the rakish pirate vessel, watching the open forward hatch, but nothing showed there. I moved down the deck a little way, keeping to one side where he'd have trouble getting a bead on me without revealing himself.

As I'd told Amy Barnett, we don't think much of that moldy old come-out-with-your-hands-up routine. I was in no mood to play cop. I simply stopped and aimed at the cabin top well ahead of my feet and pulled the trigger. The twelve-gauge shotgun slug is a blunt one-ounce hunk of lead. I was using it because it has more penetration than buckshot—anything has more penetration than those little round pellets—but it hardly qualifies as an armor-piercing projectile and I wasn't quite sure it was up to the job. But apparently fiberglass isn't very bulletproof. The slug didn't splatter or ricochet as I'd half expected. It smashed right through, leaving a good-sized hole. I shot again, at a different angle, and again, and still again, probing the cabin under my feet. . . .

"No more, no more, I'm coming out! Don't shoot, don't shoot!"

The voice was shrill with panic. Waiting, I stuffed four more shells into the magazine. The searchlight was still pointing its glaring beam stubbornly to port, the way a dead man had left it. It put a halo around the head of the figure that appeared in the main hatch nearby, probably the only one he'd ever get.

"Aft into the cockpit," I ordered the man. "On your knees with your elbows on the seat. Oh, and there could be some guns lying around, friend. Help yourself. Anytime. I'm just looking for an excuse."

"Take it easy, take it easy!"

I waited for him to get settled, then made my way aft and dropped into the cockpit, cautiously. There was no way of avoiding the blood, it was everywhere, a seagoing slaughterhouse. The three dead ones were quite dead; buckshot is for keeps if you center it only reasonably well. The only reason my captive was still alive was that I'd been aiming at his partner, and he'd only gotten the fringe of the shot pattern.

I'd been wondering vaguely why the boat's engines

had quit; now I noticed a cord attached to the belt of the dead helmsman, with a metal gadget on the end. I remembered that some of those racy boats are equipped with automatic cutoffs so that if the guy at the wheel is thrown overboard in a violent maneuver, the cord is pulled, the kill switch is actuated, and the empty boat doesn't come roaring around to chew up the man in the water with its props, which has happened.

The thug kneeling on the cockpit floor, sole, or whatever the nautical name of it may be, was rather short and plump, with thinning dark hair. He was dressed in blue linen shorts and a gaudy short-sleeved shirt. Maybe he was pretending to be a sportsman of sorts. I patted him down and told him to get up and sit facing me, which he did painfully. He was bleeding in several places. One buckshot had ripped his right ear and he had a couple in the right arm and shoulder. I thought there was a bloodstain over on the left side indicating a pellet straying widely from the main shot pattern, but the light wasn't good and the figured shirt made it hard to tell.

I said, "Would you like to die now, or would you prefer to put it off by talking a little first?"

He said, "Shit, it was supposed to be a simple hit on a dumb society broad; nobody warned us she had a pro guarding the body. You don't futz around with that shiny smoothbore, do you? Christ, what a mess!"

"You were after Mrs. Williston?"

"Shit, I don't even know who you are, mister."

"Who sent you?"

"You know I can't tell you that. Shit, man, I'm dead if I tell you that."

I shrugged. I made a production of opening the shotgun action far enough to pick out the round in the chamber. I dropped it carefully into my left pants pocket. I dug a shell out of the right-hand pocket and showed it to him.

"Number One buck," I said. "It won't spread much at this range, just a few inches, but enough to do the job." I slipped the round into place and closed the gun. I pointed the barrel at the zipper of his shorts, low down. "A word of warning, friend. I don't have the time or the patience to play with you. When I ask the question again, I either get an answer or I shoot. You can figure out what a full load of twelve-gauge buck will do to you down there just as well as I can. Okay. Question. Who sent you?"

There was a moment of silence. I shrugged in a resigned way and steadied the Winchester.

"Hold it, hold it! It was the big man, Connie Grieg himself. . . ."

A startled look came to his blood-streaked face. His eyes became big and round and shocked. He started to cough, hugging himself tightly; then the blood came pouring from his mouth in a dark flood, covering the pattern of his gaudy shirt. He slumped sideways on the cockpit seat.

I felt for a pulse and found nothing. I opened the gory shirt and looked at the chest. There was a tiny hole and a small amount of bloody leakage where one Number One buckshot pellet had struck near the left nipple. Less than twenty-five grains of lead, less than a third of an inch in diameter. I knew a girl once who was shot in the back at point-blank range with a 240-grain bullet from a .44 Magnum. It tore her up badly, of course, it required a lot of surgical cutting and stitching and patching; but two months later she was recovering well, and we were having lots of fun on the beach in San Carlos, Mexico, and other pleasant places nearby, outdoors and in. You never know what's going to kill them and what isn't.

"Helm!" It was Mrs. Williston's voice. "Hey, I hope you know you're sinking!"

I became aware that the king-sized speedboat was feeling rather sluggish in the gentle rollers. I left the dead man, looked down into the cabin, and saw the gleam of water. Obviously I'd underestimated the power of those shotgun slugs very badly. They'd kept right on going after being fired down through the cabin top, emerging through the bottom of the boat. They'd have been nicely expanded by the time they got there, tearing four holes each over an inch in diameter, maybe bigger if they'd hit something hard like a metal fitting or fastening and driven it out through the bottom of the hull. Well, it saved me from hunting for a suitable seacock.

Working fast, I hauled the dead men to the main hatch, one after another, and dumped them into the cabin, hearing them splash in the rising water. No shark food here. I gave a hasty look around. There was a life ring aft displaying the boat's name and hailing port: *Hot Rock III*, West Palm Beach, Fla. It seemed to me that although I was still a landlubber at heart, I could come up with better boat names if I had to than all these salty sailors.

I threw the life ring into the cabin with the bodies, where it wouldn't float away. I closed the hatch and snapped the lock. I switched off the searchlight, waited a few seconds to accustom my eyes a bit to the resulting gloom, and then made my way forward. Mrs. Williston had pulled the bow close to *Spindrift*'s rail. I hesitated, looking down at my feet. I couldn't see them very distinctly, but I could see the dark tracks they'd left on the powerboat's cabin top. I pulled off my shoes and passed them across.

"Watch out, they're kind of messy," I said.

She flinched only slightly as she took the bloody shoes and laid them on the cockpit seat, soles up.

Her voice was quite steady when she spoke: "Come aboard and sit down, and I'll make us each a drink. I suppose you'll want to wait and make sure it does sink. We can use the time taping a temporary patch on that mainsail until I can sew it up right."

IIIIIIIII CHAPTER 19 IIIIIIIIIIIIIIIIIIIIIIIIIIIIIIIIIIIIIIIIIIII

I AWOKE to odd splashing sounds coming in through the open port and hatch above my bunk. I started to jump up to see what the hell was wrong—after all, I was the commanding officer responsible for this ship, wasn't I?—but then I remembered that we were lying in a rather narrow anchorage about halfway down the Berry Islands, between the southern tip of Little Harbour Cay and a low rocky islet to the west, unnamed on the chart, with perpendicular shores that were only six or eight feet high: miniature limestone cliffs, curiously eroded, against which the little waves of the inlet gurgled and plopped and splashed in a disconcertingly noisy manner.

A glance through a porthole assured me that we were still where we'd been when I'd retired below to clean the shotgun, first, and then take a nap—in the business you learn to grab any opportunity to catch up on your sleep. Anyway, *Spindrift* wasn't drifting ashore. She wouldn't dare. Not after the confident way Mrs. Williston had brought us in here under power and planted—or had me plant—two anchors to hold us in position in the middle of the inlet: the Bahamian moor I'd read about in the guidebook. Apparently there's seldom room to swing in a big circle around a single anchor in those tight little island harbors. You're supposed to lie spread-eagled, so to speak, between two hooks, in order to stay pretty well in one place and leave as much mooring space as possible for other boats.

I glanced at my watch and was surprised to find that it was close to dinnertime. We'd come in here after lunch, having picked up Great Stirrup Light about dawn and found a good breeze that, with all that sail up, had sent us roaring down along the chain of little cays in a spectacular fashion that had made me very nervous; but the boat hadn't capsized and the mast hadn't fallen down and Mrs. Williston had laughed at my apprehensions. This was what *real* sailing was all about, she'd said. However, she'd informed me that even if the wind held we couldn't make Nassau before dark. We might as well find an anchorage and let her make proper repairs to the mainsail, then get a good night's rest.

Yawning, I pulled on my jeans—with daylight, the sky had cleared and it had become too hot below for me to sleep in anything but my shorts. I moved to the main hatch and looked out into the cockpit. The awning was up, and Mrs. Williston was working in the shade of it. She was one of the least domestic-looking women I'd met, but it was a domestic scene anyway: the handsome lady with a lap full of white Dacron, sewing away skillfully, but using a sailmaker's leather palm instead of a seamstress's metal thimble. She'd long since peeled off the heavy sweat shirt she'd worn last night and was clad, above the waist, in what looked like a man's sleeveless undershirt. I believe on a woman it's called a tank top, although I can't tell you why. Her shoulders were smooth and brown, I noticed; and told myself to forget it.

"Did you have a nice nap?" she asked with the

self-righteous sarcasm of someone who's been laboring while others rested.

"My God, are you still working on that?" I asked.

"I'm almost finished. But you have time to scrape the fuzz off your chin. We'll make an early start in the morning, and you probably won't have time to shave then."

"Your wish is my command, Milady. . . . What the hell is that you're sewing on? I thought the only bullethole was the one up near the spreaders where I was standing."

She was making a neat little square patch over a neatly trimmed little hole—also squared, now—near the bottom of the sail. The foot, in nautical parlance.

She said without looking up, "This is the one that went past my head when you shot the man who was pointing a gun at me."

I said, "The blast of the shotgun must have covered the report. I didn't even know he'd managed to pull the trigger. I was hoping he wouldn't."

"I'm sure you were." Her voice was tart. "Anyway, he missed. Go shave, please. I'm willing to make allowances in a long race, but we're not racing; and I prefer not to look at bristly men at dinner when I don't have to."

"Yes, ma'am."

It had been all right last night. Actually, I hadn't got my drink immediately. First we'd furled the Genoa and brought the mainsail down and taped up the knife slits with tough white patent tape from a sail-repair kit I'd bought when outfitting the boat, along with a lot of other expensive stuff I'd been told I couldn't possibly sail without. Only then, just drifting there in the dark, had we relaxed and treated ourselves to a victory drink apiece while waiting for the speedboat to sink.

Hot Rock III had settled, toward the end, very

gradually, as if reluctant to take the long dive to the bottom some six hundred fathoms below us (multiply by six to get feet). However, when she did go, she went stern first with a rush that barely gave me time to turn loose the bowline. Something about watching the boat go down like that with the bodies on board had changed Mrs. Williston's attitude abruptly, reminding her that we weren't really old comrades in arms after all; that in fact she didn't approve of me a bit and couldn't understand how in the world she'd let herself become my accomplice in the concealment of a quadruple homicide. She'd been remote while we were getting under way again, and she'd been cool to me ever since.

By the time I had my teeth brushed and my face shaved and a clean shirt on, she was putting the sail-repair kit back together. She asked me if I thought I could get the mainsail back onto its tracks and properly furled while she was cleaning up and starting dinner. I said I'd done it before and might just manage to do it again. I was finishing putting the awning back up—I'd had to take it down to get the sail onto the boom—when she set a couple of drinks on the bridge deck and came out after them, now wearing a plain white denim dress. It was quite unadorned, just a sleeveless, knee-length shift of the canvaslike material; but it fit her in a rather intimate and interesting way, and revealed to me again her very elegant brown legs. Her feet were bare and brown and not bad-looking, if you like feet.

She said, "That is one lousy job of furling a sail."

"Yes, ma'am. Aren't you afraid you'll give me a terrible inferiority complex?"

She laughed shortly. "I think you have an ego that would blunt an ax. Sit down and have your drink. How many men have you killed, really, Helm?"

I said, "Don't get personal. How many men have you fucked, really, Williston?"

She ignored that and said with sudden intensity. "So goddam cold-blooded and swift and ruthless! They were after you for some reason, but they never had a chance, did they?"

"Jesus!" I said, startled. "What do you think this is, some kind of a sport? Who gives chances, for God's sake? What was I supposed to do, invite them to a quick-draw contest at the O.K. Corral at high noon? All four of them?"

"Bang-bang-bang. No warning at all! No hesitation! Three men dead and one dying! If you told the truth about that last one and didn't just strangle him with your bare hands after you'd blasted him out of that cabin without even giving him a chance to surrender. I couldn't see what was going on beyond that damn spotlight." When I didn't speak, she said, "You haven't told me what he told you, if anything."

I'd kept it to myself, because last night had not been a good time to discuss it properly; besides, I'd wanted to think about it a little before I told her. But I'd lacked sufficient data to come to any conclusions.

Now I spoke carefully: "Shit, I don't even know who you are, mister!' "

She frowned quickly. "What—"

"You asked what he said. I just told you."

She stared at me. "But . . . but if he didn't know who you were, then why did they . . . why were they trying to . . ." She stopped, aghast at the implications that suddenly confronted her.

I said, carefully as before, "Quote. 'Shit, it was supposed to be a simple hit on a dumb society broad; nobody warned us she had a pro guarding the body.' End quote."

It was the first time I'd seen her shocked into

incoherence. "But . . . but that's insane! You . . . you mean . . ."

"Obviously somebody doesn't like you," I said. "It seems incredible, I know, but it does happen to amateurs trying to save the world in their clumsy way. I assume that's what you people are trying to do, but I'm having a hard time figuring out your method, Mrs. W."

She corrected me mechanically. "Gina, please."

"Obviously somebody doesn't like you, Gina."

"Do you know . . . did he tell you who . . ."

"Quote. 'It was the big man, Connie Grieg himself.' End quote. End interrogation. End interrogatee. Massive hemorrhage, if you insist on the gruesome details." I waited. When she didn't speak, I went on: "I've heard of a Constantine Grieg who dabbles, and a little more, in the drug business."

She licked her lips. "I . . . we never dreamed he'd send men out to *shoot* . . . I mean, that's *barbaric!*"

"What did you do to make him mad?"

She hesitated, obviously trying to put her thoughts into order. When she spoke it was without immediate reference to the question I'd asked: "We let other organizations do the protest-marching bit and wave their banners about nixing the nukes and do you want your babies to be born with uranium in the cranium." She shrugged. "Well, they do some good, I suppose; at least they keep the problem in the public eye. And of course we do a bit of missionary and educational work ourselves, corny and obvious. A group of rich socialite creeps feeling guilty about their money and trying to soothe their consciences and demonstrate how public-spirited they are by going through the proper antinuclear motions."

"Camouflage?" I said.

"That's right. To show we're quite harmless, really; just another bunch of cocktail-party activists." She was silent for a moment; then she continued: "My father used to say that a certain responsibility went with the territory—meaning with the money. Some well-to-do people donate libraries, or hospital wings, or playgrounds. We're hoping to donate a peaceful world free of the nuclear menace; that's where our money is going." She smiled faintly. "And the fact that we'll benefit, too, more than most people, since we have more to lose from a nuclear holocaust, isn't really a valid criticism, is it? The fact that you get to withdraw an occasional book yourself from the library you built for the general public doesn't invalidate the gift, does it?"

I said, "It sounds great, very charitable; but just where does a guy named Alfred Minister come in? Charity is not his big thing."

She said, "That's right, Amy told us. The fate of the world means nothing to you, does it? As long as you get the man you've been sent after."

"Considering this man's record," I said, "and the idealistic pretensions of your PNP group, he seems like a curious choice for you to employ. He puts you into some mighty funny company: first he was hired by that bloodthirsty group of so-called Argentinian patriots, then by the PLO, and now by your beautiful People for Nuclear Peace."

She laughed shortly. "Guilt by association, Matt? We'll take that chance, thank you. And what's curious about our choice? He's the best, isn't he? We wanted the best, and we were willing to pay his price, and we hired him. His past record doesn't concern us, except insofar as it indicates that he's good at his job. You managed to shake Amy's convictions, rather cruelly, by confronting her with that poor maimed woman in Coral Gables; but that's really ancient history and quite irrelevant, isn't it? We're under no illusions that Mr. Pope, as he's calling himself now, is a nice man; but he's what we need right now. A majority of the board of governors of the PNP voted in favor of employing him, myself included."

I said, "Very democratic. Suppose the majority had disagreed with you, what would have happened?"

She smiled thinly. "I might have used my persuasive powers to convince them that they were wrong; but I didn't have to. And where did you get the strange notion that we're idealistic, Matt? We're hard-headed individuals with a certain position in society who see our orderly and comfortable and rather pleasant world threatened by a bunch of madmen waving the ultimate weapon at each other. We're trying to make sure that these maniacs are placed under some kind of restraint. In the immortal words of Mae West: 'Goodness has nothing to do with it, dearie.' Idealism has nothing to do with it. We're not mushy sentimentalists like so many antibomb activists. The thought of all the little Japanese babies fried at Hiroshima doesn't bother me in the least; they started *that* at Pearl Harbor, and we just finished it for them. But the thing is getting out of control now, and nobody else seems willing to do anything about it, not even the delegates to the forthcoming Nassau convention, not really, judging by the interviews and reports we've been studying very carefully. So it's time somebody else took a hand, somebody who's willing to take drastic measures to insure the survival of our way of life. Our world, if you prefer."

"The PNP and Mr. Alfred Minister. Quite a team!"

"Opposed by one Constantine Grieg, dealer in chemical death, and one Matthew Helm, government assassin. Talking about guilt by association, what kind of a team do you call that?"

"Why does Grieg want you dead, Gina?" When she didn't answer, I said, "I'm supposed to find a mystery harbor belonging to him. Apparently it's down in

204

the outer islands somewhere. Do you know anything about it?"

She hesitated. "Yes," she said at last, "yes, as a matter of fact I do. That's what the fuss is all about; that's presumably the reason Connie Grieg is trying to have me killed, at least one of the reasons. And . . . and I haven't thanked you for saving me, have I?"

"Not exactly," I said.

She smiled crookedly. "I'm sorry, Matt. I'd never seen anybody die by violence before. I'd never heard the guns and seen the blood. All that blood! I guess I hadn't realized until then just what I'd got myself involved in, naive and sheltered me. I had never known what it was like to watch people killed. I guess I just didn't want to accept that I'd deliberately left my own world for a world where things like that could happen; I tried to make myself believe that it had nothing to do with me; that it was all on account of you." She drew a ragged breath. "I'm sorry. Please forgive me. And . . . and thanks!"

I said, "Sure. Can you thank me in a practical way, after we've visited Nassau, by taking me on to this smugglers' hideout, this Hole in the Wall? Or do I have to find it on my own?"

She laughed abruptly. "Hole in the Wall! Very picturesque. Your invention? The only trouble is, there's already a Hole in the Wall here in the Bahamas, a well-known anchorage at the tip of Great Abaco Island, northeast of Nassau. Probably a refuge for pirates and wreckers in the old days."

"I guess great outlaw minds think alike, on the sea as well as on land," I said. "And here I thought I was bringing a nice western flavor to the effete East! But whatever name we pick for Grieg's harbor, or he does, can you take me to it?"

She said cautiously, "Well, I can probably take you

205

closer to it than you could get on your own, even if you didn't get tangled up in a bunch of coral heads, poking around the banks in your landlubber fashion. It takes somebody who knows how to read that shallow water and figure the tides and currents. . . . But what makes you think I won't run you into a trap?"

I said, "Hell, I'm counting on it. Like you said, I'm the macho establishment warrior who's sure he can bust out of any trap you and your high-society friends set for him, right?"

For a moment her face had a bleak look. "I'm not sure I like this game, my dear. Sooner or later one of us is going to get badly hurt." Then she shrugged resignedly. "All right. I'll play, if you're nice to me and make me another drink. . . . No, I'll have it below, while I'm getting dinner ready." A few minutes later, turning from the stove to take a sip from her glass, she looked at me shrewdly and said, "You really liked that little girl, didn't you?"

I studied her face for a moment, wondering about her plans and motives: Was she going to guide me into a machine-gun ambush or just leave me stranded on a reef somewhere? Obviously, she'd been assigned— or had assigned herself, since she seemed to be pretty much in charge of things—to keep me busy, keep an eye on me, and take me out of action at the proper time, before I could interfere with Minister and the mysterious job he was doing for her and her PNP. For my part, I had no choice. We now had two leads to follow, and both of them were feminine. Well, Doug Barnett was presumably dealing with the Amy lead. It was up to me to stick with the Gina lead; and if it involved playing odd, schizophrenic, friend-enemy games with the lady, bluff and counterbluff, so be it.

"What brought that up?" I asked. "What makes you think I was so badly smitten?"

"She said so," Gina said dryly. "Of course, she

might have been deceiving herself, but your face says so, too. Right now you're resenting my messing around in *her* galley, just like a grieving widower hating to see another woman working in his late wife's kitchen. I'm surprised. I shouldn't think a man in your line of work would be subject to sentimental attachments."

"Oh, we kill and love with equal abandon," I said lightly.

Gina threw me a glance that had a good deal of malice in it. "Actually, she told us quite a bit about you," she said.

"Such as?"

"Well, of course she told us that you'd inherited her father's mission, to hunt down the man we'd hired under the name of Pope, but we'd already guessed that. Then she told us how you'd lectured her on the proper use of firearms and warned her what a vicious and ruthless person you were. And how you didn't seem to know too much about sailboats." Gina paused, then said casually without looking at me directly, "And weren't very good in bed."

I had the normal masculine reaction of outrage at this intimate betrayal; it seemed like an unnecessary piece of data for Amy to have passed along. Then I realized, or thought I realized, why she'd done it.

"What else?" I asked.

"That's about it, except for a few details."

My anger was replaced by a sense of relief and gratitude. Amy Barnett had carefully told her associates everything she'd learned from me and had even offered them a description of our awkward lovemaking to show she was holding nothing back—that is, she'd given them all the facts except the most important one, that her father, Doug Barnett, wasn't dead. She'd kept that secret as I'd asked her to. I was again aware of a sense of loss; and I wondered if I'd ever again see the smallish girl with the gray-blue eyes, the painful burden of guilt, and the intricate, tormenting system of loyalties. . . . I became aware that Gina had changed the subject.

"I always feel that Spam is a challenge," she said, steadying the gimbaled Shipmate stove to open the oven that neither Amy nor I had been brave enough to tackle. "I'll try to pick up some fresh meat and vegetables in Nassau; but let's see how this canned protein has turned out."

It had turned out quite well; although I've eaten too many strange concoctions off my lap with a gun handy to qualify as a gourmand even when dining at a table. But she'd dressed up the meat with brown sugar and cloves and done some interesting things to the accompanying canned vegetables and stirred up an intriguing dressing for the remaining salad makings she'd found in the icebox. We had canned peaches for dessert.

Afterward, lacking a proper after-dinner liqueur, we retired to the cockpit and sipped White Label straight with our coffee, serenaded by the small waves of the anchorage expending themselves against the sheltering rock. The sun had set, leaving a luminous starry blackness with a promise of later moonlight. There was apparently a small settlement up the inlet; we could see a couple of lights on the shore in that direction. Otherwise we seemed to have the Berry Islands to ourselves; but I'd turned on the anchor light anyway to alert any late arrivals to our presence.

"Why do you do it?" Gina asked at last.

"Do what?" Then, seeing the searching way she was looking at me in the dark, I grinned, understanding. "You mean, how did a nice girl like me wind up in a job like this? My God, lady! The tacky old question every sport asks every whore! I'll give you the tacky old answer: Just lucky, I guess."

She shook her head quickly. "No, I'm serious. It

baffles me. Why do you do this kind of work? You're an intelligent man; and not unattractive—"

I said, "And if that intelligent and not unattractive gentleman had been a normal American male brain-washed from childhood to keep himself perfectly safe and smelling sweet, and never, never spill a single drop of sacred human blood, where would you be right now? I'll tell you, Mrs. W., you'd be six hundred fathoms down in the Northwest Providence Channel, maybe with a spare anchor keeping your bloated body from popping to the surface."

She winced. "Ugh! Don't be so damn graphic!"

I said, "Don't sneer at my profession, sweetheart. There's got to be *something* out there smarter and tougher than punks like that fearsome foursome we encountered, or the world won't be a very nice place for the dainty nonviolent people who can't bear to get their hands gory. If I may flatter myself a bit, something like me. And I don't in the least mind admitting that I do it in part because of the good way it feels when they come in like that, like ducks to the decoys, thinking it's going to be easy because there are four of them and they've got guns. They've got to learn that they should be damn careful where they wave their silly popguns, no matter how many they are, because there are lots meaner people around who shoot lots better, too."

She said softly, "I'm sorry. I didn't mean to . . . I wasn't sneering." After a moment, she went on: "But the lesson is pretty well lost, isn't it, since those men are hardly in a position to pass the word."

I shrugged. "Connie Grieg knows he sent out a fast boat with four supposedly dangerous soldiers. When they don't come back, he'll start to wonder and worry, and it'll do him a world of good. And of course we don't know a thing about it, not a thing. Who, harmless little us?"

"Yes." She finished off the last of her whiskey, followed by the last of her coffee. She looked at me and spoke coolly: "Well, you probably know what's supposed to happen next, my dear; the real reason I had us anchor here. Now, of course, I'm supposed to seduce you."

I grinned. "You can't," I said.

Her eyes narrowed. "We'll probably be spending a good many nights together on this cramped little tub. Why put off the inevitable? Amy didn't say you were totally helpless in bed; and I've been told I'm not completely repulsive."

"I'm not and you're not," I said. "But these cockpit seats are pretty damn narrow and very hard, and we can't pull out either of the bunks below until we take care of all those dirty dishes so we can fold the cabin table out of the way."

Gina Williston laughed softly. "Damn these toy sailboats!" she murmured. "Well, we'd better get at it, then, hadn't we, darling? You wash and I'll dry."

TWO DIM little sticks poking out of the distant sea horizon were our first indications that New Providence Island lay ahead. They were the outlying navigational marks shown on the chart. Then the island itself began to appear beyond them: several low smudges way off where the water met the sky. The smudges gradually consolidated themselves into an un-even line of gray across our course, as *Spindrift* cruised along under sail at an easy three and four knots.

It was getting to be all in the day's work. Having already discovered Grand Bahama Island and the Berry Islands in the course of my heroic voyages of exploration, I was becoming pretty casual about having land pop out of the ocean in front of the bowsprit. Anyway, there's a considerable difference between doing it all yourself, as on our Gulf Stream crossing, and having somebody else responsible for the navigation. Here I was merely checking the Loran occasionally to make sure my handsome lady pilot wasn't up to any navigational tricks.

The fact that, dishes done, we'd spent the night sharing a bunk very intimately was quite irrelevant, of course. The last agent I knew who trusted a woman

because they'd spent the night in the same bed w:
buried young. But Gina Williston looked very good t
me this morning, even in her old white jeans and th
slightly grubby undershirt—excuse me, tank top—tha
revealed an odd bruise on one of her smooth brow
arms and some peculiar scratches on one of her smoo
brown shoulders. Well, I carried a few interestin
battle scars myself.

"It looks as if this death-defying passage migh
even wind up in the right place," she said, lowerin
the big binoculars through which she'd been studyir
the land ahead. "Right on course for Nassau, skippe
We should be picking up the fort above the tow
pretty soon. Fort Fincastle. Very picturesque an
totally useless, even way back when it was buil
Like Fort Jefferson on the Dry Tortugas."

"Or the Maginot Line?"

She laughed and studied my face for a moment. W
were sitting in the cockpit finishing our after-lunc
coffee while the Tiller Master steered the boat.

"Hey, you," she said softly.

I grinned. "Hey, yourself."

"You seem to do all right with older women. No
world-champion caliber, perhaps, but quite adequate.

"Thanks for the testimonial, Grandma."

She laughed. "In fact, very adequate," she said
bit ruefully, with a glance at her blemished shoulde
"I'd better put on a shirt before we come into harbo
hadn't I?"

"That," I said, "makes two of us."

"No problems at all. So what's the trouble with yo
and young girls? Usually it's the other way around;
takes the young ones to turn them on. Or is it jus
one particular young girl who chills you?" Gina glance
at me shrewdly. "I think I get it. She's a rathe
fragile personality, isn't she? And it would be a b
inhibiting, I guess, to make love to somebody yo

were afraid of damaging. Who the hell wants to be gentle in bed?"

"Not you, that's for sure," I said rather sharply.

She frowned at me, hurt. "Sorry. Most men don't mind talking about it. . . . Or are you angry because I took the little princess's name in vain?"

"You didn't," I said. "You don't even like to concede her right to have a name; she's always just an odd little nameless object that amuses you. What's the matter, can't you bear to talk about an attractive younger woman as if she were a real human being?" I shook my head quickly. "Don't get mad, Gina. You're a lovely lady, and I don't like to hear you making yourself sound cheap by forever sniping at the girl in that phony patronizing way. She's not all that young and helpless, and you know it. As for the two of us, what's to talk about? You can talk things to death, particularly good things like last night. So tell me what lines and fenders you're going to want when we come in, and where you'll want them."

By this time I had a pretty good idea what dockside equipment was required, but it wouldn't hurt to maintain her illusion that I was a nautical moron, totally dependent upon her instructions.

She shook her head. "No rush, it'll be several hours yet, even if the wind holds." She gave an odd little laugh. "You're a funny man, so sensitive in some ways. Considering what you do for a living. . . . Anyway, I guess what I really can't stand about Miss Amy Barnett is the way she reminds me I'm not getting any younger."

"I didn't notice any conspicuous signs of advancing senility last night. Gina . . ."

"Yes, Matt."

"The guidebook says we have to report by radio to Nassau Harbor Control before we pass the breakwater, right?"

213

"Yes. They like to be able to keep little yachts ou of the way when the big cruise liners are enterin and leaving."

"So anybody who's waiting to intercept us here wi know we're arriving just by listening to the VHF?"

"Yes. What are you driving at, darling?"

I said carefully, "It's an old maxim in the outfi 'What happens in bed has nothing to do with wha happens anywhere else.' "

She looked at me hard and licked her lips. "I don think I'm going to like what you're going to say whe you get around to saying it."

I said, "I don't expect you to betray your principle whatever they are, because of what happened be tween us last night. Don't expect me to betray min Whatever *they* are."

She laughed quickly. "Heavens, you sound as if yo thought I'd slept with you in order to influence . . .

She was trying to work up a convincing show being amused at the ridiculous idea, but the rig attitude wouldn't come. Her voice faded away uncel tainly. We sat in silence for a little, listening to th gurglings and splashings of the boat's steady pro ress southward.

At last I said, "You've made no attempt in a coup of days of sailing to run us aground or sabotage th boat in any way, so it seems that shipwreck is not o the agenda. Violence horrifies you, so it seems u likely that you really came aboard to slit my throa But you obviously came for a purpose, and what left? Why be shy about it now? You told me la night, quite honestly, that you were here to seduc me and we might as well get on with it, didn't you? seemed like a worthy night's project for two reaso ably experienced, unattached adults, so I was happ to be seduced. And I have no complaints whateve Mrs. W.; I simply don't want any misunderstandings.

214

She licked her lips. "Matt, I . . ."

When she left the sentence uncompleted, I said, "Let's assume that there's something your organization wants this conscientious government employee to do, or not do, that's not entirely consistent with his assigned federal duties. Since she was already established here on board, Amy was the logical person to do the persuading, using the customary feminine techniques; but apparently she didn't have the stomach for the job. If stomach is the right word. She hadn't had enough experience with sex to be willing to use it in that calculating way; she still clings to the naive notion that the sexual act should have something to do with affection, not to use a big word like love. So your PNP outfit pulled rookie Barnett out of the game and put in Williston, a seasoned veteran of the playing fields of *amour*. No qualms, no conscience, right? But talk about naive! The shabby old Mata Hari routine, for Christ's sake! Lady, do you know how many times this gag's been pulled on me in the line of business?"

She spoke at last: "You're the one who didn't want to talk it to death. What do you think you're doing now?"

I said, "I know, but it occurred to me that there are worse ways of spoiling it; and I don't want them to happen to us. Your head may be full of ingenious plans, Gina, and Nassau may be full of your PNP troops all ready to pounce on me as we dock, or later. Or deal with me some other way, once you pass the word that you've got me amorously softened up, an easy mark. Don't let them. Keep them out of my hair, doll, all of them. Remember what you saw, and didn't like, out in the Northwest Providence Channel two nights ago."

She said stiffly, "You're being a little paranoid, aren't you? A moment ago you were saying you didn't

215

think I'd been sent to kill you; now you talk as if you expect me to lead you into a murder trap the minute we set foot on shore."

"I don't know what to expect," I said. "Amateurs confuse hell out of me. They never behave logically by my standards, which is why I want to cover all possibilities. Let me make my position clear, Gina. I have two missions going here. Immediately, I'm supposed to locate a certain mysterious harbor, for reasons that have not been confided to me. Eventually, I'm supposed to locate and deal with a certain unpleasant individual who's been declared, shall we say, overdue. Maybe these two operations are intertwined; maybe they aren't. I don't know enough to decide that yet. Maybe you do. But whether you do or not, please don't interfere in any way. Don't let your associates interfere. Regardless of how we spent last night, I won't go around you if you get in my way. I'll go right over you, baby, and that goes for your friends, too. I'd regret it terribly if I had to hurt you; I'd regret it all my life. But there are already lots of things and people I regret, and I can live with a few more. End of proclamation."

A little gust of wind caused *Spindrift* to heel sharply. A wave sloshed over the leeward rail and ran along the deck. The knotmeter needle hit five on the dial, and then six, trying for seven. We waited to see if action should be taken to prevent the boat from being overpowered, but the gust soon died away and the speed dropped back to where it had been.

Gina spoke as if there had been no pause: "You really are an arrogant man!"

"Hell, I said please, didn't I?" I made a sharp gesture. "Yesterday you were screaming at me because I mowed down some pistol-toting goons without warning. So today, because I like you and enjoyed making love to you, I'm giving you warning; and you're still calling me names. A man can't win around here!"

She said maliciously, "I do believe he's mad at me because he's got a guilty conscience! He's had two different women in his bunk in four days, and it makes him feel terribly wicked and promiscuous. I think that's sweet!"

We glared at each other. She was perfectly right, of course. I'd made a certain emotional commitment to one lady and before I'd resolved that situation, one way or another, I'd wound up in bed with another, and it bothered me—perfectly ridiculous for a man in my line of work who'd been around as long as I had. I felt my mouth twitch, and I saw little crinkles of amusement appear at the corners of her fine eyes. Suddenly we were both laughing.

Then we stopped, looking at each other in a totally different way. More of a sailor than I, she instinctively threw a quick glance around to make sure no dangers were bearing down on us. There was a sail far ahead and a fishing vessel passing in the distance to starboard, but nothing was close enough to bother us very soon. Gina smiled and came into my arms. The knitted upper garment was no problem, or the denim lower garment, or the surprisingly pretty little nylon panties underneath that seemed to suggest she'd considered the possibility that they might somehow get exposed to my view when she'd elected to wear them today. Far from being disturbed by this evidence of calculation, I found it rather touching. We discovered that the cockpit seat, although not as soft as the bunk below, wasn't really as impractical for the purpose as we'd thought.

It felt pleasantly illicit to lie there afterward, with a couple of life-preserver cushions for comfort and a warm woman for company, in the bright Bahamas sunshine under the clear blue sky without a stitch of clothes on. The autopilot made its little whirring sounds as it guided our twenty-eight-foot ship toward the land that was gaining color and substance ahead.

Gina touched my shoulder. "I didn't realize last night what a beat-up object you are, darling. Bullet-holes?"

"Oh, that. An ancient submachine gun with corroded ammunition. Lucky for me. It jammed after three or it would have taken my arm off."

"Where did it happen?"

"That was in Norway, quite a while back. Maybe I should have my scars labeled with place and date, like museum exhibits. Do you know a tattoo artist who needs a job?"

"I'm sorry, I didn't mean to be snoopy."

I looked at her face, very close, and said, "Let's consider that your mission is a success and you have me madly in love with you, totally infatuated, all willpower destroyed. Just what is it that you want me to do for you?"

There was a little pause. "Let him live," Gina said at last. "Let him live long enough to do his job for us."

"Minister? Your Alfred Pope? I haven't found him yet."

"You will. I'll even take you to him, if . . ." She hesitated. "We discussed all kinds of ways of dealing with you, some pretty drastic. And one man's life shouldn't really count for much, considering what's at stake; but I can't bear the thought of any additional violence. Unnecessary violence. It's going to be bad enough, ugly enough, without that. So if you give your word . . . Just promise not to touch him until he's finished his work for us. After that he's all yours."

I started to tell her sharply that I wasn't as easy to kill as she seemed to think; but I'd already done my breast-beating exercises for the day. And it wasn't my place to inform her that honor and words of honor don't play a very large part in the business.

I said, "I have no authority to commit Washington or any other agents who may be assigned to the job. I can only speak for myself."

"That's all we ask. That's all I ask."

"Before I commit myself," I said carefully, "I really ought to know what Minister is doing for you."

"I can't tell you that. It's not my secret; at least not mine alone. But it's nothing you'd disapprove of, I swear it."

That seemed unlikely. Alfred Minister had never yet, to my knowledge, done anything I approved of; and there was no reason he should start now.

I said, "Okay. You've got a deal."

After a moment, she sat up on the cockpit seat to look at me, frowning. "You said that much too easily, Matt. You're holding something back."

I had a mental image of that supposed suicide Doug Barnett, very much alive, sniffing industriously along the trail of the man responsible for the shattered body, and the shattered life, of the woman he'd hoped to marry, like a persistent hound on the track of a marauding mountain lion. And I'd made it quite clear that I wasn't committing him to anything, only myself. It was a small price to pay for the information about Minister's whereabouts Gina could supply.

"Sure," I said cheerfully. "Aren't you?"

When we approached the harbor entrance and got on the VHF, Nassau Harbor Control told us to sail right in and make ourselves at home. It's a long, skinny harbor, or you could call it a wide channel, between the large bulk of Providence Island to the south, on which the business and residential districts are located, and the narrow strip of Paradise Island to the north that holds the casino and the fancy new hotels—although the enormous pink structure of the old Sheraton Colonial Hotel, which confronts you on the southern shore as you pass the breakwaters, is pretty fancy, too. The first time I'd visited the Bahamas, a good many years earlier, it had been known as the British Colonial, but times do change.

With our little diesel thumping bravely under our feet, Gina steered us past the cruise-ship docks and under the arching bridge, which, seventy feet high over the channel, shouldn't have made me nervous about our forty-foot mast but did. Turning sharply toward Paradise Island to port, she guided *Spindrift* into the small, sheltered basin of the Hurricane Hole Marina and docked us expertly in the slip to which we were directed. If I'd had any strong masculine pride in my own boat-handling abilities, I might have been envious of her skill. As it was, I simply admired a smart job of maneuvering. I wished she were equally smart in other respects. Any woman who considered seduction a reliable weapon against an experienced government agent had obviously been watching too much TV. It scared me to think of what other naive and dangerous Hollywood notions might have taken up residence in her handsome head.

"The marinas over in Nassau are cheaper," she said as we finished tying up, "but they're so big and busy it would be hard to tell if anybody was sneaking up on us there. I thought we'd be better off here; and it's more comfortable, too. The facilities are cleaner and you don't get the wash of the harbor traffic." After a moment, she went on in a casual way, "I can find out where Connie-the-Big-Man lives, if you're interested."

The Hurricane Hole Marina was surrounded by a grassy parklike area. It was bordered, in the vicinity of our slip, by a rather dense grove of trees that could have sheltered a regiment of hostile riflemen. We'd have been safer at a big open dock, no matter how crowded. I wished the lady would concentrate on the sailing, at which she was good, and leave to me the strategy, at which she wasn't. But now that we'd made our deal, it wasn't my job to second-guess her, just to follow wherever she wanted to take me, short of the grave.

"You're keeping an eye on Grieg's house?" I asked. "Your people are?"

Gina nodded. "Yes. I don't have the address in my head, but I can get it for you. We're watching both his houses, as a matter of fact. He's got another one over in West Palm; that's his respectable domicile complete with beautiful wife and cute kiddies. Two cute kiddies, one of each. But he conducts his drug operations from here, with a mistress in attendance. I can have somebody check and see if he's in residence."

I regarded her for a moment, then shook my head sadly. "There are things to be said for frankness, sweetheart. I have a lot more respect for an honest wench who comes right out and asks me to murder a man for her than for a sneaky female who just hints around it."

Her eyes wouldn't meet mine. "My God, you can't think I meant—"

"If not, why bother to tell me about Mr. Grieg? What the hell do I care where he lives and whether or not he's in residence? All I want is the location of his secret cay, and I'm not likely to get that by knocking on his door and asking."

Gina said, "You killed his men. When he learns about it, and he will, he's bound to retaliate in some way, isn't he? I thought you might want to forestall that by, well, striking first."

"I thought you were the little girl who was trying to avoid unnecessary violence."

Her voice was suddenly harsh: "That's when we were talking about human beings, Matt. Even nasty,

221

violent human beings like you. But Constantine Grieg does not qualify as human. You know what he does! You know what he sells!"

I looked at her sharply and said, "Hell, I thought we were nobly battling the nuclear menace, or you were. Now all of a sudden we're engaged in a corny crusade against drugs and drug smugglers. What a let-down!"

"You don't mean that! You can't possibly condone . . ."

I frowned, bewildered. "How the hell did we get into this? I don't know a damn thing about drugs, sweetheart. An occasional Scotch or martini does the job for me, and I've never monkeyed with the other stuff except when I had to go through the motions to make a cover look authentic. But the world seems to be lousy with people just panting to save other people from chemical perdition, and I leave them to it. Certainly at the moment I've got more important business, and I thought you did, too. Let's keep our collective eyes on the atomic ball, huh, and let the marijuana fall where it may."

"That's a dreadfully callous attitude!"

"I'm a dreadfully callous guy. And I didn't come all this way to make a touch on a pot king for high moral reasons, even if it would make a lovely lady very happy, the bloodthirsty bitch."

She said sullenly, "Nevertheless, I'm right, and you know it! If you don't do something about him, he's going to do something about you, he's bound to. And me, too. After all, he's already responsible for one attempt on my life."

I sighed. "Okay, you get on the phone and locate him, and I'll see what I can work out. I've got a couple of calls to make, too. And then let's clean up the ship and ourselves and go out and have a good dinner on the town, like a nice yachting couple relaxing after a tough ocean voyage."

"Matt." She reached out to touch my arm as I started to turn away. Her anger had evaporated, and her expression was apologetic. "Matt, I'm sorry. I didn't mean to . . . There are things you don't know about me. If you knew, you'd understand."

I said, "I'm making some guesses."

"I know. You're good at that." Suddenly she laughed and rose on tiptoe to kiss me on the mouth. "But keep them to yourself, or my lawyers will sue you for slander. God, a shower is going to feel good, isn't it? But *first* we clean up the ship, Mister, before we do anything else, or people will think we're a couple of seagoing slobs. . . ."

Later, chores done, we hiked across the high toll bridge in the fading evening light—cars two bucks; pedestrians free—to have dinner at the Bridge Inn, a noisy, colorful place that served us some elderly and inedible shrimp that Gina insisted on sending back to the kitchen. She was right, of course, but I wasn't really in the mood for hassling a waiter about a shellfish when more serious conflicts awaited me. The rest of the meal was better but still nothing to bring tears of joy to the eyes of Duncan Hines.

"What is it with us?" Gina asked softly as we sipped our coffee afterward.

"What do you mean?"

"You and I," she said. "We do get along after a fashion, we even fight in a comfortable way. I call you violent and nasty, and you call me a bloodthirsty bitch, and we're friends again. But how can you stand me? I'm a shallow society tramp who's slept with everything in pants, and a few things in skirts just for variety. A few years back, after . . . after a rather traumatic experience, I got religion of sorts and decided I'd better save the world, but that doesn't make me a very good person, really. After all, it's just a matter of self-preservation. As I think I said before, we rich folks have even more reason not to want our world blown up than the poor folks; we've got more to lose. It's only good sense for us to do what we can to keep the poor old globe in one piece. But even if I'm engaged in a reasonably worthy project for a change, it doesn't make me a very lovable individual, does it?"

This was a new Georgina Williston, humble and self-critical and a little frightening, considering the arrogant and dictatorial sailing expert I'd had to deal with on the boat.

"Maybe I hate lovable individuals," I said.

She shook her head quickly. "No. Your lovable Amy girl is just the type I'd expect you to go for. A kind of atonement. The poor kid *needs* somebody, or you think she does; and I suspect that way in the back of your mind is a nagging guilt for all the people you've damaged and killed in the line of business. Here's a way for you to redress the balance just a little; so you try to make up to her for her hating parents and the men who've used her for their own gratification without a thought of what they might be doing to the girl herself. You're kind and gentle with her, so gentle you can hardly perform when the time comes. Just what I'd expect from what I know about you. But what the hell are you doing making eyes at this beat-up society babe on her two-bit save-the-world crusade?"

"Don't run yourself down like that, Gina."

She shook her head, dismissing my words, and went on harshly: "And what am I doing, getting mushy about the kind of gun-toting macho bastard I detest?" She drew a long breath and glanced at her watch. "Seven-thirty. Enough of this philosophical crap. Let's check our weapons and go see this Grieg bastard."

"No weapons," I said. "The arrangements have been made, and it's strictly a social visit."

"I don't pay social visits to people who traffic in human suffering!"

I said, "Cut it out, Gina. Give your moral superiority a rest. And what's all this loose talk about weapons? Are you carrying?"

"Carrying?"

"A gun?" I watched her eyes betray her; and I had her purse before she could pull it away. Inside, I found a little .25 auto that I'd hidden on the boat in what I'd thought was a pretty secure place. "You've been snooping," I said. "Did you find the chopper in the bilge, too?"

"There weren't any weapons in the bilge." She frowned. "I thought a chopper was a helicopter."

"Back in the old Capone days it stood for a tommy gun. In those days they didn't have a lot of helos flying around to confuse the issue." I pushed my chair back. "Let's go see *el Hombre Grande*. The Big Man."

‖‖‖‖‖‖ CHAPTER 21 ‖‖‖‖‖‖‖‖‖‖‖‖‖‖‖‖‖‖‖‖‖‖‖‖‖‖‖‖‖‖‖‖‖‖

HE WAS big all right. Rising to greet us, he made the massive desk in front of him look like toy furniture. At six four and two hundred I'm no midget, although I'm more bones than meat; but Grieg had me beat by an inch or two vertically. Horizontally, it was no contest at all. A real mountain of a man.

With whiskers, he'd have looked like a grizzly bear in a three-piece suit. Perhaps this was the reason he was so carefully shaved, after-shaved, and talcumed, with his wavy black hair trimmed closer than fashionable these shaggy days. Even with the hair neatly clipped his head still looked plenty big enough for his enormous body. His skin was dark olive. His eyes were brown, under bushy black eyebrows. His suit was brown, his shirt was striped brown and white, and his brown tie was very neatly tied. His shoes I couldn't see for the desk.

With all this expanse of civilized attire confronting me, I was glad I'd dressed up for dinner in the only suit I'd brought along, blue, and the only tie, blue with a pattern of white; and that Gina was wearing her little white denim dress, nicely upgraded by high-heeled white pumps and some discreetly expensive jewelry, so that it looked as smart as if it were silk or satin—actually smarter in its understated way.

But the statuesque blonde behind Greig was more dramatic. She was wearing shiny, skintight, raspberry-red pants that looked as if they'd glow in the dark and a loose, lacy, sleeveless white top that made no great effort to conceal her spectacular pectoral development. She was almost six feet tall. Her piled-up golden hair and high-heeled sandals jacked her up well past the two-yard mark. The big man and woman made a formidable couple, standing there. I wondered what the wife in West Palm Beach was like. Perhaps she was a pale, downtrodden little mouse—but Gina had described her as beautiful. A clever, passionless woman, then, who was happy to share the task of satisfying the giant she'd married as long as the sharing was done in another country and didn't affect her pride or her home or her income. Or maybe she was a perfectly innocent married lady who knew nothing about her husband's illicit business or his illicit love. But it didn't seem likely.

The fifth person in the room, kind of guarding the door behind Gina and me, was small and mustached and Oriental. He looked like an undertaker's assistant in his black suit. I had a hunch that he might have helped the undertaking business along a bit from time to time at that, with the gun that showed just a little under his armpit. He'd been waiting for us outside the iron gates of the estate, coming to the taxi as it stopped and getting in beside the driver.

"I am Coyote," he'd said over his shoulder as, on his signal, the gateman pushed the button that made the iron barrier swing open for us. Then the man who'd called himself Coyote had continued: "The lady will please to give the gun in her purse to the gentleman. So. Take care of it for her, mister, please.

227

We have word of your reliability. We have none of hers. Please excuse."

We'd ridden up the drive through the trees, in the dark, getting no real notion of the place except that there was a lot of it. Coyote had helped Gina out politely at the door and escorted her inside, letting me trail along behind. I wasn't sure whether it was more a sign of his trust in me or of his mistrust of her. We'd been ushered into a big study, or office, to meet the folks.

Now Connie spoke to me, in a deep voice consistent with his size: "I got a call from Miami Beach, Mr. Velo on the line. I don't take orders from Giuseppe Velo; but I'm not too proud to take advice. He said you'd called him. He said if you wanted to talk to me I'd better let you, sometimes you made sense. So talk."

I said, "Talking is better than shooting, Mr. Grieg."

I reached into my shirt pocket, making the movement slow and deliberate. I walked forward, still moving with deliberation, placed a slip of paper on the desk, and moved back cautiously. My back felt very vulnerable. When a man, Oriental or Occidental, calls himself by a silly menace-name like Coyote, you don't want to take any chances with him. He's trying to prove something, and he might try to prove it on you. The big man behind the desk reached out for the piece of paper and sat down to study it, frowning a little.

"A position at sea?" he said. "But what's the number three thousand four hundred and eighty-six supposed to mean?"

I said, "You sail one of your ships to twenty-six degrees and ten minutes north latitude, seventy-eight degrees and twenty minutes west longitude. Then you climb into your little submersible or bathysphere and go three thousand four hundred and eighty-six feet straight down. They ought to be right there, at those coordinates, along with their hot-rod boat."

There was a lengthy silence. I saw Grieg looking down at his desk, the top of which was actually a large chart of the Caribbean, the Bahamas, and part of Florida, sealed under transparent plastic.

"Thirty miles northwest of Great Stirrup Light." He spoke without expression. "Well, that would be about the spot all right."

Sudden anger made the woman step forward to stare over his shoulder. Unlike Grieg, she didn't have a voice to match her size. You'd think she'd sing contralto, but what came out was a rather shrill soprano.

"Christ, this is Pauli and his boys the skinny bastard's talking about!"

"I know what he's talking about." Grieg spoke quite mildly. He looked at me. "You got all four of them? How? A torpedo at the waterline? A grenade in the cockpit?"

I said, "I won't pry into your professional secrets, Mr. Grieg, if you don't pry into mine. All you need to know is that they're down there and that they're dead."

"They'd damn well have to be dead, almost six hundred fathoms down, wouldn't they?" He stared at me across the big desk. "I guess you think you're pretty good."

I said, "What you should be considering is the fact that if the time ever comes that I'm not good enough, others will be sent who are. There's a man in Washington who doesn't care for civilian interference in his operations, particularly if it costs him an agent. No matter how long it takes, it will be a losing game for you in the end, if you insist on keeping it going. If Mr. Velo didn't warn you, he should have."

"He warned me." After a pause, Grieg spoke in a

changed tone of voice: "What's with you and a retired old syndicate character like Seppi?"

I said, "In the line of duty, I once arranged for the removal of a man Mr. Velo didn't happen to like. Quite coincidental; but ever since he's loved me like a son."

"That would do it all right." Connie frowned at me. "And what's your interest in me?"

I said, "Hell, until your floating goon squad tried to kill me, I barely knew you existed, Mr. Grieg."

"They weren't after you."

"They weren't going to give me a lollipop and turn me loose to talk afterward, no matter whom they were after," I said. "Anyway, I don't concern myself much with the goals and motives and life ambitions of people who wave guns at me. I simply assume their intentions are not peaceful and act accordingly. I've survived quite a long time that way." I studied him thoughtfully. "Basically, I'm not interested in imports or exports, Mr. Grieg. Your business is really no business of mine. We don't work for the Drug Enforcement Agency at all. Currently we're getting some cooperation from the U.S. Coast Guard and, I presume, giving some in return; but if I know my chief, he's not primarily concerned with illicit substances or whatever they're called officially these days. But for some reason he's ordered me to locate a certain little harbor or mooring basin in which you seem to have an interest. . . . What's the matter?"

He was scowling at me. "What are you trying to pull, Helm? Why play dumb? Your pretty partner knows all about Ring Cay; don't try to tell me she hasn't told you!"

I glanced at Gina, standing calm and handsome beside me. I said, "Take a good look at her. Does she look as if she'd tell anybody anything she didn't want to? The fact that we're sailing together doesn't mean that our purposes are identical, Mr. Grieg. Maybe you'd better tell me what's going on."

When Grieg hesitated, the blond woman in the shiny pants spoke up in her high and rather unpleasant voice: "What's going on is a goddamn hijacking, that's what's going on!"

"Shut up, Lorena!" Then Grieg shrugged massively. "Ah, to hell with it. That's about it, Helm. That bitch beside you and her friends waved all the money in the world under Howie Brasso's nose—he was one of my two top boys; Coyote is the other—and Howie sold me out." There was sadness and wonder in the big man's voice. "Hell, I loved the guy like a brother, and he sold me out!"

"I will kill very slowly," Coyote said softly. "He will make a long die!"

"First we have to find him." Grieg's voice was grim. "He took the loot and ran. Mexico, South America, Europe, who knows? But sooner or later somebody'll recognize him, wherever he is, and pass the word, and then he'll make 'a long die,' as the man says." He threw Gina an ugly glance. "In the meantime there are some others who aren't going to get away with—"

"Sold out what?" I said.

"Ring Cay, for one thing. He arranged for this bitch's friends—I don't know if she was there or not, but she set it up—to sneak up on my boys at night and take them by surprise. The fucking people for nuclear fucking peace jumping my guards with their peaceful fucking machine pistols and sending them off in their boats and taking over *my* island and *my* installations like a bunch of Jolly Roger pirates!"

"Couldn't your men fight back?"

"Hell, with Howie to tell the attacking bastards where everybody was posted, and give the right light signals as they went in, nobody suspected a thing.

I'm told it was over in fifteen minutes, not a shot fired. Sure, I could bring in a bunch of hard guys, fix them up with guns and boats, and stage a fucking amphibious assault to retake the place, like Tarawa or something; and by the time the shooting was over everybody in the Bahamas would know about Ring Cay and the place would be as much use to me as a big saltwater swimming pool."

"Anything else?" I asked when he stopped for breath. "Any other grievances?"

"Damn right there's something else! The *Carmen Saiz!*"

"What's a *Carmen Saiz?*"

"One of my ships. Five hundred and fifty tons gross. A hundred and sixty feet. Thirteen-foot draft, loaded; she can just make it into the dredged basin when the tide is high. Takes a good ship-handler, and some pushing and hauling with the little boats, but it can be done."

"What about the *Carmen Saiz?*"

Grieg threw another wicked look at Gina. "This dame and her airy-fairy society friends took all that money they seem to have lying around and bought the *Saiz* out from under me. They took her over in spite of my charter agreement with her owners. Well, those greedy bastards are already wishing they hadn't dreamed of becoming instant *ricos* off one lousy five-hundred-ton rustbucket. Coyote woke them up a little, right, *amigo?*"

"No double-cross more, I don't think," Coyote said.

I shrugged. "I should think little coastal freighters like that would be a dime a dozen."

"With the trade booming like it is, anything that floats is made of gold. But the thing is, when they took this one, my cargo was already on board."

"I can see how that might hurt a little," I said. "Where's the MV *Carmen Saiz* now?"

Grieg shrugged his enormous shoulders. "How the hell would I know? Ask her!" He glared at the woman beside me. "And ask her where my cargo is while you're at it."

I turned to Gina. "Well?"

Her face was expressionless. "Well, what?"

"You heard the man. He expressed a desire to know where his cargo is. Quite a natural desire, it seems to me."

Gina licked her lips. "Do you know *what* cargo that ship was carrying?"

I said irritably, "What is this, a guessing game? I assume it isn't lumber and it isn't coal and it isn't oil but it burns pretty good anyway. What the hell do I care what it is? Why the hell do you care what it is? I told you before, keep your eye on the ball, honeybunch. You've got something important to do, right? At least you seem to consider it important. You haven't let me know exactly what it is, yet, but I don't believe it involves saving the world from evil organic compounds. So why confuse the issue by stealing a load of pot?"

"Stealing!" she gasped. "How can anybody steal something that's totally illegal? All we did was prevent several tons of poison from being distributed to thousands of innocent victims. . . ."

"Oh, for Christ's sake!"

I stared at her, baffled. As I'd told her, I am not and have never been a user of anything but booze, in what I consider to be reasonably modest quantities. But there wasn't a chance in the world that Mrs. Georgina Williston, in the social circles in which she moved, hadn't smoked her share of marijuana, the stuff she was now referring to as poison. Hell, she'd undoubtedly sniffed her share of cocaine as well, not to mention experimenting with more dangerous and exotic substances.

For her now to go into self-righteous convulsions

about a shipload of grass, not even heroin, was disturbing, to say the least. It indicated that she must have undergone a rather extensive personality change somewhere along the line. I remembered that she'd mentioned getting religion, as she'd called it, after a rather traumatic experience, exact nature unspecified. . . .

I said, "Give your righteous indignation a rest and tell us about the *Carmen Saiz*."

She shrugged in an ugly way. "All right! We wanted to take her over before she sailed for Colombia, but the owners were slow and the paperwork took longer than we'd expected. She slipped away from us. But then, coming back loaded, she had a breakdown and put in at . . . Well, never mind where, let's just say a small, tolerant harbor not too far off her course. We'd been keeping track of her. In fact we had a man on board who was reporting to us. We had her picked up there, with the aid of her officers and the port authorities. They were, shall we say, amenable to reason."

"Negotiable reason," I said.

Gina smiled cynically. "Most people are amenable to negotiable reason, my dear, if the amount is large enough."

"What the hell do you need a ship for? Come to that, what the hell do you need an island for?"

"I can't tell you that."

Behind us, the man called Coyote said, "I can make to tell."

I saw that Gina didn't flinch at the threat. I said, "Never mind that right now. Mr. Grieg isn't interested in that. He wants to know about his cargo."

Gina licked her lips, facing me. She spoke carefully: "The cargo space was needed for . . . for other things. And we couldn't in good conscience let the lousy stuff loose on the market, could we? Even if there had

234

been some practical way of returning it to its owner. The question was referred to me. I gave the order to jettison Mr. Grieg's cargo at sea." She gave us a tight little smile. "It's happened before, when smuggling ships ran into legal or mechanical trouble. Hell, there are so many burlap-wrapped bales floating around out there that the fisherman have a name for them: square grouper."

The standing woman started to say something indignant, but the seated man grasped her wrist hard enough to make her wince, and she was silent. I heard Coyote shift position behind me. Constantine Grieg regarded me bleakly, his eyes very narrow. He was obviously exerting considerable effort to control himself.

"Do you know what that shit was worth that the bitch ordered thrown overboard?"

I said, "If the Coast Guard or the shoreside authorities had grabbed it, I'm sure it would have been worth several million dollars in the newspapers. They like to call it street value; a better name would be publicity value. But you didn't pay several million for it down in Colombia. And you wouldn't have made that from it."

"I paid plenty, friend! And I would have made plenty! And I've taken plenty from her and her fancy friends because I had a good thing going here and who wants to rock the boat? But if this high-and-mighty dame thinks she can get away with taking over my harbor, taking over my ship, and dumping my property in the ocean, and then coming here and snooting me because my business isn't exactly legal . . . Shit, what's legal about what she's doing, waving machine guns around and bribing folks and breaking ironclad ship leases? What's she got to be so fucking proud about?" He drew a long, ragged breath and spoke in a totally different tone, almost gently, "Okay, Helm. Seppi Velo says you're smart. Be smart."

I said carefully, watching him, "It would seem that reparations are in order. Is that what you had in mind?"

He sighed. "It would gripe my soul, but it would do my bank account a lot of good; and I'm not in business for my soul. Yes, that's smart. But will she play?"

Gina spoke angrily: "Matt, if you think for a moment I'm going to pay—"

I said, "Don't go off half-cocked now, Mrs. W. You were willing to buy Brasso and the ship and its officers and the port authorities in that place, wherever it is. Willing and obviously able. So why not pay your way all the way? Why jeopardize your whole project, whatever it may be, by making people mad unnecessarily?"

She said hotly, "I wouldn't put one red cent into the bank account of a man who's gotten rich off other people's misery!"

I said, "Hell, you got to destroy a whole shipload of other people's misery, didn't you? Didn't that make you feel great? Why expect your fun to be free?"

"Matt, I—"

I said, *"Listen* to me! You went at Mr. Grieg, here, with your weapon, money. Now he's coming back at you with his weapons, guns. How are you planning to fight him? Thousand-dollar bills are nice, and I'm sure you've got a lot of them, but they aren't bulletproof." When she hesitated and gave me a searching glance, I said quickly, "Oh, no, you don't! I bailed you out once because there are too many people around who don't like me, strange as it may seem, for me to let a bunch of armed, unidentified thugs get the drop on me. But if you won't be reasonable, to hell with you. You're on your own, and I don't think you can handle Mr. Coyote, there, even if I give you back the toy pistol you swiped from me." I shook my head. "Don't be stupid, Gina, just because you happen to feel so strongly about drugs. All the man wants is to be paid for the damage you've done him, am I right, Mr. Grieg?"

Connie nodded heavily. "That's not all I want, not by a long shot! But I'm a businessman and I'll settle for that."

I spoke to Gina: "You've been throwing your dough around—your organization's dough—all over the Caribbean, apparently. Now throw a little his way, and he'll be off your neck, and you can get on with your great work, whatever it may be."

There was a long silence. At last Gina cleared her throat and asked stiffly, "How much dough is a little dough? And how do I throw it? I don't suppose he'll take my check. . . ."

JUST AS we were about to go out the front door
under escort, business completed, a rather pretty
young black girl in a maid's uniform came running
and said breathlessly that Mr. Grieg would like to see
the gentleman again for a moment; the lady should
wait with Coyote, please. I went back into the
study/office to find the picture unchanged. He was
still sitting at his desk and she was still standing
behind him. Or again. As I came up, he shoved a
piece of paper toward me. I picked it up. It was the
paper I'd given him; but the position I'd written had
been scratched out and a new latitude and longitude
inserted. I looked at him across the desk.

"Ring Cay," he said. "That's what you wanted,
isn't it?"

"Yes," I said. "Thank you."

"To hell with your thanks. I just hope it helps you
screw the lousy bitch but good," Connie said.

The standing woman said, "Hell, they're already
screwing, can't you tell?"

"That wasn't the kind of screwing I had in mind "
Connie said.

Then we were driving away in the taxi that, to my

surprise, had waited patiently for us instead of returning to town. I wondered how much the bill was going to be. We'd been dealing in fairly astronomical figures in the ornate mansion behind us—well, Gina and Connie had—but now we were back on earth again; and I don't like to put excessive cab fares on the expense account, it makes for arguments with the agency money-counters.

I reflected that it would be nice to be rich. If I want a few hundred bucks cash from my checking account, I have to wait until the bank opens and take it out myself; but apparently, if you want a few hundred thousand, and your account is big enough, like Gina's, the banker will make a house call. Well, actually he'd sent the money in care of a neatly dressed young black gofer with a handsome attaché case. It had taken a while to arrange, of course. It was still night, but looking out the cab window I saw that a large orange moon, which hadn't even been up when we arrived, was now setting in the west. Coyote rode with us through the gate and got out and sent us on our way.

"A Chinaman called Coyote, for God's sake," Gina said, glancing back as we rode away.

"I don't think they like to be called Chinamen."

"Frenchmen don't mind. Englishmen, Scotchmen, Welshmen, Irishmen don't mind. Why should a lousy chink be so finicky? To hell with what he likes or doesn't like!" She hesitated, then asked curiously, "How did he know my purse had a gun in it, earlier?"

"That's easy. You were holding it as if it had a gun in it." I reached into my pocket and fished out the little weapon and handed it to her. "Just in case you feel like shooting somebody. Me, for instance. I wouldn't want you to feel frustrated."

"Hell, you probably took the bullets out of it."

"You're way behind the times, sweetheart. You

239

don't load modern guns with bullets. It's a great new invention that's going to revolutionize firearms, called fixed ammunition. Beats hell out of ramming those crummy lead bullets on top of all that loose gunpowder, not to mention messing with those lousy flints or percussion caps. You load a modern gun with cartridges. Or unload it. But I didn't, you can check."

She did, then dropped the weapon into her purse. She didn't look at me. Something was on her mind, and she was obviously stalling when she spoke again.

"I wonder if that blond Amazon likes standing around like that in her high heels, or if it's just that she can't sit down without splitting those shiny pants."

"I wouldn't mind splitting her shiny pants for her."

"Don't talk so tough and dirty. Anyway, she's out of your class, little boy. That one would wring you dry and hang you out with the wash. Matt?"

"Yes?"

"You're curious, aren't you? So ask your goddamn question."

I shrugged. "If you insist. What's with you and drugs? Or what was with you and drugs? I'd say you're pretty clean now." After a moment, when she didn't answer immediately, I spoke carefully: "The information we got said you'd spent some time in an expensive sanatorium. Nobody could find out what for."

"That's why it's expensive." She sat beside me in the moving taxi, looking straight ahead into the night. "I woke up under restraint," she said tonelessly after a little. "That's polite for being strapped down like a crazy, which I was. They said I'd OD'd on the stuff, some stuff, I never remembered what. I was trying all kinds of weird crap back then. But they brought me back and kept me from hurting myself, maiming myself, killing myself, I was that crazy. I weighed ninety-two pounds. I jittered helplessly for weeks.

I'd wake up in the night screaming. I cried for hours at a time for no reason. I couldn't think straight; couldn't think at all. When I could get out of bed at last, there was this sickening, stringy-haired skeleton-like thing in the mirror with a mouth that twitched uncontrollably in the dull-eyed skull face that didn't belong to anybody I knew." She swallowed hard. "It was a long way to come back, my dear. I've made it now, pretty much. They didn't really think I could, I could tell; and maybe they were right in a way. There are still things lurking in the dark corners of my mind that shouldn't be there. But you can understand why I hate the lousy stuff and the people who traffic in it."

"Sure," I said. "Like the fat girl, on a diet at last, hates the lousy dairy industry for having forced her to gobble all that lovely butter and gulp all that luscious cream that brought her to her awful, obese condition."

Gina started to get angry; then she grinned. "Your sympathy warms my heart, you bastard," she said. "All right, maybe what I really hate is myself for doing it to myself. Maybe that's why I've got this lousy save-the-world complex now, to make up for the way I almost wasted myself for nothing, just a few lousy kicks. But I still hate the men like Grieg who made it so easy for me."

"Is that why you picked on him? His island? His ship?"

She shook her head. "We were looking for any old island in the right place; but that ingenious concealed harbor he'd built made Ring Cay ideal. We hadn't planned on it; but we saw at once how we could make use of it. And as he told us just now, suitable ships are hard to come by these days. We wanted to be sure to get one we could get in there. We didn't want to discover at the last minute, too late, that it was too long or deep or something. The *Saiz* had made deliveries to Ring Cay a couple of times. She was use-tested, you might say." Gina made a wry face. "But maybe you're right, maybe it gave me pleasure to make the bastard hurt a little, too, after the way I'd been hurt."

I sighed. "Whatever happened to normal girls? Here I'm going along peacefully minding my own business; and I wind up with one practicing masochist and one detoxified hophead!"

"Oh, you sonofabitch!" Then Gina laughed softly. "Actually, it's kind of nice to talk with a man who doesn't feel he has to pussyfoot around it diplomatically." Malice entered her voice. "Incidentally, your pretty little practicing masochist didn't go home to Cincinnati after all. She heard her other lover calling and headed his way. Like a bee to a flower. I thought you'd like to know."

Gina obviously spoke from jealousy, to make me feel bad; but I was glad to hear it. If Amy was traveling in Minister's direction, and Doug Barnett was hot on her trail . . . But I'll admit it wasn't undiluted pleasure to think of her returning to the domination of the man she feared and had hoped to escape. I told myself firmly that it wasn't really my job to watch over screwy little girls and make sure they associated only with nice people like me.

I said, "Your Mr. Pope must be getting close to the end of the job he's doing for you."

"How do you figure that, Matt?"

I shrugged. "Obviously he's getting ready to disappear in his usual fashion—this time with selected company. He's summoned Amy because he wants her right at hand, ready to vanish with him, not off somewhere where he'd have to waste time tracking her down." I glanced at the woman sitting primly beside me without touching me. "Isn't it about time you let me know what it's all about, Gina?"

"I can't."

"You swore it was something I'd approve of, so why can't I know about it."

"I swear lots of things," she said without expression. "I swear all over the place. Don't ever take me seriously, my dear."

I said, "Let's study the basic ingredients of the situation. There's a hidden mystery harbor. There's a mystery ship to be concealed in that harbor, if it isn't already. There's a mystery cargo replacing the stuff that was previously in the ship's hold, about which there was no mystery at all. To make use of this mysterious shipment of material, whatever it may be, there's a mystery man who's good at blowing things up. And running the whole operation, with some help from wealthy friends and associates, is a mystery woman with a lot of money and a dubious medical history who keeps telling me, and herself, how violently she's against violence, meaning she's probably got something pretty violent in mind that she finds hard to reconcile with her nonviolent principles—"

"Matt, stop it!"

I went on unheeding: "And finally, on an island not too far away, there is or soon will be an international conference of important people dealing with an important international problem. If you were *for* war and *against* nuclear disarmament, Gina, if you wanted the Nassau conference to fail, the whole thing would make a lot of sense. So maybe you are. Maybe it's been a sabotage mission from the start. What about it?"

She shook her head quickly. "You've got to be kidding, Matt! Is anybody crazy enough to be for war?"

243

"Almost everybody's crazy enough to be for a war that'll gain them a lot or prevent them from losing a lot, like their freedom and national existence. If they think it's at stake, whether or not it really is. And any prowar group would be bound to call itself antiwar, wouldn't it? Just as every dictatorship calls itself a people's democracy, and our honest old War Department has long since turned itself into the sneaky Department of Defense. So your People for Nuclear Peace could actually be the People for Nuclear War—rationalizing the original name by the fact that the radioactive ashes afterward would be very peaceful indeed, perhaps the only peace we'll ever manage to find on this troubled planet."

"You can't be serious!"

I said, "Some years ago I encountered a group of rich folks very much like your organization, except that they'd bought themselves a Mexican general with the idea of taking over part of the Baja California peninsula as a defensible refuge to which they'd all retire when the world went to hell. Maybe this wealthy and exclusive PNP club of yours has a big scientific bomb shelter somewhere, designed and built for atomic survival by the best brains that can be bought or hired, from which you'll all emerge to take charge of things after a nice little atomic holocaust that'll wipe out most of us impoverished peons and make the survivors easy to govern. Instant population control. Instant dictatorship, only you'd call it benevolent world government, wouldn't you?"

"You're being perfectly ridiculous, you know that, don't you?"

I went on calmly: "Let's see how it would work. To take just one possibility: Say that secret cargo that took the place of Connie Grieg's bales of pot is a tactical missile, maybe more than one. The usual ship-to-ship whizbangs like the French Exocet may not have the range you need, but the U.S. Tomahawk should do just fine and even the smaller Lance might work, depending on just how far from Nassau this secret base of yours is located. Maybe those particular missiles aren't available on the black market, but the way arms are being passed around these days, I'm sure folks with the kind of money you have to spend could pick up something suitable. And since they're all kind of portable, at least they're designed to be hauled around the battlefield on special trucks, I'd be surprised if they couldn't be jury-rigged for shipboard use. Certainly something could. And at the right time, when all the important people from all the important nations, and some not so important, are under one roof talking peace and nuclear disarmament more or less sincerely—"

Gina laughed shortly. "Sincerely? You know better than that! They've finally got together because they've been forced to by public opinion; but they're about as sincere as a bunch of snake-oil salesmen!"

I shrugged. "Maybe. But they're important symbols to their respective peoples at the moment; symbols of peace and hope. And when you've got them all located in one spot you'll send your boom-booms on their way and blow all or most of them to hell, not only sabotaging the conference but causing all kinds of international accusations and recriminations, since nobody'll know where the big birds came from or who fired them. Hell, the world went to war once because a nut shot an archduke nobody'd ever heard of; what's going to happen when a whole peace conference blows up? You'll have your World War Three, just as you'd hoped."

Gina studied my face for a moment; then she drew a long breath and laughed again. "It won't work, my dear."

"What won't work?"

"You're trying to make me angry by accusing me of being a rabid, militaristic reactionary, plotting an outrageous crime against humanity. You hope I'll get mad enough to try to prove to you what a pure and public-spirited person I am by telling you what we're really up to." She shook her head quickly. "No, darling, you can't trick me that way. First of all, your theory doesn't even make sense; if that's what we were up to, we'd have hired a retired army missile expert, not Albert Pope. No, Matt, we're not playing with any military hardware. And we're trying—trying very hard—to prevent a war, not start one."

I said, "Well, I hope to God you know what you're doing. I haven't seen too many signs of it so far. Anybody who'll play tricks on a guy like Grieg, and then act shocked and hurt when he sends out the guns, just isn't living in the real world."

That did make her angry, and we rode the rest of the way to the marina in silence. When I asked the driver how much I owed him for the long ride out and back, and the endless wait, he shook his head.

"It is all taken care of, sah. . . . No, sah, I appreciate your kindness, but it would not be wise for me to accept any of your money. Good night, sah."

We watched him drive away. I grimaced. "Our big friend seems to carry a lot of weight around here."

"Back during the Civil War, the blockade-runners probably had a lot of influence, too. Matt . . ."

"Yes?"

"I'm sorry. I didn't mean to lose my temper."

I looked at her standing there, slender and handsome in the darkness, in her little white dress. "Now what the hell do you want?"

She laughed softly. "Is that any way to respond to a humble apology?"

I said, "That's just it. You're not a humble girl, and you're not an apologizing girl."

246

She licked her lips. "I just . . . didn't want us to waste what's left of this evening being angry with each other. Come on, all this thinking and talking has made me feel sexy as hell!"

I carefully avoided looking in the direction of the building that housed the dark office, the johns, and the public phones, as she took my hand and hurried me past them, laughing—a couple of kids running out to play, or in to play. It was one of those times when you have to go by your instincts. I had some information to pass along; but my well-traveled instincts said I could be more useful by maintaining close relations with this girl and following her lead now than by stuffily rejecting her advances and insisting on making an immediate report to Washington. I'd also be taking more risk, of course; but that comes with the territory. *Spindrift* lay motionless and lightless in her rented slip. I jumped down and helped my companion down, and we paused in the cockpit for a lengthy and rather breathless kiss that soon threatened to get out of control.

"Oh, God, not here on that damn hard seat!" Gina gasped, freeing herself reluctantly. "I've got great big bruises from the last time!"

I unlocked the hatch and slid it back. When I turned back to her, she was wearing nothing but her sexy panties. The little denim number was draped over her arm and her high-heeled shoes were in her hand.

"Give me your jacket; I'll hang it up for you, with my dress." She touched her lips to mine again, but lightly, so as not to tease the beast inside. "Just give me a moment, please."

"Take all the time you want," I said. "As long as it's no more than thirty seconds."

She laughed and disappeared into the cabin. I wrestled off my tie and got out of my shirt and pulled off my shoes and socks, waiting. Unlike her, I wasn't brazen enough to strip further in the open cockpit, even though the marina seemed to be totally asleep under the lights.

"All right, darling."

I tossed the clothes I held into the cabin and followed them down. Gina had turned on a weak light in the galley; she awaited me in the dark main saloon, to use a fancy nautical name for a space that was just big enough to hold the two facing settees and the folded table. I could see that she'd dispensed with her last wispy garment, and that she'd transformed the starboard settee—mine, if it matters—into a berth, awaiting us, inviting us. She came into my arms and winced. Laughing, she bent over to figure out the tricky revolver holster, then freed the gun and tossed it onto the other settee.

"Always so many lousy preliminaries!" she gasped, coming to me again, naked and warm and eager.

Then there was a small, springy click as, embracing me, holding me, she fired the automatic hypogun we carry, which she'd got out of my jacket, into the big muscle of my rump. I had time to hope that, working hastily in bad light, she'd managed to charge the ingenious little weapon with the right capsule, the green one. The red-and-orange ones kill.

IIIIIIIII CHAPTER 23 IIIIIIIIIIIIIIIIIIIIIIIIIIIIIIIIIIIIIIIII

I AWOKE to daylight, thinking fuzzily that it had been the green one all right, but the green what? I seemed to be lying in a cradle, rocked like a baby; and there was something wrong with my arms and legs. The thought brought me back to full consciousness. I realized that I was tied hand and foot and lying in my usual bunk; but the bunk cloth was up, a high canvas edge that you raise—with lines that secure to padeyes overhead—to keep yourself from being thrown out in heavy weather.

Spindrift seemed to be under way. In fact, we were apparently well off shore, judging by the sea conditions. We were crashing along in a good breeze, carrying plenty of sail, as was the lady's custom. We were on the starboard tack, making mine the high side of the vessel. The retaining canvas did save me from taking a quick trip across the cabin when we heeled to a sharp gust of wind; but it also gave me a shut-in feeling that was a bit claustrophobic.

With the commotion of the boat's progress, I wasn't aware that she was there until a corner of the canvas dropped and I saw her looking down at me. She had on her seagoing costume of tank top and jeans. Among the other chores we'd taken care of in Nassau was the laundry, using the marina's coin machines; so her clothes looked fresh and clean once more. But her face was shocking, gray and drawn and skull-like, with the colorless lips twitching uncontrollably.

"Damn you!" she breathed. "Oh, damn you, damn you, damn you!"

Then she raised her hand abruptly. I saw the gleam of the little .25 automatic and tried to roll aside as she fired it at my face. Bound, and still groggy from the knockout drug, I didn't quite make it. Something rapped me sharply on the left side of the head just above the ear. The blow was hard enough to turn the world bright red and make my extremities tingle strangely. I lost interest in making any further moves; I just lay there trying to cling to the few scraps of consciousness that remained to me. Somehow it seemed important to be there when the next bullet hit; it would be a shame to miss the great experience of dying.

I heard something clatter on the teak floor of the cabin. Strangely, I wasn't relieved, although I realized that she'd let the gun fall, unable to make herself shoot again. But I'd been trained to be very careful with firearms and her sloppy gun handling scared and annoyed me. Dropping it like that, she undoubtedly hadn't had sense enough to unload it first, or even set the safety. It was just as likely as not to go off, bouncing around like that. But it didn't.

I was aware that she was lifting my head—which seemed to be a long way from my body—and stroking my face and probably getting my blood all over her nice clean jeans and undershirt. A pity.

"Oh, my God, he's dead, I killed him!" she moaned, sitting on the bunk and rocking me in her arms. "Matt, please! Matt, dear, I didn't mean . . . Well, yes, I did, but I want you to understand, darling.

You've got to understand! I had to do it. It was the only logical thing to do! You'd have spoiled everything, but I'm sorry, sorry, sorry. . . . Oh, God, it's getting all over everything! But that's crazy, dead men don't bleed like that. . . . Matt! Matt, wake up!"

I made my lips move. "What the hell for?" I asked thickly. "So you can shoot me again?"

She said, "Oh, God, what a mess! Where do you hide your first-aid kit?"

I said, still speaking with difficulty, "First . . . first the gun, please. Before we take a big roll and it slides across the cabin and goes bang. At least put the safety on. I don't mind so much being killed intentionally, people have been trying that for years; but I'd hate to die from a stupid firearms accident. And you'd better check and see if we're taking water, although a twenty-five-caliber bullet isn't going to do the damage of a shotgun slug. A quarter-inch hole shouldn't sink us very fast. And the first-aid kit is in the back of the locker with the shotgun. But first of all give me a handkerchief or a towel or something to contain the gore, will you?"

She looked at me for a moment without moving. Then she disengaged herself and stood up to look down at me. Her face was human once more; and when her mouth twitched a little, it was with a hint of amusement.

"Nothing like having the murder victim take charge at the scene of the crime," she murmured.

"Somebody's got to, if the murderess just sits around with her mouth open," I said.

She reached around into the galley—on a twenty-eight-foot boat nothing is very far from anything else—and found a clean dishtowel and gave it to me. I had a hard time holding it in the right place with my arms bound together. She studied me for a moment, frowning.

She spoke carefully: "Back in the good old days when people took honor seriously, there used to be something called parole. The prisoner gave his word not to try to escape or attack his captors for a certain period. If I untie you . . . An hour, while we get you patched up and this cabin cleaned up?"

"You've got your hour," I said, holding out my wrists.

She laughed a little sharply. "Anybody would think *you* were doing *me* a favor. . . ."

Three-quarters of an hour later we had things pretty well under control. The little automatic had disappeared into a place of concealment unknown to me, I hoped with the safety on. We'd learned that the bullet had not achieved total penetration. After glancing off my skull, and drilling through the foam-rubber mattress and the plywood of the bunk, it had come to rest in a can of *chili con carne* stowed in the bin underneath after first blowing apart a can of pork and beans. Another mess to clean up. Considerable amounts of gore had been mopped off me and the woodwork. The bloody bedclothes, and Gina's stained clothes, were soaking in cold water in a bucket in the cockpit. You'd be surprised how much red stuff you can get out of a relatively small head wound. Since I was still bare to the waist, as I'd gone to meet my love the night before, I hadn't suffered any clothing damage. The crease in my skull was covered by a large Band-Aid.

"This is perfectly ridiculous!" Gina protested as, our labors completed, we sat in the cockpit, where it was hoped the fresh air would help my headache. "Sitting here like this, as if we were friends or something. . . . I tried to *kill* you!"

"Join the club," I said.

"It was the only logical thing to do," she said. "It still is!"

Spindrift was driving right along under a blue Bahama sky under the guidance of the autopilot. We were in deep water, by the color, a rich dark blue except for an occasional whitecap. We were heading east. There was land to the south, a low islet of some kind, and a ship on the horizon to the north, presumably heading for Nassau behind us. Astern, to be nautical about it. Gina was wearing her wide, pleated khaki shorts and a striped red-and-white jersey, little more than a fancy T-shirt. Her nipples showed clearly through the thin knit stuff. But that, I told myself, was quite irrelevant.

"In that case, how soon can I expect to get shot again?" I said.

The eyes she turned on me were wide and dark. "No," she said. "I can't do it again. I can't go through that again! I spent most of the night sitting right here telling myself it was the only thing. Telling myself I had to do it, I *must* do it. Telling myself there was no choice, not after . . ."

"After what?" I asked when she hesitated.

"This," she said, taking a small piece of paper from her pocket. It looked familiar. "When you went back to Grieg, when he called you back like that, I knew he'd figured out a way to make trouble. Even though he had his money, my money, our money, he still wanted to hit back at me. Well, I was right, wasn't I? And we can't afford to have the position of Ring Cay become public knowledge, at least not for another few days." With a glance at me, she tore the paper into small fragments, held up her hand, and let the wind take them off to leeward. "There!" she said. And then she sighed. "Of course that doesn't help much, does it? You could easily have memorized it."

As a matter of fact, I hadn't memorized it; there hadn't been time. I said, "You don't have to make a big mess with a gun. You seem to know all about that

253

drug kit I carry, and I suppose you've still got it around somewhere. There's some pretty lethal stuff in there you could use. Wait till I'm asleep and slip it into me. No fuss, no bother."

"You're making fun of me!" She grimaced. "You know I'm through, finished. I couldn't possibly work myself up to *that* again. And it's so ridiculously sentimental. One man's life, for God's sake! One man who can wreck everything. And it isn't as if I were a great humanitarian, for God's sake! After all, you don't hire somebody like Albert Pope, Alfred Minister, if you have a great, tender concern for human life!"

I said, "I knew a pilot who'd flown the Flying Fortresses during World War Two, dumping death and destruction all over Germany. So finally the flak got his plane, and he bailed out. On the ground, he ran into a German soldier. He had his trusty forty-five out, and he probably could have gotten away, but he couldn't bring himself to shoot a man, not face-to-face like that, in spite of all the people he'd helped kill by remote control, so to speak."

"What happened to him?"

"The German shot him, of course. And he wound up in a prison camp and came home crippled and sick and wasn't much use after that."

"Are you trying to talk me into murdering you?"

As she'd said, it was a crazy situation, and a crazy conversation, considering that all that kept me from overpowering her, sitting there, was a splitting headache and a shaky promise. However, she was no use to me as my prisoner, unless I wanted to go through a grim interrogation routine; and even then I'd have a hard time forcing her to get me into the place I wanted to penetrate. I had a better chance of reaching my goal as her prisoner; but I had to throw out enough of a verbal smoke screen to prevent her from guessing what I had in mind.

254

I said, "No, I just want you to face what you can do and what you can't, so we know where we stand. Incidentally, I'm not much good at latitude and longitude, and I don't have that position memorized."

It was an out for her. If I didn't know where Ring Cay was, I didn't need to be killed. I could see that she wanted to believe me; but she said suspiciously, "I'm supposed to take your word for that?"

"You took my word for something else."

She glanced at her watch. "Yes, and your time is almost up. Were you hoping I'd forget? Get below so I can tie you up again, there's a good boy."

Lying in my bunk once more, properly hog-tied, I asked, "What happens in a few days? You said nobody must know about Ring Cay for another few days." When she shook her head and didn't answer, I tried another question: "What is this Ring Cay, anyway? A perfect circle of an island surrounding an emerald lagoon?"

Gina laughed. "No, there is a lagoon, of course, that's the whole point, but it's rather long and skinny. The name comes from the massive old iron rings set into the rocks on both sides. They were used to secure the hurricane chains that ran across the bottom to snag the anchor of a ship and keep it from dragging ashore in a bad blow. Of course the underwater chains have all rusted away by this time, but the rings on shore are still there."

"If Ring Cay is as far down in the Bahamas boonies as everybody seems to think, it's an out-of-the-way place for a hurricane harbor," I said.

"Yes. It's an out-of-the-way place because it was originally prepared and used by some out-of-the-way people. We're told that the pirate Blackbeard rode out a storm there once."

"Sure, right alongside Captain Blood as portrayed by Errol Flynn!"

She shrugged. "I admit it could be just another Teach legend."

"Now you're showing off. It isn't everybody who knows that Blackbeard's name was Teach."

She smiled faintly, then stopped smiling. "Matt . . ."

"Yes?"

"We've established that I'm incapable of killing you, haven't we? So please don't try anything . . . anything drastic, my dear. I've got to keep you from communicating with anybody for a little while, just in case you're lying about what you remember and what you don't; anyway, I can be most useful to our project by keeping you prisoner until it's too late for you to interfere. But I think I can arrange it so you won't be hurt, if you just refrain from playing any of the violent tricks I'm sure you're dreaming up right now. Please?" Then she looked up quickly. "Oh, Christ, a wind shift! Just lie there and be good, darling."

She'd sensed it before I had; and she was halfway up the companionway ladder before the boat rose to an even keel and the canvas broke into wild flapping overhead. I heard the rattle of the mainsheet blocks and the ratchety clatter of the jibsheet winch as she trimmed the sails to the new breeze, working, by the sound of it, as quickly and expertly as ever.

She was quite a woman, but I couldn't forget the mad skull face she'd showed me less than an hour earlier, or the shot that should have killed me. And I couldn't forget a man who'd been eaten—well, half eaten—by a shark; or a terribly damaged lady in a wheelchair, put there by a gent now working for Mrs. Georgina Williston and her friends. I didn't think I'd better take her hopeful remarks about my future too seriously.

I noted that she hadn't used any of the synthetic rope on board to tie me with. It's all nylon and Dacron on shipboard these days, nylon where elasticity is wanted and Dacron where it isn't. Modern cordage is a lot springier and slicker than old-fashioned sisal and manila. It's stronger and it lasts longer, but it doesn't hold knots nearly so well. Houdini could have freed himself from the new stuff in his sleep. But Gina had used sail ties to immobilize me: lengths of soft white one-inch tape of coarsely woven and immensely strong material designed to stay tied around the furled canvas even under hurricane conditions. Smart girl. However, while she knew her ropes and knots, she hadn't searched me quite thoroughly enough. I had a trick or two left to use, if necessary; but for the moment I had every intention of being a model prisoner.

During the course of the afternoon we went through the awkward feeding routine and the embarrassing peeing routine. Later, I was aware of a change in our course. I wasn't invited on deck again, but I hoisted myself up to take a peek through the nearest cabin port. The position of the sun indicated that we were now heading southward. There were no islands in sight, but the water around us was not the rich blue I'd seen earlier. Even though it was roughened by the brisk breeze driving us, I could see that it was lighter and kind of mottled, reflecting the colors of a bottom that ranged from the brightness of sand to the darkness of weeds. It seemed frighteningly close under the broken surface, as if we were driving heedlessly across a sea barely deep enough to float us; but it was actually, I guessed, between fifteen and twenty feet down. Anyway, I'd made it at last; I was sailing on the famous Bahama banks.

I made no further effort to keep track of our progress. Even if we did sight land, I knew that one mangrove cay looks very much like another, at least to a landlubber like me. The wind faded toward evening. Eventually we were motoring through a flat calm with the Genoa jib furled and the mainsail sheeted down hard to minimize its flapping.

Half-asleep in my bunk, I was aroused by some rather abrupt course changes. Suddenly there was a grating sound, and *Spindrift* slowed markedly. The motor roared as Gina threw the throttle-gearshift lever to full ahead. I squirmed out of the bunk and hippety-hopped aft, almost thrown to the cabin sole as the boat hesitated again, the keel scraping across something rough and hard. I fumbled my way up the companionway ladder and clung near the top with my bound hands, looking around. Gina was standing on the cockpit seat for a better view, holding on to the boom of the windless mainsail overhead to steady herself. She was steering with one bare brown foot on the tiller, too intent on the channel to give me more than a glance. There was a chart on the seat, folded so I couldn't identify it, but she wasn't looking at that, either. Apparently this was strictly a spot for eyeball navigation.

Astern, the wake was cloudy with whitish silt stirred up from the bottom by the propeller wash. On either hand, the calm surface of the ocean was broken by ugly reefs and islets of coral. Ahead, I couldn't see anything that looked like a passage. Under the bowsprit was nothing but pale shallow water. It shaded off into a beautiful blue a hundred yards farther on; but we weren't there yet. The keel dragged gratingly once more.

"Come on!" Gina whispered fiercely. "Keep moving, damn you! You can do it. . . . Ah, that's my girl!"

Suddenly we were clear. *Spindrift* picked up speed again. The bottom dropped away beneath us and the shoals and reefs fell astern. Gina stepped down into the cockpit and slowed the roaring diesel. She looked at me and grinned.

"We were a little late with the tide for that particular passage off the banks," she said. "I figured it was better to drive her through than wait almost twelve hours for the next high water. Now that we're clear, how about a drink?" She studied me thoughtfully. "Another hour's parole, Sir Matthew? So I don't have to pour your booze into you and shovel your dinner into you?"

"Christ, you'd think we were back in the days of tin suits and lances," I said. "Okay, you've got your hour."

She said, "Maybe I'd better point out that even if you do break your word, and put me out of commission and take over, you don't know where we are. It would take you days to fumble your way back to Nassau, if you didn't pile up on the reefs trying. And if you're thinking of the Loran, don't. This is the area where it's totally haywire. You must have heard of that phenomenon. If you were to go by the position you read off it, you'd wind up on the coral for sure."

I had a hunch she was again playing the old salt intimidating the helpless landlubber, and it wouldn't be all that tough to reach civilization of some kind. What it amounted to was that my earlier dumb-dumb act was paying off. I had no intention of spoiling it now by showing the slightest glimmer of nautical intelligence. After a friendly drink and a pleasant meal and a couple of aspirins for my subsiding headache, I allowed myself, honorably, to be tied up again.

Darkness fell, and we motored on southward. At least I thought it was southward. It didn't really matter too much. I couldn't believe that Gina had taken herself out of the action permanently just to watch over me. She'd put too much time and effort and money and emotion into her mysterious project to leave its completion to others. She was stalling a little sailing around with me out here, she was waiting for something; but I was willing to bet that she'd wind up at the critical place at the critical moment just to make sure her elaborate and expensive plans worked out properly. Whatever they were.

I remembered, for some reason, that the conference in Nassau wasn't due to open until the middle of the week, although I still had no idea whether the fact was highly significant or totally irrelevant. Hoping that Amy Barnett was leaving a wide trail as she answered the summons of her sadist lover, so that Doug Barnett would be in position to finish the job if I'd miscalculated—hell, it was after all his job—I fell asleep.

Toward morning the motion made me aware that we had some wind again, stirring up a small sea. The mainsail had filled, and the boat was heeling perceptibly; but the big Genoa did not go up, and the motor continued to thump away steadily. It was the first time the lady hadn't taken full advantage of a sailing breeze. It occurred to me that she couldn't have had any significant amounts of sleep since I'd first seen her awaiting me on board, in the Lucayan Harbour Marina. Although her racing experience would have hardened her to standing watches night and day on a fully crewed boat, she had to be getting very tired doing it all by herself like this. I dozed off again, then was awakened by the splash of the anchor and the rattle of the chain and rope as it ran out. The motor stopped. I heard the mainsail being lowered and furled. The cabin light came on; and Gina stood looking down at me.

"Are we there?" I asked, yawning. "Wherever there is."

Gina shook her head. "Waiting. The sun's coming up; and for obvious reasons we like to make the approach to Ring Cay in the dark. I promised to take you there, remember?"

"That was a lot of promises ago," I said.

She shrugged minutely. "So we'll just kill the day right here. Besides . . ." She hesitated, watching me steadily. "Truce?"

"So you can catch up on your sleep?" Lying comfortably in my bunk, I grinned up at her. "You obviously need it; you look awful. All I have to do is wait until you fall on your face and kick your head in, right?"

"What will it get you? You still don't know where we are. Will you give me, well, three hours?"

I said, "Hell, think big, honey. Why settle for a lousy three hours? When do you really want to leave here? Wherever here is."

She licked her lips. "Actually, I don't want to get under way until this evening. That should put us at Ring Cay a couple of hours before dawn."

I nodded. "You have my parole, or whatever you call it, until six P.M.; eighteen hundred hours, if we're being nautical."

She nodded. "I'll wake up in time to cook us a good dinner." She hesitated. There was an odd sadness in her eyes. "Matt, I . . ."

I said, "I know. It would be nice if things were different, wouldn't it? We could be having quite a pleasant cruise, instead of playing captor and captee."

She shook her head ruefully. "All my life I've wanted things to be different, my dear. But they never are. Here, let me get those sail ties off you. . . . Good night. Or whatever."

Going on deck, I found that there was already light enough to see by, although the sun was not yet visible. We seemed to be back on the shallow banks—some banks; there are lots of them in that part of the world—anchored in the lee of a rather bare hump of an island. There were several other islands and islets in sight; and the whole visible expanse of water looked shoal and dangerous. Well, I'd guessed right, I told myself; she'd been unable to stay away from the action. If she expected to leave after dinner and arrive an hour or two before dawn, it meant that the elusive Ring Cay wasn't much more than ten hours away, say fifty miles at five knots. And I'd better prepare myself for an end to this kind of friendly, unreal captivity. . . .

I therefore, after catching up on my shaving and toothbrushing, exchanged the good pants I was still wearing, pretty baggy and bedraggled by this time, for a pair of tough jeans. I also treated myself to socks and boat shoes, the rubber soles of which could be useful on shore as well. I found a flat little sheath knife that Gina had either missed in her search or left where I'd hidden it. I taped the sheath between my shoulder blades where I could just reach the knife handle and pulled on over it a knitted dark-blue sports shirt suitable for night operations, in case things should work out that way. I left it hanging loose outside my belt. I was just lighting the stove for breakfast when Gina screamed.

"No, no, no, oh, God, no. . . . Ahhhhh!"

She was moving jerkily in her bunk as if fighting somebody or something; I realized that her body thought it was restrained as it had once been. Her face was pale and shiny. Her eyes were tightly shut. They opened abruptly when I touched her. A moment later I was looking into the muzzle of my own little automatic.

"What . . ." She licked her lips. "What did you have in mind, Matt?"

"You were having a nightmare."

"Oh. One of those again. I had them all the time in that place . . . well, I told you." She stared at the gun as if wondering where it had come from, then tucked it back under her pillow. She licked her lips once more. "Sorry, I misconstrued . . . I thought you were trying to . . . Sorry. Thanks. Good night again."

It was an odd, lost day. I ate, and put away the stuff she'd rinsed out and hung up to dry, and did some other cleanup work around the boat, and ate again, and took a nap although I didn't really need it, but you never know in this business when your next sleep will be. Gina awoke at last and did a few feminine things to herself and spiced up some canned beef stew for dinner in a fairly palatable way. There were canned pears for dessert. Coffee and a little White Label masquerading as cognac. Afterward I washed, and she dried. Then we went through the formality of tying me up again.

She stood by the bunk looking down at me with a crooked smile. "This is getting pretty ridiculous, isn't it? I find myself wanting to giggle. Matt . . ."

"Yes?"

She reached out as if to touch me apologetically on the arm as I lay there. With an abrupt movement, she fired the little hypogun into my biceps.

"What I was going to say was, I'm sorry, my dear. Sleep well. . . ."

When I woke up I was lying at the bottom of a big rusty iron box. A girl I didn't know was looking down at me worriedly.

THE INTERIOR of the box was coated with thick gray paint that was flaking away to expose the corroding old metal underneath. Actually, of course, it was a windowless storeroom of some kind, on a ship of some kind. It wasn't quite rectangular; ships seldom are. One side, opposite the door, had an odd slant and slope to it. Probably that was the side of the ship itself. The chamber was illuminated by a single weak electric bulb, say twenty-five watts, recessed into the wall above the door and protected by a crude, paint-caked grill. A steady vibration in the hull indicated some kind of operating machinery, probably a generator.

The space was small, with floor space enough for a couple of narrow cots and a chemical toilet that was obviously an afterthought; the space had not been designed for plumbing. The gadget stank of excrement and of its own chemistry. There was also an odor of vomit. It all brought back a jail cell I'd once wound up in, in the line of duty, in a country not my own. A ventilator in the ceiling directly above me wasn't working very hard at improving the situation. Lying on the rusty floor between the cots, I managed to learn this much without sitting up. There was some reason why I didn't particularly want to sit up until I had to, but I couldn't remember what it was.

"Take it easy," said the girl kneeling beside me. "You seem to have been drugged. Give yourself time to snap out of it before you try to get up."

"What time is it?"

She seemed to consider that a foolish question. I got the impression that she'd been locked up long enough that time had lost its meaning for her. Then she shrugged and glanced at the stainless waterproof watch on her wrist, quite a businesslike timepiece.

"It's ten thirty-five," she said.

"Night or day?"

"Night. That's what comes after beans. Day is what comes after eggs. That's how you tell, in here. You'll learn."

There was wry humor in her voice, and she seemed to be a person whose acquaintance might be worth cultivating; but my mind was clearing only slowly, and I could consider only one subject at a time. Ten thirty-five P.M. Only four hours and a little since the needle had gone into my arm. Beautiful.

I found myself grinning at the thought of how neatly my handsome lady navigator had tricked me, leading me to think we still had some ten hours of sailing left, when apparently she'd brought us well within sight of our destination before dropping the anchor. I remembered the islands surrounding us and realized that I'd probably been looking at Ring Cay without knowing it as I tidied up *Spindrift*'s deck, waiting for my honorable parole to expire while she caught up on her sleep below. Then a pleasant dinner to throw me further off guard, and some quick work with the spring-loaded hypo while I was still expecting to have the whole night in which to make my final preparations. A short run under power in the fading evening light; and here we all were in Blackbeard's old storm harbor.

"Are you all right?" the girl above me asked, perhaps suspecting hysteria. "What's funny? If there's a joke, please share it. I haven't had a laugh in a long time."

"Private joke," I said. "Too long to explain."

When I looked at her directly at last, she stirred with embarrassment and said rather stiffly, "It's been known to take a bath, given the opportunity. When properly scrubbed and dressed, it bears a close resemblance to a female human being."

One day I'm going to have one of those assignments that involve nothing but lovely perfumed ladies in gorgeous gowns, but this obviously wasn't it. Not that the girl was unattractive, although it was a little hard to tell at the moment. She'd presumably started out a week or two ago as a neat and clean and pleasant, if somewhat sturdy, young woman with blond hair cut off straight across her forehead and below the ears. The fine hair had undoubtedly been smooth and shining then, but it was soiled and tangled now. Her snub-nosed face hadn't been washed for a long time. Her light-blue T-shirt was stenciled in black across the front: I'D RATHER BE SAILING. It was rather spectacularly grimy, as were her white linen shorts; and there were splotches of what looked like dried blood, although I could see no injuries. A gold wedding band and a small diamond looked out of place on her dirty hand. When she spoke, her nice even teeth looked very white in her dirty face. Her eyes were blue.

"It isn't nice to stare," she said. "You might embarrass the girl. . . . No, please rest a little longer. You're too big for me to catch if you start to pass out and fall over."

I said, "*Carmen Saiz?*"

She laughed. "Heavens, no, do I look Spanish? . . . Oh, the ship? Yes, that's right, I think somebody did say that was the name of it. If you want to call this beat-up seagoing relic a ship."

"Mrs. Brennerman? Mrs. Molly Brennerman?"

That startled her a little. "Yes, I'm Molly Brennerman. Who are you?"

"Matthew Helm. I work for the U.S. government, too, although not in the Coast Guard." I looked around. "Where's the other one?"

"My husband died." Her voice was quite even. "He was killed by a shark as he tried to get away to get help for us."

"Yes, I know. I'm sorry." After a moment, I said, "But there was supposed to be a third—"

"Oh, you mean Ricky. Ensign Ricardo Sanderson, U.S.C.G. He's right up there on that cot beside you. Well, above you. He . . . got impatient. He tried to be brave a couple of days ago, he thought he'd figured out a way for us to break out of here, but it didn't work and they beat him up pretty badly. I'm afraid he has a bad concussion, among other things. He . . . kind of comes and goes. He should have medical attention, but they just laugh when I ask."

Another good one, I thought. It couldn't have been fun, locked up in here endlessly, the last couple of days with no company but a badly hurt youth who was conscious only intermittently; but there was no whine in Molly Brennerman's voice. I noted that while her clothes were wrinkled and dirty from long wear, they weren't torn.

"You're all right?" I asked.

"What do you mean? . . . Oh." She grimaced. "I'm Molly the Pig Girl, as you can see, after a couple of weeks—I've kind of lost track of time—in the same clothes, first of some kind of a cottage on shore and then on this filthy ship after it came in. But nobody's ravished the body beautiful yet. By now, the way I look, who'd want to?"

I grinned. "Ask me again when I'm ambulatory." I noticed that my shirt seemed to be badly ripped, although the damage was mostly to the collar and shoulder where I couldn't really see it. When I tried to raise myself and twist a bit to look, a sharp pain stabbed me in the side. Well, my subconscious had been warning me that I'd been hurt, although I had no memory of it. "Oh, Christ!" I breathed. "What happened, did they drop me on something hard when they were hauling me in here?"

"You were kicked." Molly Brennerman's voice was expressionless. "I'm afraid they found the little knife under your shirt in back, Mr. Helm. I hope you weren't counting on it too heavily. He said to tell you no more tricks like that or it won't be just your ribs he'll kick in."

I'd already determined that I still had my belt, with its peculiar buckle; one of Washington's cute secret-agent gimmicks. The searchers had apparently looked no further after finding the decoy knife, which was precisely why I'd worn it.

"Pope?" I asked.

"Who?"

"Was the man who kicked me calling himself Albert Pope? Plumpish, blondish, thinning hair, in his forties?"

"Oh, that man." She frowned, remembering. "Is he important?"

"Yes. Very."

"More important than me, you mean? Or Ricky Sanderson?" She was watching me shrewdly. "Somehow I get the impression you're not really a rescuing angel, Mr. Helm. You're more the bloodhound type."

"You get some very sound impressions, Mrs. Brennerman."

"He wasn't the one who kicked you," she said. "But I saw a man answering that description several times while they were holding us temporarily in the captain's quarters—there, I actually did get to use a shower, for a few days, and even wash out my clothes, although you wouldn't know it now—before they got this lockup cleaned out for us so they wouldn't have to guard us constantly. If you want to call this clean. The superstructure is aft, and the cabin overlooks the whole deck. The man you call Pope would come out of the hold every couple of hours to smoke a cigarette, then go back down again. He seemed to be doing some kind of mechanical work down there. At least he was usually in coveralls, sometimes pretty greasy; although once he was wearing some kind of elaborate protective clothing. But he had nothing to do with us, with the day-to-day administration of this place, the care and feeding of prisoners, security, that sort of thing. That's Junior's department."

"Junior?"

She grimaced. "Well, Ricky—Ensign Sanderson— and I started out by calling him God, Junior. Or God, j.g. Because of the way he acted. But we wound up simply calling him Junior. A fairly young fellow with delusions of grandeur. Give a certain kind of guy a lot of power he isn't used to, and a gun, and a few creeps with guns to take his orders, and I guess you've just naturally got an instant little Hitler. Anyway, he runs this installation tough and enjoys every minute of it."

"Description?"

She frowned, half closing her eyes. "Five eight or nine, I'd say; and he wishes he were taller. Regular features, dark eyes, wavy brown hair, one of the blow-dry jerks. A very pretty man. Where do all these lovely little male creatures come from? John Wayne, where are you now that we really need you?"

She made a wry face. "Maybe I'm prejudiced. Brennerman was six two, ugly as a backhoe, and built like a slab of oak. I hated him on sight, the great macho bastard towering all over those nice young men. I gave him a very hard time, until I discovered he was one of the gentlest, kindest, bravest . . . Oh, God, I'm going to cry!"

She got up quickly and turned her back to me. I pulled myself cautiously to my feet, hoping the broken rib, if it was broken, would stay put and not go wandering around. The last time I'd been kicked in the side—the other side, thank God—I'd eventually wound up in the hopsital with a punctured lung.

Molly Brennerman was leaning against the wall of our cell, pressing her forehead against the painted metal, sobbing. I turned her around and held her, and she clung to me desperately. After a while, her crying tapered off.

"Thanks, you've got a friendly shoulder," she gasped. "You don't happen to have a friendly hanky?"

"Be my guest." I put it into her hand. "Do you want to tell me how it happened?"

"I thought there was something wrong with me!" she breathed. "Not a single tear, even though I saw it. . . . That slashing fin and the great black shape of it and all the blood in the water! And the way I went dead, dead, dead inside and couldn't cry a drop; I thought maybe I hadn't *really* loved . . . Oh, God, talk about delayed reactions, here I go again. Sorry!" At last the new paroxysm subsided. After a bit of sniffing and mopping, she said, "I guess, well, you don't like to break down in front of the kiddies, it upsets them so."

"You mean the baby officer?"

She sensed my amusement at her superior attitude and said resentfully, "Don't look at me like that! I'll have you know I'm almost thirty, I've just got this dumb, bouncing tomboy body; and he's really *very* young." She giggled abruptly. "You should have heard him being gentlemanly about the two of us being locked up together. Back in that cottage, at the start, before the ship came. He told me very seriously that I didn't have to be afraid, he wouldn't take advantage of the situation. Of me. But I shouldn't laugh. He's really a very nice boy, poor boy. Maybe you'd better look at him. Maybe there's something you can do."

"I'm afraid I'm better at breaking them up than sticking them back together."

Ensign Ricardo Sanderson was wearing a red-and-white jersey and red denim shorts that had probably looked very sporty once. Now they were in the same soiled condition as the girl's clothes; worse, because he'd been sick and there was more blood. Obviously, this was where she'd picked up her own bloodstains, caring for him. He might have been a handsome young man originally, but it was hard to tell now. His eyes were practically closed by the discolored swelling of his broken nose. His lips were split and puffy, and as he lay on his back breathing slowly through his open mouth, he revealed a couple of damaged teeth. Somebody had really worked him over.

But these injuries were mostly cosmetic, I decided. What didn't heal by itself could be repaired without much difficulty if the patient lived; and I'd seen too many beat-up gents to let it bother me. What was disturbing was the ugly, swollen contusion over the right temple that made the lump on my own skull ache when I looked at it. However, there seemed to be no noticeable depression of the underlying bone.

I said, "Hell, I don't know. The pupils are the same size, which is supposed to be significant although I couldn't tell you why. Dr. Helmstein's considered diagnosis is that we'd better get the kid to a hospital as soon as possible."

"Easier said than done."

"Where there's a will and all that crap," I said. "Now tell me all about the hold."

"The what? . . . Oh, the ship's hold?"

I nodded. "I happen to know that a valuable cargo—well, valuable to certain people—was thrown overboard to make the space available for other purposes. What purposes? What's down there now? What's Mr. Albert Pope working on down there?"

Molly Brennerman shook her head. "I'm sorry, Matt. . . . It's all right if I call you Matt, isn't it? Call me Molly, please." She drew a long breath. "I'm sorry, I did watch, I knew I should try to find out as much as possible while I had the chance, but all I know is . . . well, whatever it is, it required some welding. Once he came up in full welder's regalia; you know, the face shield and the asbestos gauntlets."

"That's the protective clothing you mentioned?"

"No. That was something else. A complete white suit that covered him from head to foot like a deep-sea diver. I got a very . . . a very negative reaction from it, but I suppose that's silly."

"Reactions are what we want. Keep them coming."

"No, that's all. . . ."

She stopped as footsteps reverberated metallically in the passage outside. A key turned in the lock.

THE DOOR was opened by a short, dark, middle-aged man I didn't know, carrying a submachine gun, which was ridiculous. In that limited space, nobody but a suicidal maniac would turn loose a burst of lead projectiles to go bouncing and skittering around inside those steel walls—a suicidal maniac or somebody who didn't know much about weapons, particularly automatic weapons. The man was wearing clean khaki trousers and shirt. He waved us back against the far wall. Another one, similarly dressed and armed but blond and much bigger, took up a position in the doorway. A moment later he stepped back respectfully as a younger man appeared, whom I recognized from the girl's description. This was Junior, also wearing clean and well-ironed khakis, obviously the uniform of the local chapter of Stormtroopers Anonymous.

The girl had drawn me a good enough picture of him, as far as she could comprehend him; but she was basically a civilized person. It really takes one to know one; and for all his nicely pressed pants and prettily waved hair he didn't fool me for a moment. I can spot a born killer a mile away; but this was one of the haywire ones who do it for fun, or would kill as soon as he got his chance and threw off the few civilized restraints that still remained to him. He carried a holstered automatic pistol on his belt: the old Colt .45 or one of its numerous latter-day imitations, often offered in 9mm as well. I wouldn't know until I saw the size of the hole. I could wait.

"So you're on your feet; good!" he said. "I'm Homer Allwyn; I'm in command here. I hope you got my little message. If you try any more tricks, you'll regret it."

It was, of course, my cue to tell him what I thought of a man who went around kicking people's ribs in while they were unconscious; but this was not a movie.

I said humbly, "No tricks, sir. I'll be good."

I felt Molly Brennerman stir. She was looking at me with sudden scorn. She'd obviously expected a gallant display of Hollywood courage and defiance. Too bad; she'd seemed like a reasonably bright girl.

"Damn right you'll be good," Homer Allwyn snapped. "We'll see to that. Now move, somebody wants you topside. . . ."

"Sir?"

"What is it?" He didn't like being interrupted, but he loved the sir.

"The boy on the cot. He's in bad shape, sir. He needs a doctor."

"If he hadn't tried to escape, he wouldn't be in bad shape, would he? Keep it in mind. Anyway, there's no practicing doctor here. . . . Take him along, Jesperson."

The dark one, first in, waved his weapon at me. I realized that while he might have fired it a few times in training, he had no idea what it would do for real. He knew nothing of ricochets or disintegrating bullets spraying hot lead fragments around like miniature shrapnel. At most he'd seen himself make some neat little round holes in a hunk of paper shaped roughly like a man. That made him, in here, more dangerous rather than less; he'd actually be dumb enough to open up full-auto if he were startled. His big blond partner was obviously no more experienced; he was also handling his squirt gun in a casual way that would have got him thrown off any shooting range in the country.

I'd assumed that the directors of the PNP had paid Alfred Minister, not only to exercise his specialty in their behalf, but to recruit a bunch of knowledgeable hard cases to do whatever dirty work was required. However, it was becoming obvious that he was involved here only in a technical capacity. This elite nuclear-peace group had its own armed action force, presumably selected from the more gung-ho members. Since money seemed to be a requirement for membership, they were probably successful business and professional people—Homer Allwyn had been careful to say that there was no *practicing* doctor here, which didn't mean they didn't have a few affluent medical men around taking time out from their profession. The goon squad had presumably been recruited from those eager atomic pacifists who weren't really averse to weapons as long as they were non-nuclear.

It was good in a way, of course, since it meant I was dealing with a bunch of characters who didn't really know the score. On the other hand, I couldn't help remembering several good men and women I'd known who had died, probably amazed and incredulous, at the hands of inexperienced and frightened jerks who'd cut loose when no reasonable person would have dreamed of pulling a trigger. I reminded myself, also, that these high-class part-time warriors weren't totally ineffectual; they'd managed to take this island from Constantine Greig's cheap toughs, although they'd done it by bribery, surprise, and overwhelming force.

Outside our prison chamber, I found a short, narrow hallway that ended, in both directions, in massive steel doors, which were closed. I noted that the heavy clamp-type fastenings on the one forward could be opened from our side; but the one aft could only be secured, and unsecured, from the other side of the watertight bulkhead; if you were caught up here in a collision, and they slammed the door on you, too bad, unless you could fight your way out on deck. A steel ladder led up to a hatch, which was open. We moved that way, and the big man went up first to cover me from above; the smaller one had his weapon pointed at my rump from below as I followed. The pain in my side made the climb no fun at all, and I wasn't altogether rid of my earlier headache; but I forgot all about those pains when I came out of the hatch, because instead of the open night sky there was a roof above us.

Emerging on the deck of a ship to find myself indoors made me feel pretty unreal; and I wondered if I was having some kind of a hallucinatory reaction from the sleepy-stuff I'd been stuck with.

"Weird, isn't it?" Gina Williston was there on deck, coming forward to meet me, obviously enjoying my surprise. "You can see that your missile theory wasn't too hot; we'd have a hard time firing anything through that solid roof."

I said, "Hell, it probably opens up like an astronomical observatory. What the hell kind of an overgrown barn is this, anyway?"

I realized that the floodlighted building wasn't as enormous as I'd thought at first glance. At least it wasn't as high as I'd thought, assuming that it had to accommodate the whole ship from keel to masthead. On second glance, I saw that the hull floated in a deep basin blasted and dug out of the rock of the cay. The ground was more or less level with the deck, so that the building itself only had to be high enough to accommodate the ship's modest superstructure. But it was still quite a sizable edifice to find on a desert island.

"I thought you'd be impressed," Gina said. "Come on, let me give you the guided tour." She glanced at me. "Parole for one hour? Otherwise I'll have to take one of those gun-toting creeps along to protect me."

"You've got your hour."

"This way."

She was back in her basic yachting costume, but she'd obviously had a bath since I'd last seen her, and done nice things to her hair, and even applied a bit of makeup although she wasn't much of an eye shadow girl. Then she'd got into her rough clothes to show me around; but she was really a very handsome woman even in well-worn jeans. There was a hint of perfume or cologne tonight. The works.

"Watch yourself here," she said, guiding me around some unidentifiable marine equipment. She glanced back and smiled maliciously. "Homer's glowering after us. He doesn't trust you, parole or no parole."

"You'd better watch that guy," I said. "He thinks dangerous thoughts."

"Well, so do you."

"That's right," I said. "But I'm not supposed to be playing on your team. He is."

"Over here," she said. "Let's get outside, shall we?"

We made our way across the cluttered deck. Glancing aft, I caught a hint of movement at one of the lower windows of the ship's superstructure, perhaps the cabin window from which Molly Brennerman had watched Minister taking his cigarette breaks. Now another girl was watching from behind the heavy storm-proof glass; a girl with a sweet, familiar face framed by pale blond hair. So Amy Barnett had made it. And if one Barnett was here, could another be far behind? At least it was nice to think that Doug might be waiting out in the night not too far away. I hoped he'd call in reinforcements and not try to do it all himself; but he undoubtedly would summon help—I was the lone-wolf operator around here. I was assuming, of course, that Amy hadn't managed to lose him en route and that he was really out there.

Gina led me to a gangway, actually a two-by-eight plank, which bridged the ten-foot gap between the ship's side and the side of the basin. As we negotiated it, I could see water below. It seemed odd to be standing on bare ground inside the building; but they hadn't bothered finishing off their overgrown boathouse with a concrete floor. There was just rocks and dirt, still with a few remnants of the island's grass and brush, enclosed by the walls of the building. The ship, under the floodlights, fit into its crude dock like a loosely fitting inlay in a drilled-out tooth.

Gina let me look for a moment; then she touched me on the shoulder and led me along a dirt path to a small side door. A moment later we were outside. There was enough light from the windows high up in the side of the building behind us for me to read what was painted below them in giant letters that would be visible for miles out at sea: ELYSIUM CAY CLUB—PRIVATE.

Gina said, "In Nassau, Hog Island became Paradise Island when the developers got hold of it. Why shouldn't Ring Cay—what a dull name!—become Elysium Cay?"

I looked around. "Hell, I thought we were way off in the remote outer islands. Uninhabited. What are all the lights?"

There weren't so many of them, it was hardly Times Square on New Year's Eve; but I'd expected to see nothing but a bleak, empty island and a black sea. Instead, I was looking at half a dozen lighted houses nearby. One of them, the nearest, seemed to be fairly substantial and two stories high. There were also several lights off across the water.

"The big house is our clubhouse," Gina said. "Constantine Greig's clubhouse, I mean. It's habitable; most of the other houses you see, like this building, are really just shells. Fakes. Like a movie set. But from the water, or the air, the island looks like a going resort, with a new unit built every few months to accommodate the club's growing clientele. Supposedly growing clientele. Supposedly very, very exclusive, of course. Wealthy anglers mostly, local rumor goes, but also just rich retired folks who like a change from their Miami Beach or Palm Beach homes; a nice place where they can have their own cottages—we prefer to call them villas, please—but are pampered with good food and pleasantly supervised exercise outdoors and indoors, including swimming. Have you noticed how many people drive clear to the ocean in order to paddle around in a freshwater motel pool?"

"I've remarked the phenomenon," I said.

She went on: "Well, like in the brochures, here's the Olympic indoor pool for those who can't stand that nasty outdoors salt water. Naturally, its construction involved a lot of blasting and bulldozing—or should I say that it explained a lot of blasting and bulldozing? And of course it required a big building, not only to cover it and the associated freshwater evaporators and filters and pumps, but also to house the indoor handball courts and saunas and stuff that are supposed to be available here. Greig's Folly, I'm sure it was called; but the big man was foolish like a fox. His little ships slipped in here in the middle of the night, and the club's fleet of innocent-looking, expensive-looking, and very speedy sportfishermen hauled the cargoes over to Florida piecemeal, while the authorities were looking all over the Islands for the vanished smuggling vessel that was actually parked in the Elysium Cay Club's supposed Olympic swimming pool."

"Cute," I said. I was looking out to sea at the more distant lights. "But where the hell are we, anyway?"

"That cluster of three lights off to the left is Grouper Cay. There's a small settlement there, but they go to bed early. And Arabella Cay to the right; that's private, owned by a Miami millionaire. You can see the house, where the single light is, from this side but not from the other. Beyond it is Lostman's Rock, where we anchored. I had to pick a spot from which you couldn't get a clear view of Ring Cay—Elysium Cay—with those islands in the way. I mean, this building is pretty conspicuous, and you might have wondered. The deepwater channel runs from a mile this side of Arabella, past the end of this cay, and around into the lagoon. Eighteen feet of water all the way. There's camouflage, of course, to conceal the entrance below this supposed recreation center. It looks just like the rocky shore of the lagoon until it's opened to let the ship be warped inside."

"Sounds like one of those camouflaged sub pens the Germans built during World War Two." I drew a long breath. "Connie Grieg really had himself an installation here, before you took it away from him. He must have spent a mint on it. No wonder he was mad."

"He made out all right," Gina said. "The first couple of shiploads, several years ago, paid all the bills; since then it's been pure gravy. And he knew the authorities were closing in on him. The place had served its purpose and made him rich, but it was time to pull out. We just rushed his schedule a bit; but he got paid for that, too, thanks to you. It was only his macho pride that was hurt, not his bank account."

I said, "You still haven't told me where we are."

"Come over here."

She led me around the corner of the building. From there we had a good view of the lagoon. It was, as she'd told me once, rather long and narrow. The entrance was a break in the shore to the left. Beyond, at the far end where it wouldn't interfere with the tricky maneuvering involved in getting a ship under cover at the near end, was a lighted dock that held three sizable sportfishing boats complete with tuna towers and outriggers, and *Spindrift*, which looked small and out of place among the thousand-horsepower angling machines. There were also some smaller powerboats, presumably so the nonexistent clients of the resort could indulge in close-in fishing. There was a big sign on the dock. I couldn't read it at the distance, but it probably said something like: PRIVATE—KEEP OFF! There were similar signs on both sides of the lagoon entrance, which was narrow enough that I'd have been nervous bringing in a small sailboat, let alone a hundred-and-fifty-foot ship.

"Well, we had us a nice cruise, aside from a few ropes and bullets and hypos," I said. "Are you going to break down and tell me where it got us?"

"See that faint glow on the horizon over there? . . . No, farther to the left."

"I've got it." She was obviously waiting for me to guess, so I squinted across the sea at the vague smudge of light and said, "Hell, that could be a good-sized city, a long distance away."

"About thirty miles away. Yes, it is."

I said, "I don't think we could have made it as far as San Juan, Puerto Rico, in the time we were at it. How about Havana, Cuba?"

She laughed. "You're being silly."

"Always."

She said, "That's Nassau, my dear."

I STARED at the glow on the horizon. I'd wondered a bit at Grieg's reluctance to retake his lost harbor by force, since he felt so strongly about it. After all, it was supposed to be down among the uninhabited outer islands where a little shooting wasn't likely to be noticed. But here, so close to the big city, his resigned attitude made more sense. As he'd said, a noisy amphibious assault would have been bound to attract attention, leaving Ring Cay, even if he recaptured it, of no use to him.

Glancing at Gina, I could see that she was looking very smug, very pleased with herself. She'd pulled another fast one on me, an even better trick than the anchorage. For a grown woman, she got her satisfactions in odd, childish ways. Well, sometimes. I found myself rubbing the Band-Aid that covered the gouge caused by a bullet that could hardly be called childish.

"Oooh, what a clever lady it is!" I said admiringly. "So all that time you were sailing us around in circles?"

She shrugged, modest now. "More or less. Actually, I kept us heading generally south in the daytime when you could tell direction by the sun. Then I came back north at night. I was afraid you might know something about the stars, but apparently you don't."

"I'm strictly a Big Dipper man, ma'am. And it was never visible from the portholes, or out of the forward hatch, what with the sails often blocking up to half the view."

"Grieg was really quite ingenious," Gina said. "He planted all those rumors about his secret cay way off in the remote islands; and all the time his transshipment point was within thirty miles of Providence Island."

"But how did that coast guard boat stumble onto it? I thought they were searching far to the south and east of here. That's where I was told they were heading, at least. That's where I was supposed to be heading. That was where the body was found."

Gina laughed shortly. "They did exactly what you just said, stumbled onto it. They'd picked up a tank of dirty gas in Nassau and—would you believe it? —limped in here to clean their carburetors and change their fuel filters. They were warned off and told it was private property, a private club, can't you read the signs, stupid? The guard wasn't as polite as he might have been, I guess. That young ensign, Sanderson, apparently got mad and suspicious at this breach of nautical etiquette: who turns away mariners in distress and is rude about it? Homer Allwyn may know something about security, actually he runs a very profitable business back home providing watchmen and bodyguards and checking offices for listening devices, that sort of thing. But he doesn't know much about dealing with people."

"You don't have to tell me that. I've got a cracked rib to remind me."

"Oh, my God! He was told very firmly that there was no need to get rough with anybody."

"Maybe that's why he kicked me," I said. "And you

should see the boy officer he worked over, practically a basket case."

"I didn't know. . . ."

"Never mind it now," I said. "Go on."

After a moment, she shrugged helplessly and said, "Well, anyway, as they sputtered away on one sick engine, we could see the younger man looking astern with his big seven by fifties, studying every detail of the island. We knew who he was, of course; we knew all about the coast guard's little expedition. As a matter fact, that was why I happened to be here at the time; I'd come out to warn them after we'd learned about it. Respectable citizens with money don't have much trouble learning the plans of public servants, since they're all made in quintuplicate with information copies given to everybody around. . . . Well, anyway, watching from shore we saw him spot something, maybe a flaw in the camouflage, or something too phony-looking about one of the empty villas. We saw him point it out excitedly to his companions. So of course Homer had to go out with his cohorts and bring them back in."

I said, "Well, you can figure that you broke even. You got your ship in the first place because of a convenient engine breakdown; and then the Coast Guard people spotted its hideout because of an inconvenient engine breakdown. How did Brennerman get away?"

"That was a big, powerful man. As the three of them were being marched away from the dock over there, he simply knocked a gun barrel aside and hit the man holding the gun hard enough to break his jaw. Then he ran to the beach over on the other side of the cay. There was some shooting. He was nicked, and he limped slightly before he dove in. He'd obviously hoped to swim over to Grouper or Arabella, although the currents would have given him a hard time. But the blood from his wound was too attractive,

I guess." She shrugged awkwardly. "It was . . . pretty awful. He had a good start, they had to take a boat clear around the island to go after him—he'd obviously counted on that—but they were almost to him when the shark hit. The biggest one they'd ever seen in these waters, they said. They put what . . . what was left of him in a fast, long-range boat and took it as far from here as they could and left it where it would probably be found, where it would be expected to be found, if there was a search. As there was."

"And that," I said, "in the classic phrase, was when the shit hit the fan. And you folks stopped being a bunch of fine, concerned, respectable citizens and became a gang of bloody-handed murderers."

"It was an accident! Nobody was supposed to be hurt until—" She stopped abruptly.

"Until when?"

After a pause, she said, "There's hardly ever any way of . . . of accomplishing something in this world without hurting *somebody*, Matt. You always have to measure the amount of bad against the amount of good."

"What you're trying to say is, you can't make an omelet without breaking eggs. That's hardly an original observation, sweetheart."

She didn't respond to this; instead she said stiffly, as if I hadn't spoken: "This ship has some watertight bulkheads forward. You must have seen them when you were brought on deck. In a bad collision they'd be ordered closed instantly, wouldn't they, even if there might be some hurt crew members trapped beyond them? It would be a question of balancing the loss of a couple of men, say, as against the loss of the whole ship and the remainder of the crew."

I said, "So you're going to sacrifice a few people to insure the survival of Spaceship Earth."

"Damn you, don't sneer—" She caught herself and

went on: "Long ago we resigned ourselves to the fact that we'd have some deaths on our consciences before this was over. But when Brennerman died we weren't ready for . . ."

When she stopped and swallowed, I grinned at her. "You weren't ready for all that gore, right? The water turning red. Rags of flesh and shreds of tendons and strings of intestines trailing from the mutilated body, enough to turn anybody's stomach, right? Hell, you almost lost your breakfast a couple of mornings ago on account of a simple little groove in my skull and a few ounces of hemoglobin and other stuff splashing around. A hell of a bunch of queasy idealists you are! Like that fly-boy I told you about who could be ruthless as hell saving the world for democracy as long as he was just pushing buttons umpteen-thousand feet up in the sky but couldn't bear to slam a forty-five-caliber slug into a real live human Nazi at point-blank range."

"Just because we aren't all hardened killers . . ."

"Well, you'd better get yourself some hardened killers, baby! I mean, why the hell are Mrs. Brennerman and young Sanderson still alive? You people want to break clean when it's all over, don't you? You don't want to leave any live witnesses to your murders and whatever else you're up to. Yet you're keeping those two on ice for no good reason that I can see; and here I am, because you didn't have the gumption to put a second bullet a little to the left of the first. Jeez, what a sloppy operation! What are you saving us for, anyway? You've got some potentially good homicidal material in Allwyn. Why don't you turn him loose and let him get in a little assassination practice; he'd like that."

She said sharply, "Don't think Homer hasn't suggested it; but we'll soon have a cleaner way of disposing . . ." She paused. After a moment, she laughed softly. "You're the strangest man, always telling people they ought to kill you, when anybody else would be pleading with them not to."

I said, "It works, doesn't it? If I were on my knees begging you to spare me, you'd laugh at me and throw me to the wolves or whatever you have in mind for us. But instead I have you thinking . . . What are you thinking, Gina?"

"I'm thinking that you're right about the other two; they must be silenced," she said calmly, "We can't trust them not to break any promise we manage to extract from them. The world these days seems to be full of people who can rationalize disregarding a sacred oath whenever it becomes just slightly inconvenient; they tell themselves self-righteously that they don't have to keep their word if it was given to a spy or a criminal, or if they were coerced into giving it. But your word's been good so far, and you've had plenty of chances to break it; and . . . well, I don't particularly want to see you dead. I told you I'd do what I could. There's a way out for you, Matt."

I looked at her for a long moment in the semidarkness beside the big building. I was a little embarrassed by her trust. I wasn't at all certain how trustworthy I'd have been if it hadn't suited my plans to abide by the paroles I'd given her.

"Spell it out," I said. "What's it going to cost me to stay alive?"

"That depends."

"Don't be coy."

"To some extent it depends on how repulsive you find me."

I said, "Hell, I can't stand any woman in pants." Then I said, "For Christ's sake, Gina! You can't tell me you're so hard up for lovers you have to steal them away from the firing squad. Even gorgeous me."

She said stiffly, "Have you forgotten that you saved my life up there off Great Stirrup Light, Matt? I'm trying to pay my debt." She laughed abruptly. "Don't flatter yourself by thinking that I'm madly in love with you. But we do pretty well together, don't we? And I do owe you something."

I shrugged. "If you say so. What are the terms of my salvation?"

She said, "All you have to do is behave like a sensible man willing to change employers, for a consideration. A financial consideration, really. Substantial, we can afford it; but they'll be more likely to believe you're playing straight with us if you act just a little smitten with the lady who persuaded you to defect, if that's the proper word." She grinned at me. "That's what I meant when I said your fate might depend on how repulsive you find me. Or don't find me. I was going to wear something seductive to make it easy for you, but can you see me climbing around that grimy old ship all done up in sexy lace and satin? But I do smell pretty nice for a change, don't I?"

"Like a rose," I said. "In other words, I'm simply being offered a position with a different firm, with some interesting fringe benefits."

She laughed at the way I'd put it. "That's right. I think I can show you that what we're doing is very important, very worthwhile. And we can use a man like you; you said so yourself. What do you really owe that ruthless establishment organization you work for? Over the years, you've given them their money's worth several times over, haven't you?" She slipped her arms around my neck and touched her lips to mine. "And you do find the fringe benefits attractive, don't you?"

I said, after taking a little time to return her kiss, "You're twisting my arm. At least I think that's what you're twisting. Something. But you keep talking around the most important subject: If I do join your exclusive outfit of dedicated millionaires, what the hell will I be joining? What's going on here, anyway? What's it all about?" When she hesitated, I said roughly, "Come on, sell it to me, sweetheart! Don't leave me thinking I'll be betraying my country for a piece of tail; that's no way to soothe a man's conscience."

She released me abruptly and stepped back. "You do pick your words, don't you, right out of the sewer!" she snapped. Then she laughed. "But you're right. Enough of this circumlocution. Come on back inside, I'll show you. . . ."

She led me inside the building, past one of Allwyn's men, the big one whose name I didn't know, Jesperson's partner, who'd been keeping an eye on us out in the dark. She guided me back onto the ship, and aft to the superstructure, and inside past another guard I didn't recognize, to a metal stairway leading down— but I guess they're all called ladders on shipboard, whether they're slanty or straight up and down. This ladder deposited us in the forward end of the engine room.

I could see why she hadn't wanted to trail any sexy lingerie through here, or even her nice white dress; everything was either rusty or greasy or both. We made no inspection of the ship's ancient power plant lurking back there in the dark. Instead Gina turned the other way, leading me past a thumping generator that, shiny and obviously brand new, was an exception to the engine room's dirt and corrosion—apparently, whatever they were doing on board, they needed a reliable source of electricity. We came to a watertight door like those I'd seen up forward, but this one was open. At six four, I had to duck to get through it. I straightened up in the cavernous, lighted space beyond, the ship's main hold; but it no longer looked like a space for cargo. It looked more like a sci-fi movie.

Gina was brushing at a rusty smudge on her jeans. Before trying to determine just what I was being shown, I looked forward and spotted, at the far end of the steel room, the heavy steel door, clamped tightly shut, that presumably gave access to the passageway in the bow off which Molly Brennerman and Ricardo Sanderson were still imprisoned. Having located that, I let my attention move to the object occupying the place of honor in the center of the hold. It really wasn't very impressive, just a shiny metal cylinder about the size of a fifty-five-gallon drum. It was lying on its side, firmly secured in a massive wooden cradle bolted to the floor of the hold. Metal tubes led to the shiny thing, perhaps for temperature control. There were also heavy electric cables and some lighter wires of different colors. The rest of the space was more impressive, since it contained a well-equipped machine shop and what seemed to be a chemical laboratory of sorts.

Then I saw the sturdy little wooden boxes, or packing crates, that had been shoved aside under one of the laboratory benches. They'd been pried open and whatever had been inside was no longer there; but I could see that they were lined with lead. On the outside of each discarded box, on every visible surface, was stenciled in red the words: *Danger!*—RADIOACTIVE MATERIAL—*Danger!* I looked again at the shiny cylinder under the lights in the rusty steel room.

"Oh, for God's sake!" I said to Gina. "You've got to be kidding!"

WHEN I was a boy I dreamed of owning a certain legendary weapon: the old Colt single action army revolver, in .45 caliber of course. It took some doing since there wasn't much money and, while my parents weren't opposed in principle to having meat providers like deer rifles and duck guns on our modest New Mexico ranch, they still clung to the European notion—shared by a lot of Americans now, it seems, but not so many back then—that while a weapon fired from two hands might be morally acceptable, a one-hand gun just had to be inherently evil; a distinction I still fail to comprehend. But I was a hardworking young fellow and a persistent one; and in the end I wound up defending myself from a lot of hostile tin cans and savage paper targets, not to mention a few ferocious jackrabbits, with my faithful, .45 Colt, only to discover that it wasn't all that great. Its accuracy left a lot to be desired, the leaf springs kept breaking under hard use, it was slow to load and unload and, since it had to be cocked for each shot, not very fast to shoot. . . .

Now I was facing another legendary weapon. Not the gun that won the West but the bomb that won the East. Like the old six-shooter and its more durable and deadly successors, it had solved the violent problem that had brought it into existence only to leave society saddled with more and greater problems, leaving people wishing they could make it go away. Ban the handgun. Ban the bomb. The character who finds a way of uninventing the inventions that folks decide not to like is going to make a fortune. . . . All of which was merely, of course, the wandering of my mind as it refused to come to grips with the thing in front of me.

I pulled myself together with an effort and told myself firmly that I was a courageous and experienced gent who'd confronted all kinds of nasty homicidal devices without flinching. Facing this king-sized can of radioactive destruction, I definitely wasn't going to act all girlish and panicky like Amy Barnett when she'd suddenly found herself holding a lousy little .38. After all, I told myself, I wouldn't have been so nervous wandering into a warehouse containing a mere ten or twenty or thirty thousand tons of TNT. Or would I?

Anyway, I reminded myself, it was actually the Winchester that won the West, or claimed to have. If it mattered.

"Isn't she wicked and lovely?"

I turned to look at the man who'd spoken, who'd come up without my noticing him, a measure of my unprofessional preoccupation. He was a rather plump, middle-aged gent in a starched white laboratory smock. He had thinning fair hair, and very pale blue eyes behind horn-rimmed glasses. The dossier had said nothing about glasses, but maybe they were a recent necessity. Nobody gets any younger. His plump hands were clasped together in an attitude of loving admiration as he looked proudly at the object on the cradle. I noted that the hands looked tougher than the man;

they were callused with work and stained with chemicals.

"She?" I said.

"Anything so dangerous must be female, mustn't it? But I have her under control. I always have them under control, Mr. Helm."

I was barely aware of Gina's voice saying, unnecessarily "Matt, this is Albert Pope."

"Oh, Mr. Helm knows me, he knows me very well," the plump man said cheerfully. "We have friends in common, don't we, Mr. Helm? At least one friend; a very delightful little friend."

He was needling me about Amy Barnett, who'd left me and gone back to him. It didn't seem wise to react. Instead I jerked my head at the bomb and made my voice very matter-of-fact when I asked:

"What's inside, plutonium or uranium two thirty-five?"

"Oh, you know something about atomic weapons?" Minister's voice was patronizing; still, he seemed intrigued at meeting somebody who shared his pleasant hobby, even me.

I shrugged. "I know what everybody knows. That you use conventional high explosives to slam some subcritical mass of radioactive stuff together to make a supercritical mass; and bang she goes. That plutonium was the basic ingredient of the implosion bombs set off in the Trinity test and at Nagasaki. That the Hiroshima bomb was quite different, a gun-type job employing U235. It hadn't been tested before, but it seemed to work pretty well, anyway." I glanced at the man in the white coat and said deliberately, "As a matter of fact, neither kind seems to be very tough to make, now that we know it can be done. Nobody who's really tried has failed to come up with one that fired. As far as I know there are no fizzles on record."

His eyes narrowed. I wasn't showing proper appreciation for his achievement. "It may be easy for a great government laboratory, but under conditions like these . . . There were many problems to solve!"

I ignored his protest. "What's the cooling system for, if that's what it is?" I asked, glad to hear that my voice still sounded nice and casual, just mildly curious.

"That was one of our problems." He'd decided that he was happy to discuss his toy. "For initiating the reaction, I wanted to use a particular explosive that has some very desirable characteristics; actually a considerable improvement over what was probably used at Hiroshima. However, I had to do the preliminary work at sea; and this space is not air-conditioned. With the sun beating down on the deck above, I knew it would get quite warm down here. That particular explosive material tends to be affected by high temperatures, above forty-five degrees Celsius, say one hundred and thirteen degrees Fahrenheit. I thought it best to store it under refrigeration. Since portability was not a consideration, I also provided for coolant circulation in the bomb itself, in case conditions in here became excessive. Of course, in this location, with the ship shaded by a roof, the system may be redundant."

I said chattily, "Hell, I once carted some kind of blasting powder up to a mine in the mountains, in my rucksack, on a hot summer day. It scared the shit out of me when it started to weep; little droplets all over the inside of the plastic bags. I thought it was pure nitro oozing out and would go off if I stumbled or sneezed. It turned out that the stuff was slightly hygroscopic and some of the moisture it had picked up was evaporating in the heat and condensing on the plastic." I laughed at my own funny story and glanced at him. "So you're using the Hiroshima model."

"That's right. It's the less efficient system, but it's

considerably simpler to construct; and plutonium is hard to handle without elaborate facilities. It's relatively unstable and very poisonous. To be sure, it's more readily available in general, since it can be produced in any reactor, while U235 can only be separated from U238 by very demanding techniques; but this does not concern us. As it happens, two of the members of the PNP are financially involved in a certain experimental laboratory that made a large investment in the centrifuge process some years ago, so we had no real trouble getting our hands on sufficient Uranium 235. It was largely, I was told, a matter of bookkeeping; and somebody at that lab will be in serious trouble eventually, when the shortage is discovered. However, that is not my problem."

"As I recall, the Hiroshima bomb used about sixty pounds. That's a lot of refined uranium."

"We're using about seven kilos, considerably less than a third of what was used in that first fission-type bomb, which was really a rather crude and inefficient device. We expect a yield of around twenty kilotons. A little more than Hiroshima, but nothing, of course, compared to what is produced by one of the fusion-type devices, which would use a bomb like this as a mere trigger. However, I wasn't employed to demolish all of the Bahama Islands, Mr. Helm, just a few of them."

He said it quite casually, and I caught a hint of regret in his voice. He was very proud of his current work, he'd reached the peak of his explosive profession, but there was a higher summit beyond still reserved for the eggheads. He would love to try it, he would love to show them what a working pro could produce in the way of a *real* explosion, without the need for all their fancy degrees and facilities.

Well, there's nothing like a man who takes pride in

his work; and considering my own job I was in no position to criticize his. But I had reached the end of the long trail and the quarry I'd been hunting was within reach. . . . And the waiting silence warned me that he'd been put within my reach deliberately. If I started the killing blow that would complete my mission, I would never finish it. Alfred Minister was laughing at me behind his horn-rimmed glasses, waiting for me to commit myself. He knew that if I struck, I would be striking not only for official reasons but for personal ones: the girl named Amy whose loyalties were so terribly torn between us. That was why he'd mentioned her so possessively, hoping it would cause me to lose my head and betray myself. . . .

I turned casually to Gina. "Well, Mr. Pope seems to have done you proud; but I'm surprised that you didn't pick a different kind of specialist for the job."

"An atomic specialist, you mean?" She laughed. "If we'd got a man with an advanced degree in nuclear physics, how long would it have been before somebody like you guessed what we were up to? Instead, you spent your time of merely wondering just where we were having Mr. Pope plant his old-fashioned dynamite, and why."

I looked around easily. They weren't hard to spot, the two guards who'd moved into positions from which, if I made a threatening move toward Minister, they could blow me down instantly without damaging people or equipment—although even in this larger space, I wouldn't have wanted to predict the behavior of the ricochets if the bullets missed me or drilled clear through me. They were the men who'd escorted me from the cell, Homer Allwyn's right- and left-hand men. They looked slack and disappointed now, as the tension drained out of them. So did Allwyn himself, watching from the engine room doorway. There was also another man standing beside Gina. The fact that

I hadn't noticed his entrance indicated how totally involved I'd been with the crazy doomsday machine and the man who'd made it.

The newcomer was a tall and distinguished figure with a full head of smoothly combed dark hair streaked with gray. He would have looked well in a pinstripe suit; he didn't look too bad in jeans. I think there's a special grade of denim that's only released for sale after the customer has been thoroughly checked out in *Who's Who* and Dunn & Bradstreet. He wore a superior polo shirt above and very expensive yachting shoes below.

"Matt, this is Mr. Paul, Mr. Harrison Paul," Gina said. "He's the chairman of our board at PNP."

I shook Mr. Harrison Paul's manicured hand and said to Gina, "I thought *you* were chairman of the board, Mrs. W."

"Mrs. Williston is our president," Paul said smoothly. "Our president and guiding spirit."

"But you don't always like where I guide you, do you, Harrison?"

Paul looked at me briefly, then returned his attention to her. "To put it bluntly, I see no reason why we should all be put at risk for the sake of your amours, Gina. This government agent has already been allowed to learn too much; to bring him in here and let him chat with Pope is total madness!"

"If he already knows too much, what difference does it make if he learns a little more? Anyway, there's a way to insure his silence."

"Yes, a bullet in the brain!"

"Correct, but I'm not referring to his brain. Two bullets in two brains. He's indicated that he might be willing to join us for a consideration. Let him prove it by taking care of a certain disposal job for us." She looked at me hard. "You told me what should be done about the two prisoners up forward we've been too softhearted to kill. Well, do it."

I studied her for a moment; then I laughed. "What are you waiting for, a shocked protest, Gina? Do you think I'd lay down my life nobly rather than wipe out a grubby young widow and a beat-up kid? To hell with that, baby; that's not how I've survived so long in a short-survival business. Do I get a gun?"

"No guns, no bullets," she said. "That was just a figure of speech. You know how to do without."

I shrugged. "As you wish."

"You realize that after you've killed them . . ."

I said, "Gina, for God's sake, I've seen all the movies! Yes, I realize that after I've killed a couple of Coast Guard people for you, you'll be able to blackmail me with it quite efficiently; you'll have me under your thumb, as the saying goes. Any other corny remarks you wish to cast onto the balmy Bahamas air? No? Well, how about answering a couple of questions before I go about my deadly work?"

She said sharply, "Matt, killing is not a joke!"

I said, "No, but I've always felt better treating it as if it were. And you do want me to feel good, don't you?"

She said, "Ask your questions."

"That cannon-cracker there—"

"It's not dangerous as it stands, if that's what's worrying you," she said tartly. "There's no stray radiation, to amount to anything. You don't have to worry about your virility."

"It's not my virility that's worrying me, it's your good sense. What the hell are you hoping to accomplish with that thing? Whom are you planning to blackmail, all the nations of the world? Are you going to sneak this ship into Nassau harbor and threaten to blow up the whole town, and the nuclear control conference with it, if all the delegates don't promise to straighten up and fly right? I'm giving you credit; I'm assuming that your motives are still basically peaceful, even though you don't seem to mind a little murder on the side. But nations are even less meticulous than people about honoring forced promises. Even if you convince them that you really have the bomb, which will take some doing, do you think any country will abide by a commitment it's been coerced into making by a bluff like that?"

"What makes you think it's a bluff, Matt?"

There was a little silence. I stared at her, remembering her medical history and the screaming nightmare she'd had on board the boat. But Mr. Harrison Paul had no screws loose, as far as I knew; and it seemed unlikely that the rest of the PNP membership list was composed entirely of maniac millionaires.

It was, I decided, a question of attitude. I've long since faced the fact that, in the business I've chosen for myself, I'm probably going to die a little earlier than I otherwise might. I'll fight as hard and as dirty as I have to to keep it from happening, but I'm not about to waste a lot of effort trying to change the whole world to make it totally safe for Helms; and whether by knife or bullet or atomic holocaust, it's bound to get this Helm sooner or later. Rest in peace. But there was no such resignation in these people. If the world wouldn't leave them alone to live out their beautiful, wealthy lives unmolested . . . well, it was just too damn bad about the world, and they'd have to remodel it slightly. It was a more positive attitude than mine, I had to admit, and I didn't condemn it. I merely felt that the method they'd chosen was somewhat questionable.

I said, "You're actually going to *fire* that thing?"

She nodded. "But we're not moving this ship to Nassau or anywhere else. I told you, we picked our spot very carefully; we were just lucky that this

299

installation happened to be here. Otherwise we'd have had to use Aravella Cay, which belongs to one of our members; but that would have involved constructing suitable facilities ashore, which might have stimulated some unhealthy curiosity. This was ideal, ready-made, the right distance from Nassau, even though it meant that Mr. Pope had to do his work in a rusty ship's hold instead of a nice new air-conditioned laboratory."

I licked my lips. "Kind of a drastic demonstration, wouldn't you say? What do you think it'll accomplish?"

"It'll do just what you said would be so hard to do. It'll prove that we have it. At least one here; who's to say that we don't have another—maybe several others—elsewhere? After watching this one go up, do you think anybody'll want to gamble that we don't have other teams working toward the same goal, teams that will now find their missions much easier, since they'll have all the information we gained here?"

"Do you have other teams?"

She smiled faintly. "Maybe, maybe not. I'll let you guess about that, just as the world will be guessing soon." Her smile faded. "Isn't it time *somebody* fought back, Matt? Here they're stockpiling the horrible things all over the world and talking nonsense about survivability; and all the lovely idealists just weep and wail and throw themselves down in front of the bomb trucks crying, '*Squash me, please squash me!*' Well, we may get a little queasy at times, as you said; it takes a while to get used to blood and death. But we're not starry-eyed idealists; and we're going to give these warlike characters a taste of their own medicine!"

"Fighting fire with fire, right? And atoms with atoms."

"I can always count on you, my dear. A fast man with a cliché." She shook her head grimly. "It won't be nice. People are going to die here, certainly. The settlement on Grouper Cay will vanish. Hell, Grouper Cay will vanish; and there are other island communities nearby that'll be wiped out. The fallout . . . well, let's just say that Nassau probably won't have a very good time; and depending on the winds the Florida coast may even be affected. So? How many more would die in a worldwide conflict? And if they force us to go to phase two, and their weirdo missile silos and nuclear ammunition storage facilities start going up in radioactive smoke, there'll probably be deaths in the thousands and hundreds of thousands all over the world; but the toll still won't approach the casualty lists, or the contamination, of a real nuclear war. Damn it, *somebody's* got to put a stop to it before it starts, Matt!"

I said, "Sure. But why here?"

"What do you mean?" Gina frowned. "This is where the conference is being held, isn't it?"

I said, "Hell, the United Nations meets all the time. Why not impress those delegates instead; they're pretty influential, too, aren't they? Set off your big bang up in White Plains, New York, or down in Perth Amboy, New Jersey; and they'll have a fine view of it from their big glass tower on the East River. Much more dramatic, anyway, than blowing up a bunch of crummy little coral islands with a few niggers on them."

"Matt!"

"Don't snap at me!" I said sharply. "I'm not the rich white American lady who's decided to save the world by firing off a nuclear device in a foreign country inhabited largely by poor blacks. But you don't think the lesson's going to be overlooked by the so-called Third World, do you? They'll see whose population and real estate are considered expendable by your well-heeled peace organization—which has how many nonwhite members?"

She started to blow up angrily but checked herself. "You're being unfair and irrelevant," she said. "We picked the most sparsely populated area we could find that would serve our purpose. Without regard to race, color, or creed. Have you asked all your questions?"

"One more," I said. "There's got to be another part to your program. Constructive rather than destructive."

"There is. We've had the best political brains in the world working on it. We have a proposal. It's not foolproof; but it's a hell of a lot better than anything that's been suggested so far, certainly better than anything they're likely to come up with in Nassau, where they're all just looking for nationalistic advantage and making soothing noises to appease their frightened populations. They'll never come close to considering the problem honestly, unless somebody takes a whip to them. Well, there's the whip!" She gestured toward the shiny contraption in the middle of the hold. Her face was set in hard, fanatic lines. "Let them see what it'll be like if they don't do the work they were sent to do, and do it sincerely. Let them feel the earth shake, goddamn it! Let them see the sky light up over here; let them see the whole horizon on fire. Let them watch the mushroom cloud rise into the stratosphere. Let them run like hell from the radioactive fallout and try to wash it off when it covers them. And when they've recovered a little, those who recover, maybe they'll come to the conference table with a different attitude, they and the ones appointed to replace the ones who died! Maybe we'll have a *real* nuclear control conference for a change!"

Well, it was a tempting scenario; but behind it was

just the good old weapons syndrome that seems to attack a lot of people who don't know anything about weapons. Somebody who's grown up with guns, like me, knows perfectly well that a firearm is simply a tool for drilling a small round hole in an object, inanimate or animate. If that's what you want, fine; but don't expect a Smith and Wesson .38 or even a roaring, thundering Ruger .44 Magnum to turn you into some kind of an omnipotent deity with absolute control of the world around you. One of the saddest sights I'd seen was a young punk who tried a holdup on me and a colleague named Matson in a Washington parking lot when we were returning to our car after a pleasant dinner. The threat came from Janet Matson's side so I let her take care of it, sweeping the cheap pistol aside with the routine moves we're all taught at the Ranch in Arizona and putting three fast ones into the chest and belly of the target—as I'd told Amy, we don't monkey around when they come at us with guns. That's a for-keeps situation. Afterward the would-be holdup artist sat against the side of a parked car, dying in a spreading puddle of blood and urine, staring up at us reproachfully. Somebody'd told him a gun was all it would take to make him a big man giving orders to everybody. Why hadn't we got the word?

Somebody'd told Gina Williston that an atom bomb was all it would take to make her a big woman who would save the world, particularly her wealthy part of it. But a nuclear weapon is just another tool for making a hole; a large, radioactive hole this time, but still a hole. It's not a mind-bending force or a people-control machine; and I knew it wouldn't work the way she expected, not even if she really found the ruthlessness to order it set off—and this was the woman who hadn't been able to finish me off as I lay in my bunk, dazed from her first shot. These were the people who hadn't been capable of wiping out two dangerous witnesses against them, even after a shark had obliged them by taking care of the third. They talked very big about the death and destruction they planned to wreak; but that was, I reflected, a clue in itself. There was a good chance that they'd chicken out when the time came to give the final firing command.

The hell of it was, I hadn't been sent here to deal with any giant fireworks. Common sense said that I'd be expected to do what I could to prevent the blast; but if the members of the PNP had been all I had to worry about, I might have gambled on a last-minute change of heart. However, there was another factor: the man who'd brought me here. I looked at Alfred Minister, still standing beside his brainchild and wearing his white scientist-coat. His eyes met mine through the horn-rimmed glasses; and I could see in them contempt for the soft people whose money he was taking—the soft people and their hard talk.

He knew their weakness as well as I did; but if anybody thought he'd built this lovely thing in order to leave it unfired . . . Well, you didn't go to bed with a girl and climb out and pull your pants back on again before you'd found the release you needed, did you? I knew that no matter what orders were given, or countermanded, or not given, Minister would see that the red button got pushed. As a matter of fact, judging by the record I'd studied, his record, there were probably timing devices and booby traps built into The Bomb to make quite certain it blew eventually, even if the remote-control detonator was disabled in some way. Nobody was going to cheat this man out of his king-sized, radioactive orgasm.

So there was nothing for me to do but play along until I saw a reasonable break; and if that meant killing a couple of innocent people to gain Gina's confidence, that was just too damn bad. Nobody was totally innocent and everybody died sometime. I might die myself before this was over; and it wasn't as if they were great friends of mine. We have very few great friends in the business.

I said, "Well, I guess I like peace as well as the next guy; and you've certainly picked an intriguing way of going for it. But I'd better be getting on with my chores." I glanced at the watertight door leading forward. "Do I get that hatch opened for me, or do I have to climb those ladders up on deck and down again?"

It was Harrison Paul who spoke: "A little climbing won't hurt you. And there'll be two men with you to see that you do the job right."

I shrugged. "Whatever you say, Mister Chairman of the Board. . . ."

"No." It was Gina's voice; when we looked at her, she said to Paul, "You don't understand the kind of man he is. Put guards on him, and he'll take it as an insult and a challenge. For him to be of any real use to us, we have to trust him."

"Trust him? Don't be ridiculous, Georgina!"

"That's right," she said. "You don't trust anybody, do you, Harrison? And maybe that's why I'm Madame President here and you're just the lousy chairman and don't really have much say in what's going to happen." She hesitated. "But let me take out a little insurance, before I turn him loose. . . . Matt."

"Yes, ma'am."

She looked at me steadily. "Matt, will you swear by all you hold sacred . . . Never mind. That's foolish, there isn't much any of us holds sacred or holy these days, is there? Except, perhaps, sometimes, one thing. Matt, will you give me your personal word of honor that you'll work for us loyally and take no action against us, any of us, including Mr. Pope? . . ."

THEY TOSSED me back into my cell—our cell—without much ceremony, tripping me deliberately so that I sprawled on the rusty floor. I heard them laughing as they slammed the steel door and locked it. Well, that was all right, they had a laugh coming. Everybody had a laugh coming. Who the hell did I think I was, Sir Galahad or somebody? Who did I think I'd been working for all these years, the Boy Scouts of America?

See the ruthless secret agent who'd snuff out a couple of innocent lives like snapping his fingers if his mission required it. See the ruthless secret agent louse up said mission, and maybe foul up the whole world, by behaving like a kid with romantic notions of honor . . . *honor*, for Christ's sake, that ancient and obsolete concept! But the damn woman had sneaked up on me, with her honorable paroles and trusting truces. I'd kind of got in the habit of keeping faith with her, so that when she'd at last asked of me a promise I had no intention of keeping, I hadn't been able to give it instantly and smoothly, balking at the lie just long enough to make it pointless to lie at all.

Buy your secondhand car from Honest Helm; he'll tell you frankly that the crankcase is full of sawdust. . . .

I became aware that Molly Brennerman was helping me up and brushing me off. There was the more distant sound of the deck hatch dropping with a crash, sealing us into the forepart of the ship, since the heavy door leading aft into the hold was already closed. I looked around the cell and discovered that Molly and I were no longer alone. The beat-up young ensign had rejoined the living. He was sitting on his cot watching, sagging a little with weakness.

"Mr. Helm?" he said, speaking with difficulty because of his damaged mouth. "I'm Ricardo Sanderson."

"I know, I met your papa a while back. How are you feeling?"

"Never mind how he's feeling!" This was the girl. Her voice was strained. Well, locked up in this sardine can she was entitled to a little strain; who wasn't strained around here, anyway? She asked, "What did you learn out there, if anything?"

I said, "Not much. Just that they've got . . ." For some reason I found it hard to say. I found myself wanting to giggle like a schoolgirl. "They've gone and built themselves . . ." I heard myself snort with helpless laughter.

"What have they got?" Molly asked sharply. "What have they built?"

"The dumb jerks have gone and constructed a fucking atom bomb to save the world!" I heard myself laugh some more. "Only . . . only you're not supposed to call it a bomb, are you? You're supposed to call it a nuclear device. Like a whore must be called a lady of the evening."

"What's the matter with you, are you drunk?" Molly licked her lips, pale in her soiled tomboy face. Then she protested: "Matt, you can't be serious!"

Sanderson chimed in: "You must be mistaken, sir!

307

It doesn't make sense! I thought these people were supposed to be fighting *against* nuclear—"

Molly interrupted sharply: "You mean it's *here*? On this ship?"

"Hell, it's practically next door," I said. "In the main hold, just beyond the watertight bulkhead at the aft end of the passage, with the screwed-down door or hatch or whatever you call it. . . . What's the matter?"

She'd seated herself weakly on the unoccupied cot. She glared at me. "We're locked up next to a . . . a weirdo hellfire machine, and the man asks what's the matter!" She swallowed hard. "I suppose they're planning to set it off with us right here!"

I said, "Well, atomizing the corpus delicti with a twenty-kiloton nuclear explosion is one way of getting rid of it, isn't it? Or three *corpi delicti*, or whatever the plural is."

"This is no time for a crummy Greek lesson!"

"Latin," I said.

"Greek, Latin, Sanskrit, what's the difference?"

Sanderson asked, "Are they really intending to *fire* it, sir?"

"Yes. As a demonstration. . . ." I told them as much of what I'd learned as they needed to know. I deleted the parts about their planned demise at my hands and my display of honorable nobility. If we were to plan together, and act together, they had to be left with a little faith in the senior member of the party. I frowned thoughtfully. "What time do they serve breakfast in this tin hotel?" I asked.

"Breakfast! Who cares about food—"

Sanderson interrupted Molly's shrill protest. "They generally come around seven in the morning, sir."

I looked at my watch. "Well, it's two A.M. now; that gives us time for a little sleep. But let's figure out a few things first."

"I couldn't possibly sleep!" Molly drew a long, shuddery breath. "I'm sorry! I guess I wasn't cut out to be a heroine. Ever since my . . . since Brennerman was k-killed like that. . . . I thought I could take it, and I did for a while, but all this nightmare stuff is wearing me down! When do you think they'll . . ."

"When will they blow us up?" I hesitated. "Well, I think the first general meeting of the Nassau conference is scheduled for the day after tomorrow, in the morning. I should think our friends here would wait until the delegates are all together in one place—I suppose the PNP will make some kind of a dramatic announcement to let them know the show is about to begin. Take over the PA system in the conference hall, or something. Which means we have a day to wait. They'll probably feed us this morning, being kindly folks at heart, and maybe they'll give us lunch; after that they'll most likely be too busy getting themselves a safe distance away in their boats, maybe out at sea, maybe off in the farther islands. Upwind, of course. They'll want to be able to set off their gadget by remote control when they get the radio word from Nassau that their audience is ready, without any risk of being hit by either the blast or the fallout. And why waste food on prisoners who won't live long enough to digest it, anyway?"

"Do you *have* to say things like that?" Molly asked bitterly .

"Saying or not saying doesn't change anything," I said. "Now tell me how they bring the food. Is it the two men we've already seen; and how do they work it? If one's carrying a tray, he can't be holding a gun, too; does he leave it behind or does he sling it over his back or shoulder? Where does the other one usually cover him from? . . ." After I had it all straight, I said to Sanderson, "It's too bad they saw you sitting up just now, but I suppose you've been vertical before, between relapses."

"Yes, sir."

"Well, you're just about to have another bout of pitiful unconsciousness. When they come in, you'll be lying there dead to the world; or maybe moaning and twitching a bit, if you think that's more convincing. As for you . . ." I turned to the girl. "Are you subject to acute attacks of modesty, Mrs. Brennerman?"

She licked her lips. "I don't understand. What do you want me to do?"

When I told her, she blushed bright red and couldn't look at me for a little. Then she nodded bravely.

At six-thirty, I made the preparations. I laid out the props in artistic disarray on the floor of the cell, starting with the not very interesting part of the exhibit: one masculine shirt, mine. That was followed by the feminine display: one pair of not very clean white nylon panties, one pair of quite grimy white linen shorts, and one soiled blue T-shirt with a cutie-pie slogan across the front. There was no brassiere, which was too bad. A discarded bra, properly arranged, is always an attention-grabber, at least when you're dealing with a male audience. Well, you can't have everything.

The girl was sitting on the end of the cot nearest the door, watching me set the scene. Initially, she'd been very self-conscious about her nudity, but she was getting over it. I hadn't realized what a fine body had been concealed by the prison-bedraggled clothes. It was a stronger and more generously feminine figure than some I'd seen lately, but the waist was slim enough that, nude, she gave no real impression of sturdiness or plumpness. The breasts were bold and lovely.

"Well?" Molly said, a little stiffly. "If you're going to stare, you might at least say something nice."

310

"You mean like: Wow!"

She grinned abruptly. "Something like that. A girl likes a little appreciation when she sacrifices her lady-like modesty. . . . Matt?"

"Yes?"

"Are we . . . going to kill them?" Her grin had faded as quickly as it had come.

"Yes, ma'am. If they'll let us. That's the point of the exercise."

"I'm not sure that I can."

"That's all right. It's my specialty; leave it to me. Just keep your man busy long enough to let me get back from dealing with his partner, and I'll take care of him. Between the two of you, you should be able to manage. How are you feeling, Ricardo?"

"I'm all right." The boy lying on the far bed was, unlike me, a gentleman. He was keeping his eyes carefully averted from the naked girl sitting on the near bed so as not to embarrass her. "I'll be all right," he repeated firmly, so I knew he was feeling rocky and might leave us again at any moment.

I said to both of them, "Remember, you're not plugging for your Boy Scout merit badge in unarmed combat. Sportsmanship will get you nowhere. Smash his balls with your knee, dig his eye out with your thumb, chew his ear off with your teeth. Just keep him occupied and hurting while I dispose of the other one; and drop on the word. . . . Here we go, they're a little early this morning. Places, everybody!"

Somebody was unfastening and opening the deck hatch over the aft end of the passage outside. Ricardo turned his battered face to the wall and curled up in the fetal position, giving a practice groan. Molly let herself fall back onto her cot with her legs apart, dangling from the knees. As I knelt before her, I felt her hands in my hair, caressing me, pulling my head down. . . . While the basic plan had been mine, the detailed execution was all hers. She'd pointed out that I'd be able to react much more quickly from a kneeling position before her than a prone position on top of her. So what about, instead of faking the act itself—my idea—letting us be caught indulging in a little mouthy foreplay preliminary to the main bout; what did I think? She'd been flushed and embarrassed as she'd proposed this strategy, but quite serious: if we were going to put on such a creepy, shameless, cold-blooded performance, we might as well do it right. . . .

I'll have to admit that my heart wasn't in it—well, let's call it heart. Actually, I was embarrassed. After all, I hardly knew the lady and wasn't sure I really liked her. As I nuzzled her breasts and worked my way down her abdomen toward the critical zone with suitable kisses and caresses, I had very little of the proper reaction, if you want to call it proper. I was too busy listening to the approaching footsteps resounding metallically outside and coming to a stop, listening to the scratching of somebody trying to find the keyhole and missing with his first try, listening to the click of the bolt and the creak of the old unlubricated hinges as the door swung open. Molly's naked body arched passionately under my touch.

"Ah, don't stop, don't stop!" she moaned.

I wasn't doing anything all that stimulating; but apparently the girl was a real trouper. I heard sudden coarse male laughter from the doorway. Heavy footsteps approached me from behind. A hand grabbed me by the shoulder and flung me aside. I let myself be flung, leaving the girl lying there totally exposed.

It was a comedy routine, really. They were grown men—I won't say adults—but you'd have thought they'd never before seen a nude woman with her knees apart. A couple of real clowns. The one who'd pulled me away, the big blond one, just stood there gawking lecherously. The other one was having his look, too, licking his lips; and the payoff was that he was supposed to be covering the situation with his gun while the other man carried the food, but actually he had the machine pistol in one hand while the other hand was burdened with the tray his partner had wished off on him before hurrying forward to partake of the goodies on display. It was almost too easy. You're supposed to let the ducks get a little ways off the water before you shoot them.

Then the big gent whose name I'd never learned took a step forward dazedly, like a man in a happy pornographic dream, and bent over the inviting lady on the bed—who instantly threw her bare arms around his neck, hauled his head down, and sank her nice white teeth into his ear. It was a pleasure to meet a girl who wasn't too proud to accept suggestions. At the same time Ricardo landed on top of them. I was aware of all this only peripherally, because I'd scrambled up from where I'd been thrown and hurled myself at the dark little man called Jesperson.

The impact carried us both out the open door. Our breakfasts, whatever they might have been, went flying all over the passage outside. Jesperson lay half-stunned for a moment, having been thrown hard against the far wall. It was long enough for me, on top, to drive into his throat the little belt-buckle knife that had been overlooked when I'd been frisked earlier. I groped for the machine pistol with the other hand and found it.

There was a sudden end to farce; blood in large quantities has a way of washing the humor out of any situation. The last vestige of comedy vanished when, still trying instinctively to cling to his weapon even as his life pumped out from the severed carotid artery, the man beneath me managed to trigger off a burst, filling the small space with a brief madness of screaming lead.

313

I felt something rap me on the back of the head as I flattened myself beside the dying man—the dead man now, I saw, as I scrambled to my feet with the submachine gun in my hands. Blood was running down the back of my neck, maybe brains, too; but there was no time for investigation. I lunged back into our cell and saw that Ricardo was down. They were all on the floor; but the big man still had the naked girl firmly attached to him, her legs around his body, one arm firmly around his neck, her teeth still clamped in his ear, while her free hand worked busily at clawing his face to ribbons. There was blood running down her bare back from what looked like a knife-slash and was probably a graze from a ricochetting 9mm bullet.

"Drop!" I shouted. "Molly, get clear!"

She heard me through the haze of battle, released all holds, and rolled away. Confused, the big man came to his knees, half-blind with blood, his face a torn and gory mask. I hadn't had time to figure out the weapon I held and switch it to the single-shot mode, if available. I simply hit the trigger briefly, and the gun stuttered three times, putting all three into the broad chest where, thank God, they stayed instead of penetrating to bounce and splatter against the steel wall behind him.

Well, maybe I could have been a great humanitarian and, having the drop on him, ripped up the bedding and tied him up alive for safekeeping; but while I was doing that, what else would have been happening? Even as it was, I was too late. With the gun in my hands, I dashed out the cell door and down the passage. I was reaching for the ladder when the deck hatch overhead was slammed shut by someone; I saw the clamps—dogs, I believe is the nautical word—rammed home, probably by Homer Allwyn himself. No sentimentalist he. He'd heard the shooting and guessed what was happening. He was containing the rebellion below, and to hell with his two men still down here.

I released the ladder and drew a long breath and felt the bloody back of my head. Something hard and sharp was embedded in my scalp. In didn't feel fatal. I picked at it and pulled it out: a small, jagged scrap of bullet jacket. I threw it aside and looked down at the gun in my hands, a well-preserved German MP40 of World War II vintage, not as nicely made a firearm as the MP38 that preceded it, but much easier and cheaper to manufacture. It is an ugly beast. I've seen handsome rifles and truly lovely shotguns— the British make some real beauties—but I've never seen a good-looking machine pistol, although I'll admit the old Thompson with the drum magazine had a certain brutal charm.

I frowned at the misshapen little killing machine I held, wondering if it was a clue. You'd have thought this well-heeled gang of world-savers would have equipped themselves with something more modern, say the ubiquitous Uzi; but they'd picked a well-tested and reliable, if elderly, piece of equipment, and maybe that was what counted. Or maybe it was just what happened to be available on the arms market the day they went shopping. . . .

I awoke to the realization that there were still things to be done and I wasn't doing them. Reaction, I guess. I checked the door at my elbow, the door to the main hold, where the big bang awaited the signal to blow this part of the Bahamas to radioactive hell. I discovered that there was a way of releasing the door clamps, dogs, whatever the nautical term may be, in emergencies, from the forward side, our side, with the proper tool to fit the hexagonal sockets. I saw the bracket that had held the tool tucked away behind the ladder leading up to the deck, but it was empty.

315

With sudden hope, I hurried back to the man whose throat I'd cut, remembering that there had been a cigarette-package-shaped bulge in the pocket of his khaki shirt. I got the cigarettes out gingerly, wiped my bloody fingers on his pants, and extracted the book of matches he had tucked inside the cellophane. I went forward and opened the heavy door at that end of the passage and used the matches to look inside. But Allwyn, or somebody, hadn't missed any bets. There had been an emergency tool here, also; but while the bracket remained, that wrench, too, was gone. I determined that the only way out of this dark forward compartment filled with mysterious, decaying gear was back the way I'd come.

I returned to the body sprawled across the passage in a mess of blood and spilled food and excrement— he'd actually fired both barrels while dying, and the stench was overwhelming. I got two extra clips from the pouch on his belt. I retrieved my little knife, cleaned it, and returned it to its primary duty of helping to hold up my jeans. With the blade hidden inside the leather of the belt, it looked like a very ordinary buckle, as it was supposed to. Having taken care of the details out here, I stepped back into the cell, where the second dead man remained very dead. With three 9mm slugs in the chest there was no excuse for him not to. It's not much of a cartridge for single-shot kills, but with multiple hits it will get the job done.

Molly was kneeling beside Ricardo Sanderson. She was fully dressed again, even to her shoes; and she'd already bled through her T-shirt back. That made two of us, after I'd pulled on my own shirt. Well, to hell with the gore.

"Help me lift him onto the cot, please," she said. "Gently, he's got an ugly hole in his hip from one of those screaming ricochets. But I think I've stopped the bleeding."

When we laid him down, the boy's eyes opened. "Like with mosquitoes," he whispered.

"Shhh, don't try to talk," Molly said.

"I mean, you hang out a gooey strip of something and it attracts all the mosquitoes around and they stick to it and don't bite you. Well, you hang out a Sanderson and he attracts all the clubs and bullets around so they don't hurt you. . . . Did we win, Coach?"

"The game, yes," I said. "The series is still in doubt."

The girl beside me stirred irritably. "I hate professional optimists!" she snapped. "You know perfectly well we're still locked in here; I heard the hatch close. We killed two men for absolutely nothing."

I said, "You're looking at it backward, sweetheart. There were two doors beween us and freedom; now, whichever way we go, there's only one. There were, say, a dozen men between us and freedom; now there are two fewer. And we were unarmed; now we have a gun. I consider that pretty good progress."

She looked at me for a moment; then her lips twitched and formed a reluctant grin. "All right. Sorry again. If that's the way the game is played, I'll be a little Pollyanna from now on. I'll be so cheerful you won't be able to stand me. But I must say, if this is what you do for a living . . ." She hesitated, then went on: "I know it's horribly self-centered of me to say it with a dead man on the floor I helped kill; but I don't really like being turned into a wild animal, particularly a naked wild animal. I must have looked perfectly ridiculous and quite disgusting!"

I said, "In other words, Mrs. Brennerman, you'd prefer to die dignified rather than live undignified, is that it?"

She shook her head ruefully. "You can twist any-

317

thing around, can't you? But I owe you an apology. I thought, when you were being so polite and humble to that pompous little prick, calling him sir, sir, sir . . ."

I grinned. "I know what you thought. The point is that he thought it, too. Very useful word, sir. I learned long ago in somebody's army that you can generally castrate a man with one hand and he'll never even notice it as long as you're saluting him with the other and calling him sir. . . ."

"Hey!" That was young Sanderson, weakly trying to attract our attention. "If you two senior citizens will stop arguing . . . I think something's happening out there. I heard a funny noise."

"Sit tight," I said. "Molly, maybe you can take that other mattress and use it as a shield for both of you; it could stop a ricochet if more lead starts bouncing around. And don't stick your heads out into the passage. I want to be able to shoot in any direction without clobbering any friendlies."

I moved across the room and stepped into the passageway cautiously, gun ready. As the kid had said, something was happening. There were scuffling and rattling sounds from the other side of the door to the main hold. I heard the squeaky noise of rusty metal moving against rusty metal, like a half-frozen nut being forced to turn on a corroded bolt. Okay, Friend Homer, for some reason, had decided to come in after us; but he wasn't about to descend that exposed ladder in the face of a submachine gun he had to assume was now in enemy hands. This time, instead of using the high road over the deck, he was taking the low road through the ship's hold.

I looked around. The doorway of our cell was the obvious cover from which to shoot; but all Allwyn had to do, once that watertight door was flung open, was have a couple of machine gunners outside spray the metal passage at different angles. Sooner or later a bullet would take the right bounce off a wall and solve all his problems, or at least his immediate problem: me. I put a fresh clip into the MP40, slung the weapon over my shoulder, and started up the ladder. The cracked rib didn't help, and I was still conscious of the groove Gina had put into my skull, and the new nick in my scalp wasn't exactly comfortable; but we stoical heroes of the undercover services are, of course, quite immune to discomfort and pain. Or supposed to be. I settled myself as securely as I could at the top of the ladder right below the deck hatch, looking down at the door through which they would come. Clinging there, like a monkey on a pole, I wasn't in a good position for pinpoint marksmanship; but at that range, with that quick-fire weapon, William-Tell–type accuracy would not be required.

I heard the final fastening yield to the accompaniment of a muffled grunt of pain as somebody barked a knuckle. The door swung open creakily. Somebody stepped over the high sill and paused. Almost directly above—I seemed to be making a habit of potting them from the trees, so to speak—I couldn't see clearly for my own knee in the way. I wanted to scream at the guy to go on, get moving, and bring all his friends. I wanted them well inside the passage where I could mow down the lot of them before they mowed me . . .

The figure below me moved forward into the clear. I clung there under the ship's deck, steadying my weapon awkwardly, finger ready on the trigger, just waiting to see if a few more wouldn't move into my sights before I took this one. I wasn't looking at it as a human being. I was regarding it simply as a target with the ten-ring clearly marked between the shoulders. Then the shape below me paused to suck at its

319

skinned knuckles in a way that was wholly feminine; and I realized that I was looking at the silver-blond hair and slender figure of a smallish girl I'd once got to know pretty well.

I released the trigger pressure hastily and drew a shaky breath. I said, "Amy, what the hell are you trying to do, get yourself shot?"

IIIIIIII CHAPTER 29 IIIIIIIIIIIIIIIIIIIIIIIIIIIIIIIIIIIIIIIII

BELATEDLY I realized that I was taking for granted that the girl below me was on my side, just because we'd once made beautiful music together—and actually it had been a little off-key. Well, I'd also been told she'd refused to play Delilah to my Samson for the PNP, wherefore Gina Williston had replaced her as my sailing companion.

On the other hand, when Minister had summoned her she'd apparently run right to him; and he'd recently referred to her in a very possessive way. In any case I was acting very trustingly for an agent of my age and experience. This seemed to be my day for naive behavior; and the situation could easily blow up in my face, now that I'd revealed my trap and given away my position. I waited for the lights to flash, the sirens to wail, and the guns to fire, signaling the end of another dumb agent who'd made optimistic assumptions about the wrong wench; but nothing happened. Amy merely turned her head to look up at me curiously.

"What in the world are you doing perched up there? . . . Oh." She shook her head quickly. "You don't have to worry about them. They've all gone to the boats; they're getting out of here. Matt, do you know what they're *doing*? Do you know what they've *got* in there?"

"Yes, I know."

"How crazy can you get? I mean, it's the thing we're all fighting *against*, isn't it? When I learned about it, I knew I had to do *something*. . . . Anyway, I couldn't leave you trapped here to be, well, incinerated, could I?" She giggled abruptly. "You look very silly up there!"

I dropped down beside her, getting a clear look at her at last. "You look pretty silly yourself," I said. "Is it raining outside?"

Actually, she didn't look so bad. In a pretty dress, or even a pair of smart slacks, she'd have been a mess; but you can be dripping wet in a snug black jersey and blue jeans and people can hardly tell the difference. Her clothes were a bit saggy and shapeless, to be sure, and a small puddle was forming about her blue canvas shoes as she stood there; but the most obvious flaw in her grooming was the lank, soaked hair. You'd have thought I'd have spotted this earlier; but what you notice looking down the barrel of a quick-fire weapon, or any weapon, isn't quite what you notice under normal social circumstances.

Amy glanced down at herself and said ruefully, "It seems as if, ever since we met, whenever I go away from you I come back a sodden wreck, either with booze or with seawater." She squeezed the wet hair back from her face. "But it isn't very nice of you to make fun of the girl after she's just swum through a sea of sharks to save you!"

"You came across the lagoon?"

"Just the entrance channel." She hesitated. "I had the captain's cabin here on the ship. I think you saw me at the window last night. I meant for you to see me. . . ."

322

"I saw you."

"Anyway, when they said we were all leaving just now, I was assigned to a boat like everybody else. I was supposed to go on Albert's boat, of course; the flagship, you might call it. Albert's and Mrs. Williston's, and Mr. Paul's. The one from which . . . *it* will be fired. The other two boats, with Homer Allwyn in charge, are simply going to head straight back to the States with the rest of the PNP action group. They'll all disperse until they're called together again for another project. . . . Well, anyway, I told them that the Dramamine they'd passed around in preparation for the sea voyage was making me very sleepy and I wanted to go to the boat and lie down a little. But on the way I dodged in among the villas and sneaked past the dock and around the far end of the lagoon. I came up this side of the island while they were all going down the other, well, back and forth along the other side, to load the stuff they want to save from their private atomic Götterdämmerung." She stared at me bleakly. "Matt, I had no idea, before Albert told me about it the other day, very proudly, that they were planning anything so totally, utterly mad! I mean, even with the best motives in the world, how can they dream of deliberately doing exactly what we're trying to prevent everybody else from doing! We've got to stop them!"

There was moral outrage in her voice; the atom bomb seems to affect some people that way. As far as I'm concerned, a weapon is a weapon; and the primitive gent who, way back at the dawn of history, first chipped out a crude stone knife advanced the world along its homicidal path just as significantly as the modern scientific characters who figured out the latest H-bomb. But she was right; it had to be stopped.

"We'll give it a try," I said. "But let me have the rest; did anybody at all see you coming here?"

She shook her head. "I don't think so. They were all very busy with last-minute stuff, particularly Albert. He wasn't worrying about me; he was making the final tests and checks on his . . . well, I guess you'd call it a transmitter, wouldn't you? A long-range detonator?"

"Where does he keep it on the boat, up on the bridge or down in the deckhouse?"

"On the bridge. He's built a weatherproof box for it there. I guess it's pretty sensitive; and there's no protection up there, just a windshield and the controls and something to sit on."

"Go on," I said when she paused.

She licked her lips. "As I said, I think I got away unseen. Swimming the channel was no fun at all; I kept waiting for something to grab my leg or . . . me. But there was a good tide rip, wind against current, nice and choppy; I don't think anybody spotted me there, either. Crawling ashore, I put my shoes back on and sneaked up here. The last ones were just leaving with the last loads. When they were gone, I slipped into the building and climbed aboard the ship. It felt very strange, all dead and deserted. I went to the cabin I'd been in, but they'd already taken my things to the boat. No dry clothes. So here I am, still sopping wet, just in time to get my head blown off by the man I came to rescue." She hesitated. "Oh. Here. I didn't know you already had a gun. Looking for something to wear, I found this in a bureau in the cabin next door, the one *she'd* been using."

It seemed that Amy was having as hard a time bringing herself to use Gina Williston's name as Gina had had using hers. I didn't allow myself to crack a smile. Amy lifted her soggy jersey in front and pulled out a familiar weapon: the .38 Special revolver, complete with clip-on holster, that I'd been carrying earlier, that Gina had hidden away after putting me to sleep the night we'd paid our visit to Connie Grieg. I found myself rather proud of Amy, and of myself. She could probably never have brought herself to touch a fearsome firearm—she wouldn't even have been thinking in those terms—except for our little weapons-training session out in the Gulf Stream.

"Thanks," I said, slipping it onto my belt after checking the cylinder: full house. I asked, "How much time do you figure we have?"

"Until tomorrow morning, when they get the coded message from Nassau that'll tell them the convention delegates are ready to appreciate the fireworks. . . . Matt, how did I ever get mixed up with these high-class lunatics, anyway?"

I couldn't answer that; but at least I'd figured the time factor correctly.

"Who'll have the honor of setting off the blast?" I asked.

"Albert, of course. It's his pride and joy; and anyway, only he knows how it works." She grimaced. "I still think of him as Albert; I can't get used to his real name. When he gets the word, he'll warm up his magic box, go through the safety routines he's set up to prevent accidental detonation, and push the pretty red button that says 'Fire.' "

"From where?"

"I don't really know where we're supposed to go, just that we're going to anchor the *Cuttlefish* behind some island a safe distance away, to await the signal from Nassau. *Cuttlefish*, that's a kind of squid, isn't it?"

"Or octopus; I forget, exactly," I said. "Which one is the *Cuttlefish*?"

"It . . . she has a blue hull. The other two are white."

I said, "He didn't by any chance tell you anything that would help us disarm it?"

"No." She hesitated. "Well, he did let something slip, but it's not very helpful. The bomb is booby-trapped. He always does that, he said, so that if somebody does catch him after he's planted it, he'll have the consolation of knowing it'll probably go off anyway."

So I was right again; but, as she said, it didn't help a great deal. I said, "Nice playmates you pick."

"That's right," she said dryly. "One blows them up with high explosives; the other shoots them with guns."

I grinned. "Touché. Well, I don't know anything about defusing bombs. We're going to have to get to *Spindrift's* radio and get help in here as soon as they're well clear. They're not planning to take the sailboat, I hope."

She said, "It wasn't mentioned. Just the three big powerboats."

We stood there for a moment in the narrow passage, awkwardly, not really knowing what our relationship was now. I understood that the fact that she'd come here to release me didn't necessarily mean that she'd rejected another man in my favor. It wasn't a gesture of love. Not that she minded saving my life, but mainly she'd needed my help to do something about the immoral device in the ship's hold, the thing she felt must not be exploded under any circumstances.

"Well, we'd better go," she said. "The coast should be clear by the time we get out there."

"I'll bring my fellow prisoners."

But when I entered the familiar little cell, Molly Brennerman didn't greet me as eagerly as I'd expected; and young Sanderson, lying on his cot, didn't greet me at all. His face was gray and shiny and his eyes were closed.

I said, "We've got to leave, Molly."

Sitting on the edge of the cot, she glanced at me

irritably over her shoulder. "Don't be silly, he can't be moved, can't you see? He's in shock and he's still losing blood."

"It's the last boat out, sweetheart; and I mean that literally. We're going to try to get some expert help in here to deal with the gadget next door; but it's booby-trapped, so I can't risk trying to disconnect it myself, or pour water over it, or whatever you do with the damn things to kill them. And if help doesn't get here in time, it'll be a long, fast ride straight up unless we start running right now. At six knots, all *Spindrift* will do, it's going to be close, anyway; we may get all the way clear and we may not."

She said stubbornly, "He'll bleed to death if we try to move him."

"Then we'll just have to leave him and hope we can get back here in time with a doctor, if we can find somebody to deactivate the thing. If not, well, it won't help him to have you blown up, too; it's not a situation in which companionship counts for much. Come on."

"No."

She rose and turned to face me, a girl of medium height with a snub-nosed tomboy face and a figure that wasn't boyish at all. The fact that she wasn't in top sartorial condition didn't matter a bit, at this moment.

"I can't do that," she said softly. "I've done a bit of whining, I know, but I'm not going to run away now. I know you'll find a way of stopping it, and you don't need my help. He does. It could make the difference to him, my being here." She smiled crookedly. "After all, he's my superior officer, Matt. I can't just . . . just go off and leave him lying wounded on the field of battle, can I? I'll stay here and do what I can. I've had some first-aid training. Come back as soon as you can, with help. And if you can't . . . well, I'll know

327

you did your best; and . . . and I didn't really mind fighting alongside you in that very unladylike way."

They're turning out a very good grade of female human beings these days. I wanted to kiss her, as a token of respect and admiration, but although we'd played a fairly intimate scene together, that had been strictly stage stuff. I didn't really know her well enough to kiss her; and shaking hands seemed inadequate. It was no time for pretty gestures, anyway.

So I just nodded and turned away, passing Amy in the doorway and signaling her to follow me. The door to the hold stood open as she'd left it. As we approached it, I could see beyond it the shiny drum of destruction on its crude cradle in the middle of the open space. The ship was almost silent; but the generator was still running back in the engine room. I considered shutting it down, but that would have left Molly and her patient in the dark; and Minister wouldn't have made it so easy to disable his toy. Maybe interrupting the current would actually trigger the device. I hoped next time, if there was a next time, Mac would pick me an assignment that involved things I knew something about, instead of sailboats and nuclear gadgets. Well, actually, I was catching on to the sailboat racket to some extent; but I doubted that I'd ever be a great atom-bomb man. . . .

"Drop the gun, Helm!"

Entering the hold in that preoccupied fashion, I'd walked right into it. There he was, rising up from behind one of the workbenches along the wall to my left, with his .45 auto in his hot little hand. Both hot little hands; he was using the two-handed grip and the approved crouch. Great style. The chief storm trooper himself, Homer Allwyn, still in his natty khakis. Something moved behind me. I glanced over my left shoulder to see Gina stepping out from behind the swung-back steel door to aim my own little .25 pistol at my back.

"Drop it!" Allwyn's voice was shrill.

I flung the submachine gun away from me convulsively, as if in abject panic; throwing it to the right. There was a kind of sickness inside me: *I didn't want this, dammit!* They followed the ugly firearm with their eyes, of course. They had to see if it would go off when it hit, didn't they? I went left, fast, without waiting for it to hit, deliberately throwing myself past Gina and the little automatic in her hand. They never come to it prepared; it always takes them a while to make up their minds to it, particularly if it involves someone they know; and if she did do it, the chances of a little .25 bullet disabling me instantly weren't overwhelming. But she didn't fire in the moment I was directly in front of her gun. Then I was past her, hearing Allwyn's big automatic go off with an impressive roar. Concentrating on moving fast and getting out the .38, I still heard the smack of the heavy bullet hitting flesh, and Gina's shocked gasp as she took the slug meant for me.

After that it was easy because, as I'd known he would, Homer Allwyn was staring open-mouthed and bug-eyed at what he'd done. I had all the time in the world to finish drawing the Smith and Wesson and shoot him three times in the chest. In the movies they're generally hurled backward dramatically when they're shot. Here, in real life, Allwyn simply stood motionless for a moment, dying on his feet; then he pitched forward, still holding the big .45.

The gunfire had been very loud inside the steel chamber. The silence afterward had a ringing quality; or maybe the ringing was only in my ears. I stepped back and picked up the .25 Gina had dropped. Hugging herself tightly, as if trying to hold herself together, she'd slid down to a sitting position against the gray-painted bulkhead, by the steel door behind which she'd hid; but I didn't have time for her yet. I went over and pulled the .45 out of Allwyn's dead fingers. Then I gathered up the MP40 I'd thrown aside. It seemed to be in functioning condition except for a bent magazine, which I removed, replacing it with a fresh, straight one. I worked enough 9mm cartridges out of the damaged magazine to fill the partly used one I was also carrying. That gave me one full thirty-two-round spare. I threw the crooked clip away. I found a length of insulated electric wire on a nearby workbench, coiled it up, and stuck it into my pocket. Business attended to, I went back to Gina.

Amy, kneeling beside her, gave me a reproachful look, which was par for the course. Any time the damn fools get themselves killed, the bystanders reproach the smart ones still alive. For just being alive, I suppose. Who'd first pointed guns at whom, anyway? Gina watched me squat beside her, cowboy fashion. Quick-draw Helm, the terror of the Islands.

"You knew!" she whispered. "You knew I couldn't shoot you in the back!"

"They never can," I said. "At least not fast enough."

"And you knew he'd . . . You had it all figured out, damn you!"

I said, "For Christ's sake! Of course I knew. That he'd shoot, yes. That he'd shoot behind me, yes. How can you swing with a fast-moving target when you're all crouched down like that with the pistol frozen in that rigid two-hand grip? Oh, the FBI boys can do it, but they practice. I'll bet that bastard never shot at anything but a motionless piece of paper in his life. Did I know that he'd either hit you or come so close he'd be paralyzed with guilty shock? Yes, indeed, I was counting on it. Any other dumb questions?"

"You're angry," she whispered. "Why are you angry? I'm the one who's . . . hurt."

I said harshly, "There seems to be no way of keeping some people from killing themselves! Jesus Christ, I've been giving my little lecture about dangerous Helm every night for a week, but you've paid absolutely no attention. Hell, I even put on a demonstration for you, four men dead or dying in about three seconds; and still you try to take me with your silly .25 and your totally incompetent security genius! Would you pick up a bag of clubs at the local hardware store and stroll out to take on a bunch of professional golfers, betting your life on the game? Then what makes you think you can casually pick up a stray firearm and deal with a professional gunman like me? Christ, I can't help it if people commit suicide around me! Damn you, Gina, I tried. . . ."

But her eyes were looking far beyond me and seeing nothing but darkness. I closed them and got to my feet. It's supposed to be all right for men to cry these days; but the trouble is that when you need to cry you usually have no time for it. And I doubt it does all that much good, anyway.

"You loved her, didn't you?" Amy said, trying to make a tragic romance of it.

"Hell, I love everybody," I said. "Just the little lover of all the world, that's me. Come on, let's get out of here."

Our departure was watched only by the dead and by the shiny object in the middle of the room, silent and waiting. We made our way past the cheerfully thumping generator, the only happy thing in the ship, doing its work and doing it well and having a fine, noisy time of it. We climbed the metal stairs. The daylight on deck, even filtered through the windows of the sheltering field house, or whatever Elysium Cay called its supposed recreation center, was a real shock. It seemed as if I'd been buried alive for years. I stopped at a place where the deck was reasonably clean.

"Turn around and put your hands behind you," I said to Amy.

Her eyes widened. "Matt, what in the world—"

"Do as I say!"

She hesitated and swallowed hard, then turned away as ordered. I hauled the length of wire from my pocket and cut it into two pieces, using the buckle knife from my belt since my little pocketknife had been confiscated along with the decoy weapon I'd worn under my shirt behind. I used one piece to lash her wrists securely together.

"Matt, I don't understand—"

"Sit down against the deckhouse there."

She sat down reluctantly. I knelt and tied her ankles with the other wire. I rose and looked down at her.

Her face was very pale. She whispered, "You think I betrayed you!"

I shook my head. "No, Amy."

"Yes, you do! You must! Why else would you be doing this to me? You think I was working with them. You think I opened that door for you just to lead you out into their . . . their trap. Matt, I didn't, I didn't!"

"I know you didn't," I said. "They either spotted you making your channel swim or, more likely, they saw that you were gone when they brought your luggage to your cabin. They figured out where you must have headed. They couldn't just sail away, guessing that you intended to turn me loose and that I'd be heading for a radio. They had to come back and stop me." I shook my head again. "No, it's nothing like that. You're a sweet lady and I appreciate your help; but if you think hard, you'll figure out why I have to do it this way. Don't try to free yourself, you'll only hurt yourself; and if things work out, somebody'll be along to release you shortly." I made a wry face. "And if they don't work out, we'll all go to hell together, and it's been nice knowing you."

I heard the distant sound of a boat's horn, the kind they blow for fog and bridges. Somebody was getting impatient at the other end of the lagoon. They were saying clearly: *Get your asses back here fast or we'll leave without you!* After a last look at Amy, glaring up at me hurt and resentful, I hurried off the ship and out the back door of the building. The sun was very bright outside, unreally bright at first; and the water surrounding the island was very blue, except close in where the reefs made a pale pattern. Two big white sportfishermen were in sight. That was the flotilla that Homer Allwyn had been scheduled to command; he must have put somebody else in charge and sent them off, while he came back to deal with me. Out toward Arabella Cay, one of the vessels had already cleared the reefs and fired the afterburners. It was riding high and throwing an impressive wake. I estimated twenty knots, but it could have been more. The other was still cautiously feeling its way out through the shoals. Their part of the great atomic adventure was behind them, and the PNP rank and file were heading back to their respectable, civilized homes and offices and to their wives and kiddies.

I hurried to the corner of the big building and looked around it without exposing myself any more than necessary. The blue sportfisherman was still at the dock, waiting. It was the *Cuttlefish*. Not the most appealing name in the world for a boat, but they do pick some odd ones. As I watched, the horn blew again. Maybe Alfred Minister was getting restless. He probably was; but I had a hunch the hooting was being done by Mr. Harrison Paul, chairman of the board, arrogant and impatient and panicky. Keeping the building between me and the distant dock, I made my way down to the shore where I couldn't be seen and fought my way along it toward the entrance channel, the way Amy must have come not too long ago; but at least I wasn't dripping wet. There seemed to be a lot of gutsy ladies around. I tried not to think about the fact that there were fewer, by one, than there had been.

It was tough going, over big broken rocks that were as rough as pumice but a lot harder. The fact that I was weighted down with firearms until I walked bowlegged didn't help; but I didn't dare jettison any of them. I couldn't risk the noise of test-firing the MP40; and if it decided not to function after all, after being bounced around like a basketball, I might wind up trying to stop a twenty-ton sportfisherman with a palm-sized .25 automatic after emptying the .45 and the .38, neither of which was fully loaded.

When I found the right spot, hidden in a rocky crack just above the channel, the two men on board *Cuttlefish* had said to hell with waiting longer and were casting off their lines. I saw them both clamber up the ladder leading from the cockpit to the flying bridge. Some cruising craft have inside steering stations as well; but sportfishermen are mostly equipped only with the topside controls from which the helmsman can watch the angler in the cockpit fighting his fish and maneuver accordingly. I wished I knew where on the bridge Minister's detonator was located; and if it would trigger the bomb if I hit it with a stray bullet. That Minister would explode it himself in a last defiant gesture, if he saw himself trapped, I had no doubt whatever.

So it was a gamble at best; but the fact was that if he got away he *would* push the button as soon as he was clear, now that he knew things must have gone very wrong on the *Carmen Saiz*. He wouldn't wait for any signals, and he'd ignore any orders Harrison Paul tried to give him. The operation had got all screwed up at the very last moment; but he'd made the thing, and it was the best thing he'd ever made, and by God he was going to fire it before somebody had a chance to tinker with it. And I hadn't been sent here to protect the Bahamas from nuclear disaster anyway. I'd been sent here to get a man, and he was moving into range now, very nicely, like a mallard coming to the decoys. . . .

Hunkered behind my rock, waiting, I felt my stupid conscience give another twinge: I'd promised a woman who was dead to let Minister finish his job before I took him. I told myself firmly that was okay, he had finished; and I'd never promised to let him push the button. I checked the MP40. It had a curious safety. Strictly speaking, it had no safety at all; you just hauled the operating handle back a bit and dropped it into a retaining notch, putting the weapon out of action. When you needed it again, you released the handle from the notch and you were back in business. Not exactly a speed rig, but simple and inexpensive. I readied the weapon for firing, with the folding stock extended for greater accuracy, and I waited some more.

Minister was taking it very easy. I had a feeling that he wasn't comfortable at the controls of the big vessel, in these close quarters, although he knew the moves. I couldn't help sympathizing with him a bit: a fellow landlubber. I could see his head and shoulders above the plastic windshield. The chairman of the board was beside him; but as they approached, Harrison Paul rose and made his way to the ladder and started down it, presumably to tidy up the docklines trailing around the deck before one blew or washed overboard and got tangled in the prop. Although he was sheltered by a corner of the deckhouse as he descended, I could probably have reached him through the boat's structure—those jacketed 9mm bullets have a lot of penetration—but I had nothing against Harrison Paul except that he was a prick, which was not a capital offense. Minister was the one I had to hit, without warning, hard and permanently, before he could activate his firing device.

I watched him start the turn that would take the big sportsfisherman straight out the channel past me. Range, seventy yards. *Come on, make your swing nice and wide now, amigo* . . . Range sixty. Fifty. Forty-five; and there was no way for him to check the momentum of the twenty-ton fiberglass monster now, and no place for him to take evasive action in that narrow slot without running aground. I rose up fast and lined up the sights and started firing, holding down the trigger and hosing down the bridge until the gun went empty and silent, stinking of scorched oil and burned powder.

Somebody went out of the cockpit in a flat dive: the chairman of the board, abandoning ship. Second clip. Range still closing. I ran it off deliberately, the bullets hammering the flying bridge into splintered wreckage; and blood was now running out through the scuppers and down the sides of the cabin below. Mission accomplished, I hoped. The big boat, never properly lined up for the channel, ran up onto the rocks within twenty yards of me, with a great, grinding, rumbling noise. And things were happening around me now, men emerging from the sea in glistening frogman suits. Two of them had Harrison Paul in tow. Hauling him ashore, they set him on his feet. He didn't look as good in wet jeans as somebody else I knew.

I saw Doug Barnett wading out of the water toward me. Well, it was about time he turned up;

whose lousy mission was this, anyway? He looked like a goddamn wet black seal with flippers on. For an older man, he indulged in some peculiar sports. Maybe I was jealous because I don't swim that well.

"Damn you, he was mine!" Doug said.

"Sure. He's all yours now," I said.

Belatedly, I realized that even with all my shooting, the doomsday device hadn't fired. Well, concentrating so hard on my target, I probably wouldn't have noticed if it had.

I WATCHED the two men studying the shiny cylinder resting in its cradle in the hold of the *Carmen Saiz*. They seemed to know their business. They couldn't really get to work until the rest of their equipment arrived and the island and the surrounding cays had been evacuated, in case they goofed and, quite literally, blew it; but they were getting the feel of the thing.

They'd questioned me at length about Minister and his record and the types of bombs he'd been known to use, and the tricks he liked to employ. I was waiting around in case they thought of anything else to ask me. It wasn't the most relaxing place in the world to wait, with that thing staring me in the face and the men scrutinizing it warily and checking it cautiously with various oddball instruments—including an ordinary stethoscope, for God's sake! I kept telling myself that being here was really no more risky than being anywhere else on so-called Elysium Cay, since if detonation should occur for any reason, the whole island and everything on it, including me, would simply cease to exist.

Outside, I knew, the activity was tapering off; but it wasn't my activity. My job was done. I'd seen

Georgina Williston carried away on a stretcher, under a blanket, dead. I'd seen Ricardo Sanderson carried away on a stretcher, under a blanket, alive. I'd been told that the prognosis, in the latter case, was favorable. Ricardo's papa, Admiral Antonio, the Coast Guard officer in charge of the amphibious assault upon the island—well, in cooperation with a Bahamian counterpart—had been grateful to me but more grateful, rightly, to the girl who'd stayed with his son and cared for him when it wasn't easy. I hadn't seen Homer Allwyn carried away, or his two dead henchmen, and it didn't bother me a bit. I'd had no good-byes to say there.

"Matt."

The voice behind me was quite soft; nobody was speaking loudly in here. I guess we were all afraid of startling the gadget into premature activity. Considering that guns had been fired on this ship and men had died, and a woman, it was a little ridiculous, particularly for Molly Brennerman, who'd been here through it all. She sensed what I was thinking and smiled ruefully.

"I guess my voice isn't likely to set it off, but it's kind of like being quiet in church, isn't it? A church dedicated to the Devil instead of to God? And that's the crummy altar!" Molly shrugged a bit awkwardly. "I just wanted to say good-bye."

I looked at her for a moment. Somebody'd given her a big blue coast guard windbreaker to cover her grimy prison costume; and I knew she'd be well taken care of in other respects, and not only because she was Coast Guard herself, widowed in the line of duty. She was a brave and competent and attractive girl, and it would be a long time before I forgot our little love charade; but the odd thing was how we had nothing for each other in spite of it. I could see that she felt exactly as I did. I was a nice enough older guy and a handy fellow to have around if you needed some shooting done, but in spite of the charged situation we'd shared, no spark of any kind had passed between us. Now the time for guns was past, and it was only left for her to say good-bye politely and forget the whole ugly incident, as far as it could be forgotten.

She held out her hand. I took it; and suddenly she was blushing fiercely. "Gee, that was some crazy act we put on! Good-bye, Matt. Take care."

"You, too."

I watched her depart hastily, fleeing her own embarrassing memories. The older of the two defusing experts, whatever they called themselves, was beckoning to me. I went over there.

"What can I help you with?" I asked.

He had the stethoscope around his neck, doctor fashion. "The bastard's ticking," he said. "Very faintly; but there's a timing device running in there somewhere. He must have rigged a simple clock backup in case he wasn't around to fire it by remote control. How long would you say we had?"

I glanced at my watch. "About twenty-four hours. He wanted to have the fun of setting off his toy himself, so he'd leave it as late as possible in case the signal from Nassau was merely delayed for some reason; but if somebody interfered with him, or his remote failed, he'd want the thing to go off while the conference delegates were still in session, before they adjourned for the day. That's just a guess, of course."

"Your guesses are all we have, mister. Okay, thanks."

"A suggestion."

"Give."

"There are electronic timers around that don't tick, aren't there? If he put something in there you can hear, it could mean he wanted you to hear it and go for it, maybe overlooking some other nasty surprises he'd fixed for you. He was a very tricky fellow."

The man was smiling faintly. "The thought had occurred to us."

"Sure. Nothing like telling an expert how to do his job."

"I didn't mean it that way. We're happy for all the help we can get. Well, if we've got until tomorrow, we'll do it by the numbers and not rush it. Now you'd better get the hell out of here."

I said, "If I'm wrong about the time, sue me."

He grinned. "You can count on it," he said.

I went outside. A helicopter was just lifting off, making the usual horrible racket. I watched it make its crabwise way toward Nassau, disappearing in the distance. I remembered an ancient book on airplanes I'd once come across, written back when just getting off the ground with a pair of wings and a prop was a real feat, in which it had been proved conclusively that helicopters couldn't fly, it was aerodynamically impossible. Well, whoever wrote it had had a point. It still looked impossible. People in uniform were still milling around, but there were fewer of them than there had been. I made my way through them, as another helicopter settled into the place the first one had left vacant. A real military evacuation. I felt the wind of the rotor before it stopped. I went past and down to the dock, where the sailboat still lay, looking lonely and neglected.

"You and me both, girlie," I said.

They'd found somewhere, and returned to me, my confiscated belongings, including my keys. I stepped aboard and unlocked the hatch and went below, thankful that Gina Williston had been a very tidy lady and hadn't left any personal items behind. I opened the forward hatch to let a draft blow the stale air out of the cabin. I turned on the main switch for the batteries,

341

found the right Bahamas chart, and spread it on the chart table, turning on the light since it was a dark little corner of the cabin. I determined at last exactly where we were and how I'd have to sail, or motor, to get out of there. . . .

"Ahoy. Permission to come aboard?" It was Doug Barnett's voice.

"Permission granted," I said. "Come on down and have a drink."

By the time he'd descended the ladder backward, the way you do on a boat, and turned around, I had the plastic tumblers ready. I put one into his hand. We faced each other in silence for a moment.

I asked, "How's Amy, besides mad at me?"

"She's all right. In fact, she . . ." He checked what he had been about to say. After a moment, he said instead, "I don't suppose you could have saved him for me."

"I figured you were probably somewhere around, but I didn't know where," I said. "It seemed best to take him while the taking was good."

"Anyway, it got done," Doug said, dismissing his vengeance and Alfred Minister, who was now defunct. Considering that it been his goal for several years, I respected him for this; but he had another bone to pick with me. "I had a chance to stop in Coral Gables a few days back. Marsha . . . Mrs. Osterman showed me her jewel box. A certain opal ring. A certain capsule. What the hell do you think you're doing, Matt?"

"She asked for it and I gave it to her," I said. "She's an adult; she has a right to make her own decisions. If she'd asked you, would you have refused?"

He hesitated. "No, I suppose not. But why you?"

"Because I'm not a doctor, who wouldn't have given it to her. And I'm not you, whom she happens to love. She didn't want you to have it on your conscience.

She couldn't care less about mine, as she made very clear to me. A fine and courageous lady. And now that she's got it, it's your job to make sure she has enough to live for that she doesn't use it, isn't it? Now that you've finished your stint as the Relentless Avenger."

He glared at me for a moment. Then, surprisingly, he grinned. "How does it feel to run other peoples' lives for them, hotshot? Maybe you ought to give a little thought to your own affairs." He raised his glass to me, then drained it. "There's somebody top-side who wants to see you. I haven't done much in the papa department in the past, and it's a little soon for her to forget my lack of faith in her, although I'm hoping; but you'd better be good to her or I'll have your hide."

I said, "You and what other six superannuated crocks?"

He chuckled, then stopped smiling. "Since you're so free with advice to the lovelorn, I'll pass some out, too. I've done some checking and got an opinion from one of our medical experts. The girl's got problems; but her biggest problem is that she doesn't like her-self much. She wants to punish herself, and be punished, for being such an awful person, right? Well, I've kind of forfeited the right to build up her confi-dence in herself, but maybe you . . . Oh, Christ, I feel like a pimp, turning my own daughter over to a lousy old lecher like you! But I'll be grateful as hell. . . . Why do we always seem to get the ones with the broken wings?"

I said, "Hell, the number of wings we break in the line of duty, maybe it's only fair that we fix one or two."

"Yeah. Well, you'd better get this tub out of here so the bomb-disposal boys can get to work. Matt . . ."

"Yes?"

343

He was frowning thoughtfully. "Don't you wonder a little . . ."

"You mean, maybe we should have let it be fired? Maybe it would have shaken some sense into people?"

He nodded. After a moment, he said, "But of course it isn't practical. If everybody who wanted to save the world got to fire off a nuclear device, we might as well have a war in the first place. Well, I'll see you around."

Then he was gone. I waited, but nobody came down the companionway ladder; so I put some ice and whiskey into a clean glass and set it, along with my own drink, on the bridge deck. I climbed out into the cockpit. Amy was sitting at the far end of it with an elbow on the tiller. She was still in her creased jeans and saggy jersey. Well, that could be fixed; the clothes she'd bought for her honeymoon as Mrs. Penelope Matthews were still on board. At the moment, it could hardly be called a formal party; I was in my well-worn Levi's jeans and the sport shirt with the torn collar and the bloodstains down the back. I noticed that she had managed to brush her hair very smooth, and that in spite of her rough-dried clothes she looked very good. Somehow, with all the action and excitement, I'd forgotten what a pretty girl she was.

She watched me gravely as I sat down beside her. I passed her the drink I'd made for her. When she reached for it, I noticed that her wrist was bandaged; that both wrists were bandaged.

"I told you not to fight it," I said.

"You forget, I'm the little girl who loves hurting herself. Or being hurt. But I know why you did it, now. You were going after him, after Albert, and you knew how I felt about him, how I couldn't help feeling about him in spite of myself. You didn't want me to have any part in killing him and blame myself, so you tied me up and left me behind."

I shrugged. "Maybe I just didn't want to be bothered with a clumsy dame trailing along."

She said quietly, "Matt, I don't want to be like that. Like he wanted to make me. Can you help me?"

I shook my head. "If help is what you want, go to a psychiatrist. All we offer here is bad food and seasickness and sunburn. And a little Scotch, and maybe . . ."

"Maybe what?" she asked when I hesitated.

"A little affection. And now, if you're willing to settle for that, we'd better fire her up and get the hell out of here so the boys can do their work. . . ."

"Matt?"

"Yes?"

" 'Affection,' " she said softly. "Could we . . . could we maybe change that word to 'love'?"

I looked at her for a moment. "Well, we could try," I said.

We did.

About the Author

Donald Hamilton has been writing Matt Helm novels for over twenty years. An expert yachtsman, he has also written nonfiction books and articles on sailing. He and his wife live aboard their yacht, *Kathleen*, and in Santa Fe, New Mexico.